D0193115

Also by John Rolfe Gardiner

The Incubator Ballroom

In the Heart of the Whole World

Great Dream from Heaven

Unknown Soldiers

Going On Like This

Somewhere in France

To Mike —

With admiration —

And appreciation for

leading us over the Divide

John Rolf Gardiner

Somewhere in France

John Rolfe Gardiner

Alfred A. Knopf   New York   1999

THIS IS A BORZOI BOOK
PUBLISHED BY ALFRED A. KNOPF, INC.

www.randomhouse.com

Knopf, Borzoi Books, and the colophon are registered trademarks of Random House, Inc.

Library of Congress Cataloging-in-Publication Data
Gardiner, John Rolfe.
    Somewhere in France / by John Rolfe Gardiner.—1st ed.
       p.   cm.
    ISBN 0-375-40740-5
    1. World War, 1914–1918—France Fiction.   I. Title
  PS 3557.A7113S66   1999
  813'.54—dc21   99-15603
                                                CIP

Manufactured in the United States of America
First Edition

To Ann Close, my editor,
and Wendy Weil, my agent

St. Mark's on Seine

$\mathcal{O}$n October 3, 1917, a few days before his American medical team arrived to join him in Chaumont, Major Lloyd entered the Hôtel Rive Haute for a final inspection. As a roving officer of the Chief Surgeon's staff, he had requisitioned the building for Base Hospital 15 of the Allied Expeditionary Force. A few French casualties were temporarily in beds on the ground floor, attended by a single French doctor.

From somewhere inside, a husky voice rang through the marble columns and echoed in the stairways:

> "Where is the pity for those who have none,
> Who can forgive what the Germans have done?"

"Be quiet!" he called out.

The singing continued, and he cocked his ear for its direction.

"Quiet, I said! This is the commanding officer!"

Only for another day, until Colonel Hanson arrived.

"This is a hospital!"

The song was finished, but a humming continued. The Major despised this sort of insolence. He came through a doorway at the back of the lobby, into a large bathroom. A small fellow was on his knees, scrubbing the floor. The man stopped, did not turn, but gazed upward with a saintly patience at the urinal in front of him. There was a powerful smell of ammonia around him. It was perfume to the Major's sense of hygiene. This, and the picture of the poor man at his thankless task, turned the officer's mood, filled him with pity and self-reproach.

Good enough, he thought, the man must come with the building. I'll make a place for him in the table of organization. "Well done. What's your name?"

Still he would not look up, but went back to his chore. His exertions had pulled the shirt from his trousers, exposing his back. Closer, Major Lloyd saw that he'd been quite mistaken. He was staring down at a woman's waist and hip. Quickly, he turned away, and asked again, "But who are you?"

The deep voice, the pants, military-issue, and the rolled sleeves. All this and the bobbed black hair had deceived him. At last she turned to him. Her lively round face was red, and wet with perspiration; her large gray eyes, accusing.

"My name is Jeanne Prie," she said. "I am a nurse. I will work for you, if you please. But not in such filth."

At the Major's request, she did stay on after the French patients had left. And on. Without the usual papers or references because she so clearly knew what she was about, and worked harder than any two others. For several months, there was only brief mention of the nurse as "my French wonder" in Major Lloyd's mail home, though she was making a name for herself through all ranks of the hospital.

Within a year, the Major's family could sense her presence and influence in all his news, even when her name was not written. By then, Lloyd knew that her presentation of herself as a charwoman on her knees had been a clever bit of theater to ensure herself a part in the coming practice of military medicine in Chaumont.

October 20, 1917
Somewhere in France

The rear of an army in battle is the most discouraging sight. The Adjutant here, a bad penny from my school days, is the worst sort of scoundrel and ought to be horsewhipped. The nurses, even the untrained, do adequate work, though the morals of my Americans are sometimes lax. We have a French wonder who puts them all to shame. The hospital's enlisted men are sluggards. The German prisoners, the intelligent ones, believe their cause lost, and only fight on to inflict as much damage on the world as possible.

Dr. Lloyd's observations pressed against the censors' nets like determined Sargasso eels, and many passed through, making their way across the Atlantic to the Lloyd drawing room in Manhattan. Here they wriggled under the watering eyes of his wife and mother, as the women thought again of the husband's, the son's, honorable duty and danger.

The two were eager to share whatever words survived. Once a week, or once a month—the irregularity of delivery was unconscionable—the widow-mother, Mrs. Helen Livingston Lloyd, would arrive in the city from the old family plantation at Moriches on the South Shore of Long Island, carrying another letter, or at least a tin of pastries to sweeten the commiseration with her daughter-in-law, Emma.

"Why does he write so misshapenly?" Emma scolded on one of these visits.

"A pretty script is only a vanity," the older woman, pulling irritably at the retractable chain of her pince-nez, defended her boy. Years earlier when she had asked the same question, one of his schoolmasters had said, "A true intellect rushes on with what it has to say without stopping to admire its penmanship." He had nothing like the fine hand of so many of his peers.

And so her only child, her "Boykins," her "Billy Lengthwise," her "Buster," had been sometimes a hero even by default.

"Don't call him those names," Emma pleaded. He still offered his mother the childish endearments, while Emma made do with "William" at the end of a letter. He was forty-four years old and a major, commissioned at Allentown, where his unit from Roosevelt Hospital had been trained in June of that year, 1917, before shipping off to his "somewhere in France."

It was a somewhere with a Roman triple-arched stone bridge and a fifteenth-century church with magnificent glass, and wonderful walks, "if there were only time," beside fields worked by shaggy-footed draft horses. "Even here in the zone of advance, you'd hardly know there was a war on."

It was selfish of her to suspect that he took a secret pleasure in the heroic mystery of his "somewhere," and the mother-in-law, Helen, dismissed Emma's quibble. It was the censors they should blame. Her Billyboy, now Major Lloyd, had told them how silly the rules were. How matters of far greater moment were published daily in the papers, how the French sent letters to his unit giving name, rank, organization, place, on the *outside* of their envelopes.

In Helen's and Emma's mail from France, there was sometimes a blot of ink where a proper name should have been, a person or a place. And some of their letters had the text washed completely black where Dr. Lloyd must have attacked the week's news with a cavalier indifference to regulation. Emma would be furious with him, but the mother, Helen, again blamed the ignorant sentries. She turned their insult into public shame, as if new insights from the family hero had been denied to the world. Information such as this, already received:

The Poilu is a marvelous, filthy, courageous, ignorant fighting man. . . . I pass my life among men who have looked death in the face and been unafraid. . . . The French officers of the rear are delightfully reassuring and totally ineffective. . . . The health of the French people is remarkably good.

Thanks to you, Emma, I have the Emerson at my bedside. I hope you've bought another copy so that you and the children will not be without his advice; two copies, in fact, one for the city and one for Moriches. The boys especially should have another go at these essays. I believe they went right over Willie's head on his first try. And Louis may have been too cocky to listen to anyone's counsel. Keep reminding them that Nature manifests the rules for their conduct. That's the key to it all. They've just got to open their eyes to Nature, God's first Bible.

More of their man's handsome generality, while Emma yearned for a messy detail that might give his sacrifice useful edge. In April of 1918—he'd already been abroad ten months—came another sheet painted black by the censor, and written somewhere in France to "My Dear Emma from Your William." She ripped it to pieces in front of William's mother, as if the woman had only raised her Billyboy to torment her, and she rubbed her face red in the scratchy horsehair of the parlor's Biedermeier sofa. An immature excess, which the mother-in-law thought to ease by preparing tea.

Helen thought back to her earliest warning to her son about Emma. "The stock is fine, William, but you won't be marrying her family. Emma is so easily frightened." His reaction had been quick and perhaps a little disloyal: "I know she's excitable, Mother, and she's got a regular Delafield pudding of a face. But to me, it's beautiful." In Emma's wide-set eyes he read accurately an unfailing affection. If she was a bit jowly straight on, in profile she was a silhouette cutter's dream. You'd hardly know the nose was not as precisely chiseled as a Lloyd's.

Helen had always imagined someone more assertive for her son. This Emma Delafield was nicely educated, but gentle to a fault. When she had someone down, she was far too softhearted to squash him, though it might be well deserved. It was both hard and cunning that Helen foresaw this as a failing that could destroy a marriage.

It was true enough that Emma could be overmatched by life's deceits and its untoward surprises, and what better example than her husband's choice of patriotism over family, which obliged her to present a reasonable bitterness as pride. Yet her self-assured mother-in-law could not frighten her. Each of the women thought she was reaching more than halfway for accommodation with the other. So their hands might touch while their thoughts slipped past each other to settle on private grievances.

Now they wrote a letter together to shame William from his continuing carelessness, Helen holding the pen and editorial control as Emma dictated: "No more names, no more places. Let us fill in the empty spaces."

And he answered: In this army, it is not such a coincidence to find someone in your unit whom you knew as a boy. And unless you are the same rank, this is bound to lead to awkwardness. In my case, the bête noire is ———, whom I was forced to room with for part of my last year at St. Mark's. He is our Adjutant! And as thoroughly corrupt in the army as he was in school.

/   /

As it turned out, they were able to fill in the blank easily enough a week or so later. On her next visit, Helen overstepped her pity for the too-emotional Emma, bringing a gift in a shoe box from the country.

"Here, dear, no one censored these."

It was all the mail her son had sent home from St. Mark's School in Southborough, Massachusetts, some thirty years earlier, letters numbered from 1 to 196. Each year of his school life, from twelve to sixteen, tied in a separate packet with thin green twine, and put away till now.

If she had read them over, she would have become a censor herself. But her memory of those years had sweetened with time. Overcome with the sentiment of her own gift of letters, she embraced Emma and said, "I'll tell you what. We'll call his posting St. Mark's on Seine."

"You think the Boche have reached Paris?"

"No, calm. Remember? The zone of advance does not always mean the front."

Emma was already opening the first packet, marked 1885, about to learn: The trouble about my bed has only happened once this week. Matron sets an alarm for me that rings at 2 a.m. The clock is under my pillow, but Tisdale and Willis, who sleep on either side, can hear it and have told the others.

"Poor thing," Emma said, "he never told me."

Already the older Mrs. Lloyd wished she could take back her well-meant gift. "I'd almost forgotten. But he was only twelve years old. Everyone had a theory. We were told he'd have to be shamed out of it."

Major Lloyd, ordered off his compulsive naming of military friends and acquaintances, and away from geographic precision, could still make clear to his family his elation at service in uniform. The old place at Moriches, he said, had sent one son to the Revolution and one to the Civil War, and he would not run from his duty to honor it in this, the Great War.

He had toured much of France, scouting for hospital sites, arguing with hoteliers, preparing for the coming Expeditionary Force; now he was speaking French lickety-split, amusing his French counterparts, letting verbs take whatever tense and person they pleased, and the nouns choose their own gender; for a while he did autopsies, studied lung tissues scarred by gas, and recommended new combinations of counteragents and filter systems to be employed in Allied masks.

A very busy, very happy man, to hear him tell it. Then back to Base Hospital 15 in XXXXXXXXX, where he expected to be placed in command.

"St. Mark's on Seine," Emma agreed they would call it.

Wherever he went, making himself indispensable. But Emma suspected her husband was not indispensable to an Allied Expeditionary Force. Even as she knew he would be working overtime to distinguish himself. It annoyed Emma that Helen should turn his reports into a kind of boasting, by which she could distance her son from the less sanguine volunteers and from the misguided pacifists who had to be pushed to the draft, though, thank God, there were only a handful of them.

He wrote that the failure of the United States to come through on schedule was disgraceful: Have to go north this week to meet the Boston Dr. (you know his name) who clips people's shoulder blades. I now wear a gold **V** on my left sleeve, four inches above the wrist, indicating I have been in the zone of advance for six months. Remember, this doesn't mean the front.

He wrote to his mother that her idea of a weekly telegram was no good. Far too expensive, and as likely to be delayed as ordinary mail. It could only make her worry more if she became dependent on weekly confirmation of his safety. Odd, he thought, that she should have given Emma the school letters:

Oh well, no harm. But is Emma taking proper precautions for the children against infections? She writes me, yes, but is she too upset to be making wise decisions? I have autopsied a number of fever victims here. Something different is happening; a deadly strain has appeared in France, and Americans are being blamed for it. The tissue of the diseased lung is heavy as a wet sponge in your hand, saturated with fluid. Breathing becomes difficult, then impossible.

He still couldn't believe that one of his letters had been washed black. As if a week-old report of the weather conditions in a northwest salient could help the Kaiser, when, for God's sake, the rain was general all over northern France, and the only thing moving over the trenches at the time were acute lung irritants, a new British lachrymator, a paralysant of hydrocyanic acid that no side would own to, and the standard German mustard.

By May of 1918, Emma knew that her mother-in-law had kept some of William's news and advice from her, had not shared every letter from France as she'd promised to do. Helen was pretending it was her own idea that the children should come to Moriches that summer for the fresh air blowing off the ocean. Actually, Emma knew from her own mail that her Major had ordered his mother to get the family out of the germy city, even if it took a threat of disinheritance. A horrid thing for him to suggest, and she wrote him so, and received his apology as plans were made to obey his command.

Still trying to make himself a man in the eyes of his mother. In the old mail, Emma could see him at twelve, writing what amounted to a weekly confession to his parents. Like a frightened papist child, she thought, forced to invent trivial sin, rather than claim seven days with none at all:

I don't know how to bridle my tongue when I get excited. The other day in the gymnasium, I was wrestling with a fellow and turned him over once, and Fairbanks, who was watching, said he knew my knack. I said I hadn't one, but he had guessed it. He told me what it was, and without thinking, I denied it. I hate to tell you such things. I have prayed to be forgiven. But this has spoiled two or three days for me.

He had sinned, too, in his leadership of the stamp-collecting craze sweeping through the school in his third-form year. He and other boys were acting as agents for stamp dealers in the city. An educational activity sanctioned by Headmaster Peck, but commercially tainted, with a premium on sharp trading: A boy wanted me to sell to him on Sunday. I gave him the stamps but did not collect his twenty cents until Tuesday.

Was that wrong? If you think so, I'll give the money back. I don't think I can expect him to return the stamps.

He had promised his parents he wouldn't borrow, but there were pressing obligations: I have pledged fifty cents to some friends of Mr. Peck who are starting a church in Florida, and now I am in debt. Please send me two dollars. Don't send it to Mr. Peck. Send it to me.

Emma pitied her little-boy husband-to-be more when she read: I stand thirteen in my class of seventeen this marking period. That is dreadful and I feel terrible about it. Some of the boys say I deserved to stand much higher. The dirty little rat, Mr. Wilmer, is responsible for my trouble. I'm going to try my very best for you. I would like a picture of you and father for my alcove.

Later that same month, little Billykins was disgusted by another boy he wrestled, who had got him down and tried to do something dirty on him, and they could be sure that he would never wrestle with that boy again.

What kind of school was it, Emma wondered, that would have a boy "run the gauntlet" on the day of his arrival: I didn't get hurt. There were no stones in the handkerchiefs this year, only knots.

Pledges, doubts, confessions, pleas for small change. For Emma, so many years later, the school letters were clear evidence of tyranny over an only child. But her sympathy for William was mixed with a distaste for his showy submission: In my free time, I am reading only the books on the list you and Father approved. Song of the Way West by MacIntyre is bully

And why had all this Billyboy-Billikins-Willytop pabulum survived into manhood, now to be pressed on Emma's children? The ready-mades for William junior; for Louis, "Loulou," which would be confused with the feminine Lulu; while Helen, the youngest at fifteen, and the prize of her absent father's lap, was distinguished from the grand-mother Helen with "Nellie" or "Nelliebelle." Emma knew her children loved their long visits to the great farm at Moriches and saw that they accepted the endearments as the common fare for all children of loving families—the privilege of a grandparent.

As William soldiered on somewhere in France, he was becoming a different man in Emma's eyes. The pride and satisfaction that Helen took in his service, Emma reappraised in light of their antecedents. Since the child was father of the man, and the childhood was documented, her husband was laid open to an easy scrutiny. She saw a danger in this. But still she moved ahead through the boyhood letters, though only a few each day so as to put off a time when there might be no news of her Major at all, new or old.

The old mail gave her a hold over his present wandering, a compensating power over his insensitivity to her loneliness. Why did he keep telling her he was so happy, and so happy with himself? It was no special comfort to know where his passion for approval had come from. Still twelve:

I am not so fresh this term, and now I want to begin to get in favor with the school in general.

Imagine a child that young calculating his institutional progress! And thirty-two years later, he was writing to Emma:

I wonder how my experience here will affect my return to Roosevelt Hospital, and what sort of assignments I should look for—autopsy (one never has enough experience at this), administration, treatment of the wounded. Lately I work all day and well into the night. Neither my car nor my driver can keep my pace. I'm giving them both a week off. So the car can be taken to the shop and the driver can take to his bed.

Emma read for the first time that he longed for the day he would return with honor. There's a blackbird that sings beautifully over here, he told her, but I miss the song sparrow. He was learning to speak better French and she should do the same to keep up with him. Someday he would bring her to this beautiful country.

She could settle for these palliatives or jump back three decades to the news from St. Mark's when he was "putting aside bad thoughts and bad language and giving up chess for Lent," and had been surprised by a man who had come to lecture the school on the Indian question and taken the part of the Indians.

From France, he gave her a rather pathetic account of a weeklong bout with "gyppy tummy," which he believed he'd acquired on a motor trip to XXXXXXXX to give two generals their physical examinations. Even intestinal misadventure could be chased into the past:

Ate some pork scraps and got the diarrhea squirts. The doctor came to the school hospital and gave me a powder.

Helen's boy had kept no secrets. She remembered his problem as "autointoxication," too much inward energy that could turn him pale. But it was clear to Emma from the early letters that her William had been primarily afraid of God, and then of his parents as His agents on earth. So much so that he had confessed to everything, inviting his mother and father each week into his guilty conscience.

And from father to son, the burden had passed again. Emma liked to recall a scene from the Moriches summer when her own son Willie was only ten. The boy had carried a sand bucket of green apples from the orchard down to the dock. He and his father, William, were throwing them as far as they could, into the water, aiming at a dinghy tied up behind an unfamiliar crab boat. The larger boat swung around on its mooring, putting it in the line of fire.

Father and son kept right on throwing like two naughty children. Some of the apples were bouncing into the cabin. And smash! The crabber's glass windscreen was broken and scattered over its little foredeck. Emma, watching her husband and son, was more astonished at what she saw next—the two of them laughing and running up the meadow, away from their mischief.

She called at them to stop, and they realized, with fallen faces, they'd been caught. They came to her sheepishly. "You two devils!" she said. They doubled over in convulsive laughter. There was never another incident like it. Such a happy moment between father and son. At a time for scolding, only impish glee between them. Emma loved the recollection, but the story had aged and was no longer useful in rescuing Willie from his father's thorough disapproval.

Emma saw her in-laws as moralists whose own livelihoods had been well favored by advantageous family and business connections, and who had driven their only child to intellectual achievement and professional accomplishment well beyond their own limits of perseverance.

But they had saved the family plantation, at least twelve hundred acres of it, no small accomplishment.

When they had first taken it on, Gus had not been so wealthy. Helen boasted that in lieu of a fine piece of jewelry for a wedding present, she had accepted a sloopload of manure—organic matter, please—from her Gus, the nitrates that drove ten profitable acres of asparagus shoots out of the sandy loam.

Flax had been the cash crop once, but the market for the linen fiber had collapsed. In a moment of defensive pride, Helen had informed Emma that though it was her husband Gus's birthright farm, it was the wealth of two of her own celibate uncles that had built the comfortable house here, and her own family furniture—grand pieces from England, secretary and sideboards, and a later style of cabinetry from Newport—that furnished it. Of course, her Gus had later prospered marvelously on a tip from Mr. Morgan, whose sister shared a childhood with Helen. Yes, he'd had ample means to leave his stock brokerage behind and move his life to Moriches as a gentleman farmer.

The country effort was understood among the Lloyds and their cousins to be a courageous venture restoring a family institution that had fallen close to extinction with heavily mortgaged lands, and farm buildings rotting from the roofs down. Helen and Gus surely loved the land and its natural bounty—the duck hunting, the fishing, the orchards, the grain and livestock.

Gus's claim on the place descended from a line of farmers and states-men here, beginning with the immigrant Welshman Richard Lloyd's purchase of five thousand acres in 1678. Richard's grandson, William, held on to three thousand, and with no education, but a farmer's recti-tude, shambled into the Continental Congress, representing his Long Island brothers of the land, and later into the Constitutional Conven-tion, eventually ambling back to his farm, a "Signer," giving cachet to those who followed in his line.

This William's great-grandson, John Gelston Lloyd, forsook the farm, once worked by slaves, to follow his conscience into the House of Rep-resentatives, where his abolitionist oratory scalded compromisers high and low. He let the plantation run toward ruin in penance for his fore-bears' black-stained gain. John's grandson Gus arrived two generations later to rescue the property from failing cousins, who were ready enough to pass title to any Lloyd who would assume their debt.

The rebuilding began. The new house, funded by Helen's uncles, was conceived on a large scale but with little thought to outward charm; the opulence all inward, according to Helen's design, rooms measured to suit the dimensions of her furniture waiting in the city. Two high-ceilinged stories and a spacious attic, a wood-framed rectangular box, built four feet above the ground against the high water of storm or equinoctial tide rising across the flat plane on the Great South Bay only a quarter mile distant. The front, with two ill-proportioned dormers, faced east across Forge Creek toward Center Moriches. And running the length of the front on the ground floor was a screened porch, called "the cage," where they sat during the long summer evenings, trapped inside by hordes of mosquitoes.

The siding was round mustard-colored shingles, which Emma thought of as the hue of dyspepsia. But the home's most hideous outward feature was a sleeping porch built on four twenty-foot stone pillars, an addition that Gus had called "the camel," and which gave Helen the screened fresh air she expected of country sleep, and a vantage from which she had a commanding view of the farm's low-lying acreage. One could see across the creek to the roofs of Center Moriches, and to the south, across the bay to the Fire Island shore. There was a four foot megaphone kept on the porch, which, on a quiet day, could summon a farmhand or a child a half mile away, or, in emergency and with the help of an offshore breeze, bring someone off the bay.

Since America joined the Great War, the camel had become Helen's military observation post. It was not just a rumor, she assured Emma—hadn't William promised them it was true?—that German spies disembarked from time to time from submarines, and these had made their way across Fire Island to steal small craft and float stealthily over to the South Shore beaches.

Emma's children arrived at Moriches that summer one by one. First William junior, Willie of the green apples, who was twenty-one and attending Dartmouth again after two years as a Wall Street runner. A bighearted, blustering failure, scorned by his father for academic laziness. He might have had a happy, productive life learning to manage the farm, Emma thought, but more was expected of him, and so more must be tried. College and a profession.

Some asked a more difficult question—why the middle-aged father served abroad while this able-bodied son shirked. The father, over there, and waiting to hear that Will junior would soon be adding his name to the lists, while another doctor had justified the boy's deferment with diagnoses of poor pulmonary function and the occasional palpitation.

To look at him, one would suspect nothing wrong, and Willie would admit to no infirmity, preferring to appear in control of his nonmilitary destiny. He could be roused from his easy amiability to a thundering temper, and his siblings dared not question his reluctance to serve, but what would his father say to the apparent malingering?

It wasn't that college was difficult, Willie told his mother, Emma, but much of it too trivial. All that study, as pretty and weightless as a butterfly. And like a butterfly, it kept flitting off beyond his reach. He had dropped out for two years and then been allowed back. Moriches without his father would be like a school without masters—all sport and no tedious books—and he left his classes and came hurrying home at the first encouragement. He was taller and heavier than his father, with a pretense of worldly experience that kept his more gifted siblings at awestruck heel.

When Louis arrived in June after his examinations, Emma heard the older brother chide him for risking his life to city germs for such an airy conceit as a few lines of Chaucer. What could a dead scholar add to the family's reputation or fortune? Louis, easily bullied, accepted a fishing pole and prepared for a season of leisure with his brother on Moriches Bay.

Nellie, fifteen, came a day later, released from academic jail, and the boys circled around her, avoiding her attempts to hug them. She flew into Emma's arms when they pretended they were actually afraid of her extra day of exposure in the city. "Valetudinarians," the grandmother called the boys. The fearful spawn of a doctor, but two of Nellie's schoolmates were in the hospital and one of them had a brother already dead from an unnamed fever. Emma thought a few days of confinement for her daughter would be prudent, though it made little scientific sense, because at mealtimes and each evening the two of them had a little cry in each other's arms.

Nellie had tight brown curls, a minor overbite that did no special harm to a pretty mouth, and eyes dark with a family love that was lost on oafish brothers. As a girl, she escaped the professional expectations that kept the boys ever under the father's critical eye. She could read hours on end in her grandparents' library without fear of being called to account for intellectual achievement.

Still, Emma knew it was no small hardship and insult to be kept apart for a week. And she forgave her daughter for rummaging through the shelves for grown-up literature and rifling the drawers of the tall secretary, the repository of her dead grandfather's office paraphernalia, which, in her distress, she spread about the room: hole punch, compass, pens and nibs of all styles, cloth measuring tape, penknives, pipes and pipe cleaners, playing cards, letter openers, sealing wax, dozens of seals, folding rules, inkwell, magnifying glasses, mucilage, opera glasses, a spyglass, a kaleidoscope, paper clips, pins, postcards and embossed stationery.

Down and down she must have gone through the drawers until at the bottom she found the shoe box full of the St. Mark's letters, where Emma had secreted them, letters proving to Nellie the obvious, that her own father had once thought like a child and written in the hand of a child.

Emma removed the letters and hid them, but much too late. Nellie had already had four days alone to absorb them, flaunting her new knowledge of her father in front of mystified brothers. And soon they pried the source from her, and they, too, had pored over their father's juvenilia.

Helen thought Emma might take more pride in her husband's military progress, the personal achievements that set him apart from the other volunteers, from the training in Allentown to the present. How he had arrived all alone in a French town with no American but his chauffeur anywhere near, and in charge of the biggest hospital job in France, traveling to acquire and organize all the medical units for the coming American forces.

There had been his voluntary instruction of men on the steamship crossing when others were loafing, his study of French while others played tennis, the researches on mustard gas with so much more thoroughness than the studies of his fellow officers (how could Helen know that?), the preparation of the facilities in his mystery city, the arduous trips to acquire hospital materials, then the request for service with the Chief Surgeon's Office during a doldrum when others were content to sit on their hands. Helen declared that he had everyone's confidence and was given responsibilities far beyond his rank.

Oh yes, Emma knew, just as he'd translated his Latin with honest diligence when all the rest of his class had cribbed it. But she bit her tongue. After all, there was a report the Germans were bombing some of the rear hospitals. Helen's bragging was part of the brave front she put up against the real fear of her son's danger, and all for the benefit of the family. They did have some kind of hero at war in France.

His somewhere was Chaumont. Not the one their guidebooks would have told them about. Not on the Loire, but the Marne. Here in Chaumont, he still hoped to take full charge of Base Hospital 15, a sanitation nightmare, a compound of eager and wild American nurses, their meek French counterparts, sisters from a convent in Reims, a too-randy staff, and all manner and ranks of itinerant patients. Far too much of the kiss-me-quick business going on, he wrote to Emma. Too much like a service-sanctioned bordello. "In a foreign country, they think themselves free from public opinion, and licensed by the uncertainties of war, they debase themselves."

He lectured the American women, told them their fame had spread to Vittel and might soon reach the trenches, and that soldiers joked about them: If you're wounded, ask for the girls at Chaumont. They'll take your pulse all right! That's the place!

Was that the kind of reputation they wanted?

He gathered them together in a corner of the makeshift hospital's grand lobby. He had requisitioned this building against the bitter arguments of the proprietor. Now, maybe about to take charge, he feared it was becoming a hospital Sodom.

The tall nurse, Prudence Plume, stood up with a flashing eye and demanded to know which of them he was accusing. There was no doubt he had seen several of them in the evenings leading men by the hand out of the ward—the hotel's large dining hall—and up the stairs to private rooms. He had no intention of following these trysts to their seamy conclusions. The women must police themselves, or be gone.

"No," Prudence told him, "you slander us all. Make a direct accusation or take back what you said. Don't you know when the lavatory is crowded, that some men have to be taken upstairs? And the stairway is used for exercise."

He apologized, and said that others, with less clear consciences than hers, would know what he meant. He was losing the nurses' confidence and cooperation, the worst that could happen in a hospital. He spent the next week passing out compliments, repairing the damage.

He was able to write at last that though he'd made a botch of it at the start, he now had earned back the nurses' goodwill. They were doing splendid work for him, and his hospital would be on the road to full recovery if he could only get rid of the miscreant Adjutant Lieutenant ————, who assumed that as the commanding Colonel ————'s aide, he spoke with the Colonel's authority:

The scoundrel imagines charge over me because my promotion to Major was only by dint of assignment of a pay grade suitable to my profession.

This man from his past was countermanding Lloyd's orders, slinking around with one of the nurses, and conniving with the mess sergeant to feed the officers well while denying decent food to the patients and common soldiers, and pocketing the difference. Stealing!

The Major tried to improve morale in the command by organizing a baseball game in which nurses, officers, and enlisted men all took part. But the enlisted men made ill-bred remarks about the nurses and spoiled the function. Nurse Plume, on reaching base successfully, wiggled her behind in triumph. And Latoni intimidated the umpiring private, and was damnably skilled with the bat.

For a brief time, Lloyd was made Summary Court Officer and President of the Post Exchange Council. He took this opportunity to examine Adjutant Latoni's procurement records. There were erasures, contradictory entries, and faulty or false addition. He gave his findings to Colonel Hanson, and was quickly replaced as Court Officer by the frightened Colonel. This only made the Adjutant bolder. He was courting a clique of favored henchmen among the enlisted personnel, leaving others threatened and discontented in their work.

The Colonel was a gentleman with no medical knowledge and no taste for scandal, a man hoping to embarrass no one. The result was dissolution, misbehavior, frequent trials, and ineffective company punishments. There was garbage left in buckets at the kitchen door—rat bait—men and women debasing themselves, drug chests left unlocked, morphine disappearing, and Latoni, still giving orders, though a party to all the worst that was happening.

·

In Moriches, Emma was losing control of her family. Willie, who should have been shamed by his father's mail from France, showed no contrition. Instead of reforming, he was affecting the scholar's wrinkled brow like his brother, Louis, who was suddenly given to showy displays of shallow philosophy recycled from the cocky tongue of one of his college instructors.

"Prayer, the way it's practiced around here, is a thieving selfishness."

How dare he? In front of them all at the table.

"I don't want to hear any more from your Mr. Fiskett."

"It's not my Mr. Fiskett," Louis assured his mother. "It's *your* Mr. Emerson. The one you and Father insist that we read, and he says quite clearly that prayer for a particular narrow end suggests a duality in nature. Him and us. When all the evidence is of unity. He *in* us."

She dismissed Louis from the room, but his argument was left unchallenged, a subversion hanging over the table for the consideration of William and Nellie. No need to trouble her husband with this problem. Instead, she wrote to him of the family's "halcyon season together," all fitting into the old house as if they had grown up there.

Nor did she mention that Louis, against his grandmother's rules, had brought an uncleaned fish into the house. One of the flat kind with both eyes on one side, which he'd lifted, still alive and flapping about, from his fishing pail, placed on the kitchen's marble counter, to tap it with a wooden mallet.

Unflustered by his mother's sudden appearance, he had turned to her and said he wanted to see if he could make the thing take the color of the countertop, the way it would camouflage itself on the floor of the bay.

"Father approves of using animals in scientific experiment," he reminded her.

He thought of putting it on a background of plaid cloth to see if this produced a nervous reaction. Emma was horrified, but her letter to the Major referred only to "Louis's new contact with nature afforded by the farm and its salutary effect on his curiosity."

Willie was a different kind of problem. Under the gruff pretense, he could be such a warmhearted soul, her favorite, though she would never admit it, even to herself. The big lad couldn't prove himself academically, so he was forced to find other ways. He only appeared to be the head of the gang, dictating the day's activity to his siblings.

The Doctor and his first son had a recent history way out of place in Emma's loving family. Loud arguing, shocking language, and Emma forced to be referee. Each of them on his own was such an amiable fellow, yet the first word between them could set them off.

Instead of healing, the prospect of a family separation had fanned the bitterness. The weekend before the Doctor left for Allentown, they had gathered in the city, and Louis and Willie had put their heads together in defiance of all the college patriots and a whole country's banner. Willie was the one with the showy nerve and the perverse sense of timing to declare that the departing support personnel for the Expeditionary Force were doomed to be "ineffectual meddlers in other countries' affairs." As if his father might actually reconsider his coming tour in France.

In fact, this was pure Louis. Louis, the family thinker, who had enough foresight to try the idea on his broad-shouldered brother before announcing it himself. Emma knew it was not meanness that would make Willie attack at the heart of his father's life. It was not a premeditated ugliness, but more a compulsion to confront the man who seemed determined to make his first son's life an academic misery. He could not help himself from provoking his father.

Separate rooms were not sufficient boundaries to the war that followed. Emma got them on separate floors and demanded that both apologize. Later, Willie told his father he was sorry, that he had not meant to be disrespectful, and that he wanted to work harder than ever in the coming semester. The Doctor listened, and then he laughed in Willie's face. And Willie never forgot it.

The Doctor gave the back of his hand to his son and and went back to making a final balance of his checkbook before turning family finances over to Emma's management. Weeks later, from Allentown, he wrote to Willie that he had been pleased by his promise of scholarship, but all Willie saw was his father's upturned lip, and all he heard was the soft laughter absorbed forever in the rug of his father's study, a room he hoped never to walk in again.

June 9, 1918. The Germans were moving suddenly, advancing three miles a day. It wouldn't have surprised the Major if they took Paris, or came close enough to destroy it by shell fire. An American sick train had arrived at his base hospital in Chaumont with 250 new cases, and Adjutant Latoni, nurse-mistress on his arm, had chosen this difficult time to take three-day leave.

In a memo to the unit, Latoni had ordered that all personnel with problems requiring command decision should go directly to Colonel Hanson. They should not bother Major Lloyd, "who will be busy with his doctoring."

In the chaos of that week, some lax practice was slipping by uncited. Beds missed on morning rounds, nurses screaming in frustration, talking back to the doctors. The Major was watching it all, but there was far too much to correct all at once. One morning, he saw his French nurse going down the line of fever patients, calm as you please, bending over to talk to each privately, saying things that made them smile and reach out for her hand. He saw her touch one lightly on the forehead as she whispered in his ear. And the same down the row for two others, her forefinger on their brows, making some sign as she spoke to them. It was unsettling, as if she were giving them last rites. And the following day, all three were dead.

The Major mentioned this to no one. Could he be sure of what he'd seen? What might this woman know that she was not telling the rest of them? If he told the other doctors, Latoni would hear of it and try to make more trouble for her, blow it into a scandal. Lloyd was able to satisfy himself that Jeanne Prie simply had more experience than any of them. She might have seen signs in these men that she would not even be able to name.

The Major knew by then that he'd be spending the rest of the war in Chaumont if the German onslaught could be repulsed; he would not be running up and down the front doing autopsies on gas and fever cases. But he would never make the hospital run smoothly with Latoni in his way. Referring to him only as "the scoundrel," or "our miscreant adjutant," he tried to explain the situation to his mother and wife. The fact was, Latoni made Lloyd uncomfortable with himself.

It pleased the Major that Emma was now privy to his successes at St. Mark's through his own childhood mail. It might help explain to her his compulsion to volunteer. He'd been a leader at the school, first among the Harvard contingent. He'd left Southborough with happy arms in the air and a victory lap around the buildings. Long forgotten were self-penned doubts, which fascinated his wife and children in Moriches. Doubts such as:

I have a great deal of trouble not to say or do anything impure. I said something yesterday not exactly impure but bordering on it, which is almost as bad, and it reminded me of something I said last term, which was worse and which I forgot to speak of while I was home.

He did remember difficult times when his parents, not the masters or Headmaster Peck, seemed to be the main obstacles to his success. Especially in the last year. And a term that began with Mr. Peck assigning the boy with the Italian name, one of the fast kind with shiny shirts and pants, whose admission to the school was a mystery, to be his roommate. A boy who never thought of saying his prayers and swore awfully, and threatened to run away if his father did not bring him home.

Although Mr. Peck would not change the room assignment, he did call William in with several other boys to ask him to be a monitor. A great honor and one that he'd carried through life with pride. In France, he forgot the early doubts, the unflattering details that filled the shoe box, the self-incriminating things that his children were studying in fascinated leisure, way ahead of his wife:

We're supposed to report any vice we see and don't feel able to stamp out by ourselves. I see lots of things among the fellows that I have no power against. I can't go to Peck and report all these things. There'd be no end to my peaching.

Thirty years later, and once again in position to peach on scoundrels, Lloyd remembered few of his earlier words, though he was easily reminded of a separate embarrassment. It came back to him as the season he had written Emma Delafield asking if she would dance with him at the spring hop—months in advance.

And that led him back to the previous summer's house party at Edith Sands's home in Englewood, where Elsie had been one of the guests. It was to be a gathering of cousins and school chums—six boys and seven young women, several of whom had already charmed him into a stammering adolescent admiration. He had begged to be allowed to go. It was the thing he had most looked forward to. And he'd worked his way up close to the top of his form that semester; they couldn't say no.

When the party gathered, Edith gave him her brother's bed to sleep in, a prize, it seemed, as she showed them all to their quarters. The first day and night, they had reveled in openhearted congeniality, flirtations, and barely acknowledged pairings. On the second evening, he drank far too much cider. Retiring that night, he lay awake, waiting for the faintest urge to use the commode before falling asleep. He dreamt wonderfully, first of Edith, then of Edith's noisy friend Eugenia, who had touched his hand at table while asking for pepper.

The dreams were warm and affectionate beyond appropriate imagery and sensation, and he prayed in his drowsy state to be forgiven. He was most confused by his imagination's fickle wandering from a favored girl to a lesser for no apparent reason.

At dawn, in half sleep, he was luxuriating again in the security of the weekend's affability and fancied attachments. Moments later, he felt a warm wet spreading out from his center, already turning cold at the edges. He had discharged a full bladder through his pajamas, through the bedclothes, and into the brother's mattress.

His only hope was an open window, a drying breeze, and the discretion of the chambermaid. When it was time to leave, and all the young people were in the front hall making manners, Mrs. Sands singled him out for praise he'd never forgotten: "And you're the well-raised fellow who makes his own bed. But of course we strip them all after company. Edith says you must visit us again. Oh, I've made your cheeks red!"

He could only guess at how many there would share the knowledge of his habit. Worried that he had written himself out of the *Social Register,* his early invitation to Emma Delafield the following year had been a way of testing his standing. There had been no mention of his disaster. The terrible business never happened again. His father said it was because the mind within the mind had built its final barrier against the humiliation.

Major Lloyd thought of his wife's delight in reading of his triumphs in the gymnasium, and her pleasure in coming to that time when, after grinding like the devil, he had risen to first in his class. The respect he'd at last won from Mr. Peck, the masters, and even the matron of the Sixth Form House.

Then came a surprise at the end of one of Emma's letters about the children's progress on the farm. "I think we've found it! Is Latoni the name of your miscreant Adjutant? Yes, we're sure of it. Jerry Latoni." Pulled from his schoolboy correspondence and sent to him somewhere in France. The boy who had been dismissed from St. Mark's for escorting a young girl from the town onto the campus, and sneaking her into his room.

It surprised him now because it jumped forward as such a horrid and enlarged shame—one that did no credit to himself, though he could still rationalize his part in the dismissal. Latoni's adolescent stare of hatred and contempt was brought back to him with Emma's mention of the name, the irreverent Italian boy, flashy and crude. With the long black hair made slick with the pomade. He used to make a foul gesture with his whole arm and fist and call Lloyd a shit-heeled swell.

Something had happened to Latoni in the years between school and his entry to the army ranks; something had brought him down from a showy wealth to a dependence on the vulgar opportunities of a career soldier stuck in grade. The Major believed he could see right through the Adjutant. For Latoni the Army was just another class of dupes, and the war, a great play, a notorious comedy staged for his traveling amusement and financial benefit. His uniform was a silly costume, easily shed when he took leave for Paris. He had matured into the kind of man who needed a second shave by midafternoon, who used his dark beard and nature to intimidate. He still had that jaw-thrusting arrogance that won him a bully's share of friends. And a crude way with women, boastful and suggestive talk that he had practiced as a boy. It was contemptible that one of the nursing staff would blush and bend to his will.

Major Lloyd recalled that fall in 1889, when he carelessly followed his roommate on and off the St. Mark's campus on a Saturday-afternoon escapade of crime against his school and against his family's trust. Taunted, "Come on, momma's lamb, what are you afraid of? I'll show you what we're here for," William had followed. He stood outside Miss Crowther's room as Latoni rifled through the housemother's sewing box for a thick needle and heavy thread.

Parker, passing through the hall, whispered, "What's this about?" and William waved him off, already incriminating himself in front of a witness. Then he was following Latoni out the back door of the house, walking casually to the woods at the west end of the campus. They made a brief stop in the groundkeeper's shed, where Latoni swiped a pair of pliers and a spool of wire. A moment later, they were into the covering trees and heading for Chauncey Lake, where, the cool thief said, someone was waiting for them.

The boy had sensed that William, hanging back, was thinking of deserting and reporting him off bounds without permission. "Go on, pet, what do I care? Tell them whatever you want to."

He was having some trouble keeping up in the heavy underbrush; hadn't supposed the sport-shy Jerry could be in such good condition, and by then he wondered if the boy knew where he was going or was lost.

"Hurry up, if you're coming. They won't wait forever." "They" turned out to be she, and she was "Poxy Jane," as the St. Mark's boys called her. One of the town girls who gave them the eye of cold appraisal, the sneer of the poor for the rich, of the free for the chaperoned, from the back table of Dutch's drugstore in Southborough, where the older boys might be allowed for Saturday outings at the soda fountain if their grades and deportment were satisfactory.

"You're late," she said scornfully, not even turning from her seated position on the outcropping from which Foster had jumped the previous year and broken his arm. She flipped the cigarette she'd been nursing into the water.

"What's that you brought with you?"

"Lloyd. I told you about him."

"What's he for? There's nobody here for him."

"Nothing. Doesn't matter. Did you bring the umbrella?"

"You didn't notice it ain't raining? Yeah, I brought it."

William has never met a girl like this. Not to talk to. So unhappy and sour before anything had been said to upset her. Mouth turned down, or she might be somewhat pretty. Though as you got closer, you could see she used a thick lotion to cover the pocking on her cheeks.

"What are you staring at, boy?"

Her full shape was immodestly defined in a snug white blouse beneath the bib top and wide straps of her dress. And the dress was far too blue, electric blue, cut several inches above her ankles.

"I told you, didn't I?" Latoni looked to William, who wasn't sure what he was being asked to confirm.

"You told him what?" Jane said. "You told him nothing."

"I did. How easy you are to look at."

"You didn't either." The flattered girl looked to William, who was stubbornly refusing to tell a polite lie.

"Get down."

Latoni was reaching for one of her bare ankles. Jane screamed and slapped his hand away.

But then she was taking his other hand, staring into Jerry's eyes, and accepting his help down from her perch. Jerry handed William the umbrella and told him to open it, turn it upside down, and wedge it between the outcropping and another rock at the water's edge.

"Now," he said, "get up there on the bank and dig me some worms."

William, a monitor, didn't have to take orders from a fresh roommate, a boy who had no standing in the school, a boy he could get rid of with one short session of tattle in the headmaster's office. But he obediently began to gather worms from under the rocks close to the water. Where should he put them?

"He'll be going to the university in Cambridge," Latoni said.

"Oh, well then!" she said. "That explains it."

Jerry made a little worm prison of small flat stones, and William followed his order to fill it. He'd found several dozen before Jerry said they had enough and told him to sit on the big rock with Jane and learn something. Jerry threaded the stolen needle, then began to thread the worms through the length of their bodies. They watched the worms twist their ends away in futile refusal of the needle's point.

Jane turned to William. "Don't get any ideas," she said. "We're not doing anything in the woods."

"Never mind," Latoni snapped at her. "Pay attention."

He worked at it until he had something like a ten-foot-long worm, and then he began to roll it up as if it were a thick yarn, into a ball.

"Not too tight," he explained, "you don't want to kill them."

"Uck, it stinks!" she complained. But it didn't smell at all, and William saw that she was fascinated, climbing off the rock and placing her hands on Latoni's back, leaning over his shoulder.

When the ball was finished, Jerry wrapped it in a few more circles of thread, then hung it from a piece of the wire he'd taken from the shed. Jane flicked another half-smoked cigarette into the water.

"This better be good," she said. "I don't know why I waste my time."

"Time?" Jerry said. "What time?"

"You're paying for it. I want another packet of cigarettes."

"Sally doesn't ask for anything."

"So why didn't you ask her?"

William had never heard such a disagreeable flirtation.

"You won't catch anything with that," he said, "not without a hook."

"Five dollars?"

Jane stood up on the rock and told William, "He never saw that much money."

Latoni dropped the ball of worms, reached in his pocket, pulled out a wad of green bills, and riffled them under his thumb.

Jane sat down, silent for the moment, reconsidering her approach. William, who was not intimidated by the sight of money, but amazed to see so much of it in the hands of his roommate, asked, "If you're so rich, and you hate school so much, why don't you run away and do what you like?"

"You're ducking the bet, Lloyd."

"I'm not."

He wouldn't be shamed in front of this wild-bred girl, though he was flouting the school's strict rule against gambling or any kind of wager for money. Quickly, Latoni was standing on the rock and dangling his ball of worms into the lake.

Through the clear water they could make out a muddy bottom and the slimy trunks of birch and pine tress rotting under the surface. Something darted at the ball and grabbed it, and the wire was almost pulled from Jerry's hand. From the water he lifted an eel, which was hanging by its mouth. It was thick as his wrist and long as his forearm. How could it be—how could eels have found their way into this fresh-water? William was stunned.

"Come to poppa."

Jerry moved the line slowly around the rock and shook the eel loose over the inverted umbrella.

"Five dollars." He began to whistle. A pompous scatter of notes with no tune or rhythm. William, who didn't have five dollars to lose without going penniless for the rest of the semester, said the bet had been only for fish.

"The hell you say." Jerry glared at him. And he soon proved the catch had been no accident, snagging another eel. And then a third. When they bit at the worm ball, their teeth were caught on the thread, and he had them dangling helplessly until he shook them free over the umbrella.

Satisfied with his catch, Latoni took out his pocketknife and the pliers. He cut slowly through the neck of one, looking up at Jane, who obliged with a shudder. With the head dangling by a flap, Latoni cut an inch down the eel's length, then took hold of the body with the pliers and yanked in the other direction with the head, turning the skin inside out and leaving the naked body writhing for life already lost.

"That's disgusting," Jane said.

"You're going to help eat them, aren't you?"

"No!"

Jerry began to prepare a small circle of rocks for a fireplace, and a spit on forked sticks. He sent William into the forest for firewood, but this time when he returned, Latoni and Jane were gone. The skinned eels, woven into a slimy embrace, were still.

William remained there by the lake for an hour or more, not waiting for them—he knew he'd been played for a fool—but dithering over what to say when he returned to school. Complete honesty was expected and would be ruinous. Not just for Latoni but for himself. He'd been a party to theft and had wagered for cash. He'd lost a bet and then denied it. His conscience, racing here and there for cover, found none.

Back at school, his house was in a frenzy of gossip about the flashy boy from the Bronx. Tisdale had gone looking for William, and found Latoni in the room with Poxy Jane from the village. Not just in the room but lying on William's bed, the two of them embracing.

When William got back, Tisdale was still in the room, agog, going over the story in all its fantastic detail. "Didn't even cover the girl up. Just rolled over and said, calm as ever, 'Won't you just give us a few minutes, Tisdale?' and went back to his business."

Tisdale had gone quietly for the housemother, and her scream brought the English master, Mr. Bosman, who took Latoni into custody while the rest of the faculty was called into emergency session with the head. Latoni had secured his ticket out of Southborough. It remained to be seen what he had in store for William, who scurried to gather the five dollars to pay his debt.

As far as the Major knew, the only problem on the home front was his fantasizing mother, whose medicine must be a carefully turned lecture, which he hadn't the time to write that day. He had just been told there wasn't enough morphine to answer the needs of the moaning ward.

He ripped the Adjutant's memo from the dayroom door and marched across the street to the Colonel's quarters to report missing drugs, to demand a clear chain of command that must acknowledge his own rank of major as superior to that of the Adjutant, a mere lieutenant.

The news was sent home to Moriches something like this: The CO went to XXXXXXXX and was gone for a week. The miscreant Adjutant returned with his smirking nurse and a suitcase of morphine. "Just what the doctor ordered," the Adjutant said, offering an unlikely account of its acquisition from a French hospital in XXXXXXXXX. A drunken orderly had looked the other way in return for a quantity of American cigarettes, and no paperwork had been done.

Who was to vouch for the purity of the stuff? But the Adjutant was making him look a prissy fool, and the marvelous French nurse, Jeanne Prie, who had been here before the sisters or the American girls arrived, a woman who put the relief of pain before regulations, had already begun to soothe the suffering with the new analgesic, which proved satisfactory. This time, Lloyd did not scold. He went up and down between the beds, doing his best impersonation of an excellent diagnostician and competent doctor, which he was, and a man in full command of his domain, which he was not.

They always had several German prisoners in the hospital, those in such serious condition that no guard would be needed. Sucking chest wounds, leg amputations and such. He had watched with pleasure as Jeanne Prie showed her concern for the sick or wounded enemy and he encouraged the American nurses and his nuns to do the same.

To keep the family happier at home, he decided to tell them the humorous things: about the barber who started with his nose hair and eyebrows, and about his sharp-tongued laundress who thought he wanted her to share his bed, when he'd only meant to ask her if she could wash his sheets.

Altogether, he wrote, I live like a prince. The girl who takes care of my room is excellent; she does my mending, counts my wash going and coming—doesn't trust that laundress—cleans and dusts, shines my boots, and does not scruple to slap soldier or officer who insults her. For all this, I pay only seven francs a week.

The Major's room was on the corner of the French Officers' Quarters in a solid stone and mortar structure with a ceramic-tiled roof. There was a cement floor covered with a dozen throw rugs; electricity, steam heat, and a hole in the wall for a coal stove. The officers' section made an **L** with an enlisted men's barracks, joined together by toilets and showers at "Latrine Corner."

We sink to the Poilu's sanitation level because the Poilu refuses to rise to ours, he wrote his mother. Sewer pipe has no trap. Opens at upper end into large shallow bowl with corrugated foot plates to prevent slipping. The Poilu stuffs his old clothes in the pipe and wipes his hands on the walls. A good thing I learned to squat in the meadows at Moriches.

The French had asked him back to one of their hospitals that week to evaluate one of their cases, a soldier bruised all over. There was spontaneous hemorrhaging, loose teeth in bleeding gums. He knew immediately what it was. Fruits and vegetables had been available, but this man would eat none; he was dying of scurvy. Blood vessels leaking all through him, too late to save him.

As a precaution, the Major wrote out an order to his own mess sergeant that there should be more citrus fruit and heavy greens in the hospital diet, but the paper did not make it past the Adjutant's desk. Again the miscreant prepared a memo of his own, which said that medical staff were welcome to make dietary suggestions but that orders for procurement of foodstuffs must be left to military officers with contracting skills and experience in the local markets.

For the moment, he transformed his anger into love for his children. Writing Emma: You tell them how proud I am of their work on the farm, which, after all, is just as important as what we do here. Though I'm sure they would be here if they could, especially Willie. Did he tell you I wrote to him? Please tell him again that I forgive him and love him.

Now, Emma, I want you to tell Mother to get a grip. I've never been to the trenches and I've never been addressed by President Poincairé.

We all look the same when photographed in service hats. The picture she saw in the paper was not of me.

I've written to Mother about this business, but tell her again that on the night of June 3, I was safely in my room. There were no German bombs falling here. The Boche don't bomb hospitals, for fear of reprisal. These thought-transference games are all right for the parlor but have no place in wartime. They're going to make her sick.

I see a great deal of idealism, even among the men committing indiscretions. So your question about morality here has no simple answer. Perhaps I've given you the wrong impression. Low-class immorality is not the point. In fact, we suffer from too high a class in our personnel. Many of the enlisted men are college boys, some are independently wealthy, and some very wellborn. And the wellborn become the despised targets of a man like the miscreant Adjutant, while other officers show them too much deference. The intermediate and undefined rank of the nurses blurs the chain of command. In short, we haven't found ourselves yet.

For my own part, I sometimes have more influence with the Chief Surgeon's staff—for which I've done a number of things—than in my own hospital. The Chief Surgeon has told my CO, "If there's anything rotten going on, give Lloyd all the stick he needs. He'll clean it up." But the CO, for all his earnest effort, is the blind monkey here. Hates a row. Won't shovel the muck because he can't see it.

The Major must have forgotten that he'd already written about the German infiltration in America, because he told them again: I'm sure there *are* German spies all around you, in the city and on the Island. I know there are submarines off the coast, and you should have no lights to seaward at night.

I'm surprised by your fear of my part in the dances. Of course I have to attend to support morale. And if I'm there, I can't very well refuse when the bossy Nurse Rountree pulls me onto the floor. Most of the time, I crank the Victrola. Some romance that is!

My energetic French girl, Jeanne Prie, I've scarcely told you about her. I allowed her to stay here after the building was turned over to us. She's been the mediator between the two factions of nurses. On fire to save her country. No, she's not the one who carries the nail file with her wherever she goes. That's Lucille. She has an intuition about many of our patients that is quite remarkable.

I believe the Adjutant tried to use Jeanne as his contact for grafting with our suppliers, but this has only thrown her into my camp. Jeanne is thoroughly clever. I've ordered her to correct my French grammar, which she does without apology, though her English takes an odd turn here and there.

There's a deal more to tell you about her. She can barely hold her tongue when she hears a flawed diagnosis, but she knows it's a nurse's duty to listen and obey. The other day, she told me that all medicine runs forward and backward in history. And eventually the ends meet. I asked her to explain. She said that folk remedies and modern germ theories will be unified when microscopes of the future see into the smallest matters of the cell. An ordinary nurse volunteer talking this way? Actually, there's nothing ordinary about her.

You'll get a laugh out of this. She's hoping for a chance to prove to me the curative powers of the hot waters at Bagnoles de l'Orne. Of course this is a peasant mythology, charming but not worthy of her scientific mind. Don't worry, she would amuse you.

"She would not," Emma assured Helen. "And don't you find it odd that the names of nurses routinely pass the censors, while the men are protected with oblivion?"

"You mean anonymity."

"No, oblivion. This censorship is the army way of preparing us for permanent losses." There was a time when she could not say such a hard thing without blubbering, but unending fear has made her heart an unpredictable matter, sometimes granite, sometimes jelly. And her man has not been completely truthful. They know now that Germans have been bombing Allied hospitals. The pictures are in the papers. An operating table in a room with no ceiling, gurneys laden with bandaged mummies lined up in a courtyard full of rubble.

The farm rhythm at Moriches was supposed to settle Emma's nerves. Instead, she felt a guilt of indolence as she watched the scythe men move across the hay fields. In the slow, deliberate back-and-forth she saw not the blade of harvest but the pendulum of death, and she heard the careless voices of her own children, laughing and arguing points of shameful inconsequence.

A horse-drawn mower was broken and no part available for repairs. From Helen's despair—"What of the harvest?"—Emma heard the prosperity of the farm teetering on the want of a single gearwheel and cotter pin, though the place had been no more than marginally successful since Helen and her Gus had resurrected the windmill and repaired the roofs. Corn, hay, and mangel-wurzels were only harvested to support the livestock. The farm barely sustained itself with cattle, swine, orchards, fish and game, and modest income from the careful husbandry of the asparagus beds.

Emma could see the war brought with it a new national purpose, a grand spirit that foretold a concomitant prosperity. Of course, there was some grousing, some class resentment. You could occasionally overhear it in the village and in their own barns and kitchen, though the driver-handyman, Peterson, would not abide it in his presence. "If it's a rich man's game," he asked Willie, "why aren't you playing it?" Stirring trouble right under Emma's nose.

"Forced conscription is a national disgrace," Willie snapped at him, and Peterson pretended to wince, as if the boy had landed a body blow. "There's more liberty in Germany." Willie was talking like a Socialist, and worse, defending Mr. Debs. Probably after more instruction from his brother.

"And what's wrong with Debs?" Louis raised his voice to Emma, as if he were arguing with street rabble on a Cambridge corner. "A committed internationalist, just like Liebknecht on the other side. The Germans put Liebknecht away for a few months, but we want to lock Debs up for life!"

"What do you know about it?" she asked him.

"Mama, everyone knows that Viscount Grey and the capitalists in

London were as much to blame as the Kaiser's men. They pushed Germany into this."

She suspected these arguments, too, were coming straight down from his college. Was this what a gentleman's education had come to?

She looked to Willie again.

"I only go to Dartmouth," he said. "Father wouldn't put much store in my opinion."

"What do you mean?"

What was happening to her big fun-loving boy? Deferring this way to Louis, who would not give it up.

"Mother, it's just not as clear as you want it to be."

Nellie's ears were perked again for subversion while Louis, encouraged by his siblings' rapt attention, was explaining that, "For centuries the whole point of British diplomacy was to make sure that no significant military power established itself on the shores of the North Sea. When Germany went into Belgium. . . ."

Willie, who'd been nodding his head like a dodo bird, took the argument back to finish it: "The English are fine at getting other countries to fight their battles for them."

"Stop!" Emma ordered, but with no counterargument other than "the brutality of the German army and the sacrifice of so many Allied patriots," her children shied off into another afternoon as wastrels, and she sat down to write her husband the next installment of civilian life in Moriches.

She explained how all was going so splendidly on the farm. A few inconsequential breakdowns, nothing serious, and the children turning to with a will. She lied, too, about the good humor of the help. Secretly, she wished Helen would fire the insinuating driver, Peterson. He had come to the Lloyds as a young fellow very eager to please. But years of service had made him cocksure here, imperious. After Mr. Lloyd's death, he supposed himself indispensable to the widow. His proprietary interest in the Bouton bordered on outright ownership, as if all trips in Helen's car must be approved by him after his estimation of weather and road conditions. "You won't want to be driving today, missus."

And Peterson upset Charlotte, the cook and housekeeper, with his kitchen talk of city mayhem. Country mayhem, too. And more power, he said, to the vigilantes going after the antiwar bums. And it was every citizen's duty to report the slackers to their draft boards. Peterson made sure they all knew where he stood.

Such an unpleasant man, Emma thought, for all his patriotism, and far too attentive to her daughter's emerging beauty, arranging Nellie's lap rug just so with a familiar pat before a drive, and staring into her eyes too long for approval. Now he was fomenting political argument in the household with gratuitous questions about Willie's draft obligations, knowing full well the embarrassments that would ensue. She thought his daily mail run into Center Moriches and infrequent driving duties for Helen were hardly sufficient reason to maintain his noisy mouth at the farm's board.

Emma knew that Peterson had once made romantic appeals to Charlotte in her kitchen, and Charlotte had rebuffed him firmly, reporting his troublesome attentions to Helen. By making the unwanted advances immediately known in the household, Charlotte exonerated herself from any blame in promotion of a liaison so odious to her. Helen said she had been more amused than concerned when she saw the rejection did nothing to disrupt the household management.

Peterson continued to take his meals in the kitchen with Charlotte and the two of them could still chat away the hours in mutual umbrage at radical behavior, in political harmony. Dr. Lloyd had pointed out that the two of them were of a common facial type, with narrow jaws and palates that crowded their teeth forward into V's rather than arches. This, it was noticed, gave a pinched cast to their conversation, and suited the ferretlike tenacity of their sermonizing.

But in her letter to the Major, Emma said how lucky his mother was to have the extra help of a character like Peterson, who could engage the children in such lively conversation. As she wrote, she was actually thinking how her mother-in-law weighed her down, even the older woman's clothes, which were always the same, regardless of season. A full skirt of buff-colored cotton to the ground, a belted overblouse of the same material inset with lace, and under this a boned net guimpe covering her little neck all the way to the chin, threatening respiration. Along with low-heeled slippers made dainty with grosgrain bows, her uniform of constant civility was a reproach to Emma's relative informality—a single-piece dress, all the corsetted discomfort she could stand.

Emma closed her letter with troublesome lines about the children finding so many mysteries in his early mail. "Things I certainly can't answer. Except they wanted to know what could have become of that bounder Latoni, and this I was able to tell them. They were amazed, if you aren't. But explain to us again. As Adjutant, is he in charge of you, despite your rank? Or vice versa?

"Willie grew quite warm at Louis's suggestion that you might have been responsible for your own roommate's dismissal. So, in spite of all his argumentation, your oldest son harbors quite a respect for you."

It was not Emma, but Helen, who still believed there was a certain kind of family that had far too much money for its breeding, those who made tasteless displays of wealth, embarrassed themselves in foreign travel, played games like golf without a notion of the etiquette required, and flung their children at institutions where they were bound to be outclassed. It had been just so with the Latoni boy, Helen supposed. Their fathers indulge them, and look what happens to them in the end.

In fact, William suspected that the cash Latoni had displayed back at St. Mark's had not come from home, but from a clever cornering of the money supply within the school, whose source was monthly allowances, small fractions of the discretionary incomes of law partners, stock brokers, doctors, bankers; pried free of their scholar sons by Latoni's street cunning, by sharp trading, gambling, and outright thievery, though the last had never been proven.

When Latoni walked down the house corridor for the last time to be taken to the station, he looked at each of his housemates with a casual indifference, as if to say, You poor fish, you're already in the net, and you don't even know it. And William knew that he had been saved from early disgrace by that indifference. Latoni hadn't cared what the school or its headmaster thought of William, and therefore he said nothing to incriminate him. Though William had never been sure of that.

It had seemed like a sensible separation. Jerry hated the school, and most of the school hated him. A mutual good riddance, and forever. But a week after Latoni had gone, William still felt the hot flush of guilt on his neck whenever Mr. Peck glanced his way. It did not seem natural that he would not have been called to the headmaster's office.

There should have been pages of confession and extenuation mailed to his parents. Instead, he prayed to be forgiven, and waited for Peck to call him in. As the remains of that semester crept on toward his graduation, he spent his anxiety on still more rigorous study. And as his class standing approached the top again, his fear became lost in activity and in his sense of goodwill toward his fellows and the school that was about to bury his difficult season and write his name in Latin on a fine imitation of parchment. To release him to the Harvard zoology labs, unscathed, honored, on his way to medicine.

One afternoon, with the boys indulging themselves in the sailing skiff, tacking across to Fire Island, and Nellie gone on one of her beachcombing meditations, Emma sat in the orchard, staring up at a delicate white canopy of apple blossom, and heard "Emma, come at once" whispered in her ear, as if the bees had learned English. Or her Major, in extremis, was exhorting her with a telepathic love from across the sea.

Dismissing these conceits as war nerves, she sat up straight against the apple trunk, in an attempt at military posture, and was spoken to again. "Emma . . . this minute." She stood to look up and down the orchard rows, and the voice was suddenly louder and more demanding, now riding a favoring breeze from Helen's megaphone.

Emma found Helen on the sleeping porch, agitated by several things missing and several things added to the landscape. "Look there!" The rowboats gone from the Smiths' docks, and the Smiths had not even arrived from the city. And there, in the shallows beyond Forge Creek, one of the Careys' duck blinds was missing. Helen was certain she'd seen it only yesterday. But most mysterious, and she handed her binoculars to Emma, as if Emma could confirm the sudden appearance of a minute island or floating pier far across the bay.

"I've seen their lanterns on the water," Helen assured her. "Long after midnight, when none of our people would be showing lights out there." Where Helen saw suspicious alteration, Emma was more inclined to find the normal transformations of storm and tide.

"No need to tell the children," Helen thought.

On the contrary, Emma believed the discoveries, even if delusions, might help plant the seeds of national duty in her children's fallow hearts. And if Nellie supposed the fears well founded, they might throw a proper fright into her, put an end to her melancholy strolling on the deserted beach. Better all of them should be alert, aware of their opportunities and obligations in counterespionage.

Instead of complaining, Emma wrote how his mother contrived in her wardrobe to maintain a perfect defense against the dusk swarm of Moriches mosquitoes—"an armor that covers every inch of skin, including face and fingers. While Nellie and I race for the house, your mother puts on her long gloves, pulls down the veil of her bonnet, and refuses to be hurried. She sets us such a measured example.

"The children continue with their endless questions about your school days. I'm sure now that I should never have left the letters where Nellie would find them. Naturally, they're more curious than is good for them, even impertinently so. All together, you know what a mischievous threesome they can make. I believe they're ready to get some real work done here, and your mother is always reminding them of Mr. Hoover's promise that 'food will win the war.' Nellie has a wart on her knee. Is there some new remedy to replace our old superstition? I've told her not to pick at it."

Actually, the Major was pleased that Will and Louis might be learning something from the record of his young manhood. What it had taken in courage and diligence to prepare for medical classes, the honors he had won along the way, the hard-earned respect of the masters, all his victories over the petty adversaries of childhood.

He recalled the testy Miss Crowther bursting into his room on a Sunday afternoon to find him roughhousing with three mates and singling him out for punishment. "You, Lloyd, you of all people," because he had taken Communion that morning, and she thought he ought to have more self-control. He organized a boycott of the woman—no speaking to her unless spoken to—and then had to apologize to her, and confess the ungentlemanly conduct in a session with Headmaster Peck.

He remembered such sessions with Peck not with shame but a sense of pride in his own nerve, and a memory of the headmaster's underlying admiration for a forthright explanation of circumstances. He never came away from those confrontations with tail between his legs like some of his classmates. But with a satisfaction that the man had seen his side of the thing, that a mutual respect had been gained, that the two of them had risen above a matter of little moment and gone forward with no grudge between them.

He cherished the memories of his school, almost all of them. As a senior boy, he'd made himself superior. Whatever his class ranking, which was high by then, he knew his destiny included service. Whatever that last wink from Mr. Peck meant as he handed him his diploma and squeezed his hand.

*T*he large dark rooms of the Moriches house were suitable for ghost fantasy and brooding. Emma saw that nightfall was an especially grim time for her daughter, Nellie, who teased her own melancholy, pacing between the two gas lights in the long front hall, so that two shadows of herself moved past each other in opposite directions as she went back and forth. Everyone looked pale in this light, and the Major had promised his mother that her victory prize would be a Delco machine in the gas house, and electric lights in every room.

"What's the matter, Nellie? Nellie, stop that. It provokes your grandmother."

"Mother, does Father really think Dartmouth is a terrible place?"

"Where is this nonsense coming from?"

"What was Father's habit?"

"You've been at his letters again."

"William says it was wetting his bed. He says Father couldn't control himself."

"Nellie dear, that's when he was small, and it's none of our business."

"Louis says if it still happens when you're thirteen, it's a disease, and there are pills for it. But if you take too many of them, you get silly in the head and are only good for a soldier."

"Louis is a tease and disrespectful show-off, and he ought to be ashamed."

Emma reminded Nellie that her father wrote articles for medical journals, was revered among his colleagues, and that it was a great honor for him to have been chosen by the Roosevelt Hospital as a top officer of its expeditionary unit. "When you write him, you should tell him how proud he makes you, and listen to me, Nellie. Your brothers are not living up to your father's example."

Peterson, out of sight in the kitchen, could be heard speaking to the same point in the kitchen: "The things those boys are saying! Ought to both be in jail. They'd best keep it to themselves."

And Willie, who had come through the front door with two hare dripping blood on his grandmother's Persian hall runner, called back, "What the devil would a chauffeur know about it, who gets all he knows at the cracker barrel?"

Peterson stepped into the hall and stared past Emma at the boy. "Look at you! Have you no respect for your grandmother's house?"

I've my own war to manage right here, Emma could have written her Major by then. A confused chain of command. A rogue adjutant— Peterson—who was presumptuous and deriving authority through Helen's sufferance, with discontent and subversion in the ranks. But still she refused to burden her soldier in France with this kind of news. If he could report a fine turn in hospital morale, she could respond with news of the children's joy in the bounty of the farm.

The following week, the Major's letter was all about his design of a new hospital bed. Drawn hastily in an early visit to a manufacturer in XXXXX. (How stupid! She could read Nancy under the blot.) A prototype had been made, which the Chief Surgeon's Office considered excellent. A hundred more were ordered, and if these turned out well, twenty thousand more would follow. "The French call it 'the Lloyd chaise.' Wouldn't it be strange for me to attain fame through a bed?"

Odd to catch herself thinking, Far better that than on one, since once again his letter argued on the side of the angels: I am not going to smile on adultery no matter the extenuation of war and loneliness. It is no great sacrifice that a man should make do with his sweet sorrow for a distant wife.

As Emma read, she was considering the lecture she must give her children, with whom she was losing patience. If they could not take the reasonable side as to the guilt of the warmongers, they had better, by heaven, decide whose governance they could accept when it was over. Could they accept among the nations those who warred like monsters, bombing civilians, returning to cities they had overrun to smash the stained glass from their cathedrals as the Germans had done in Malines, indeed all through Belgium? And might do in France. If men like Father did not turn them back.

But Emma was hopeless at lecturing. She floundered in the stress of her sincerity, drowning her well-planned arguments in emotional puddles.

"Oh Mother! Don't cry again. Every time you have something to say to us, you start crying. It's not fair. Remember what Father tells *me.* Tears may win sympathy, but never arguments."

"I'm not arguing, Nellie."

But Emma was thoroughly flummoxed by her daughter's cool appraisal of the weakness.

"Willie wasn't denying that Father is a patriot," Nellie went on. "All he said is that there can be patriots who don't believe in this war."

"That's right," Willie said, "and it's a crime to put them in jail."

From the kitchen, Peterson was again raising his voice to the cook so that all in the dining room would hear: "Jail is where he'd be going if he spread that sort of talk in the city. I doubt he's got the nerve for that."

Louis whispered behind his hand to Emma's end of the table, "Why does Grandma keep that man?"

"He's been very faithful," Emma said, "and taken on extra duties since Grandpa died."

"What duties?" Louis asked.

"Busybody duties," Nellie offered.

"He takes care of the gas house now, so that *you* have light to dine by, Nellie," Emma reminded her. "And he does a wonderful job with the car."

Now Louis raised his voice so that he could be heard in the kitchen. "Doesn't even know when to retard the spark."

"You keep your hands off that car, young man," Peterson sounded his retreat, banging the back door behind him.

"Off to give the Bouton its one o'clock dusting," Nellie supposed, drawing snickers from her siblings. At that moment, Emma despised the privilege to which she'd trained her children and blamed herself for their arrogance. But strange to her that the hired man should still feel free to shame his employer's grandchildren. Perhaps he had another Bouton waiting for his chamois in another South Shore garage and was provoking his own dismissal here. A firing from which he might plead ill treatment and ask an excessive severance.

The children were of an age now when they should be gathering the rewards of their father's industry, learning by his example the habits of study and discipline of mind. But he was abroad, making good at his patriotic duty. "And instead of knowing him as a man," Emma complained to Helen, "they take their father for a child. From those letters. And excuse their own shortcomings by comparison."

There was another letter from France that arrived in Moriches on June 28, the same day the news came to them of more death in the trenches from unidentified fevers. This time, the Major praised the foresight of his mother for making him study French as a child, along with the measure of German she had forced into him. "Just enough to make the difference here. Enough so that Jeanne Prie has had something to work with. She really is a marvel. Our American nurses adore her, and why shouldn't they? She's everywhere, doing things for everyone without complaint, and gives them all the credit."

Emma remarked that in their growing file of letters there was nothing said of the French nurse's physical appearance.

"Why would there be?" Helen chided. "Has he ever described the other nurses?"

It was Jeanne, the Major said, who had begun to turn company opinion against the scoundrel Adjutant. At a dance.

Always at a dance, Emma thought, reminded of what she'd read about soldiers in one of the journals: "The Boche, the Blokes, the Yanks, the Poilu, the Russians—all are the same. When fear overwhelms them, they organize a dance."

At a dance, he said, Jeanne Prie had snatched away his job of crank-ing the Victrola, which he confessed was a way of keeping himself off the dance floor and controlling the tempo of the revels. While she was turning the handle, the Adjutant had sashayed across the floor with his strumpet nurse and pinched Jeanne Prie in the most inappropriate place. Jeanne slapped him smartly and turned away.

"What was that for?" the Adjutant had asked, all innocence. And she told him, *"Si on est bête, c'est pour longtemps."*

The Victrola's needle moaned to a halt; the dancing stopped.

"I don't speak Frog," he said.

So Jeanne translated for the whole room, "I said, 'If you're stupid, it's for a long time.'"

While most of her people wear the look of patient endurance, the Major wrote, Jeanne keeps radiant with the promise of victory. She has infected the place with optimism, the very germ we've needed. She makes my job so much easier. I can't keep her out of things. She's been fussing around at night with the equipment for our new bacteriological lab. Making inventory of the hypodermic syringes, needles, slides, vials of sugar of one kind and another, gas burners, centrifuge, and two mag-nificent microscopes. Zeiss, she noticed.

"You Americans had better learn to make your own," she told me. Do you know what she calls the centrifuge? "A merry-go-round for blood." And of course that is the way one prepares serum from raw blood. You would love her. The way she takes control by force of character, by so often being right about things. And she turns aside when the praise comes down.

And here it came at last:

Her black hair is short and ragged. She cuts it herself, grabbing a bunch with one hand and shearing it off with the other. As if she were nothing more than a wild animal. Sometimes I think she's making sure that men won't find her attractive. By habit of observation, she's risen above herself. Some of our doctors are actually deferring to her judg-ment. You know how unlikely that is in any hospital. If some envy her skill and success, others are won over by her sense of humor. All but the Adjutant and his whorish Nurse Wilkins, who spread the vilest gossip about her and call her vampire, and witch doctor and a name that I will not repeat.

/ /

From too little news of this woman, there was now too much for the women on Long Island. And it continued: It's a fact that Jeanne's medical knowledge surpasses some of our men. The younger ones are less apt to find it insulting. Where it comes from is a mystery. "I pay attention and don't forget," she says. No formal training as far as we can tell. She was simply here when we arrived, available and competent. As if she'd been waiting for our hospital to grow up around her. She has a memory for the regimen of every patient without so much as a second glance at their charts. Making rounds with her I sometimes find myself asking for her advice. Though we try to give all our nurses equal shares of responsibility to keep peace among them, the others are more than willing to be led by her.

She hears reports from Rome that her namesake Jeanne is sure to be canonized. She believes that she, too, has been led into this mission of hers by holy voices, though she asks me to keep this to myself, not wanting the others to think her deluded or conceited. If that's what it takes, I wish a few more around here could hear the same voices.

Among them, the children had very nearly memorized the most intimate details of the St. Mark's letters, and when Nellie asked "What *was* Father's impurity?" Emma, who had been pacing herself through the old mail to make it last longer, was not sure what her daughter was getting at. She answered that any impurity involving Father must be of the most trivial sort.

But if trivial, why had Grandma made such a thing of it? Nellie wondered.

"How would you know what Grandma did way back then?" Emma turned, wondering if Helen was close enough to hear them.

"Because," Nellie said, "the next time he wrote, he said he was sorry his letter had caused her so much grief."

Willie, embarrassed by his sister's innocence, came to her rescue.

"Nellie means the time he lost his monitorship for harassing the fresh boy."

"It was for poor judgment," Louis remembered. "The school was just making an example of him. He wasn't really in trouble."

"No, not that time," Nellie persisted. "I mean when Father wrote—"

"You don't know what you're saying," Willie interrupted again. But his sister wouldn't be stopped.

"I do. I mean when Father wrote, 'I have had some little trouble with my impurity just lately, but I hope to overcome it by a little determination.'"

Emma, who considered herself a progressive woman, put the question back to her daughter. "What do you think it means, dear?"

Nellie supposed it meant he had let his imagination take improper turns about girls.

"Well, that's probably a good guess, Nellie, and I think we can leave it there. As a little boy, your father was honest to a fault, and look what kind of man he's grown up to be."

"A soldier?" Louis asked.

"Not a soldier! A doctor! Serving his country and humanity, according to his doctor's oath."

"And his oath as a soldier," Louis added with a strained patience. Emma despised the arch tone the boys now took when they spoke of their father.

College did something horrid to young men. She couldn't abide it. As if intellectual analysis of a matter could trump a lifetime of experience, as if her children shared the burdens of the workingmen they defended with their idealistic dogma.

"What are *you* going to be, William?"

"I'm not going to be drafted."

"Is that a lifelong profession?"

They heard laughter from the kitchen, and Emma saw Willie's face darken.

"If the man's such a help to Grandma, why is he always in the house bothering Charlotte?"

"Do you know what they did last week, Mother?" Louis pleaded for her common sense. "They locked a man up in Chicago for publishing parts of the Declaration of Independence!"

"I'm sure they had good reason." But she was not at all sure, so she began to talk to her children about the duties of privilege, and when she faltered again, in search of the phrase that would sting their consciences, Louis asked her if she didn't think it was odd that a country like America, which had never had to lose a night's sleep over this war, should be the nation that woke every morning with the highest war fever.

"Yes," he went on, pleased with his figure, "and can't tolerate anyone who wants to shake down the thermometer."

The boy's satisfaction with himself, the way his mouth pulled to one side to admire its own argument, galled her, and if Nellie had not been watching her so intently, Emma might have screamed scorn on him. Instead, she melted in love for all her family's weaknesses, for the sincerity of their passions, for the safety of her children around the ancestral hearth. And thank God she had them quartered here on their own wide coastal acres, with a whole ocean to shield them against the mustard wind. And out of the cities, where, if the boys carried on this way, she knew they *would* be arrested and jailed.

The children had left her so far behind in their family reading that she decided she must skim ahead and find the letters that had drawn their attention. The difficult scrawl made it hard to absorb more than one or two at a time. But wasn't it a shame, she thought, that Nellie would pass over the happy details of her father's childhood—the top-spinning craze, the stamp collecting, the hunting for squirrel nests, the sledding, the skating, the day of school missed to visit a "bully smashup of a train wreck"—and fix her imagination on the mysteries of "my habit" and "my impurity"?

Emma took the box of letters to her bedroom the next evening and skipped ahead in them to his last year at school, 1889. No matter what his sense of guilt or religious conviction, it was still a wonder to her that after a letter in which he explained that two boys were to be bounced for smoking, he wrote another the same week all about smoking on the train on the way back to St. Mark's.

Then a retraction: Of course I won't smoke while up here. When was he going to stand up and fight them? At the end of October 1889 came another confession:

You'll be sorry to hear I've been suspended from my monitorship. Not on account of anything really wrong, only for cutting up. My punishment is twenty-five hours' time, and bounds till the end of term. It was just a little nighttime hazing. Mr. Peck says he will reinstate me before the end of term if my conduct is good.

Then the lines Nellie had fastened on: I have had some little trouble with my impurity just lately, but I hope to overcome it by a little determination.

The little devil, Emma thought. Had he supposed he could slip this by those vigilant parents without a remonstration? And then she came to the one she'd been waiting for. Her man finally standing up to them, and she imagined her mother-in-law's surprise when she'd received it:

In the first place, the boy was not hurt in the least. Mr. Peck told me it was not a breach of trust so much as nonappreciation of duty. I would think you, Mother, would be capable of the distinction. And I hope, Father, that I am still "a gentleman," whatever you may think me. I doubt you could show me a healthy boy of my age who has not broken some rule in his career. And Mr. Spalding has assured me there is nothing "cowardly" about hazing among schoolboys, that it is only a little careless. To read your letters, one would think I had sunk to the lowest manner of vice. There is no more chance of my being expelled than of flying to the moon.

I have been as good as any of the monitors here. In fact, last term all of the other monitors took part in hazing. And listen to this. When I first came here, I was hazed, badly hazed. What's more, Mr. Peck caught two boys locking me up in the coal house and all he did was charge them for a new padlock when they lost the key.

I see nothing wrong in getting up at night and kiting around the house a little and then going to bed again.

Emma felt herself cheering him on as she read:

The impurity is all passed now, and I trust was only temporary. Yes, I'm sure it has left me entirely. Fellows from the age of sixteen until they get married have the hardest struggle of their lives, and no one can help falling sometimes. Every man must have those yearnings, and it is his business to put forth strength and sand to get the better of them. No, I have not become a slave to such thoughts and actions. Though once in awhile they get the best of me, I've always been able to snuff them out. I hope this shows what a false impression you have.

/ /

"Tell them, you little scoundrel, tell them," she whispered to herself.

"What are you saying, dear?"

Helen had walked unannounced into Emma's room, ostensibly to open the windows, the same room that had been her son's as a child, perhaps the way she had surprised her Billykins years earlier, ever watchful for the influence of the devil. And Emma resented it now, for her own sake and her husband's.

"I didn't hear you knock."

"No, I thought you were still down with the children. See here, Emma. I hope you won't mind my saying so, but I think you've got to take a stronger hand with them. You submit to them so easily in argument. I confess I had the same problem when William was a child. But I overcame it, and I'll give you the hint."

Helen sat down where Emma had spread the letters and began to lecture.

"If you've got something important to get across, you have to gather not just the appropriate words, but also your emotions. But look here, I've made you cross."

Emma waved a dismissive hand at the apology, though disgusted by this intrusion and the insinuations. And Helen continued.

"I've got a little plan to patch things up between our Billikins and Peterson. We can't have the two of them at crossed swords all summer. The thing is, Peterson is an unhappy man, and I do let him overstep. Charlotte understands this, I believe. His rabid patriotism *is* a caution. But it seems to answer for some of the regrets of his sorry life."

Emma, eager to get back to the letters, was forced to hear how Peterson's wife had gone back to her family with their children, leaving the man with little more than his injured innocence and an overbearing portion of propriety.

Helen went on, describing an impossible scheme by which she meant to use Willie's and Peterson's mutual interest in her car, the Bouton, to make them chums. A shared chore of maintenance.

"Good luck with it."

With that, her mother-in-law left the room, and Emma was left alone to read as her man went on the attack at last. Giving it back to this same woman with whom she could not argue:

It's useless to argue with you. When will you understand? You say the fact that the fellow was not hurt in no way excuses me. Mr. Peck's "delicate" discrimination between breach of trust and nonappreciation of duty does not seem so exquisitely delicate to me, and I have no intention of acknowledging this as a great disgrace. If you can't see how ridiculous your position is, you had better read no further.

I'll tell you exactly how Mr. Peck explained it to me. He said a story might get around that barbarous treatment of new boys was allowed to go unpunished. And then what would the reputation of the school become?

Now, as to impurity, since you can't come off the subject, the only trouble I have ever had has been of very short duration. You still seem to think I'm a slave to it. I don't mean to be disrespectful, but the preoccupation with the matter seems to be yours, not mine.

Emma slapped the bed in amazement, aware of how much had changed in a single generation, how impossible this exchange would be between herself and her own children. Her Willie would turn a speechless red. Neither a confession nor a defense was conceivable. Freedom gained in this new age, she supposed, had come at the expense of honesty lost. Should she despise Helen for overbearing moralizing or envy her for the intimacy of her debate with her son, which had turned so testy:

I object when you criticize something I have not done. I've expressed no views on matrimony. When I said a young man has this yearning until he is married, I did not mean I thought that was the whole object of marriage. In fact, a man who marries with such a single thought is a low order of beast.

What you say of Harvard is ridiculous. You'll find a bad and a refined set in every college, and a man, like the birds, will find those of his feather. You show your ignorance of the schools when you speak of Dartmouth, a place where the scum of the land is dumped.

If, as you say, poor marks and poor behavior go together. Consider that I now stand second in form and fifth in school with an average of 8.85.

Emma came to a note on the headmaster's stationery, from Peck himself, dated February 10, 1890.

> *My dear Mr. and Mrs. Lloyd,*
> I hope you will not feel too anxious about William's future. I'm sure he has learned that a position of trust and honor carries corresponding responsibilities.
> I have not a catalogue of Amherst or Dartmouth by me, but a change made now in William's preparation would be a great disadvantage to him.

Emma went on with her reading in spite of a commotion downstairs, a row over which of her children would have the longest candle to take to their bedrooms (Helen still wouldn't allow them to light the gas sconces in their rooms). And Willie joined the dispute for show, as if he ever took a book to his bedroom. Poor Willie.

These troubles ran briefly across her mind, pushed aside by the more early news from St. Mark's:

The nurse bathed my head with camphor and cold water twice. I think it would be useless for you to come to visit. When you have tonsillitis, the way you spit is a caution to rats. I must have spat a good-sized basin brimful of phlegm. I gargle my throat every two hours with potash and some red stuff.

Dated a week later was his report that scarlet fever had broken out in the school. "But practically no danger for one like me who has had it already." Peck's own daughter had it, and the headmaster was changing his clothes each time he went from his quarters into the school.

And in France, Emma thought, still brave, or foolhardy, as if a knowledge of medicine and his doctor's pledge were inoculation against all the fevers. As she read:

Every precaution has been taken and Mr. Peck's part of the house has been completely shut off. Don't act hastily. Taking me home now would spoil all chance of passing my exams. I hesitate to tell you that there is also an epidemic of pinkeye going through the school. But so long as you keep a private towel, which I do, there is no danger of catching it.

And only a few days later:

If you are afraid of the chicken pox, you had better drop this letter like a hotcake. Had a fever last night. Woke feeling better, but then I looked in the mirror and saw my face covered with pimples, but not pimples.

Not only that but he had pinkeye and was laid up in the infirmary again, unable to read, gaining no advantage on his classmates.

The commotion below ceased. The children sorted out their dispute and went their separate ways into the night. Emma heard Louis pass her door and enter his room; he must have won the long candle. The door of the screened front porch slapped twice, which meant that both Nellie and Willie had set off on brooding walks, and Emma knew that Helen was watching them from the camel as they faded into the darkness. She heard the old woman fussing at them through her megaphone not to wander too far, to remember they lived on the dangerous edge of a country at war, to be careful and keep clear of strange lanterns on the beach or any lights drifting toward the shore.

Emma didn't have to watch. She was familiar with the way the two of them took their separate ways, Nellie on the wagon lane, lifting her skirts over the spilled seaweed fertilizer, and Willie with his frog spear on the creekside path; both of them pretending they could not hear their grandmother calling to them from the camel: "Watch for their lights! They don't take prisoners!"

Already July, and the children were wheedling for permission to put the torches to the farm's huge Fourth bonfire. Permission denied. Without Louis's clever protests, Willie might have been content with his grandmother's explanation, but excitement was his birthright. In fact, he was a little ashamed that a political argument, which he did not fully understand, prevented his service in France. He had taken a stand and would stick to it.

Emma thought again of what Helen had said: "My son, William, sees the world as a duty; my grandson Willie sees the world as a ball to be danced, or played with." Emma told herself she must go back to first principles, as her husband would do. She must explain, as Dr. William had on so many occasions, that this family's religion was more difficult, more exacting than simple Christianity. As Louis had pointed out to her, the Christian duty of prayer was problematic and must be sorted through for the transcendent purity advised by Mr. Emerson.

Prayer for Allied victory and international peace? Yes, of course, if it did not interfere with a higher earthly purpose. But prayer for the early return of Dr. Lloyd? No, this was a thing to be devoutly desired, but it was far too narrow a concern to have standing on the Founder's chart. They were, by God, Christians, she insisted, but Christians for whom most churches were far too selfishly pastored. Lloyds sent their children to Protestant academies not because these institutions approached moral perfection but because there were no schools available to provide a higher guidance.

And what good had these standards done them if they treated their mother with such scant respect, and laughed into their hands as their grandmother whispered too loudly to herself the names of the cards she held at bridge? Tomorrow, Emma could review her new volume of Emerson, and his distinctions between self-assurance and self-reliance, prepare herself thoroughly to deliver the grand comeuppance to her children. With the old news from St. Mark's still scattered on the bed around her, she drifted into sleep with a disturbing vision of her William, so anxiously naughty at sixteen, green from a cigar, bent over the train's commode, leaving his lunch on the rail bed to Southborough.

Emma woke with a stiff neck, sweaty and uncomfortable in the dress she had never even loosened. There were footfalls, surely Willie's, passing her door, not quite muffled by the hall's carpeting. A moment later, the mechanical rumbling of the hall clock gathering strength to strike the hour made her sit up, ready to measure his disobedience of the eleven o'clock curfew set by Helen, her way of getting them off the dangerous beach. It was 3:00 a.m. He would have to be punished severely.

But was the beach really dangerous? It puzzled her that William would reinforce these fears with warnings from France of Boche infiltration here. Emma supposed the children's long night walks along the bay were also a way of proving their grandmother wrong. The boys were furious with her for her decree that the bonfire would not be lit this year. Was she afraid that Germans would be drawn like moths to her flame among all the lights that marked the American shore?

Always yearlong projects, always the largest in the county, the Lloyd fires of the Fourth were known to reach into the sky far above the fearsome heights of great barn blazes, and they were seen with admiration five miles distant over land and water in all directions. Each year, many neighbors, village folk, and even strangers came uninvited because the primal rite of so huge a fire was its own invitation. The annual blaze was public property.

The gathering of windfalls from their acres of woods—branches, brush, any combustible matter—began as soon as the last spark died in the ashes, then continued for twelve months, until another pile stood higher than a house and a hundred feet or more across, ready for another anniversary of independence. A pile of this size could not be left to haphazard accumulation. There were rules that must be followed and an architecture, which had been supervised by Peterson in this year of the Doctor's absence. A central cavity was always left like a chimney in the middle of the debris, the secret of the fire's awesome upward reach. And all year there had been Peterson's doleful forecast of lost majesty if a careless hand left a trunk protruding into the carefully engineered central column.

"Thank God the Doctor's not here, or you'd be hearing what for!"

How did the Lloyds pile wood that high? It was not easy and it was not always safe. As the pile grew, there must be a firm stairway of limbs left on each side as a means of pulling more material toward the top. The largest windfalls were drawn by teams of horses and then advanced up the sides of the structure with ropes and pulleys. Several years earlier, a man had broken his leg at the summit and had to be brought down by laying three orchard ladders against the stack, end to end, lashing them to interior branches, and sending up a rescue party of three agile men summoned from Moriches' volunteer fire brigade.

To have this year's excitement canceled on the dotty assumption of its abetting German war aims was more than Emma's children could bear. And they hectored their grandmother all the week long, first wondering aloud about the effect on the region's morale of forbidding their grandest patriotic rite and pleasure, and then reminding her of the metaphysical implication of interrupting a century-old tradition. Wasn't the Lloyd bonfire the family flame of freedom, and thus funeral pyre to the Huns' tyranny?

Helen, unmoved by the clever rhetoric of their sudden patriotic conversion, made her decision clear and final. "No bonfire this year, Willieboy."

"But see here, children," she reflected, "won't we have a celebration next year? With your father home! And a fire twice the size! Won't that be a spectacle!"

They had looked at her balefully, as much younger children might have, and Emma had been so ashamed of their rude silence. College-age boys? She rose and marched down the hall to Willie's room, entered without knocking, and caught him in his shorts as he was checking his features in his dresser glass.

"What do you see, Will? Anything to admire? Do you know what time it is?"

"You must have heard the clock, Mother."

So, insolence, on top of disobedience, even as he appraised himself in the mirror. Was he pleased by his reflection, or doubtful? Vanity of face disgusted her. But looking at himself, he seemed to her the exact image of his father, not just in handsome profile but in complaisance; in his desire to please, though, there was the same jaunty angle of the head.

"Why can't you be more like your father?" she said.

"I don't want to go back to college," he told her.

"And what's wrong with your college that a few less Socialists wouldn't cure?"

"Didn't you know? It's where society's scum is dumped."

"Where have you been tonight?"

"Swimming with the eels. In the seaweed. With all the other scum."

"And after that? Is your sister in bed?"

"That's all. I was just on the beach with the slimy oysters. How would I know where she is? It's three o'clock."

"What's got into you, Willie?"

"Maybe dregs. Or slime. I don't know."

"We'll talk about it in the morning."

The letters should have been burned. Emma went down the hall, checking into Nellie's and Louis's rooms for the sound of easy breathing, for the sleep of the innocent. But Nellie was moaning "no, no, no," whether in debate or putting off a terror, Emma couldn't say; and Louis was sitting up in his own troubled dream, rocking back and forth like a member of a rowing team. An odd family? she wondered. Or just ordinary in their peculiarities?

The next morning at ten, Peterson had not yet been seen in the kitchen, and Helen was already sitting in the cage, the screened front porch, waiting patiently for her ride to the village. Willie was asked to check the driver's rooms over the garage, but he shirked the chore, and Louis, too, shied away. The boys seemed to know that something was way out of the ordinary. Sending Nellie up to the disagreeable man's quarters was out of the question.

Charlotte, the cook, eventually went, setting off with her customary complaint. "I sweat and slave around here, and what do I get for it? A royal kick in the behind. That's what!" Taking some pleasure in her role as martyr to the family's convenience. She returned, amazed with her own news: "He's nowhere about! But his clothes all laid out, and his bag half-packed! If he's going, he can't be gone yet."

There was a search through the farm, all hands questioned, and a car sent into Moriches to ask around the village, where, Charlotte suggested, he might have wandered the night before to give his notion of leaving the farm for good the benefit of what she called "the whiskey try." "He'll have gotten himself in a state and been taken in by the constable."

No, the constable knew nothing. Hadn't seen Peterson for a week.

Helen was quickly sure of foul play, and she knew the foul players would be German. Her not-so-faithful Peterson had walked down to the beach—didn't they all walk to the beach in the evenings, each on his own path, and each for his own chance at solitude and reflection?—and here Peterson would have gotten in the way of a team of German infiltrators on their way to do propaganda and sabotage in the city. Yes, she thought she might have had a premonition of this in her sleep. A deadly scuffle in the sand, a drowning, and a body riding away on the outgoing tide.

"For heaven's sakes, Grandma! He's only been gone a few hours. He's got himself lost in the woods, for all we know."

Helen's gaze bore in on Willie's insolence.

"Your mother's right about you," she said. "You're fresh as paint!"

The boys were too far gone in disobedience and deceit for Emma to pretend any longer in her mail to France. And Peterson's disappearance was news she could not deny the Doctor. Initial reports from the village had not been quite forthcoming. Both Willie and Peterson had been in Moriches the night the driver went missing. And both had been part of a public spectacle that shamed her son.

With all this on her mind, she was still able to begin her report: "You would be so proud of Nellie—Nellie canvassing for Liberty Bonds, and pitting peaches and sending the pits to the Red Cross, which makes a charcoal of them and sends them to you as filter material for your gas masks. So excited to think she's actually working with you!

"And Charlotte sees to it that we follow Mr. Hoover's advice. So we are wheatless Monday and Wednesday, beefless Tuesday, and porkless Thursday and Saturday. Really no great hardship; we could do more. Now, dear, a line or two that may trouble you."

Emma thought her mother-in-law should have known what would happen to the huge woodpile, considering the community's expectation of it. That such a grand anticipation would produce its own spark. On the night of the Fourth, many were turned away at the farm entrance on the Moriches Road. Others coming cross-country on foot over the creek and through the woods had to be sent away disappointed. Most of them could not believe there would be no fire, supposing instead that they were only being denied entry on the place out of some new proprietary selfishness that Dr. Lloyd would never have allowed. A good number remained lurking in the woods and along the fences until the excitement of the flames would be a passport to all.

Helen, who woke at midnight and saw light flickering through her east window, said she knew at once what had happened. She almost fell to the floor from the big four-poster, limped to the open sash, and could already hear the crackling fire gathering its first strength from the breeze. "Emma," she called down the hall, "where is Willie? Where is Louis?" already accusing them of a treasonous arson.

Emma came into the hall just as the boys and Nellie threw open their doors, and the whole family stood dumbfounded, regarding one another's bewilderment. Emma and her children were dressed in a flash and rushing out to share in the glorious disobedience of the celebration. By the time she reached a line where her face was too hot to advance, there were a hundred or so people already admiring the blaze, giving full throat to Independence cheers.

In minutes, the fire was licking up to its majority, gathering new fury, gulping air and creating a loud wind in the center tunnel, hurling light and sparks at the stars. Charlotte appeared beside her, murmuring, "God help the rabbits." Emma turned toward the house clear in this giant elemental light, and saw her mother-in-law in silhouette, standing with her megaphone behind the camel's screen, blowing impotent commands into the hot wind, which only blew them back at her with doubled fury.

And Charlotte, who seemed to be asking for an answer, said again, "God help the rabbits, ma'am. And the birds. And any other thing that's in it."

It was more like prophecy than prayer. And Emma was answering not Charlotte but the hypnotizing fire, repeating a line she wished she could take back from a letter already mailed, a letter she would as soon were torpedoed. Why had she closed the account of Peterson's disappearance with such a non sequitur: "Children have a thousand tests to pass, but remember, William, a child never passes his parents' final examinations. Consider your own." Somehow turning all her troubles at home into a riddle of family dynamics that must be solved by her hero in France.

The French Angel

He was sent from Chaumont to Cannes on special assignment to see if any of the seaside hotels could be used as convalescent hospitals, long-term care facilities far enough from the front to ensure peaceful recoveries. He was not impressed by the Mediterranean. Far too gentle, he wrote Emma, no more surf than Moriches Bay, and the houses are a fright. Expensive, no unity of design, ugly. Here a Roman villa, there a Swiss chalet, and hard beside that, a country mansard under cupola.

In Cannes, he was given credit for devising a plan by which seven hoteliers would share their profits with an eighth, who agreed to turn his grand stone palace on the beach over to the American army. The details were worked out with the intercession of the mayor, who told him his bad French had been responsible for the success of the negotiations. The bacteriological laboratory to be set up in Chaumont would be shared with the French. And never mind that he had unwittingly agreed to pay in full for the hoteliers' lost revenues when the war was over. Another star by his name on General Ireland's chart.

He returned to Chaumont, to find that new cases of trench fever had broken out in his hospital and that four men expected to recover from their fevers had succumbed. Jeanne Prie was beside herself with grief, taking responsibility for the deaths, as if germs had snuck into the ward like thieves when her back was turned for one negligent moment. As if she could have recognized the culprits by sight and turned them away at the door.

"The French angel," the patients had called her, and now there were some doubts. Her growing responsibility in the wards coincided with rising morale and some unusually rapid recoveries, but her greatest fear and concentration was with the fever patients, who were arriving from everywhere. That week, she was in tears much of the time. The Major feared she might make herself too sick to work.

Jeanne came to his office one evening and closed the door. Off duty, she dressed in the brown trousers and shirts of the American soldier, like a man, and her close-cropped black hair, her androgynous features, soft-edged and childlike, and her odd English constructions were so completely asexual that if he accidentally touched her or she brushed against him in the course of their daily rounds, he could as well have been bumping into a metal leg of the new Lloyd chaise.

And when she spoke, it was without hesitation, or calculation—straightforward, defying cynicism. He had aligned himself with her. He believed that together they made a single-minded agent of medical salvation. It was this of which he was so proud, this out-of-self, ennobling cooperation that he could not seem to explain to Emma without evoking a troublesome jealousy, this fear of hers that he was drifting into some selfish preoccupation.

He had only been sharing his amazement with his wife. And who wouldn't have been amazed when this French "knockabout-nurse," as the Colonel called her, explained why the Major was losing too many men to infections. "She's shown us a form of sepsis we never saw in civil practice, a gas gangrene," he wrote to Emma.

Disinfection and sterilization weren't enough, not for wounds full of the manure of farmers' fields. "We were so stubborn, but Jeanne was right. The poison grows in dead and bruised tissues. We have, therefore, to cut away all damaged flesh, make a total surgical cleansing. Asepsis, not antisepsis or exercise of tissues, wins the fight. Jeanne, 'the French Angel', revealed this simple truth to us. And with absolute modesty, as though we'd discovered it for ourselves. The French, the Belgians, the Germans have been aware of this since 1916. It makes me quite ashamed of our late entry here, and our failure to keep abreast of elementary battlefield medicine."

So. How silly of Emma! Of course he was preoccupied.

It was all his shame and none of Jeanne's that he felt obliged to step around her and open his office door.

"Fresh air," he pleaded.

"You mean let everyone listen."

"Do you know," she asked, "why I'm here in Chaumont?"

"To save your country, to save France," he said.

"You patronize with your great talk," she told him, and she was right. But so, he thought, was he.

"Do you have any idea what the map of the United States looks like in a German schoolbook?" Jeanne asked him. "The geography they teach their children?"

He did not.

"America is divided into three parts," she said. "The zone of the blacks, the Indian territories, and the land occupied by Teutons."

Perhaps she thought this would clarify his understanding of the beast they were up against. Instead, it reflected back on her as a bit of remarkable knowledge that he would never have expected from her. Each day she could surprise him with something new.

She was still the mediator between the two halves of his nursing staff, the untrained sisters from the convent in Reims and the volunteers organized by a relief agency in New York City. The one group, hardly out of veils, tiptoed around with heads lowered over the bedpans they carried, as if excreta were more interesting or less threatening than daylight or a familiar face; and the American contingent with eyes ever alert for adventure, as if casual romance were the quid pro quo of selfless service; and between them, Jeanne Prie, bridging the divide.

Remarkable enough that this stray nurse who had been waiting there for them without papers, but with a forthright pride, had transformed herself into their tacit leader and his most trusted aide among the women. The others had sponsoring organizations and résumés, while she proved herself with double shifts, a memory for detail, and an uncommon gift in diagnosis.

Where was Latoni getting the horrid things he had to say about her? How dared he? The IG had *him* under investigation for procurement fraud. In front of Colonel Hanson, the miscreant called her "the Major's little shit-handler."

Ashamed of his awkward propriety, the Major rose and shut the door again.

"I want you to tell me a little more about yourself."

Jeanne began with a village called St. Crouen in the north, where her father had been the undertaker, and her mother a morbidly religious laundress who dressed up in the white sheets she took in and came groaning over her children's nursery beds at night to impress on Jeanne and her younger brother the hellish fate of the faithless. The father had made the children accompany him when he went to measure for a coffin, and he locked them in the room with the corpse to "strengthen our minds."

Was it a wonder she had run away to Brussels to live with an aunt, whose only religious rules were prayers each night, bare knees to stone floor of her cottage? The aunt was married to the building superintendent of a Protestant hospital, where Jeanne was taken to clean rooms and empty bedpans every day when school was over, starting at age nine.

"And that was your medical training?"

"I was there for so many years," she said. "I had to learn something. I couldn't just carry the bedpans." And then, when the war began, she had waited for her assignment. He presumed she meant a military order, not a call from saints.

Why would the French let go a person of her skills?

"Ha. Why do you think?" The answer too obvious it seemed, beneath her consideration. He supposed she meant that her abilities, her medical knowledge, might have been an embarrassment to doctors less willing than himself to be instructed or corrected by a nurse.

And how had she learned English?

Flemish first, then some German, she allowed. As if the acquisition of two other languages could explain proficiency in a third, and none of them her birth tongue.

"Our Latoni has reminded the Colonel we have no papers on you. We have to get something in the file."

Jeanne retreated into her faith, spoke of her visions again, dreams in which she, blessed by God, was told she would leave Brussels to follow an army. Extraordinary enough. But the father, back in St. Crouen, was having the same dreams. And what could he be expected to think?

Wouldn't he naturally assume that his daughter was only running off with soldiers to service their revels?

How could the father know that she would also be told by the voices of Saint Margaret and Saint Catherine that she must one day use every skill and wile she might possess or conjure, use them to save the soldiers guarding France, to save them from mysterious mortal fevers? He couldn't know that frightening visions were revealed to her under a crown of brilliant light—the manure of farmers' fields, horses' blood, lice, intestinal pestilence and excrement, the mire of battle, with her in the middle of it all. She took it to mean that out of the mire she must find the germ of cure.

Her father, fearing that his own dreams foretold her whoring off with soldiers, sent her brother to Brussels, on her trail, to see if she had fallen into a life of pleasuring the Poilu, and if so, to drown her. And if the brother refused, he would come and do it himself. She had been warned of her brother's mission by the aunt in Brussels and she had been told by the voice of Saint Margaret to come here to Chaumont, where the work she was meant for would reveal itself to her. "And, you see, it has."

Major Lloyd listened in mild shock; her religiosity was far more like superstition than a respectable faith, but the details of her tearful story were their own confirmation. He had no idea they were modeled so closely on the life of the Joan of Orleans. Her work in the ward must be its own evidence of loyalty. She could not send back to her colleagues in Brussels for letters to confirm her story. The Germans, now in occupation, had killed or captured them. But she must provide something to put in her file, something to satisfy the Colonel. Latoni would never let the matter drop.

"Why is that man still here," she asked, "when you know he steals?"

"In due time," he promised, "he'll be gone."

She rose and touched the Major's shoulder as if blessing their mutual effort to fight *all* the infections that threatened their hospital—bacteria, pride, and greed. The door swung open and there by ugly coincidence was the leering Adjutant, cheapening the moment of affirmation.

"This is about her," he said, handing Lloyd a page fresh from the orderly's typewriter, Latoni's charges written in barrack-house legalese. The volunteer woman from Brussels, it said, had been observed after midnight by swing-shift nurses "leaving a proscribed area, a secure room," the newly equipped bacteriological laboratory, or, as the Adjutant came to call it, "her germ factory."

The more important question was how had she got the key, which could only be granted by Major Lloyd. When asked by the other nurses what she was doing, she had said, "Preparing the blood," and walked away, carrying a small box believed to contain hypodermic syringes and needles. Latoni's report concluded: "We know more about the woman's activities."

"The Colonel has a copy," he said. "And let me tell you this, that nurse speaks German like a Boche."

With that, the Adjutant made a lazy turn and walked out of the room.

"And what do you have to say for yourself, soldier?" He began to question her in Latoni's voice. They broke into laughter before the Adjutant was quite out of hearing.

"Yes, what about *le clef?*"

"He should be *sous clef*," she mumbled.

"Latoni has it?"

"No, under the key," she said. "He should be in the prison. The key is in your desk."

"Prison key?"

"No, funnybrain. The key to the laboratory. I put it back where I found it."

"Funnybrain is no English word."

"*Eh bien*, more's the pity."

"You told me you spoke only a little German."

"Someone has to ask, 'Where does it hurt?' eh? And there is Wolfram. Asking every day why he lives. Someone has to tell him?"

Wolfram was a German corporal who had hopped into one of the French trenches on mangled legs, which the doctors took the rest of the way off at a field hospital. And here, another limb, gangrenous, lopped off at the shoulder on the Major's order. Now he was not much more than a torso with a droopy head and left arm dangling, cursing in German between his twice-a-day injections of morphine.

"He thinks we have taken him apart, one piece at a time, for the doctors' spite, because he has nothing more to tell the intelligence. I only said a rhyme for him. Your Adjutant throws him a ball and says, 'Catch this, Max.'"

Jeanne's bold manner reassured the Major, but what he really wanted at that moment was someone to share the weight of another letter in his pocket—his mother's version of the news in Moriches, where his wife's moodiness is wearing out the Chopin rolls on the player piano, and Nellie has been picking at a new wart on her knee in an unsuccessful effort to make it disappear, and has withdrawn invitations to two houseguests on that account. And, making these complaints pale, his first son, Willie, has shamed the family with public statements about the evils of conscription.

Jeanne was preoccupied with something else, which left him in the middle distance of her vision, gazing past him toward Bologne or perhaps as far as Joinville. He was an obstacle to be got around if she could first borrow his bicycle.

"I only want it for a day. Tomorrow."

She meant to see what a twenty-four-hour absence would do for her anger with the Adjutant, who, she said, not only abused patients but wished to destroy her experiments, as well.

"When I'm gone," she said, "I want you to watch what he does. My room, no. My laboratory, no. Keep him out."

"Your laboratory?"

"My researches, eh?"

And where would she be going?

"Away, away. As far as my legs take the bicycle in a day."

"Joinville is more than fifty kilometers." Would she be safe alone?

"Not to any place," she explained. But to some field along the road, a destination with no name, where she might catch her lunch in the river and build a fire to cook it. Someplace where the trees bent down over her to watch the water flow by. And later she would gather more sticks for her evening fire and smooth the ground for her night. And she would make a solitary communion with the rising moon and stars.

He'd never heard her talk this way before. As if there were, after all, a romantic spirit, trapped behind her duty. She'd never asked for time to indulge herself; her life was service. More peculiar, her imagined day seemed an incitement, an unnecessary declaration of her singularity and, therefore, a provocation. Shouldn't someone be by the Marne the next evening, watching from a discreet distance over the safe sleep of his irreplaceable nurse?

On her way along the river from Chaumont, how many strangers might a lone woman trust in wartime? In his own reverie, he was drawn into her idyll, and he began to imagine how he might follow after her as chaperon, how he could accomplish this without detection. Perhaps suspicious of her escape or a little envious, he couldn't say which.

"*Mon Dieu,* Monsieur Lloyd! I ask only a day, maybe two. The devil has your tongue!"

"Of course, Jeanne."

She took his hesitation as a selfish concern for his bicycle. It was agreed she would set out from the Chaumont bridge at 6:30 the next morning, before the midnight shift of nurses came off duty and before the orderly room people, the despised Latoni in particular, might notice her departure on the Major's bicycle.

Satisfied again of his support, she asked, "Now what is *your* sadness, William? Tell me."

He opened the letter from his mother, worn thin along its creases from all his nervous folding and unfolding, and began to explain the failings of a son who had taken his antiwar talk into New York City and barely escaped a street crowd's bare-fisted wrath.

He'd hardly begun before Jeanne seemed embarrassed to be taken into this sorry confidence. Already impatient with his account, she interrupted to secure his promise that his bicycle would be ready at the bridge the next morning. She'd picked a good time for her respite; 215 patients just shipped out of the hospital—but so many of them with another unnamed fever—and 307 more expected on a sick train that would arrive in Chaumont by the end of the week. The week of the Fourth, which would pass here without ritual, and for which he'd have no news of the Moriches celebrations for at least another two weeks.

In the morning, just as she'd promised, Jeanne started north along the river toward Condes and Riaucourt with a box tied to the handlebars, some extra clothes, and a blanket lashed to the platform over the rear wheel. He tried to give her a few extra francs; she wouldn't take them. If this was to be an overnight trip, it would be dependent on a local civility. A rank cheese made itself evident under the closed lid of the wicker box, where she claimed a fine loaf was also secure. Nothing more.

He had left word the night before that he'd be traveling the next day to the field hospital at Joinville, actually making his own plans for a day off along the river, the first time off he'd taken. And after watching her disappear over the bridge and beyond the first rise in the road, he set out in the same direction on foot. His fast walk was not much slower than her riding speed, and after several kilometers, he caught sight of her walking beside the bike, up a long incline where the road left the river to accommodate a small group of houses perched on the hillside.

He held back, not wanting to spoil her day, only making sure that her bivouac would be sensible, safe, protected. If he fell too far behind her, he'd have enough French to inquire after *l'infirmière avec la bicyclette verte*. The day was fresh and his rapid walk hardly made him perspire. He was renewed, traveling in the wake of her hardy spirit, which seemed to dare the road to present her with an enemy, maybe one of those French-speaking German agents who lurked in the countryside, spread false numbers of new French casualties, and occasionally killed if his identity was suspected.

Jeanne never reached Riaucourt. Watching from several hundred yards behind her, he saw her turn off the road toward the river, and he hurried ahead. Another man appeared from behind a hedgerow, turned once to look around him, and ducked under the branches, following her. The stranger looked quite heavy, not like a soldier, but some village lout on a dark errand.

The Major trotted forward down the middle of the road, winded by the time he turned into the bushes where the man had gone. A moment later, he was watching them in rapid conversation at the river's edge. The fat man presented her with a paper package and a jar, both of which she placed in her basket. A two-cheek embrace and their meeting was over. The fellow disappeared along a path up the river and Jeanne sat down to eat her lunch.

Lloyd watched the heavy man move away along the bank, and then he made his own way down the path to Jeanne's side. She wasn't the least surprised to see him.

"You followed me. I saw you."

"Your rendezvous—who was that?"

"You want me to work for you under suspicion? Always suspected of something else?"

"What did he give you?"

"Blood and eyeballs," she dismissed his question.

"Jeanne, what are you saying?"

She reached for his hand. "Really, I hoped you would follow," she said. "Do you think I would show you my way if I wanted it secret? I want to think you follow me because we have the same desire, the same enemy. Not just Germans. Whatever else is extra. It means as nothing."

Whatever she meant by "extra," she was pulling him down to sit opposite her, diverting his attention from the bicycle basket, which held the fat man's gifts.

"Why do you wear the harness?"

She reached out to touch the shiny brass buckle of the Sam Browne belt that went over his shoulder and around his waist, and of which she knew he was a little vain.

"Will you pull a wagon?"

"Part of the uniform."

He was still looking at the wicker basket, waiting for a full explanation, and she exhaled sharply, as if this obstinacy had already destroyed their moment together.

"Look yourself!" she ordered, exasperated, pointing to it.

"Who was the man?"

The butcher of Condes, she explained. The one who supplies your Adjutant with horse meat.

"Beef."

"No, horse meat."

"But I think the butcher is your friend."

"He does what he can," Jeanne said. "What can you expect in these times?"

The Major opened her basket to look for himself. Inside was a copper-lined box. He removed the lid and found several small chunks of ice, a jar of dark liquid, and a package of waxed paper. Unfolding the paper, he saw that she had not lied. Four soft, shiny balls, larger than shooter marbles, bloodshot whites and black centers, rolled to and fro on the sheet, as if turning in horror from the living world.

"You didn't believe, eh?"

These were indeed the eyes of a team of oxen slaughtered the day before. The butchered animals, too, would soon be on their way to the American hospital. For the officers' table.

"Your appetite," she shamed him. "And your man pays twice the expected. And gets more than a *pourboire* in return."

"In the jar . . ."

"I told you, but you don't believe. Before he kills the mayor's cob, he takes the blood. I give him the needles."

"But this man is your friend?"

"This man is the butcher. No one else is the butcher. Do you understand?"

"No."

"I'll tell you more about me. It was no lie. Only the name. But there is more. Very more."

"Much more?"

"Very much more. Here you must call me Jeanne. But my name is Lucienne de Crouen."

She waited for some sign of recognition. He could not oblige her.

"*Une chasseuse des microbes?*"

Still no comprehension.

Someone who cleaned up after the professors at the institute, she explained. Until she learned more than was appropriate to her work for the men in Paris.

A blank.

"And was passed along by Pasteur to Bordet as a lab maid. You have heard of Bordet?"

At last he could say yes. And there was a place for her to carry on with her story again. This time in the great man's quarters in Brussels, where she said she had kept cleanliness and order among the beakers, slides, and test tubes. Was even trusted to wipe the lenses of the microscopes. And over those lenses, she reintroduced herself to the little engines of disease, the microbes.

Just as the unassuming Bordet, "so mind-absent," had watched silently in the wild Metchnikoff's laboratories and drawn his own conclusions. So had she, Jeanne explained. She had questioned Bordet's theories in the germ-killing ways of blood, until she was obliged to leave that man's service, as well.

She went back to the Belgian hospital, where she was, in name, just a nurse, but, in fact, a secret researcher in bacterial disease. Another microbe hunter, but a doctor without degree, whose usefulness was understood by the Germans when the war was under way. She gained access to the hospital's lab by a nervy stealth and stayed there, against the better judgment of men, by suggesting that her findings must, of course, be taken as their own.

Her story was scarcely believable. He could grant her a measure of exaggeration. She was much too valuable to insult. But she was poking again at his silly belt as she invented herself once again for his approval. The hypnotic chatter reminded him of the bedside balm she practiced on her special cases—the gentle lilt that healed in four languages. She offered a charming explanation of the war:

"The germs started it, and the germs will finish it. Don't you know for twenty years the French and Germans calling 'liar' at one another?"

She explained for him how Pasteur and his French champions all stood behind Metchnikoff's microbe-eating phagocytes, the wandering white cells; and the Germans yelling, No, idiots, the blood itself conquers the germs. Liar! Fraud! Back and forth like that in the scientific journals.

"When people hate like that," she said, "where else to go but war, where the germs will finish more soldiers than the bullets."

It was almost plausible. He was charmed, if hardly convinced. She took his hand again and looked at him as if he were missing something elementary, as if this, too, were simple. He could almost believe that she was there at his disposal, that his welcome use of her might signify as little as a politeness at a time when a selfish passion would be inappropriate.

Their real passion must be behind the laboratory door, where she was going to show him what moved this week in the ox-eye bath—some crooked rods he might never have seen before, swimmers from the blood of the helpless German corporal with a fever that rose and fell with the sun, and who had nothing else to live for but the nurse who spoke German.

There must be a way to explain to Emma the difference between nurse Plume, who shook her business for the soldiers like a flag of rut, and this remarkable Jeanne, who marched her short, full figure through the hospital like utilitarian machinery of cure but now, on the riverbank, turned her lap into a pillow, squeezing his fingers one at a time, as if each might be a separate channel of receptivity, and asked with a forthright urgency, "Would you like to make acquaintance with my lice?"

Willie! Why was it always Willie who brought disgrace on himself and the family? A college failure, an absentminded Wall Street runner who, one summer, had cost his firm several thousand dollars when he delayed delivery of a trading slip so that he might take a leisurely lunch of three pastrami sandwiches and a double lager by the river. His father had been asked to help defray the loss, a concession that saved Willie, temporarily, from being fired. Perhaps better that he had been, since his release came only a few months later, after another error of omission, one more sign, his office suggested, that William had not yet found his calling.

Now, several days after the fire, with smoke still rising in scattered trails from the great pile of ashes in the meadow, Emma ordered him out of the house with her for a little walk along Home Creek, trying to get to the truth of the night before the fire. She was given only grunts, evasion, sullen silence, and an occasional flash of anger.

"How many times do I have to tell you? "

"But you haven't given the same story twice. Didn't you tell the sheriff's man you went around by the road into Moriches?"

"Uhm."

"Is that a yes?"

"Uhm."

"Speak up, Willie. The most important thing you'll carry through life is your honest reputation. . . . What?"

"I didn't say anything."

"But why *aren't* you saying anything? Stop mumbling."

"All right, I went along the beach. And then across the Mercy farm. As Nellie said."

"Why didn't you tell the deputy that?"

"He's against me, like all the others. He was watching when they knocked me down. Laughing with the rest."

"This isn't about that, Willie. They're looking for Peterson now. Everyone's looking for Peterson. Nellie saw you arguing with him on the beach. Were you arguing with him on the beach?"

"Umh."

"Were you?"

"Do you want me to call Nellie a liar?"

"So you were?"

"Umh."

"God, Willie! What's wrong with you?"

"Well, the silly ass thought he was going off to be one of Creel's four-minute men."

"What?"

"Yes. Walking out on Grandma. Going off to carry the war spiel across America. Seventy-five thousand of them, so why shouldn't he be one? As if they'd train a chauffeur for one of their propaganda puppets."

"If that was his care and passion, why not?"

"Peterson? He couldn't make Charlotte cook a custard."

"Never mind. And you came home the same way?"

A musty smoke was drifting with them down the path, and she looked back in irritation at the long bed of ashes that would smolder for several more weeks under low barometric pressure and a gray sky. The weather was conspiring to remind them of the community's and the children's disobedience. Coughing and sore eyes, and Helen was furious, unable to sleep on the camel, her bronchial discomfort the subject of her own pitiful letter to her Boykins doctor somewhere in France. It could take a month before the coals at the bottom consumed themselves, before men would be hired to rake and spread the remains over the whole farm. In the meantime, it teased and reproached them all as a dawdling cremation of their mischief.

"You see what you've done?"

A long and petulant sigh.

"I want you to write a letter of apology to your grandmother. I want you to tell her everything that happened those two nights, everything you did, everything you saw."

Another sigh.

She wanted a forthright written confession from him, like the elemental honesty of her husband's childhood mail. For all its pleading and vanity, it had shown his ability to speak up when the occasion called for it:

I think that you will not send me to another school, or at least, I hope not, for I have bad enough influence around me here, and I should have much worse somewhere else. Much love and hope that you will cheer up and make the best of the circumstances, and give me another trial. I am not "as ever," but your same old
   Boykins

And she thought again of the intimacy of his confessions, the trust implicit in another plea that haunted her: When you answer Mr. Peck's letter, don't mention the other trouble, for he does not understand the terms we are on.

The terms they were on. Were still on. Not available to her and Willie, who was walking slower, falling behind her, as if that could remove the nuisance of this conversation.

Helen had been unforgiving after the fire, insinuating that Willie's behavior was no Lloyd inheritance, but must come from somewhere else. And just to prove it, she thrust yet another letter in front of Emma, as if letters hadn't done damage enough. This was something William had written home as a college boy preparing for medicine, his head bowed half the year in zoology texts, but still with time to spare to gratify the mother and father, who, when he showed them a glimpse of sainthood, pressed on for divinity.

Was this one to be the last, pulled from the family scrapbook chockablock with William's awards, certificates of achievement, diplomas—this, the ultimate demonstration of docility and filial obedience that Emma must now read in front of her mother-in-law? All of it reflecting so marvelously on Helen and her Gus.

Dear Mamma & Papa,

I've just read your long letter over. You have sized me up exactly. I don't know how you could describe my present nature more accurately. I'm going to give up this idea that my character is weak, and see if I can't make a much finer stand against temptation than I have thus far.

As yet, I am very immature and underdeveloped, but I am starting to see the importance of the tone of my present life on the man I hope to become. For some time past, my existence has been like a series of impressions, a kind of imagination life, stuck in its own complacency. With a deeper and more demanding analysis, I believe I can grow out of the two great weaknesses you point to, carelessness and indecision. And I will, or bust.

About the farm, you mistake me. You say I might debase myself to the point that I forget where I came from. Never. I love that place beyond everything. Living there ennobles me as nothing else in the world. I have all the hereditary affection for it, coupled with my deep love of nature. And these forces assert themselves more strongly than any others in my undeveloped state. You need not fear that I will ever desert the old place.

I won't destroy your letter. It's the best you have ever written me. I'll write again at midweek. Till then, good-bye and love,

Will-o

"Do you see, Emma? He wasn't perfect, oh no. We knew he was playing cards, and drinking wine at the weekends. He told us as much. You see, there was nothing he was afraid to tell us, nothing."

"You wanted to know everything?"

In her bitterness, Emma imagined specimen bottles of the young man's urine, even excrement, put away with his baby shoes and diplomas, to be brought forth some day to prove their worthiness against the competition of the next generation. These people who had hovered over their boy with moral fervor and censure had yet been rewarded with confession after confession, and, in the end, a docile devotion.

Looking back, Emma saw nothing but love and forgiveness in her rearing of Willie, the same as with her other children, and a supreme injustice in this generational joke being played on her.

"Well?"

"Whun?"

"Did you hear me?"

"Hear you?"

"About the letter?"

"I think you said you want me to write a letter to Grandma. Who is living here in the same house with me."

"You're going to write an apology. A full confession of what you did those two nights. Explain yourself like a man. And ask for her pardon. Or you're not going to stay here."

Willie tossed his head and suddenly turned back toward the house at a fast walk. Emma began to shake, more fearful than angry. Suppose her ultimatum sent him packing? The world beyond his family had no tolerance for his blather; his privilege vanished at the farm's boundary. Emma saw no place for him but these open fields and the water, which she knew he loved. He could have worked here in perfect happiness, except for his father's insistence on another career for him. Willie had arrived a generation too early, or too late.

Emma went back to the house, ready to apologize for being too hasty, wanting to compliment him for something, wanting to turn the whole thing around, to start again with a loving rapport. It had taken courage for him to face the toughs in Moriches. He wouldn't be afraid to face them again. No coward, he could have disposed of them one at a time. But they were a gang.

Helen was in the parlor with the deputy, who had come to ask more questions about Peterson. Emma heard her explaining how common it was in this modern world for people to be taken in and gulled by trusted help. Peterson, she said, was just such a deceiver. How else to explain his bag, half-packed for departure, and his willingness to turn on a member of the family that had supported him for fifteen years, holidays paid?

"July Fourth was not a holiday?"

"You don't pack all your effects, sir, for a single day's leave."

"Your grandson is here, Mrs. Lloyd?"

"I have two grandsons."

"The one who came to the village and gave such a talk in the street."

"And was that against the law?"

"You know I'm not a lawyer, and . . ."

"Just so. Your job, I think, is to keep people who have no special knowledge of the law from taking it into their own hands. . . . Oh, Emma, is that you? Come in. Deputy Barrow's here again, the one who saw the men attacking Willie. Do you have anything to ask him . . . because Willie has been limping, hasn't he, and is unable to raise a pitchfork still? They could have broken his back."

"Quite a help around the farm, then, is he? He seemed quite all right when I sent him home."

"Sent him home?" she snapped. "Is there a curfew now in Moriches? Yes, well, a doctor will have to decide about his condition. Perhaps then we'll have more to discuss with you."

"Mrs. Lloyd, we'd like to have a look around the farm again, in the woods and so forth. In the barns and sheds. The sheriff says we could help you put the fire out. Unhealthy for you, all the smoldering, I think you told him."

"You will please keep your men away from the ashes, Mr. Barrow. Once started, a bonfire must be left to a complete combustion. Or we'll have charcoal all over the fields. Go on about your search and leave our fire alone. And where were you when they started it? What about your curfew then?"

"You said curfew, Mrs. Lloyd. I never did."

Emma was surprised by Helen's argument because she'd heard her give the order to her own help to extinguish the remaining coals if they were still burning the next day.

"Your grandson Willie," the deputy asked again, "would he be hereabouts?"

"We have not seen him today," Helen lied. "Hadn't you better get back to your village and see that he's not thereabouts? Making your streets dangerous with his politics."

A few minutes later, she heard the deputy in the yard cursing "the Doctor's bitch mother" as he gave orders to his several men to search the woods for the queer driver who'd gone missing.

"You see, Emma?" Helen pestered. "You see what happens when the men go off to war and leave the women to the drugstore patriots? Look here, dear, I want you to leave Willie and me alone while we have a little talk. I've sent him up to the camel to wait for me. He's made quite a confession already. Quite ashamed of himself. You sit there in the cage and see they don't pour water or go poking about in the ashes."

Only a day ago, her mother-in-law, the flinty patriot, might have pilloried Willie for a disobedient coward, and now she was taking up for him against an odious constabulary. Appeased by some confession. The old lady's eyes were still watering from the acrid air drifting over the property; it could have been the stink of a whole town's garbage set afire; something horrid in these ashes, and yet she refused the deputy's help in shutting down the hot fetor. She had not wanted it started, and now she did not want it put out.

Emma sat for a while in the cage, as she'd been told, wondering how her Willie could yield to the overbearing grandmother things he denied to herself. She saw one of the men coming out of the woods with a long pole, approaching the remains of the fire, and watched as he began to stir the ashes red at the edge. A voice came booming from above her.

"Get away from there!"

The man jumped, as if someone had snuck up and struck him on the shoulder. He slunk away into the woods again, driven off by another command delivered across the plain from Helen's megaphone. "And put that stick back in the woods where you found it!"

Emma stayed only a moment more on the porch before going silently up the back stairs and making her way along the corridor toward the sleeping porch. Close enough, she leaned her head back against the camel's wall until it became a sounding board for the conversation within, where Willie was asking, "Does Papa have to know about it? Are you going to tell him?"

"Have you put his gun back?"

"Yes."

"Have you cleaned it?"

"Yes."

"Does Louis or Nellie know anything about it?"

"No. No."

"All right, then, we'll just say nothing more of it. You've made a clean breast of it to me. That's the important thing. You've admitted your mistake and you're ready to start over with a clean conscience. See here, Willie, sometimes telling others has a way of implicating them in your troubles. Unless we're going to tell the whole world—and I don't think we want to do that—we'll do your father and the whole family a favor by keeping this to ourselves. Yes?"

If Emma meant to put a stop to this, this was the moment to burst in and ask just what kind of pact was being made here. The inconvenience of admitting her eavesdropping was nothing to the shame of what might be afoot. Her fear of knowing more had turned her to a stone. But a stone with ears, and the intrigue continued:

"I think you love this place as much as your father, Willie. When he comes home, there'll be time enough for you to go off and make yourself worthy. Stir your stumps. Have you thought about how you'll do that? Now listen to me. Pull yourself together."

"What if they find his . . ."

"It was much too hot for that. There'll be nothing left but ashes. I want you to find your brother and sister and take them off for a swim. They're spending far too much time in the library."

Emma made her way down the back steps and was sitting in the cage again when Helen came down to assure her that everything would be put to rights as soon as they could be rid of these nosy men the sheriff had sent from Moriches, the ones sniffing at the fetid air, through the woods and in every corner of the farm. "Willie's going to be fine. He's very sorry about the fire."

Emma hardly comprehended what the woman was saying to her. She was too busy reorganizing her thoughts; all ideas of a drowned Peterson, a bloated body wafting away on the bay's gentle swell, were burned off in her mind into crematory ash. She supposed the fire's white-hot center could have managed that. And her boy was easily strong enough to drag a body up the brush stairway and send it hurtling down the carefully arranged chimney.

That Helen might accept this horror as her own privileged information confused Emma. All that talk of the family's difficult religion, more rigorous than Christianity, with the Bible only a primer, the guiding but simplistic legend, to be supplemented by Mr. Emerson's transcendent message, the real Lloyd text, the one for those unafraid of a higher human responsibility and independence, all this began to make a private sense.

It was coming clear that Helen was the family church—Mary, Paul, and Jesus—holy mother, explicator, and deity. The ultimate confessor. The oneness in nature held this selfish corollary, an allness in the grandmother. The fastidious manners and dress were the lay guise and costume for a supreme force within, the soul of a priestess who could pass upon any corruption so long as the culprit knelt to her. In the process, stealing the boy's loyalty and devotion from his own mother.

No. Emma would not have that! For a moment, she hardened into total disaffection, then recognized the folly of a grudge, which could lead them only into damnable silence. She would have to come to the truth with a tactful determination. No counting the times her great oafish boy had put her through this change. But so many times, he'd been the injured one, the one forced to accomplishment beyond his means, to angry confrontations, while the brainier Louis tutored, and then hung back from the consequences of his dangerous counsel.

"Willie!" she yelled frantically toward the beach, pleased when the older woman covered her ears in pained protest.

"Willie!" Louder. But Willie and the other children were already pushing the sailing skiff into the bay.

"Look, dear, this has come for you."

Emma took her letter and turned away.

"Won't you share it?"

Ignoring Helen, she made straight to the study for pen, ink, and paper. Armed with these, she marched out of the house. Gauging the breeze, she took herself upwind of the wicked stench, across two fields to the edge of the woods, and, on a seat of moss, her back against an arrow-straight poplar, she prepared to spill her heart's new grief and terror to her soldier in France. But first she must read the incoming news.

It was another rehash of the Adjutant situation. If a major outranked this man, she asked herself, why couldn't a major just relieve the man of duty, get rid of him? Apparently, it was more complicated than that, but the complications bored her. Military nonsense that could only be a hindrance to medicine; her man should put himself above it.

And how could he go on about the French angel again, the nurse accused by the Adjutant, this time of farmyard witchery? What now! Accused of spinning a horse's blood in a centrifuge? Of frightening to death the domestic animals of Brethenay, of nighttime adventuring in the barnyards with a hypodermic? Of a grotesque interest in the bedpans of her patients?

"A lay person might assume the Adjutant has raised some honest questions," the Major wrote. "Never mind. Jeanne's scientific curiosity is at once innocent and sincere, and her selfless nursing, her palpable compassion, easily give the lie to any doubts about her. If you could see the tears rise when she comes out of the ward, and yet she never allows the patients a glimpse of her distress. You say I worry you with all my admiration for her? This is a silliness you must put behind you."

Emma dropped the letter to the ground in disgust and took up her pen. It was an added annoyance that his news was one month old, and that hers might be equally stale or older when it reached the doctor.

"I am almost pleased that I shall not see you when you receive these lines. Will you be standing? Sitting? Regardless, your anger will not avail any more than will my tears. It is too late for the whip, too late for Scripture. Our Willie is what he is. And if he has done the terrible thing I suspect, he may not be ours to instruct much longer. You already know that he was bloodied by young patriots in the city. This is worse."

She recounted the evening of July 4, working backward from the awesome fire whose windblown sparks had threatened the house; the arrival of the Moriches Fire Brigade, summoned not by alarm but by flames visible from the fire station; the fire set by a more than willing town boy, whom they think was put to his mischief by the disconsolate Willie. Willie, who had not been able to wheedle permission for the blaze from his grandmother; Willie, who only the night before had been followed over the Forge Creek Bridge and into the village by Peterson.

It was Peterson who had pointed the village hard boys in the direction of the disobedient son, who in an act of foolish courage, or self-destruction, when dared to repeat an antiwar sentiment, called the American adventure in Europe one of the most tragic and foolish campaigns in the world's history. No more or less than his circumspect brother had been explaining to him for a month. No more or less than he'd done a few weeks earlier in Washington Square. With similar result.

These events had been related to her by the postmistress, Mary Rose, whose rooms were directly above the commotion and whose sleep had been interrupted. And Emma, who had once agreed with Helen to spare their soldier any home-front grief, was sick of her own euphemistic deception. Angry enough to revel in her spite, ready to make up for lost opportunities, reconstructing the long quarrel between Willie and Peterson. So disagreeable. And now, the horrid man's disappearance. The stench hanging over the fire's remains. And what in heaven's name could be causing that? Let the Major suffer the same suspicions as she must:

"Your gun was missing, the one in the middle of the rack that does the two-barrel trick, the one you always took with you to the Adirondacks. I know Willie had it. I heard him tell your mother so. I'm sure they have an enormous ugly secret. It is most unpleasant here."

Emma couldn't go on. Her anger gave way to despair. It was days later before she was able to finish. The same unpleasantness, she explained, had continued through the month. No word of Peterson. The grown children indulging themselves as if nothing had happened to disrupt their own household. As if the dead of Passchendaele, and the mire of Flanders, were another planet's misery. In the skiff, towing one another across the bay like happy whales. And Helen, reluctant to leave the camel, where she must keep a sharp eye peeled for German action, would no longer criticize her grandchildren.

At last, the sheriff came with warrant and deputies to do what Emma knew he must. She walked right behind them as Helen watched from her porch. They went sifting through the cold ash until, at the very center of the pile, their metal rakes clicked against the hard evidence of bone. A deputy picked up something that fell apart in his hands. There was a bleached haunch of some kind, and other pieces thin as twigs—what was left of them. They hardly looked human.

Her report to the front said:

"Thank God, no skull. The deputies stayed for hours. I heard one say, 'Look for the teeth. And the watch.' Whatever bits did not crumble as they picked them up, they wrapped carefully in cloth and took away. Willie went to the city this morning. I didn't try to stop him."

She waited so long for him to understand the situation in Moriches. Had her letter gone to the bottom of the sea? Could delivery be so slow? There was another from him and he was still oblivious:

My Dearest Emma,

Now that our expeditionary troops have arrived in force, the censors are overwhelmed, and I am going to tell you things that I might not have dared before. Not the names of colleagues, or exactly where we are; I don't wish to flout the regulations, but there are certain developments here, which I'm bursting to share with you, and with a clear conscience. Medical research and scientific advances ought to be the property of the world, and since I would, and do, treat German patients on stretchers with the same care as our own, so I'd have no regrets if these lines should be read by the Kaiser himself.

So. The most extraordinary week here. Something horrid going on between the Adjutant and the Colonel. And I fear they have me in the middle of their ugly feud. Using me, both of them. Of course I would side with the Colonel in a moment, except that he refuses to rid us of the miscreant, and thereby reveals his weakness, perhaps, and, I tremble to suggest it, his own tacit involvement in the miscreant's graft.

Imagine! In the middle of a continental slaughter, when the little good we can accomplish is so outweighed by the massive count of the dead—into the millions—we have two men at the top of a command fighting over the credentials and duties of a single nurse!

His French marvel's eyes were sinking deeper each day behind dark rings as she went so often sleepless. It couldn't go on that way. The Major tried to slow her down, restricting Jeanne's hours in the ward. But instead of sleeping, she would hide herself away in the newly equipped bacteriology laboratory. (Still waiting for research volunteers from America. What is wrong with America? Doesn't it understand the death struggle here?) And this is where she had brought the Adjutant's ignorant and jealous suspicion on herself.

And this led to such a revelation. To the Major alone, she confessed her real identity, and together they began work that would be of significance far beyond the lives saved in their hospital! No, Jeanne was not the unwashed provincial patriot that she first pretended to be. An ordinary nurse, yes, but only in her first informal training. I've seen small miracles of healing that convince me of her gift. It seemed to Emma he was trying to convince himself:

In fact, Jeanne is Lucienne de Crouen, who worked among the most remarkable European men of medical science before the war. She says they called her *"la chasseuse des microbes,"* or *"la doctoresse sans grade."* Reviled for making herself such a valuable pest in the laboratory of the celebrated Pasteur. Then as the research assistant of Bordet.

Remember Bordet? We read his papers when Louis had his frightful childhood fevers. Most revered of European pathologists. A pioneer in the theory of immunity and curative inoculation. Well, our Jeanne worked right at his side. And she forgot nothing.

Instead of running from the Germans, Jeanne—Lucienne— stayed on in the laboratory of her hospital so as not to lose the results of her research into a Belgian fever (one of the trench fevers?). Of course, the Germans meant to steal her work, and she was forced into political stealth. The statements she made then were held against her by the Germans. In so many words: The soldiers will settle the arguments among nations. We are here to defeat something smaller and more dangerous. I know it sounds grandiose and pompous. But if you could only see her in the ward!

She survives her awkward history by her clear devotion to her work. She stayed in Brussels too long to be trusted again by the French, and when she finally escaped the Germans, of course she had to assume a new identity. She arrived before us, having guessed where a welcoming hospital would appear. So the turnabout wind of war blew us a rare gift, and it has been given to me to help her re-create some of her work that the war has destroyed.

So far, the Colonel accepts my assurance of her value, but the Adjutant still spreads ugly talk of her doings behind her back. You can imagine what kind of effect that sort of rumor has on some of our patients. We do our best to keep him out of the ward.

As I say, there is rapid turnover here, as in all military hospitals. The sick and the wounded come and go in great batches. Few stay for more than a week or two, and there is not much time for the Adjutant to infect them with doubt. But with each accusation, Jeanne must come to me for support. It's up to me to see that she maintains the Colonel's confidence. And I must calm the staff. I have supported and encouraged her laboratory stratagems, which follow one after another.

Emma, I am reborn in my work with Jeanne Prie. We are not just saving the occasional soldier's life but also looking each disease in its microscopic face and scheming to beat it at its own game. Don't despair for my affection or my faith. Here, too, we only verify Mr. Emerson's rules of unity. From the tiniest malignant germ, we concoct its health-giving counterpart. Disease and health are built of the same materials and it is given to us to induce them to fight among themselves until only the healthy order survives.

Now, about the children. Do you remember how Pasteur chased the atheists from his door? The ones who claimed that germs sprang up spontaneously in the brewer's yeast. No! he said, the germs fly into the brew from the air and are themselves a product of regeneration. Maybe this will be useful to you in clearing your conscience of responsibility for the nonsense you say now afflicts the minds of our boys. We know the sort of infection that issues from the mouths of college professors and is borne through the classroom air to impressionable ears. If we are clever enough, we find the appropriate antidote. And the young people get over it.

Emma cursed. "What would he know about 'get over it'? Only a page left, and still he raves about the French tramp!"

Emma, if you were only here to see this firsthand. If you could only share the wonders of the laboratory with Jeanne and me. Just imagine the three of us looking through a microscope at B typhosis growing in a drop of liquid from an ox's eyeball. (You mustn't think we're ghouls. This is the nourishing medium of choice for many bacilli.) Together, we marvel to see a field covered with little rods that dance about with abandon.

Then, come into the ward with us to the bedside of Corporal X, out of his normal wits in a fever. Watch as Jeanne draws blood from his arm, and pay no attention to the patient up the line calling, "Vampire." How could he be expected to understand? Now, back into the laboratory, where we prepare a clear serum of the sick soldier's blood. Under the microscope, the myriad rods still do their turns in the drop of fluid on the slide. But we add a drop of our serum to their waltz and see the revels gradually subside. The dancing bacilli fall into one another's arms, gather in clumps; they become lifeless organisms. We have made a vaccine against the very strain of typhus that afflicts our man! We do the victory dance. Behind the lines, we fight a universal enemy, and it may help if you imagine yourself here with us in this exhilarating struggle. Your devoted, William

Emma was chastened for the moment. Still, he was so selfish in his enthusiasm! Besides, this was already old news. What had he done with his French sorceress in the meantime?

"Would you like to make acquaintance with my lice?" The Major did not recoil in disgust; rather, he was smitten with the boldness of it. The forthrightness of a vulgarity almost beyond belief. Jeanne's honest warning of the price to be paid for an indulgence on which she placed so little value. It aroused not the moralist in him, but the forbearance of the doctor.

A healthy woman, near forty; so many travels in a dangerous world. It was possible to imagine some lout misusing her open zeal, forcing her affection, and leaving his crawl and spore on her. He could clean her up, make her whole again. No one else need know there had been a stain. No, there was no way to explain all of this woman to Emma.

"Jeanne, you don't have to live with the little devils." He had an astringent that would kill them, and a cream that would finish off their eggs.

"Kill them?"

Forgetting the gifts of the butcher—they would be made useless by a long day in the sun—the two of them gave themselves up to lazy hours beside the river. She entertained him with recollections of the men she had meekly served, the "mind-absent" Pasteur, whom she once had to advise to fasten the buttons of his pants. Metchnikoff, who had let one of his lab girls swallow cholera bacilli, and purposely infected a volunteer medical student with syphilis to prove the agency of his calomel ointment. And Bordet, drooling unawares into a vial of serum, so that an experiment in its final stages had to be started all over again.

The Major took his harness off to please Jeanne—he was luxuriating in this human side of science—and the jacket, and he rolled his pants to the knees. Likewise, she rolled hers. They went downstream to a shallow place, and he waded into the dark water with a net she fashioned from the supple branch of a tree whose name he did not know—she called it "children's sorrow," often cut for switches—and a piece of mosquito netting.

The water, muddy from the rains, showed them no fish, but in the next quarter hour, two short, thick eels swam into their round seine. Proud as a man who'd invented survival, he made a fire to cook the homely things, then began to skin them in the manner he'd observed as a boy.

"We used to do this at school," he said. "When we had a day off on the weekend." Taking his pocketknife and cutting most of the way through one eel's neck, trying to remember what he had learned from Latoni years earlier.

"Now you need something to grab with," Jeanne said, as if she, too, had seen this operation before. She fetched a small bicycle tool from her basket and watched as he used it to rip the skin from the body.

"It doesn't suffer," he assured her.

"No?" she said. "It moves but does not feel? Who told you so? You don't know that."

Her face, shiny with perspiration, glowed red over the fire. A rumble of artillery to the northwest quickened the Major's heart, and like a mind reader, she reached for his wrist and felt his pulse.

"Yes," she said. "You see it happens to me, too." Taking the fingers of his right hand, she placed them under her chin, against the pulse in her neck. "Fast as a rabbit."

"Scared of the guns?" No, he thought, not this far south on the river, though German nostrils were still flared for the perfume of Paris.

"Not of the guns. Of what can happen to ten thousand men at once."

She skinned the other eel. She, too, knew Latoni's technique? They skewered the meal on more children's sorrow and held it over the flame. The Major watched her heavy lips labor at her earnest argument; certain he had her meaning now: a cloud of gas descending over a regiment, or the front and rear trenches becoming ready conduits for the exhalation and inhalation of a germ that killed all up and down the line. He looked down at the soft hair on her thick ankles, considered the possibility of lice roaming in her nether parts, and moved closer to her. Poor Emma, he thought, and other women of her stalwart kind, so uncommonly tidy.

Jeanne was explaining the spirit of sacrifice in Metchnikoff's entourage. Several of them, young French women hoping for the smile of the Russian. "What they would do! It stops the heart!" Bacilli injected, bacilli scratched into lesions, bacilli swallowed.

"No," the Russian told them, "I am not asking this of you. You must not." But for these women, he knew his protests would only be further enticement, and they made themselves sick for him. "But none of them died," Jeanne said triumphantly, poking the Major again as she made her point. "Too much to live for. We need this again, don't you think? People to take a chance with the life."

Lloyd, unsettled by the turn in her conversation, turned back to the lice, not wanting to appear squeamish. He could as easily have been a man of the trenches as a doctor, picking nits off a comrade's scalp.

"I'm not afraid of them."

"Afraid of them? Why would you be afraid of them?"

It came to him suddenly that she must think him terribly silly. Again, what could he have been thinking? A nurse like her! As many soldiers as she had treated for lice. But she needn't be coy, he told her. His New York practice wasn't so sheltered that he didn't know the difference between the head and body varieties. And as attending physician at Roosevelt Hospital, he'd learned the little crabs had no respect for class. Jeanne needn't be ashamed.

"Ashamed of *les poux?*"

She laughed and promised him warmly that he knew her well enough to be making their acquaintance soon. But for the moment, was he familiar with the work of the American Smith, who proved that the Texas fever in cows was carried and passed by one generation of ticks to the next? Yes, and no easy job when his laboratories were only fenced fields.

And then she was back to her time in Brussels, where, she said, they had asked the clergy to coax the children of their congregations into giving up their guinea pigs to the great goals of medicine. And the children, pressed by their parents, had made teary sacrifices of more than a hundred. These were separated into three populations injected with three experimental serums, which had caused one group to hemorrhage internally, another to grow obese without becoming immune to enteric, and the third to copulate in a frenzy.

"Three poisons and no remedy," he offered his condolence.

"Three?" she teased. "Perhaps two."

She brushed a strand of hair from his eye, led him up the path to a grove covered with a wild yellow flower. She drew him down to the ground. He was composing a protest that he never made, fighting against an image of Emma's stricken face. They rolled once on a gentle incline, and were stained all over with the wildflowers' pollen, her face, too, covered in the golden dust.

Clothes were coming off. And, painted like gods, right to the skin, they might have taken the gods' privilege. But Jeanne began to betray her excitement in shocking rapid movements, in a way that might suggest habit more than novelty. And very quickly he felt more monster than god. His life of preparation against just such a temptation, almost wasted. Would he become a hypocrite now, who could only lie by omission in all future mail to Emma? And here in France, his Pucelle, his Saint Jeanne, nearly corrupted by his acquiescence to her fevered generosity. He lay in a silent shame, counting on her discretion to ignore forever the thing that had not even been finished, and a return to their proper concern, their war against wounds and bacteria.

She rewarded him immediately with a complete disregard for the unconsummated act. "*Un rêve*," she called it. "As light as nothing," and as she rose from their nest, she was already gathering up the items tossed into the real world from their dream, parts of his uniform so she could wash away the yellow stain in the river. Some dozen miles away, he knew the same river ran red, and the seeds of the same yellow flowers on the banks had been driven by 100,000 boots into the quagmire.

"Your Walter Reed," Jeanne said, as if the subject had never changed, "he understood that guinea pigs were not enough. Guinea pigs don't get the yellow fever."

Did he feel the itching, the biting already—raking his fingernails across his pubes as she collected his clothes? Naked, she looked curiously short, her fine bosom thrust out in a pride of health. He wished she would cover herself. Jeanne again seemed mindless of all but her mission: "He needed the brave men. He needed the volunteers who were not afraid of the mosquitoes."

She went to the water still half-naked, his pants and jacket slung over her shoulder, and he was free to examine himself. Bent over, staring dumbly, pulling aside the hair, but it was vain with his eyesight. He would need the big glass he used to read the finer script of Emma's mail.

A half hour every night in the week that followed, in his room with the door latched, bent over himself with the magnifying lens, straining for a glimpse of one of the little creatures. A horrid time for him, as Jeanne went among her patients with a new tenderness, coming to them with the needle of relief from pain. Their day on the river seemed to make her forget her problems with Latoni. Given her own key to the laboratory, she was happy at last, and confident.

She asked for and received his permission to ask another of her disabled German patients, who also had a trench fever, for cooperation with one of her little experiments—a morning and evening donation of blood. Another died and she made black armbands for a few of the survivors who begged to attend services but were too sick to rise from their beds. One more German amputee, grateful for her tender care and the lieder she hummed softly over his pillow, asked if he, too, could wear the black armband to honor the dead. Jeanne spoke German with these men much too quickly for the Major to follow.

When another patient was carried out, she put a band on her own arm. There was confusion in the hospital as the bed count grew suddenly from three hundred to five hundred; dozens of doctors and seventy nurses struggling to keep up with the ever-faster flow of sick and wounded through their doors, scribbling histories and instructions on charts that were more like prayer boards than useful protocols.

Efficient medicine frequently gave way to intuition or carelessness. It was the luck of the patient whom he drew for doctor or nurse, and the whimsy of the general order that might force his transfer to the next hospital, which could save or end his life. The Colonel recognized the chaos under his command but was reluctant to do anything about it. He was expecting Major Lloyd to shape things up before Chief Surgeon Ireland's next inspection.

The Major wrote Emma: I've told you the Colonel is not a doctor. And neither, as it turns out, is he a military man. He's here through the misplaced confidence of a friend, the kind of mistake we get when ranks are mustered directly from a peaceful cadre into soldiery. For all his posturing, I think it rattles the Colonel to give an order with the force of law and summary punishment behind it. He doesn't understand that in the army, authority without rank is no authority at all. He sets me up for intolerable insolence from men who are my equals in rank but far beneath me in medical knowledge. American soldiers are at last here en masse. The patients are cycled through here much too quickly.

Jeanne showed the Major her new laboratory notebook. There were some German words—some medical terms for which English offered no translation—and her French scrawl was almost illegible. He watched the purple level rise in her syringe over the shriveled arm of a dying man as a pulse flickered. Not protocol, but he permitted it. Jeanne taking blood again before it was lost to science. The man in the next bed grabbed the Major's arm, and through a mask of white tape and gauze wheezed, "Had a finger in his bum, too."

He pulled himself away from the deluded fellow.

"Not the trench," she said quietly, "the enteric. This man, we could have saved him." And in the laboratory, she showed him how she might have stopped the swarm of microscopic rods by agglutination, with a scant drop of another clear serum she'd prepared. She claimed to have a serum antidote made of three types of typhoid germs.

"You brought this with you?" he asked her. "Impossible. How could you maintain the temperature?"

"I make it here," she said. "But the blood is not the first test." For three days in a row, she said, she had gone into the man's rectum for specimens of the excreta. "Each time, no typhus under the lens."

The Major was incredulous. "You couldn't wait for the stool from his bedpan?"

"But of course one must have it when one needs it."

She made his squeamishness seem an American character flaw, pushing his head down over the microscope, over her pungent slides, and then over the recently drawn blood, now teeming with the B typhosis bacilli.

Jeanne explained something he knew already: that B typhosis, taken into the body through the mouth, grew in the intestine, then after two weeks, spread into the blood. Also that one drop of blood might not contain enough of the germ for it to be recognized. A sample might have to be incubated.

Instead of being insulted, he was awed again by the audacity.

"We can make some a little sick to keep them from getting dead."

Her eyes shone with the joy of healing.

Yes, he was well acquainted with the theory and practice of prophylactic inoculation, but he warned her very slowly, very precisely, "Jeanne, we don't do experiments on our patients."

"No no no no no no no." She rattled her agreement like a Long Island woodpecker. "Of course, no." Then: "But the ones who have so small a hope, they beg to volunteer. What of them?"

He went to his rooms and wrote the letter about Jeanne, *la chasseuse des microbes,* that had so flustered Emma, already in despair in that week of volatile patriotism when every exploding firecracker reminded her of gunshot, and every gunshot, of the missing Peterson. There was another page she had first ignored in her dismay:

Jeanne was raised humbly, and a Catholic. We need not hold that against her. Like us, she gets her divine message direct, without interlocutor. In her case, it comes from two saints who speak in her ear, and for all I can tell, it's practical advice they give her. Her common origin and her ease with life's vulgarities are a caution, but they do make her a marvelous nurse.

Now, Emma, do me a little favor. Since my knowledge of German is rudimentary and mother's is complete, would you have her translate something for me? Of course you can't breathe a word of German around here without arousing contempt or suspicion. It was in one of Jeanne's notebooks.

Wolfram wird mein Stechnadelkissen sein.

Wolfram is one of our Germans. A terrible case, which I won't describe to you. I think the line may be part of a rhyme Jeanne made up to take his mind off his condition. She couldn't explain it to me.

For all his self-inspection, the Major found nothing, no crawling itch. His body was clean, but what of Jeanne's? Had she been linked in a carnal chain of sin that could only provoke the Allied God? Who nevertheless was pushing back the Hun this month.

Lloyd was called in by Colonel Hanson to be told that an English doctor, a Captain Armond, who had been at the field laboratory in Poperinge, was being sent at his request, to act as their clinical pathologist. "He'll be a great asset to us. Extraordinary things being done now in diagnosis. Preparation of vaccines on demand. It should put an end to the Adjutant's troubles with our Jeanne. Of course, I don't believe half the stories he tells."

Why wouldn't the Colonel look him in the eye as he spoke?

"She does a fine job, no doubt. But proper procedure comes first. We can't have these germs thrown around carelessly. About yesterday."

"Which germs?"

"Latoni says a tube flew out of the centrifuge and blood spattered all over the place."

The Colonel swiveled in his chair, away from counterattack, collected his argument, and began again.

"So, all for the best. You're too busy to take that on. No criticism, but you'll be taking command when I leave. You won't have time for microscopes. If I were you, I'd tell our French gal to forget the germ hunting, too. That's it."

But there was more.

"Is there something you're not telling us about her? For God's sake, William, you know we can't have a nurse telling doctors what to do, not in a hospital!"

Had the Colonel forgotten Jeanne's protocol against gas gangrene — cut all the mess out, right back to the healthy tissue—the total surgical cleansing that had put their antisepsis dogma to rout? She might have saved twenty more arms and a dozen legs if they'd listened to her sooner.

But the Colonel was swiveling away again, turning to the wall map next to his chair and marching his fingers to the northwest, from base hospitals to field hospitals, up the Allied path of medical mercy in which he took special pride, coming to rest on Poperinge, so close to Ypres, in Belgium's seaward corner.

"That's where our man's been, right under the German cannon."

A hero? Coming their way, to tell the boys in the rear what war was? When the Major told Jeanne about the new germ man coming to Chaumont—Captain Armond—he was surprised that she already knew of him.

"But why Armond, here? He's just a big show-off."

Yes, she said, and he was in Brussels before the Germans came. And there Armond had claimed to have something to share with the world. His theory that the cure for all intestinal infestations could be found in the foodstuffs of the same country where the trouble was ingested. Not so stupid, Jeanne thought. But what good to anyone in wartime? You couldn't feed an expeditionary force of this size on local corn and honey. Useless. But the British let him follow his nose to Gallipoli, where a whole army's bowels had been cursed.

"And now he comes here?" she asked. "A man of so little science and so much pride. Why do the English send him to us? Just ask yourself."

Emma went about the Moriches farm in a dread that the truth of the Fourth of July weekend would be revealed to her through the instruments of public justice—sheriff's men, warrants, summonses, courts, public prosecutors. Willie, and perhaps Helen, who might tell everything, had some sort of pact to say nothing more about it, and Emma could only hope that whatever her boy's troubling part, it had been by accident of passion, not premeditation. For Willie's sake, she was thinking beyond the retribution of men to the mercy of God.

In August, the farm's fertility—the acres of asparagus now gone to fern, fields once white with potato blossom now in flourishing green rows, and second-growth stands of hay waving in the offshore breeze—only increased her shame. A plenty beyond their deserts, even if the farm was a marginal enterprise. And when the old deputy with white hair and the jumpy hand appeared, Emma supposed the sheriff had chosen the most decrepit of his department as courier of accusing papers to humiliate the family further.

But no papers. The deputy caught his breath on the screened porch, waiting for Miss Helen to be summoned from the camel; his news was for her alone, not for the mother of the cowards, or anyone else on the disgraced property.

"We know what happened to your Mr. Peterson."

"What do you know?" Emma interrupted.

"If you don't mind . . ."

The man reached out with his palsied hand, led Helen to a private corner of the porch, and began whispering to her. Out of ignorant spite, Emma supposed. The news would have to come to her filtered through her mother-in-law's dark lens of family propriety.

"Everything's going to be fine," Helen promised her again when the man was gone.

"But what of the bones?" Emma demanded.

"Which bones, dear?"

"You know well enough."

Emma said she was returning immediately to the city.

"With Nellie and the boys? The chance of infection? You can't do that, dear. William would never forgive you."

"They'll have to learn, won't they. Everyone will have to learn. I won't be made a stranger to my own children."

And then she was accused of being melodramatic. Imagine. Controlling her anger, and wondering what surprise she'd be hearing from across the Atlantic next time, because heaven knew what kind of nonsense the old woman had been writing to her Boykins.

Imagine, Emma composed without benefit of stationery, your mother, the suggestible duenna of Moriches, who fancies Germans in every rowboat on the bay, who calls an alarm through her trumpet every night so that strollers on the beach assume we have a madwoman in the house, calling *me* melodramatic.

Emma pushed past her, through the screen door, on her way to pack up. Helen reached out to stop her, grabbed her blouse, and held fast.

"Let go of me. Why do you insult me?"

"Take hold of yourself."

"I will, believe me; I'll take them back to the city." It occurred to Emma she should have done this weeks earlier. Her mother-in-law would not care to be left alone after growing so accustomed to their company and her control of their lives.

"See here, Emma, sometimes it is better to hold back."

"Better for whom?" she snapped.

"Listen to me; the police have found Peterson. He's quite all right. In New Jersey, working for a taxi service."

"Alive? Thank God. But why didn't you tell me?"

"He'll speak to no one here until William returns."

Emma pulled away again.

"You kept me wondering all this time?"

"Wondering?"

"If Willie had . . . had been responsible."

"But dear, I never imagined you were thinking that. Not after the sheriff came and found nothing."

"Nothing?"

"Oh, you goose! Let me explain it all."

"Willie had a terrible Independence Day. The night before was such a disgrace for him."

At that moment, Nellie, who must have been listening from the living room, started a little coughing fit, perhaps to avoid what she sensed was coming next, and Helen's story was put off for the moment. Emma, wild to hear the rest, had to agree to a stroll out to Lon's Creek with her daughter, who said everything on the place looked "so glorious and abundant."

But the walk itself felt more like a diversionary tactic than a spontaneous celebration of the farm's bounty, because Nellie was asking awkward questions again, all of which looked backward rather than ahead to the generation whose future was now in question—Willie's, Louis's, and her own.

Of Lon's Creek, she wanted to know, "Who was Lon?"

"I think he worked on the farm a long time ago."

"Wasn't he a slave?"

"Well, yes, I believe he was. But why do you ask if you already know?"

"Grandma said she *thought* he was a slave."

"Grandma knows he was a slave."

"Why are you and Grandma arguing?"

"What makes you think that?"

"Is it about Daddy?"

"No, we were discussing your brother."

"He had a fight with Peterson, didn't he?"

"What do you know about that?"

"Nothing. Except Willie said I didn't have to worry about Peterson. That he wouldn't be putting his hand on my knee anymore."

Nellie's innocence was stained everywhere with half knowledge and impudent probing. Emma was not sure whether her daughter would be acting as Willie's informer, or only trying to move the family from a contention that might destroy the season here and send them all back to the monotonous and dangerous city.

"I think Daddy must have been awfully naughty when he was younger."

"Really, Nellie! Not that again! What have you got there?"

It was one of the letters from St. Mark's.

"I mean he was older than most of the other boys when he graduated."

"You've been told he missed a year with scarlet fever. Before that, he was ahead of himself."

"But he must have been in some mischief. Surely as bad as Willie, I'll bet you."

"What does that say?"

Abruptly, she pulled the letter from Nellie's hand. It was the one about the railroad accident, a schoolboy's fascination with the chaos of disaster. Masters and scholars set free for a whole morning to study what happens when a train of varied cargo, including a dozen Estey organs, slams into the back of a milk train. An engine dashing into a caboose, setting the whole business in front and behind afire. The organ pipes, those not consumed in flame, or in smithereens, gurgling with scalded milk.

It made Emma wonder how much the little doctor-to-be had actually seen that day and how much was made up to amuse the insatiable parents. But it wasn't the train wreck that had caught Nellie's eye. It was the mention of more girls and dances:

If you give me an entertainment over the Easter holiday, I'd rather have a dance than a theater party. If you do give me one, let me have something to say about the girls, please. Edith, of course, and the two Julias, Cornelia, and Elsie Littell. By the way, Albert Huideckope decided to dance at the hop, and since Davis's sister Hannah is his sweet, of course I had to give her up to him.

"Mama, was Daddy what you call a flirt?"

"Of course not. Stop this nonsense."

"Willie says he must have been."

"Willie's opinions are not reliable."

"I suppose not. He and Louis joke awfully about the letters."

"What about them?"

"About Daddy's habit. About his impurity."

"Nellie, shame! We will not discuss this again. Your father is a grown man. A volunteer! Do you understand that? Now listen to me."

She told her daughter that the boys' disrespect was their way of compensating for failing to measure up to their father's standards. It was not till later that evening that she was able to get from Helen the full explanation of what had happened over Independence weekend, and the same night she began to set it all down for William:

"You must get used to the idea that you will never see the great buck again, after all the years you protected it like a ward of the farm. Gone, like that! Not shot by some poacher from town, but your own son—I don't have to tell you which. A wanton act. William, when I learned of this last night, I was actually relieved. This is how bad things are with your family. You see, when Peterson disappeared, I thought Willie might have done away with him. The hatred between them was that profound. And when bones were found in the ashes of the bonfire, I froze. Could not bear to ask. I was told nothing.

"Your Mother knew what had happened, but I was left to brood on this without a clue. Willie has been ever more secretive, going back and forth to the city, though I ordered him not to. He refuses to explain himself. I cannot control him, and doubt that you could, either. He is hardened in his shame, and minds no one. I've no doubt you would banish him from the farm. But what would we, or the world, gain by that? Another city derelict, I expect.

"Your mother explained to Louis and Nellie what Willie had done even before she told me. In such a short season, she has appropriated the children's allegiance and affection. Through it all, I have maintained my civility out of loyalty to you, supposing that, as they mature, the children will sort this out for themselves and see it for the injustice it is.

"Helen says they were all afraid I'd tell you first thing, and you see how right they were. Isn't family deceit the worst kind of all?"

/   /

Emma read that much over, not sorry at all for the anguish it would cause. Perhaps it would wake him from his swoon into medical mysteries with his French nurse. Who did not seem to be a nurse at all, but, by Emma's intuition, the kind of interloper who seduces with a pushy virtue. Hadn't Emma heard enough stories about the nurses at Roosevelt, not the young ones who followed the doctors around like devoted puppies, but the seasoned hussies, whose hands and eyes had laid on every human part and frailty until innocence was turned, perforce, into a brazen knowledge? These woman knew far too much for any man's good, regardless of their altruism in the wards.

Emma could imagine Willie wandering off to the beach with the gun so late on the night of July 3. After he'd been knocked around and made to kiss the fatherland on its muddy lips outside the Moriches pharmacy, he'd come home in a rage. Into the house for the gun, and back to the beach, where he expected to find Peterson. Peterson had told the young men in the drugstore all about Willie's draft dodge. No palpitations, no asthma, as far as he knew, not as long as he'd been working for the good Mrs. Lloyd, the older one, which was "most of the shirker's life."

"There he is. That's him." And they'd come filing out of the pharmacy into the street, where Willie defied them all with his rehearsed piece, most of it learned from his brother, about Mr. Debs's elemental honesty, and the international forces of oppression.

He was in pain, his cheek swollen, his arm wrenched, according to Helen's secondhand account. Willie still refused to talk to anyone else about it. In Peterson's version of what happened later, the one he gave to the police, he was on the beach in the first small hours of Independence Day. There the boy approached him with the gun and threatened to blow his head off if he didn't get off the property, and told him never to let his shadow fall on Lloyd land again. Peterson didn't even come back to the house for the clothes he'd already started packing, but went to spend the rest of the night with Mrs. Smith's driver in Moriches. Too proud even to claim the possessions in his quarters through the proxy of a constable, he left the next morning for New Jersey with a small stake provided by Mr. Smith, enough for a week's lodging, and found work immediately at the taxi company in Newark. There he meant to begin taking instruction in public communication as a four-minute man.

"Well, thank our stars that Willie turned the gun on an animal. Surely out of his wits at that moment, for he knew how you treasured the creature and your orders to all who came on the farm that it must not be destroyed. He was so ashamed of what he'd done, he dragged the carcass to the top of the brush and logs and dropped it in the center to be rid of the evidence. At daylight, our nervy devil snuck back into Moriches and promised the Carter boy a dollar if he'd torch the whole affair after dark. Of course, that wasn't necessary. A half a dozen of Carter's village friends were waiting to do it for no payment at all. But I'm curious to know how much of this your mother has already told you."

Jeanne had warned the Major about Armond, the British bacteriologist, who'd been passed up and down the rear lines like a smelly fish and had now been sent to the Chaumont hospital to get the germ laboratory into shape. A thin, bald captain with his own car and driver. That kind of mobility, the kind the Major had enjoyed, went beyond rank. It might have meant Armond was considered too valuable to be tied to one post. Why just a captain if he was so important a figure? The tedious detail of his instructions and orders would be left behind for others to implement.

So many places to reform, so little time. He might clean up the lab, show them how to make a vaccine in the field, and be on his way. His latest authority came straight from General Ireland's office, and it soured Lloyd, because it was the very same flattering language used to pass favor on the Major: If there's anything funny going on in that laboratory, give Armond all the stick he needs. He'll clean it up.

/ /

If and when Colonel Hanson left, the Major would have an overhaul of his own in mind. In the meantime, he must not lose the cooperation of Jeanne, who was under a new kind of investigation. Armond seemed unnaturally interested in her. She said she felt the man's eyes following her through the hospital.

Armond told Hanson and the Major they had a bad situation here. Germans mixed in with their own men. And this volunteer from somewhere, this woman who called herself French, speaking German to them, and no one to translate what was being said. And the fevers all jumbled up together. A hodgepodge in the laboratory, where the same woman played with death-dealing germs and horses' blood. What the hell, he asked, could they be thinking? A nurse?

Armond got into her laboratory notes. "Very revealing," he told Lloyd. The evidence, he said, was of a jumbled and careless searching for some panacea serum that could restore the blood to a healthy order, no matter what its invader. "Look, Major, someday we'll have an inoculation for every fever, but she won't be the one to find it. Show me the patient who calls himself her pincushion."

In the officers' mess Captain Armond's voice rang over the wooden tables: "A diet of yogurt could have cured half the dysentery victims at Gallipoli, and the other half, the ones with amoeba in their intestines, got them from Turkish vegetables. I'm quite certain they could have been purged with enemas of Turkish coffee." A raving idiot, Lloyd thought, but with portfolio. The most dangerous kind of zealot.

Malassise was his exemplar of good war-hospital order.

"Set it up myself," he said. "Give a medical unit a good model, and they'll make the most of it. What I suggest we do here . . ."

Hadn't been in Chaumont two days, and had already given orders for sterilization of all equipment in the lab and destruction of the confusing slides. And then he was lecturing Lloyd and the rest about the Malassise system. Two hundred beds in the monastery for the wounded, and a large field of tents for the infectious diseases, separated into camps for measles, rose measles, scarlet fever, diphtheria, and so forth, each with a separate latrine. Never mind that this was Chaumont, this was a town of close quarters, with no place for a field of tents.

He would like to have stayed, Armond said, when Malassise had been overrun, as several other doctors had done to remain with their patients, and accept whatever fate the Germans handed him, but his services and knowledge were considered too valuable to be sacrificed to one camp. The decision had not been his, he said, though probably a wise one, considering what happened at Aisne.

As if Lloyd and the others should be familiar with what happened at Aisne.

"You haven't heard? Three hundred cases brought in during the battle. The CO and three other officers stayed behind when the camp was overrun, and the Germans let them continue treating their sick for three weeks. Then sent them away with the others as common prisoners.

"But . . . that . . . uh . . . I don't know . . ." Gossiping like a nanny about *his* war. "In Malassise, quite pathetic. The poor who came in could speak only Flemish. It was rather like a veterinary practice for us. On the other hand, they could tell us no lies."

Now he was offering a rudimentary lecture on "the immune body," preparing them all for the magic he meant to visit on the troubles here. His mouth worked like his own little pill factory, spitting out a medicine of *mots*. "We can neither weigh nor see it, whatever manner be it."

"So?"

"So, in time of war, we don't waste time looking for it or theorizing about it. We prepare the antidote and let it do its stealthy work."

"Yes?"

"You ask again? Let me tell you a little story, Lloyd. At Poperinge we had a couple of chaps always at each other's throats about how immunity develops. Does the disease exhaust the nutrients in the blood on which it depends? Or does the disease create the antidote to itself? They made such a thorough tangle in the laboratory, they were both sent back to England. Meanwhile, I made a serum that saved two dozen men. That's the business."

And as an afterthought: "God knows how many hundred more we saved from the fevers with prophylactic inoculations. You know, giving men the disease in so slight a form that it renders them immune while making them only slightly ill." As if he'd invented the procedure.

"Clever of you to mark the Boche with black ribbons," Armond said. Can't be too careful."

He had mistaken the memorial armbands for a hospital labeling system. Let him live with his ignorance. Lloyd wrote home that a visiting Englishman, only a captain, had destroyed some of Jeanne's good work and some of her reputation, as well. Only when Armond was gone did the Major realize that Armond's raving was a cover for his investigation of the base hospital for General Ireland. Coffee enemas for dysentery? No, no, no.

This didn't come to him all at once. But Lloyd saw that this man who presented as an Englishman with a French name must, in fact, be an American. Brussels before the war, where Jeanne had first become aware of Armond, had been a European hub of learning and argument in germ theory and immunology, and, as the war started, it was the place to loot for medical advantage, a nest of medical espionage. Germans, British, French, Belgians, all with their noses in one another's work, while an American played the fool for them, even as he took notes on everything they were saying and made copies of their lab notes. Isn't that what Armond had done here in the name of reform? Hadn't Jeanne seen the same tactics in Brussels? Now he was a snoop on General Ireland's staff, kept inconspicuous by his rank, and further disguised as a mad theorizer.

Lloyd could not have been sure of all this, but it's certain he thought it true, because the same conjecture was written in separate letters to his wife and mother, a week apart, in mid-September of 1918.

Lloyd regretted that he'd been so stiff with the little peacock, and gullible, since as Jeanne's apologist, any report would also reflect on himself. He had allowed his reputation to be tied to her, and was happily defiant in her praise. He became more extravagant. In a letter to his mother (which he expected would be shown to Emma) devoted completely to a defense of his French nurse:

She is a blotter who has absorbed the blood and the ink spilled by Europe's renowned men of epidemiology.

She quotes Lavoisier: "Public usefulness ennobles the most disgusting work." When I asked her if Lavoisier hadn't got the guillotine for his trouble, she looked at me as if I were a very small spirit indeed.

But Mother, I do get discouraged at times. The war does its best to turn us into a thermometer hospital. Fever after fever, every kind. All different in their cycles and duration. As I explained before, the wounded come in and are shipped out usually within a week or two. *If* they don't contract one of these dreadful heats, which can kill very quickly. And so we treat the delirious. One man went up to 107 yesterday and came down to normal in time to eat his supper. But he never woke for breakfast.

Two of our American nurses under the Adjutant's influence refused the serum we prepared for them. They passed away yesterday. Both had worn their germ masks faithfully and were exquisitely careful. I will lead memorial services for them this evening. Otherwise, our staff seems strangely immune. Jeanne says this blesses us with the opportunity to take further chances in our work. Don't worry, I discourage this kind of talk.

As you asked, I've written to Willie, but it will do no good if you offer him the shoulder of sympathy. I won't tell you exactly what I wrote, but I do not want him at the farm, spoiling the good fruit with the bad. It never occurred to me that you and Emma could not keep a compatible household. I've written her that she must not coddle Willie. And I ask the two of you to put your differences aside and make a common stand against his malingering. Save your tears for such as these women I will eulogize tonight. They didn't have to come here, but served of their own will.

Jeanne's laboratory work was destroyed, Latoni himself hurling the little glass tubes and slides and retorts against the sides of the trash cans for the sound it made; too satisfying to be left to lesser rank. But instead of the hysterics the Adjutant had predicted—"She'll smash the works and be gone before I can say 'court-martial'"—Jeanne saved her remonstrance for Lloyd alone.

"If Monsieur Latoni is not careful, he'll cut his hand and catch the death."

And she asked the Major to her rooms, across the bridge, well away from the hospital and barracks where the American nurses were quartered. It was a little flat she'd been given by a grateful old lady of the place. Like many of the services Jeanne negotiated, it was with a special understanding between her and one of the local population, as if she, too, were a native of the place. They gave her run of the town without questions. Wherever she pleased in the surrounding countryside, she ate, she drank, she slept, on the community's hospitality.

Should he dare go to her quarters? He'd had fair warning of the temptations she practiced in the name of science, even a preview of his susceptibility. It was time—*"enfin,"* she said—for him to meet the lice, her lice. And so he went with a lecture in mind, and an order from the Colonel that she must stay out of the laboratory and be treated as all the other nurses. And, too, he came with the cure—a small bottle of the astringent and a tube of the calomel—as though he was saving her the embarrassment of asking, herself, for these telltale specifics at the dispensary.

He was let into the little house by a bent-over woman who had to turn her head sideways to look up at him, and who did not attempt English, but reached up to touch the oak leaf on his shoulder. *"D'or!"* Her eyes lit up as if she had guessed the all-too-human purpose of his visit. And she pointed down the unlit hall to a narrow stairway that would lead him up to *"les chambres de l'infirmière,"* the nurse's rooms.

He climbed the stairs with a deliberate heavy tread, preparing a military attitude, and knocked firmly on Jeanne's door, as if announcing to other tenants in the building that this visit was anything but the business of a furtive or stealthy heart.

"Himmel! Doucement! Quiet!" Irritation from within fired at him in three of her four tongues. Jeanne opened and pulled him in. "What's the matter with you, William? Is this the American invasion?" She was in her stocking feet, and she ordered him to take his shoes off as well, in consideration of the family directly beneath them. "Do you want to disturb everyone?"

It was odd to see her out of her normal American army clothes. She was all in black, the color of European widowhood, of mourning sustained for whole lifetimes. But this wasn't a dress she wore; it was a shift, high-necked and loose, under which her short-coupled figure was disguised as shapeless. So much the better for the Major's troubled oversoul.

Rooms? There was only one room, lit by several candles. His eyes moved around the perimeter from a dresser with a fine bevel-edged mirror to an unmade bed, a chair, a stool at the long table under the front window. As he grew accustomed to the dim light, he saw the microscope on the table, a rack of test tubes, slides, retorts, and the hand crank of a centrifuge. And beside these, a little wooden pharmacist's cabinet with dozens of tiny drawers. He wondered how much of this equipment she might have taken from the hospital laboratory, anticipating the Colonel's quit order.

Seeing his confusion, she said, "Men like Latoni, men like Armond. They can't stop us, eh?"

"Our friends are in there," she said, pointing to the small cabinet. "You have brought your poisons for them. But no, you must be nice to our friends."

Friends? Lice? A cabinet full of them it turned out, both head and body varieties. She had brought her own populations from Belgium. Lice removed from healthy men who had never been to the trenches, put in tiny glass containers, catalogued in the cabinet drawers, and fed from time to time, Jeanne explained, on the blood of her own body. *Eh bien,* a few other bodies as well, she confessed. I was hoping you would help with them. Do you remember?

That had been her plan for him on the road to Joinville? His healthy body for a company of her little invaders from Belgium. And maybe for their descendants. Just a temporary thing; she would help pick them off, and the nits, too. He was for the moment dumbfounded. How wildly mad had they all become, waiting while the trenches swallowed the men? How mad was she?

He could imagine committing her somewhere for war nerves. The English were the only ones doing any good in that field. The French had no time for it, and the Americans, in steadfast denial, no sympathy for it, even when confronted with cases of paralysis, losses of speech or hearing. But what of a woman feeding her lice on the bodies of her friend's men?

"And what are you doing with all your healthy lice?" he asked her.

"Not all healthy," she said. "These are very different." She was pointing to one of the drawers and pulling it open. "In here are the ones that ask for a sacrifice, the ones we will learn from." She showed him a half dozen of the little glass containers, each marked with its own code.

"Your doctors don't know one trench fever from another, or what is enteric, or influenza until the soles of the feet are black. But with the help of *nos amis* . . ."

"But what can they tell you?" he demanded. He warned her again against using the sick under his care and command in any experiment that would risk their health.

"The Germans with the armbands, all of them will help us," she said. "And Latoni will be *sous clef*," as if this followed in some logical order. "He's leaving," she repeated brightly. "The Sûreté, yes?

"But you will be the Colonel. Hanson is leaving next month. You, in charge. Think what we can do here.

"About Mr. Latoni," she said, closing the lice back into their little compartments, "he spends too much time with the Germans. And now perhaps he will be sorry."

Latoni had been outraged at Lloyd's order that the Germans under their care would receive treatment equal to that given their own men. The Adjutant was furious that they were treating any Boche at all in these overcrowded conditions. And he was used to making a daily round of their beds, just to assure himself that none of them was ambulatory or capable of the war crimes he was sure they were still contemplating in their German brains.

"I told you," Jeanne said, "he throws a ball at Wolfram and says, 'Catch.' To a man with one arm and no legs. And do you know what else? He takes the black band off Wolfram's arm and says, 'We don't need your Kraut sympathy.' Like this," she said, taking a scarf from her bureau, pretending to unwrap it from her arm and then, with two hands, rubbing it back and forth against the back of her head as if she was drying her hair. "You know he hates me and says I am crazy."

Jeanne was concerned about something else, close to tears.

"The French know that he stole their morphine from the dispensary in Vittel," she explained.

But surely this wouldn't upset her so. Lloyd advised her to put Latoni out of her mind. There were some men, he said, who were raised without love or pity, and so they could not be expected to feel these things themselves. Men lost to humanity, who were selfish sores on society. Latoni was one of these, he told her, the kind who might never feel the sting of his own conscience, and for whom punishment could never be restorative because there was nothing there to restore.

Jeanne touched the Major's hand gently and then took hold of it more firmly, but only to lead him to the door. "Yes," she agreed, "perhaps we should forget about the Adjutant, though he will not forget about us. I'm telling you to leave before they talk about your visit." She pursed her lips and pointed to the apartment below.

The Major's expectation for the evening had been turned on its head. He was being shown out. She had no use or thanks for the treatments he had brought her. He'd hoped she would have given him the opportunity to decline some small intimacy, but he was on his way down the stairs, moving past doors that had been opened to witness his dismissal.

"Go on, get out," someone called behind him.

The next day, the Major learned that Jeanne's prediction was more than wishful speculation. Latoni, who for the time being had maneuvered his way out of trouble in Chaumont, had been caught out by the French, who had good cause to take him into custody. He was picked up by the Sûreté on his way south with his favored nurse. She returned to the base, frantic, cursing the Frogs, and demanding a military response to the insult.

The base hospital's charges against Latoni had been dropped at Colonel Hanson's request. Lloyd had confined his disrespect for the Colonel's pampering nonsense to his own mail home, fully aware of how reckless he was being, but preserving a measure of his self-respect in the telling: If that's the sort of fellow the CO wants for his right-hand man, he's welcome to him. Not for me to insist that the man he chooses to assist him is a grafter who keeps a nurse-mistress no better than a harlot. Now with French assistance, we'll be well rid of all three— Colonel, Adjutant, and Adjutant's whore.

Kessel's Fever

It wasn't just her imagination, Emma decided. There *was* something missing in the Major's mail home. The indirection of it, the decorum; by omission, denying the things that she knew, from other reports, must be all around him. The gas-burned lung, the blood gurgling in the throat, an arm blown away, a leg sawn off, an eye shot out of its socket, a brain rearranged into a new kind of pudding. By sparing her all these, he was making the war sound like his own administrative nuisance, which he was going to overcome by strength of character, by willpower. Just as he'd conquered the lesser forces ranged against him as a child.

In the middle of August, Willie went to the city again, against his mother's wishes. He told Emma that he had business there that might keep him away from Moriches indefinitely. She knew no more than anyone else in the village about what was actually happening. He'd been ordered to Manhattan for another physical exam, to be given by a doctor approved by his draft board.

Not much of an exam, more a vindictive ruling on the boy's failure of will. How could this so-called doctor hear the thump, regular or syncopated, through his stethoscope while he was talking, delivering a gloomy set piece on the blood-drenched hands of the Huns and American malingerers who indulged themselves while the end of the world approached?

"What the hell would you know about it?" Willie demanded. And the doctor only bore down harder on the nib: "Attitude: seditious.

Physical impediments: none. Moral fitness: advise remediation. Induction: immediate."

Willie was asking for a horrid time in the army, and the army gave it to him. First at Camp Devens in Massachusetts, where his name was put on a list with other recalcitrants who must be hurried through training and shipped over without delay as a reward for their attitude. He nearly lost two fingernails in the scalding, greasy water of the pot-and-pan sink in the recruits' mess. There was no pity for his asthma attack during gas training, nor for his subsequent bronchial infection.

These complaints did nothing to delay his transport to France or his reservation on a troop train to the front, where he received a piece of mail from his mother and declined to answer it. But even before he was off the train, he wrote to his brother, Louis, whose commiseration would be further incitement to his complaining. He told Louis he felt like a caged animal.

"I don't think I'll get through this without something terrible happening. If they order me out of a trench, I'll obey and run right into a bullet. This will serve Mother and Father twice. They'll have the hero they wanted, and be rid of me at the same time. But running into a bullet isn't what I meant by something terrible. They have a capricious power over us here and the only defense against it is a spineless submission. This won't work for me. In training, I was singled out for extra work scrubbing the toilets, and seven straight days in the kitchen.

"But I'll tell you something that should give us hope, Louis. You can pass this along to our friends. I hear that some of the Frenchmen are refusing to come out of the trenches. That's mutiny! There's no other word for it. The Poilu are brave, but not fools. Maybe we, the common soldiers, can bring sanity to the generals, though some of us may be shot for our common sense.

"You can tell Mother that my not writing to her is not my way of punishing her, as she will complain, but simply a case of my having nothing to say to her for now, or to Father, for that matter, wherever he is. What could I have to say to parents who only laugh at what I believe and may as well have disowned me already?"

That letter never reached Long Island. But late in October of 1918, two weeks after Willie had arrived in France and was put on his train for the front, a Captain Grayson visited at the farm in Moriches by the afternoon train from the city. At last, a personal emissary, a colleague of the Major who had served with him at Base Hospital 15, hand-carrying a letter from her husband. Uncensored, and a rosetta stone for all future mail from "somewhere."

From then on, the somewhere would be big *C* for Chaumont on Marne, and little *c* would be Commercy; big *V* would be Vittel, and little *v* would be Vessoul; the big *H* would be the CO, Colonel Hanson, and *L* would be the miscreant Adjutant Latoni. "But never mind them, they're almost out of our hair." A full page of initials, a simpleminded code for places and people, as if this were sufficient encryption to fool the Boche.

"Don't worry," he explained, "it's enough to satisfy our people and the French. Everyone does it the same way. By the way, I've asked the kind Captain, Dr. Grayson, to spend a little time with you, give you a chance to read this, and then answer any questions that occur to you. It's no use your asking him where Willie has been sent. He has no more idea than I would. And tell Mother it's no good writing more letters to the President. Of course his office doesn't have time for that sort of thing. It's a wretched conceit to think otherwise. They will simply ignore her."

Captain Grayson was short, very overweight and round, which made his military uniform a contrary joke. Lucky for him, Emma thought, that he was only fighting disease. She and Helen held the Captain at the farm for the whole afternoon. There were two servings of tea, with a slow stroll to the beach in between; later, a walk through the orchard, followed by tea again. Grayson seemed somewhat reticent and without sentiment. And quite military in his pronouncement that their Major was in fine health and serving with the energy of an ox, helping transform a hospital that had once been a disgrace into a model of humane efficiency.

Grayson sounded very much like her William himself. Emma had hoped for a session in which the finer truths of her husband's military life would be opened to her, that personalities would come clear, that the bickering and feuds she knew existed would be acknowledged and more fully defined—in short, that the Captain would confide in them as a friend made closer by the searing experience of war surgery that he shared in common with the Major.

But in his oral report, he could as well have been the Major's secretary passing along a dictation, a memo that could be read by the world at large without embarrassment. And Emma began to repeat herself. By the end of the afternoon, she could sense that Grayson was tired of this and anxious to be gone. He had already assured them it was quite safe in Chaumont. And, no, the Germans had never bombed there. Yes, William got along quite well on very little sleep. No, he had not heard of German gas bombs being dropped behind the American lines. Grayson offered nothing extra. Not until he was about to leave, and Emma saw her chance evaporating, did she ask as casually as she could manage, "Are the nurses performing well? I suppose they're behaving."

"Behaving?"

The question surprised the Captain, and for the first time that afternoon, he became voluble.

"Oh, yes, Mrs. Lloyd, they're really quite wonderful. William must have told you. As a group, they've received a special commendation from the Chief Surgeon, who thinks the combination of nuns and our girls has been a capital experiment, and one of the finest examples of international cooperation. The kind of selfless integration of purpose that men could learn from."

"Really?" Helen said, saving Emma the awkwardness of her misgivings. "That wasn't our information at all. We thought perhaps there had been a lapse in—what should we call it, morale?"

"Lapse? No, I wouldn't say that. Oh, no, you have nothing to fear on that account."

Here the Captain slowed, as if he was reconsidering. "No, why do you ask? What has Major Lloyd told you?" He looked to one and then the other, the women deferring to each other, unable to state the dark rambling of their imaginations. And this obtuse man, instead of putting their fears to rest once and for all, only gave the matter a universal absolution.

"Oh, I suppose there's the occasional indiscretion, the normal portion of human failing. No more than one would expect and forgive under the circumstances."

This man doesn't know my husband very well at all, Emma decided, ready to let him go. He'd brought them the useful letter, and that would be all he was worth to them. Now he was going on about the imminent loss of the Adjutant and the difficult period of readjustment that must follow the departure of a man who had shouldered so many administrative responsibilities. Helen, who was probably as disgusted as Emma with all his tolerance and blandifying, looked the Captain directly in the eye and demanded, "And hasn't the Adjutant taken one of your nurses for his mistress?"

"I wouldn't know about that. If that's what Dr. Lloyd has told you, I'm surprised."

Why had William sent them a blind messenger to natter on about the mission? ". . . the health of several million American soldiers. We're there to mend their bodies, not their ways." This turned Emma's anxiety into a shameful selfishness.

Helen wasn't having any of it. "You're not one of the Roosevelt Hospital men, are you?" It was almost an accusation.

"No, I'm not," he said.

Of course not. They already knew he was from Boston, and that he would have been home by now if William had not prevailed on him to make this generous detour, which they were turning into tedious chore with their insinuations.

"Maybe," Emma ventured, "you could tell us more about this French woman. William writes so warmly about her."

"I expect you mean the nurse Jeanne Prie. Yes, actually I'd call her headstrong. A bit off-camp, you know, a bit of a freelance . . ." Captain Grayson hesitated.

"But quite the miracle worker, we understand," Emma encouraged him.

"I don't know if I'd say that. It would diminish the work of the others. But just how much has the Major told you?"

Emma and Helen answered simultaneously.

"Everything."

"Very little."

Taking opposite tacks to draw the man out, they only made him more wary of them, and to settle him again, Emma asked, "When will you be going back?"

"I'm finished!" he said. "After all, victory's at hand. No, the doctors will be needed here now. You're aware of the shortage."

"Oh yes," Emma said.

"But the French woman," Helen persisted. "She has the knowledge of a doctor, isn't it so?"

"You're very concerned about her," Grayson observed.

"But it is odd, isn't it . . . that she takes this extra part as a scientist?"

"Let me assure you, the situation is under control now."

"'Situation'?" Emma stopped him.

Helen stared at her as if she were an imbecile and said, "Of course we knew there was a situation."

Emma, who would not be her fool in this, no matter what advantage it might gain them, said, "What situation, then?"

Helen, imperturbable, directed her reply to the Captain alone.

"We knew it couldn't be quite right. . . ."

"Ladies," Grayson said. "I'm sure the Major couldn't have told you everything. There would be no way delicate enough to put it. I think it's enough to say that the woman's extra activities have been curtailed, and she confines herself now to her nursing responsibilities. We had a very good lab man assigned to us, Armond, English. He's sorted out some of the tangle. The rest is off-limits, a lot of it gossip, I expect."

That was all he'd say about Jeanne, though Helen tried to provoke him again.

"I shouldn't have thought a woman so willful could be a very good example to the others."

"It's lovely here," the Captain said, admiring a line of Canada geese that had circled out over the bay and returned, and now were honking overhead, announcing their landing rights in a far field of the farm.

Grayson said he'd thought at first it had been his car coming for him from the Moriches station. Which the women recognized as a pretty lie.

"Isn't it wonderful," he said, "that the Major was able to get away to de Chastelain's for the week of hunting? Going at it so hard for so many months."

"No," Emma said. "I didn't know."

"But yes," Helen said. "The French doctor with the big lake. William told us he'd be going but wouldn't say where. The French doctor who didn't even know how to make duck stool. Or how to use it. I'm sure I showed you the letter."

Emma could only console herself with the idea that in writing separate letters to them, her husband sometimes forgot what he had told one or the other. She cried a lot. Anger, jealousy, and now her fear for Willie were making this fall of 1918 the most awful season of the war. Why should she have to curry favor with Helen for news of William? Why should she have to kneel to one son for news of the other? When she stared at her looking glass for more than a moment, her eyes locked onto their reflection, making her feel crazy.

*T*hough the train moved from platform to platform at a crawl, Willie felt himself being whisked off to war just as quickly as, two weeks later, he would be yanked back from it in shame. He believed he was heading for an American encampment somewhere north of Paris. As the strange spellings of towns and villages slid by on station walls, he mumbled them to himself, but they were forgotten in a jumble of fears about how he was going to die. Would he feel a bullet passing through his skull or would it be over too quickly to notice?

Well aware of the American army's censorship of his father's mail, he thought himself very clever in passing his last letter for Louis to an English-speaking French soldier who stepped off the train for a moment in one of those bustling stations and sent it on for him through the French post.

A friend of only an hour. This bright and amiable French boy, Paul, a kindred spirit. Like Willie, there in uniform against the more admirable side of his own conscience. They were twin martyrs to the will of their mad nations. In whispers, they shared the remarkable likenesses of their brief military histories; they both had corporals, sergeants, and lieutenants whom they already despised, and who despised them in return.

They traded fantasies of how grand it would be if the misused soldiery on all sides simply refused to fight.

"But how would you manage that?" Paul asked.

"It would be quite simple," Willie assured him. "I think some of your men have already shown us how." This talk didn't square at all with the general drift of their conversation toward the inevitability of their own tragic deaths.

"No," Paul told him, looking at the envelope Willie handed him. "It won't work like that. It won't go. You have to put your name and company on the outside."

Paul mailed the letter and then squeezed back into his place beside Willie on the wooden seat. For the rest of the journey, through the herky-jerky of a dozen station stops, as the train gorged itself on bodies for the front, the two young soldiers announced to each other their readiness to die. Foch and Pershing had both declared the highest purpose of their soldiers' service was to die for a finer civilization. It was easy to be romantic about decisions so completely beyond their control. Shoulder-to-shoulder with Paul, Willie was proud to be part of an international brotherhood of skeptics.

But this trip was soon over, and he was back in trouble again for the scowl and desultory pace with which he answered the simplest commands of his platoon sergeant, a man thoroughly scared of dying himself, and more than ready to transfer his fear into the petty discipline of his men. It was his own shame to be in command of such a collection of dissident spirits. Now they were at a staging camp, a place with no name at all.

The know-it-alls, the kind of men the NCOs called "the shit house lawyers," the enlisted men who could tell you your rights against military abuse even as they performed their company punishments—these men never knew where they were, but they could always tell you where you were going, casually forecasting the company's fate on the Somme, at Verdun, at Passchendaele, as if there were to be reprises of all the grandest slaughters just for themselves and for Willie.

And by then, Willie understood that he had no rights here, only his poor reputation and continuing retribution for it, in the latrines and in the mess. The company commander, a career failure named Captain Preston, was already sick of Willie's name. They were at the wrong staging camp. Whose fault was that? Who'd have rank ripped from his shoulder this time? Not Willie, who had nothing there to rip. He was put on another train with the rest of this spiritless outfit. He got off at a station stop, thinking himself as casual and clever as Paul, and a moment later was whisked away, without explanation, by two guards of the Sûreté.

Now Willie sat between two rank-smelling French guards on the wooden seat of another train, heading away from the front and his appointment with death. But just as fearful, cast out of the barrack of one whimsical master into the guardhouses of another, who would feel no responsibility for him at all.

Going south maybe? As usual, he didn't know where he was. And no one would tell him. His duffel was under his seat. His name and a number had been written on a heavy piece of brown paper and pinned to the tight jacket of his uniform. The Frenchmen who had him wedged in the middle wore shoulder belts and pistols. One of them spoke some English. That was why he'd been chosen for this demeaning duty, transporting a green Yankee malingerer, perhaps a spy. He prodded and shoved to prove his contempt.

"Why am I here?" Willie asked. "What have I done?"

Either the man didn't know or wouldn't tell him.

"Where are you taking me?"

The angry answer sounded like Mah-say.

But first, they were out of the train at a stop where there was not even a platform, and into a truck as small as a car; he was still between the two hairy guards, who were greasing their mouths with a foul soft cheese and wiping the grease away with bread. The one who knew no English passed the cheese under Willie's nose as if to tease his appetite. Seeing that it made him queasy, he continued the game for sport.

At last, names on a building, names that held still long enough for him to read and remember—Ministre de Sûreté de Noyon. It was a dark stone building with soldiers of the Sûreté going in and out. "Move!" He was pushed inside to a courtyard where he could look up to a balcony and a tier of rooms with bars on the doors. A prison.

His pockets were emptied of a billfold and penknife. He was turned over to an officer who denied this was a prison. "Here," he said, "we only ask questions. First you will be fed; then you will talk to me."

He was hustled away so quickly, the response he'd prepared only echoed in the dark passageway: "I'll speak to someone from the American embassy. No one else!"

Humiliating laughter followed after him from the office and more fell from the upper tier. After his meal of bread and soup, they took him upstairs, locked him in one of the rooms, and left him alone. The space was dimly lit by a small window, too high to reach. There was a bunk with a straw tick and a porcelain bucket for toilet. The floor was gray tile, cracked and broken; the walls smooth stucco, whitewashed, but defaced everywhere with pencil marks, foul pictures, writing, most of it in English.

Was this a cell for Americans and Englishmen? Clear enough, the Sûreté was encouraging his insolence, too. Stubs of two pencils had been left on the floor, with which he could incriminate himself. No, Willie thought, they wouldn't catch him out that way. The first word he might put on the wall would begin to define him and would be used against him. And the very act of writing on the wall—they were sure to call a vandalism.

They left him alone a whole day, giving him only bread and soup, and with nothing else to do, he read the walls. There were pictures and doggerel, piggish figures with captains' bars and colonels' wings, and rhymes to skewer them. Stuff scribbled by men who had not been afraid to show their contempt. And mixed with these were whole letters written to the world at large, and some "To Mother" by men who had lost hope:

I am not a deserter or a spy. Whoever reads this, please contact Mrs. Oliver at the Squinting Cat in Harrogate. If she does not receive my watch, the guards here have stolen it. Mrs. Oliver should tell Cynthia to do as she pleases.

Willie's heart sank, his eye drifting down from misery into common filth:

Over the top, says Captain Tim,
That's your weekend pass,
And the only gas he ever breathes
Is blown from a French tart's ass.

What could he think now but shame on his brotherhood of dissent? "Why don't they come to question me?" he asked of the guard who brought him his evening bowl of soup.

"But you said you wouldn't talk to us," the man teased. "Are you ready now to talk?"

Willie said nothing, and he was left in his solitary confinement for another day. From time to time, he heard someone sing out in full throat into the courtyard, a single phrase, "So long, Leicester Square . . ." Interrupted by a louder guard: *"Fermez!"* There was life here, and rebellion, and these moments renewed his hope. The French bastards in their clownish hats were going to regret their mistake, kidnapping him in broad daylight right under the eyes of his unit still on the train, and now holding him here by a clerk's error perhaps—in fact, with no charge lodged against him.

Their soup had given him diarrhea and their train had left him with fleas in his clothes, and more. His head with a fiery itch. He scratched his scalp and was appalled to find a tiny white thing, barely visible, crawling along the quick under his fingernail. He'd never seen one before but was sickened by his certain knowledge of its name. If there was one, there were dozens and would soon be hundreds, crawling on invisible legs through his hair, scissor mouths breaking skin and feasting on his blood.

He screamed through his door, "Lice! I have lice!" His panic was answered by an international chorus of laughter. He could as well have been a man at a beach announcing, The ocean is open today. Guards pacing the courtyard and upper tier laughed along with the prisoners, and Willie's belligerence fell away into contrition, an abject prayer for medical attention, and a new plan for polite response to interrogation if they would only give him a chance to explain the mistake they had made.

But for the next two days, the walls of his room and the thousands of words written on them were his only diversion. The scribblers—there had been several hundred, the earliest dating their residencies here in 1914—had followed a practice of small script, tightly lined, as if to leave room for all future inhabitants, enough clear slate for the naysayers' chronicle of this whole unending war, the self-wounded, the absent without leave, the anarchistic graduates of the trenches, accused spies, the moralists, and the deviates. All of them, by their own witness, falsely accused. Just as Willie had been.

Each innocent in his own way, and thus each had left evidence of his own disgust and frustration, and, especially in the stick figures and naïve drawings, their disrespect. It was either that or be assigned by their jailers to the undifferentiated population of sedition and spinelessness that threatened France, and shipped down the rail for export, leaving no sign of their passion. Lucky for them, Willie thought, that the British and Americans among them had not been ultimately subject to French justice.

Returning to the wall after his noon nourishment—a broth barely darker than water and no thicker—he was brought up short by the final line of some singsong poesy, whose author—Corporal Roberts, Leeds—claimed to have thrown down his rifle and wept for his part in the godlessness:

Tomorrow they shoot me for saying my "Peace."

Could they actually have shot a British soldier here? Was there a firing squad? Far more likely, this had been the simpering of a fevered imagination. Or maybe the French themselves had added the sorry ballad to the cell's chronicles just to frighten new arrivals to their prison, to loosen the stubborn tongue.

But one inscription begged for attention above all the rest, if only by the playfulness of its design—a circle of words that led in a tightening spiral until there was no room left at the core, and, not finished there, continued in a horizontal line from the center, through spaces left in the concentric rings, until it stuck out the side, free of the maze. There were no capital letters in this composition that flowed from one thought to the next with scant punctuation. If it was meant to be poetry, there was scarcely any rhyme. Louis would have loved this. It was like the wordplay in one of his college literary broadsides. But Louis wasn't here to decipher it.

It was awkward reading, half the time having to turn his back to the wall, and then bend his head down and to the side to make out the upside-down portions, just as the author must have done with his pencil as the verse spiraled in. Here at last was all Willie could have hoped for in preparing for his interview with Monsieur le Directeur—a model of honesty, defiance, and the sting of a final contempt. Above the circle of words, the title:

the song of edward

hey monsieur le ministre i volunteered for this got in a ship and took the ocean's curve to drive an ambulance—instead i get an interview with you bully boy one two three you shoot your questions and when they miss the mark four five six they take gravity's fall chase me around in circles it was my own side accused me of going frog going to war in dirty clothes, the charge was consorting with the allies, they dumped me in your laundry you didn't wash me you took my cigarettes and pen and asked if i had anything in my shoes. my feet. you close your contemptuous eyes i'm here for palling about with b whose mail is full of treason, any complaint is out of season, i wrote a letter with him dear undersecretary for french aviation could we be transferred to the lafayette escadrille partial to french sky, you ask why wouldn't we keep to our own kind, join our own air force, do we hate the germans, no we love you. your questions wind tighter there's nowhere to go nowhere for you, but for me, a gap here to slip through and another there pulling my tale behind me—eec.

The last dozen words wending their way in a somewhat horizontal line through spaces between the circling words until the initials eec were free of the maze. eec had made good his escape.

Willie was thrilled by the impudence. He copied the words in their pattern on a scrap of the paper the guards had given him to write his confession. Louis must see this. But how was he going to show his own independence? A fever had weakened him till he was more inclined to whimper for mercy than argue with them, and when they finally came the next day to march him from his cell to the interrogation room, he had forgotten the speech he meant to deliver. In front of le Directeur, he fell into a muted ramble about the high standing of his father in the American command. He was faint and dripping sweat.

"Private Lloyd," le Directeur stopped him, "if you are from such a patriotic family, why would you hope to make a mutiny against France and your own country's interest?"

"I am for peace," he said softly. "I don't expect you to understand. When will I be released?"

"Did you write this?"

Le Directeur held the letter out to Willie, who reached for it, but the page was drawn back and the man began to read:

> "But I'll tell you something that should give us hope, Louis. You can pass this along to our friends."

"Hmmm. Yes. Isn't this your letter, Mr. Lloyd? You would encourage a mutiny?"

"I want to speak to an American. I want to speak to the Red Cross. I am sick. I am not going to say any more."

"Mr. Lloyd. I have been here since the beginning—months, years, and I can tell you, men have been shot for far less than we already know about you. You are shaking."

"I have a fever."

"You are afraid, and with good reason."

He was not afraid, but exhausted. They led him back to his cell, with le Directeur calling after him, ". . . more careful of the friends you make on the trains . . . another chance tomorrow."

Willie's diarrhea was worse, his bucket half-full and stinking; it was up to him to call a guard to escort him as he carried his own waste to the sewage wagon in the yard below. So depleted, he'd sooner sleep with it beside him. He was shaken awake the next morning and told to gather his kit for another journey.

They were transporting several dozen from the Noyen triage station—destination unknown to the prisoners of mixed nationality, mostly French, but six Americans among them. Their names were penned again on strips of brown paper and pinned to their uniforms. As promised, another train ride. They were marched to the rail station and herded together into a converted passenger coach whose crude wooden benches were loosely bolted to the floor. Guards were posted at either end of the car.

The prisoners, still in their countries' uniforms, were each given a round piece of white cheese the size of a lemon and told it would be their only food for the next twelve hours. There was water in a large glass jeroboam, with a single tin cup for all. The men could mingle and sit where they pleased.

Aware of the Sûreté's tactics, this time Willie was careful whom he spoke to. But of course the six Americans of the same call and feather flew together immediately and perched in the middle of the car, as far from their Frog guards as they could manage. They began to debrief one another at once. The one officer among them, with a lieutenant's bar and no name tag, tried to establish his authority, first asking trick questions to establish their Yank authenticity, then giving orders.

"Private Woodly, get water for the squad."

Squad? Woodly looked doubtful but obeyed.

"All right, I want to know what each one of you has been accused of."

He was looking at a Corporal Davies, who spat on the floor and said, "Who the hell are *you* to be asking *us* questions?"

The Lieutenant pulled a pad and pencil from his breast pocket, and wrote down the name, moving his lips, spelling D-a-v-i-e-s, c-o-r-p-o-r-a-l.

"What are you playing at, Latoni? Do you want me to tell these boys what you've done, what you're accused of?"

"Shut up, Davies, if you don't want your stripes pulled again."

It was clear enough to the others that Davies and the one he called Latoni had a common army history. Whatever their stories, they had come from the same unit. And Willie sat silent and smug, already quite sure what that unit was. Against what wild odds would this be the Latoni of his father's correspondence and so much family discussion, the one who had deviled the doctor as boy and man? It would be good sport to play along with his questions until Willie was sure this was the army grafter and womanizer from Base Hospital 15 who, as a bounder and sharper in training, had been bounced from the St. Mark's School thirty years earlier with a nudge from Willie's father.

The train lurched forward, and those who had not braced themselves for departure tumbled backward into the legs of the prisoners behind them. Up and down the coach, men were cursing in half a dozen languages and lifting themselves from the floor. The water jug fell from its pedestal and cracked open. A guard spat insults down the aisle.

"What did he say?" Willie asked the boy next to him, who was laughing.

"He said, 'The Yanks can drink from the toilet after the others fill it.'"

"You, boy, let me see your name."

Willie turned his chest, making his name tag clearly visible to the Lieutenant.

"You look sick, Lloyd. Come're, you sit here. Lemme feel your head." He was pointing to the place beside him on the bench. And Willie obeyed, rather than cause more trouble for himself.

"Didn't anyone teach you to say 'Yes, sir,' boy? What's your first name, Lloyd?"

"Will."

"You have a father over here, don't you, Will? He's a doctor, isn't he?"

"Wouldn't be much chance you knowing him, would there?"

"Oh yes! I know Dr. Lloyd. First-rate." He was putting his hand on Willie's forehead, a hot, sticky hand.

"God, you're hotter than I am," Willie said, pulling away from the Lieutenant in disgust.

"You're shaking. You're scared."

"I'm cold. I'm shivering."

"Caught the chills, eh? Where's your jacket, soldier?"

"Lost it."

The Lieutenant was taking off his own dirty woolen jacket and placing it carefully around Willie's shoulders with the tenderness of a nurse, behavior completely at odds with his bullying and rank pulling, and Willie looked up at him with weak and wondering eyes.

"Your old man wouldn't think much of me if I didn't look out for his boy."

Was this the same man his father despised? Willie was pleased to have plumbed a hidden compassion in someone his father had dismissed as corrupt and useless. Sick as he was, he held this weightless medal to his chest as he fell into a fevered sleep. And the stations crept by, one by one, hour after hour. It was an uncomfortable journey on a train that, to the prisoners, seemed unable to make up its mind whether it would stop or go. They were impatient for an end to it, even knowing the hard-earned destination would be only another jail.

Willie was propped against the smirking Lieutenant's shoulder while a second rank of lice deserted the dry collar of the borrowed jacket for a blood feast on the private's hot scalp, and the Lieutenant imagined and cheered for a host of invisible crabs scissoring into the arrogant boy's head, transmitting a real fever of death, the same that he feared now ran in his own blood. "Turnabout's fair play"—the schoolboy prattle of Major Lloyd and his moralizing friends.

A Colonel was he now? Yes, Latoni thought, things were winding down, the end was in sight, and the generals didn't mind giving the short-timing wonders a little boost to their vanity, even Lloyd, who'd been given command of the base hospital, though his haughty tenure would be short. A couple of months perhaps and then the army would be back in the hands of men like himself who knew how to make things run smoothly and profitably.

As Lloyd, who announced his promotion without fear of censorship on the next envelope to America (it was hand-carried by a field officer being hurried home to New York for a delicate surgery)—Colonel W. Lloyd, Base Hospital 15, AEF France—explained to his wife, the business with their son and Latoni was not the impossible coincidence one might imagine it to be. If two Americans—a careless-mouthed malcontent and a narcotics thief—ran afoul of the Sûreté in the same season of heightened French fright, it was natural enough that French officers might snatch one off a street, as with Latoni, or off a station platform, as with Willie. Having hard evidence against them, they would not scruple to ask for extradition or worry about the political stink that might follow.

Willie would eventually be returned, he told her, and so, unfortunately, would Latoni. Lloyd had far more troubling news for Emma.

Both Latoni and Willie had been taken to Noyen for triage, and they eventually found themselves on the same train to Ferté-Macé for further investigation, disposition of their cases, and threatened trials. Never mind that; there would never be any trials.

He told her he was doing what he could, both through Allied headquarters and the embassy, to secure the details of Willie's case. But neither the French nor the American command was responding. He said their son, who had refused to send his news to her before his arrest, had, in extremis, suddenly found his tongue, or his pen, and had been able, through weekly contact with a representative of the Croix Rouge, to pass letters out of the prison and into the French post, addressed to him at Base Hospital 15. Lloyd passed along Willie's misery:

"He wrote to me on October 19 that he was not altogether well, though his hand seemed steady enough on the page. He wrote, 'Father, do you know what? By quirk, or what some call the odd wind of war, I've met your Adjutant! And I think you've been so wrong about him. Of course, he's not a socially capable man, but, to me, he's been the very example of kindness, of course within the restraints of his rank over me. On the train, he did seem officious at first. He was in wretched condition himself, yet he took off his jacket and placed it around my shoulders. Since then, as our senior officer, he has interceded on my behalf for my rights as a prisoner of conscience. I hope, when we are all back in New York again (if I make it back—the French doctor, who visits here on leave from a veterinary practice, has no idea which fever I have), we will be able to make it up to him. Imagine, Latoni is the one who suffers most here. I'm afraid his fever may carry him away. He says he's terribly sorry for the trouble he's caused you there for allowing himself to be taken by the French while on liberty. He's even ready to testify on your behalf in case you should be involved in a court-martial. This is why I must think of him as a Christian friend. Father, I think you and I are both in a position to do each other some good.'

"My God, Emma. What have we spawned? What can he think I would be court-martialed for? Our silly-billy asks for political influence, when what he surely needs most is a medical diagnosis and treatment. I'm making every effort to have him released. In the meantime, I'm agitating to be allowed to visit Ferté-Macé as an inspecting physician. Of course, I would be expected to report on the condition of all Americans held there. We understand there are a dozen or more. If this were known to the general American public, it would cause one h— of a thunder.

"The French are unyielding on any sort of seditious behavior, but of course they have to deny they hold any American soldiers as political prisoners. Publicly, they charge these men with criminal acts, while behind the scenes, they investigate each case for themselves and then present their evidence to our general staff. The war will likely be over before Willie is released to his command, and G— knows what shame they'll have in store for him before they send him home.

"Jeanne Prie, whom you know is our true resident expert in blood work and fevers, has agreed to accompany me when permission comes through. She'll be a fine asset, not just on site but also in transit, since she slips through petty barriers with the brass of a general and the fair wind of her countrymen always at her back. She makes friends so easily. It's like traveling with a celebrity, though I wear the colonel's hardware, and she the boots, pants, and jacket of a common American soldier. Such a fuss, then a wink and a Godspeed."

One thing Jeanne could do little about was the French trains. Lloyd, now a Colonel, left Chaumont with her in a private compartment on a Friday morning and arrived at Bagnoles de l'Orne three days later in a converted cattle car. In between, they had journeyed on seven trains, with unscheduled stops at and between uncounted stations, where Jeanne served as guide from cafés to platform water closets to the unreserved seats they fought for on a tour around what might have been all of France, for all the hours it took.

Jeanne could be far more relaxed in the war swarm of her own people than in the fussy hierarchy of Base Hospital 15. And without an audience of American military, Lloyd felt he could relax and be led by her, rather than pretend to a false authority.

On arrival, when he looked at a larger map, he saw the comedy of the route they had taken—as serpentine as the Seine between Paris and the Channel—which would lead one to suspect either dishonest ticket masters or a careless travel agent. He had put himself in Jeanne's hands, and now she was hard-pressed to explain that her chosen route had actually avoided even further delays and had always been based on up-to-the-minute telegraphy between stations, passed along to her by compliant trainmen who were persuaded of the urgency of her journey.

Most of the time, they had been pressed together, standing or seated in the little French cars, which seemed like miniatures to Lloyd, who was used to the grand coaches of the Pennsylvania and Long Island railroads. The two of them should have been thoroughly exhausted after three days of this, wearing the same clothes night and day, sweating and drying and sweating as temperatures shifted. They were sticky and grimy, with nowhere to change or bathe.

Sharing small loaves of bread, cheese, and wine in dirty glasses sold from the station platforms, they spoke in whispered English of what they might do for Willie, first as doctors, then as emissaries of the Expeditionary Force. She had brought her needles and syringes, and a valise whose contents were not fully known to the Colonel.

Instead of complaining, they resigned themselves to their inconveniences. In the middle of their travels, he caught the scent of her monthlies, and though she tried, she could not make a complete secret of the cloth she had to rinse and dry as they advanced from station to station. On a siding at midnight, waiting for three duty-bound troop trains to pass, she made his blood jump, recounting Napoléon's scandalous on-the-march message to Josephine: "Home in three days; don't wash."

The air around them became their private musky cocoon, shutting out the other odors of the train. He accepted the crush of soldiers all about as the convenient agency of an innocent intimacy with her. Her head lolled on his shoulder as they took turns dozing and the train lurched through the night. Once, he woke to squelch a warm and untoward pleasure at his groin, which had almost escaped his control.

Awake, he whipped his conscience, dwelling on the shamed son for whom he traveled. There was still a day and night more of the curious journey before they'd reach Bagnoles de l'Orne, from which they'd have to hire a car for the short trip to Ferté. One didn't have to speak French to understand that the voices rising to a clamor at each station foretold a war almost won.

Lloyd, too, might be able to celebrate when Willie was healthy again, and sailing west. On the last segment of the journey, as he gathered the wool of victory sitting there in his gamy uniform and they waited for yet another train more important than their own to pass them, Jeanne shifted suddenly into French, as if for the benefit of the Poilu around them: "You need a horse's bath. I'm going to give you a horse's bath," loud enough for others to hear. The Poilu cheered, and one of them started singing a version of "Yankee Doodle," which his comrades thought terribly funny.

Lloyd was blushing and angry with her for encouraging their impudence. It wasn't the first time she'd spoken in a provocative riddle. Jeanne took the Colonel's hand to reassure him and stared with pity at the rude young men. They couldn't be discouraged from their fun.

"Don't worry," she told him, "your baths are Les Bagnoles de l'Orne."

When the Poilu heard the name of the town, they broke out in a chorus of *"Quelle chance!"* and *"Bonne chance!"* The rest of it, he assumed, was disrespectful, full of elisions and slang, which made it difficult to translate. A conductor climbed into the car from the siding and pretended to scold them, but he, too, started humming along at "Yankee Doodle" as he walked among them, counting heads and asking a few for their orders, though none of them paid fares or had tickets.

Lloyd understood later that one of the men, cocky and fresh, had introduced himself to Jeanne and asked her destination and if she could imagine his companionship there at the end of the line, in a household where they would make children together and be happy. The man's comrades were urging him on. Someone should have boxed their ears. Not the Colonel, who hadn't been sure of what was being said.

Jeanne accepted the banter as a pardonable sin of her country's exuberant army. She looked at the boy with a motherly concern and told him she was sure the war had made him a hero. She thanked God that he and his friends had been spared and said she would pray they could forget the horrors they had seen.

The soldier hung his head in shame. Jeanne forgave him and blessed his mother, and this made tears well in the young man's eyes. *"C'est rien,"* she told him. "It's nothing." The other men had shut up and begun to listen to her. She was speaking in French again, but very slowly, so that her American Colonel could not mistake her meaning.

She told of an old horse named Rapide, which had been close to death and in such misery that its failing owner, who had ridden it for years through battle and famine, had been obliged to destroy it. But he hadn't the strength or will. Instead, he let Rapide wander off into the forest. Some days later, he was astonished when the steed returned to him in fine health.

The man followed Rapide's tracks to a spring where the horse had bathed. He submerged himself in the waters, with the same revitalizing effect. These, Jeanne explained, were the health-giving springs of l'Orne, the spa called Bagnoles de l'Orne, where they were all heading, and where the infirm among them might do themselves the same favor. "Eh, Colonel Rapide?" And she pulled on his Sam Browne belt again as if it were a horse's tack.

He did not answer, only shook his head, doubting that a woman at the frontier of blood science could seriously be advocating a folk remedy. Was she implying that his earlier reticence with her was not a moral decision but simply a sign of frailty that might be overcome with a treatment of mineral waters? The farther she got from Chaumont, the more brazen and familiar she was becoming.

He drifted off again, and when he woke up, she was tugging once more on the shoulder harness and imploring him to grab his kit and hurry off the train. They had arrived in Bagnoles de l'Orne and nearly missed their stop. They were the only ones disembarking, and the Poilu, who had become drunk on some bottles of wine passed into the car at an earlier station, were cheering them again: *"Bonne chance,* Monsieur le Colonel!"

It was after eight in the evening, and chilly, with no one about in the town. The single taxi that worked from a stand beside the station was off for the night. The sweeper in the waiting room told them there'd be no transportation to Ferté-Macé till the next day.

He pointed them in the direction of the lake, though Jeanne was already familiar with the place. She had come here to stay once when a healer in Crouen had recommended the water cure for the swollen and contracting fingers of a schoolmaster's hands. The hotel was boarded up now, and so, with bags in hand, they walked around the south end of the lake, along the promenade that led to the watering place. They'd had no supper, and they might have entered several public houses along the way, but Jeanne had a destination of her own in mind, and Lloyd followed.

The water of the hot spring ran down toward the lake into three successive wooden-lined pools, each enclosed in long bathhouses—the first and finest for the men, the second for women, and a third for the poor. The first two huts were padlocked and the windows secured. The third had no windows, but its door swung in the breeze, and it was into this rude structure that Jeanne carried her duffel and signaled the hesitant Colonel to follow with his bag.

Whatever she had in mind was not to be shared by others. She closed the door and drew the wooden latch into its keeper, and he had only a moment to take in the simple surroundings—a wooden deck around the pool and a double bench built against three of the walls—before they were in complete darkness.

The air over the pool was warm and moist and faintly sulfurous, and with the long room closed to all but them, the interior became a comfortable temperature long before his eyes could discern the least hint of her movement across the pool. A few moments later, she was asking, *"On est prêt? Are you ready?"* and he heard her slipping into the water. Girded by the formal style of her question and the cover of night, he shed his own clothes, and let himself down into the warm bath, and once there, he vowed to himself to keep his hands on the wooden boards at his side lest he be tempted toward the middle of the pool.

It was unusually warm on Long Island in that last half of October 1918. The old-timers in Moriches knew this was the weather and time of year for what their grandparents had called "oyster fever." They weren't inclined to give up the sovereignty of a death-dealing disease to Spain or any other nation. Not until it carried off two dozen village citizens in a single month, including the postmistress, two farriers, and all four children in the Ethical Culture Society's kindergarten. After that, Emma noticed she'd get no argument from the druggist if she called the hateful germ "the Spanish flu."

Instead of sending Nellie and Louis off to school and college that fall, Emma kept them clear of the pandemic to the best of her ability, sequestered on the farm, and strictly forbidden to go into the city, or even into the village. If they met a stranger on the beach, they should keep a distance at which any germs on his breath would be blown away in the wind.

They were told their brother was sick and in disgrace. The effect was to turn them further from dutiful behavior into a pair of outright family renegades who were shameless in their discussion of the mistakes and character flaws of their parents. They made solemn oaths to each other that they would never fall into the same traps of pride and folly as these old people who had amnesia for their own childhoods and were driving the younger generation across the sea to their deaths.

Peterson came back to the farm quite humbly at the end of October. The government no longer needed men trained to whip the public halls into fevers of patriotism and enlistment. He'd been turned away, and after that, he tried for a chauffeur's position in Smithtown, but without a reference from Mrs. Lloyd, any such job was out of the question. He asked for his old position.

Helen lectured him on loyalty. She could never take him back, she said. Not after his part in Willie's fall into France. She agreed to write a note of tepid approval to whom it might concern, which helped him secure a basement room and doorman's job at a small hotel on lower Lexington Avenue. She could advise all, without qualm, that he was a clean man and sober. But his employment at the hotel lasted only a week or so. He couldn't stand the indignity of walking the tenants' dogs round the block.

Peterson was seen again in Moriches, knocking about aimlessly. And the Bouton, which had never needed major repair, stalled on the way to the village and would not start again. Helen was ready to blame it on the inexperience of Louis, who had become the family chauffeur. At the garage, she was told the valves were fouled and the fuel line clogged. They knew it was vandalism—perhaps the work of the village brothers questioned by the police about lighting the Lloyds' July Fourth blaze? But Louis thought it was Peterson.

He came calling at the Lloyd house again, asking for another interview with Helen. She met him in the yard, where he suffered another of her lectures. He was so contrite and expressed such concern for the condition of the Bouton and its need of full-time protection that Helen offered him temporary reemployment. He worked at furthering his return into the Lloyd fold with hat tipping to Emma and regular expressions of sympathy for the situation of Master William junior, who, he said, had been a soldier after all.

He might have done better not to mention Willie. It only reminded them again of his part in the family's misfortune. When the mechanic called to inform them that the car would require a new engine block, he began to speculate on the probable saboteur, maybe to switch attention from the month it would take for shipment of the parts and his wildly high estimate for the repair: "Sugar in the gas tank, not easy, not easy."

With no one to scold in the household, Charlotte had gone into a prolonged bout of melancholy. Helen assumed that the constant presence of a spurned suitor must actually have been more an amusement to her than a worry. Louis and Nellie, supposing Charlotte could use their company and a little political education to offset their mother's and grandmother's propaganda, had taken Peterson's place in the kitchen, sitting for hours, explaining the misguided war and the honor in their brother's apparent misfortune, until Charlotte had to tell them that their talk made her nervous, and to please leave her alone. At Peterson's return, she experienced a marked emotional lift, and Helen supposed taking Peterson back might have been the right thing after all.

With no one left who would sit still for their argument, the brother and sister walked on the beach and discussed plans for Willie's escape from the French military police barrack where he was being held, fantasizing a furious flight that left his captors in the dust. Had they known how weak and fever-worn he was at that moment, they'd have tried to conjure him into a hospital.

Louis and Nellie could not disguise their impatience with their mother. At mealtimes, they made only perfunctory conversation with her. She knew they blamed her as much as the draft board or Peterson for Willie's predicament. Her tears, which had run so easily for so many months, could not move them. She felt guilty enough without their insinuation. The house was split into generational factions. Children and mother-in-law cutting her loose on either side, leaving her to float back and forth between them.

Their father would wake them up when he came home. They wouldn't dare this affect of diffidence in front of him. It hurt her most that her daughter could take a side against her. Never before. But Nellie had forsworn her war duty. No more gathering of peach pits, no more knitting for the boys over there. Right in front of Emma, she'd called the war "a damnable slaughter" and those who took further part in it "fools." Emma knew it was her children's only way of standing with their brother Willie, and she might have forgiven them on this account except for their refusal to allow her a place beside them. When she scolded, it only drove them further away.

*T*he water was as hot as any he'd ever bathed in, and the Colonel let himself in gradually. He winced as he went under, then quickly surrendered his whole body to the luxury. His feet touched the wooden floor. His chin was at water level, and the steamy scent of the mineral solution penetrated his sinuses and lungs. He opened his imagination to health-giving water seeping into his pores.

His conscience was as clear as his head. A righteous cleansing in the face of temptation; more pure because what wasn't going to happen here could be a secret forever from the rest of mankind. A locked door, and sun behind the planet, no one else near them in the black night.

"Where are you, Jeanne?"

There was no answer. He went along his side of the pool, which became shallower in the direction he was moving. At the end, he was able to sit on the bottom with his back against the wall and head out of the water.

"Jeanne?"

He could see nothing.

She came up out of the water, gasping for air. He could tell she was moving away from him.

"Be careful," she called. "You can be overcome by the heat if you remain too long. People have drowned."

Jeanne said she was going to sleep on the bench for a while. He could hear her climbing out of the pool.

"Here?"

"Of course here. Too late to find somewhere else. You are safe."

"What are you doing?" he asked her.

"Drying with the old clothes."

A moment later, he was drying himself. He, too, tried sleeping on the bench, and dozed off for an hour or so till a wind came up outside and it became cooler in the building, a little too chilly to sleep comfortably. So into the water again, where Jeanne had already returned.

They made their way to the shallow end and sat side by side. He felt a well-being, now on the verge of rescuing his son, a first step toward the honorable reunion of his family. He understood that Jeanne was proud to be soaking in the pool where common people made do with water that had already bathed the bodies of the wealthy. And he, though a colonel now, was also pleased to be swimming with the common men, though there were none in sight.

"Does the medicine come right through the skin, monsieur?" she asked him, remembering a question she'd heard asked a dozen years earlier in this very place by a crippled mother of seven children who watched from the benches for a miracle.

"Yes, madame, and once under the skin, it washes away the germs."

"But must I drink the water?"

"*Jamais!* It would make you sick. It must be taken through the skin. Think of the water entering your pores. There, do you feel it?"

The Colonel could imagine exactly what Jeanne looked like as she took this part of the naif, and he the quack doctor of the public baths. She would be cooked red as a Renoir, but in far more appealing definition than one of those pâté-fattened women. Not lounging on a sofa, nor standing like a flesh-burdened animal attending a man's fateful decision, but alert, ready to make judgments of her own.

Again, she was out of the water ahead of him, trying to sleep once more. And again, he followed her example, drying off and stretching out on the bench. They continued that way through the night, the strangest night he'd ever spent. Naked and chaste, hot and cold, wet and dry. They declared themselves not tired in the least from the journey, but incredibly refreshed, and in this regard, they were no smarter than the poor whose pool they shared, giving credit to something in the water.

Jeanne talked for a while about her separation from her family in Crouen, and Lloyd encouraged her further in this direction. Back to the earliest years of her life, which had started in poverty, where all fairy tales began. Maybe thinking twice told would be once convinced, she related again how she'd been rescued from demonic parents by an aunt, led into scientific enlightenment by chance of her menial employment in a hospital, and finally whispered to by saints who set her on her patriotic quest.

Jeanne's work in Bordet's laboratory had been verified by a Belgian doctor whom Lloyd had met in Nancy while suggesting some improvements in the Lloyd chaise. He confirmed that a young woman who called herself Lucienne de Crouen, who had once been a room maid in a hospital in Brussels and then trained as a nurse, had come to Bordet as an assistant and eventually gained his full confidence, but was obliged to leave him when an experiment of her own created a confusion of credit and loyalty in the laboratory. As for her mystical religious directives, Lloyd only wished that his American nurses' motivation had so passionate and selfless a core. His later mail to Moriches showed that he began to doubt the value of his own contributions in France as he recognized the scientific acuity of Jeanne.

After the Ferté trip, he wrote Emma about Willie's fragile condition and the rigors of the journey: I arrived with the nurse Jeanne Prie in Bagnoles de l'Orne long after nightfall. Without accommodation, we took refuge in the public bathhouse and slept on its rough benches. We must have been a sight, scrambling to stay decently out of each other's way in the pitch-dark. Someday I'm going to bring you here to take these remarkable waters.

At Bagnoles de l'Orne, Lloyd was forced to see Jeanne as the daring other half of himself. Informal and spontaneous to a fault, the side of himself he had been trained against. "Do you see why we might have doubted your stories?" he asked her.

"If I had credentials but no abilities, perhaps. But the other way around, no."

As a hint of dawn came through the building's cracks, he saw her silhouette standing in the shallow end, facing him. He turned away, taking his pleasure in the water, and when he looked up again, she was drying off on the bench. A moment later, she was fully clothed in a clean outfit from her kit, outlining her part in the day ahead of them, preempting whatever plans or orders he might have for her, and ignoring his embarrassment as he fumbled to cover himself.

"Blood samples from all of them," she insisted.

They walked back to the station and hired a car for the ride to Ferté-Macé, stopping first for breakfast at a café on the edge of the lake. They were no sooner in the café than the whole village seemed to gather there for breakfast with them. They were the object of all eyes and whispered conversation.

Jeanne looked over her shoulder into the room and raised her voice: *"Honi soit qui mal y pense!"*

He remembered the phrase painted in black over a house door at St. Mark's, but you might have thought Jeanne was reading it from the Bible. The crowd in the café went back to their morning business. The taxi driver, not so easily shamed, taking directions, paid his respects to Jeanne as "Madame le Colonel," and she refused to respond even to his innocent questions for the duration of the journey. It was the first time Lloyd had seen Jeanne denied the respect of her countrymen, and he knew it followed from their night together in the bathhouse.

First thing the doctor saw at Ferté was his own car, now repaired, which had been sent after him and had arrived there the day before. Many messages had preceded Lloyd and his nurse's arrival. The two officers who greeted them, piqued by the delay, were not sympathetic with the medical mission. But they were aware that Lloyd was the father of one of their detainees.

From the Colonel's description of the Ferté sojourn and its aftermath, it was clear he knew that the Directeur there had already decided that the Doctor would be allowed diagnostic examinations of the Americans, in which only medical matters would be discussed. This restriction would apply to his son, as well. And a camp officer would be present in the room to ensure the directive was obeyed. Lloyd was furious, and he threatened to expose the horrific sanitary conditions that already assaulted his senses.

There was a different kind of French insouciance at Ferté—something he hadn't seen before. A "do what you will and be damned" attitude. He was told to report anything he wished to whomever he pleased.

A three-man commission—an officer of the Sûreté, a lawyer, and a police captain—came to the camp every three months to inspect conditions, to hear the cases of the detainees, and to rule on their guilt or innocence. If found guilty, one became a "prisoner" and was sent to a regular prison camp for the duration of the war. If innocent, the man was supposed to be set free. But the commission was not due there for another three weeks, and Lloyd had heard that many lingered for months at Ferté if the commission's finding was inconclusive.

He wanted to see Willie last of all the Americans held there, to be well armed with details of camp life and the general condition of the men before making a judgment about the medical treatment of his own son. Instead, he and Jeanne Prie were shown to Willie first. The stench from the boy's waste bucket greeted them at the door. The doctor looked at Willie and could say nothing. Willie stared blankly back at him. From bunkside, the Colonel went straight to the bucket and carried it himself down the stairs and out of the compound, pushing it furiously under the noses of the guards as he passed them.

When he returned with the cleaned pail, he found Jeanne sitting on the bunk beside Willie, replacing something in her valise and singing softly in German to her new patient. Again, he was speechless. She read the boy's temperature, then, distrusting the number, stuck the thermometer in his mouth again and lifted his wrist to take his pulse, nodding her head to the beat. She said, "Sometimes the others have better words for what we want to say."

"What words are they?" the Colonel asked her.

The guard seated across the cell said, "You will speak in English or French. Nothing else or you will leave."

Jeanne nodded toward the guard to indicate she had no choice in the matter, and she gave Lloyd the boy's temperature, 104 degrees.

"He is dehydrated. Feet as hot as his head."

"What is it?"

"I don't know which one."

"Father," Willie said slowly, "this isn't where they keep me. It's all right. There is one big room for everyone. I am not scared. I did nothing."

The guard said, "You will speak only of the illness."

"How long have you had the fever, Will? How long have you been in this room?"

"I don't know. We take turns carrying the buckets."

The guard stood and said he was going to take the doctor and his nurse out of the room. Lloyd turned to him in a fury.

"Shut up!" he said.

"What food are you taking?"

Willie shook his head. "You should know that your Adjutant Latoni has done everything he could for me. He even asked that you be allowed to come here. So you see?" His voice trailed off in a delirious contentment, and he fell asleep.

Lloyd wrote out a series of instructions for his son's treatment. The list began with immediate release into his custody. In case this was not allowed, the boy should be transferred immediately to a hospital. First thing, deloused. Then, cold compresses during periods of high fever, plenty of liquids. . . . He looked to Jeanne, whose eyes held no answer but compassion. She put her head close to Willie's and began to comb her fingers through his hair, gasping at the swarm of tiny white life that infested his scalp.

The Doctor wrote, "Pending further instruction from Colonel Lloyd, Base Hospital 15, Chaumont."

"I want to see the room where all the prisoners are kept," he told the guard, and instructed him to inform the Directeur. Instead, they were shown downstairs to a waiting room, and when the guard fetched them again, they were taken up to the same cell, where another American now lay on the bunk vacated by Willie.

They're showing us the sick ones first, he thought.

It was Jeanne's opinion they would all be sick, and she proved to be right, though some of the dozen Americans were in easier stages of their fevers. One man had sores all over his body such as Lloyd had never seen before. The patient described a cycle of welts that were open lesions before scabbing over and healing, and then breaking out all over again somewhere else. He had the fear of death in his eyes, and longed to be told there was a simple cure for him. Lloyd also pressed for release of this man into his custody, but no chance. He'd been accused of a vile crime on a child, to whom he'd transmitted his skin disease. He was only there waiting transfer to a court jail for trial.

Most of the other detainees Lloyd diagnosed could stand and take nourishment. Latoni, whom he saw next to last, was in a weakened condition, with a mercurial heat that kept no regular pattern, and was seated on the bunk, leaning against the wall when Lloyd entered.

"So they made you a colonel? Well here . . ." He threw off an insolent salute, like a drunk brushing a fly from his forehead.

Lloyd turned to Jeanne.

"Not her. I know her."

The man was trying to sound menacing, but he was too thin and weak to have much effect. Until he began to talk about Willie.

"Your Junior won't last much longer here. He needs me. Do you understand?"

The guard marched forward with his swagger stick and poked Latoni in the chest.

"Medicine only."

When Jeanne took her needle out of her kit and prepared a syringe and clean vial, Latoni stood and raised his hands in protest.

"She's not sticking me."

The guard, fascinated by the prospect of a needle to be used on a prisoner, rose again in support of the procedure.

"No!" Latoni yelled, rising and stumbling toward the door. In the end, his arms had to be tied to his sides and an extra guard brought in to hold him down on the bunk while Jeanne drew her sample of blood.

By midafternoon, they were in the car and on their way back to Chaumont. They drove straight through, the Doctor in the front seat, in charge of the map this time, giving instructions to the driver and organizing his thoughts for a report to the Chief Surgeon. Jeanne rode in the back, in a fitful sleep, mumbling to herself about the shape of microscopic swimmers in the twelve vials of American blood she'd collected at Ferté. She'd fallen into a rhyme that her ear must have liked, because she kept repeating, "Shepherds' crooks and long fishhooks," backed occasionally with "Wolfram is my *Stechnadelkissen*."

Lloyd turned in his seat to see what she wanted. When he understood that she was only talking in her sleep, he answered her in kind with a phrase that his father, Gus, had given to a kind of cloud formation that sometimes hung over the Great South Bay, "Pony tails and mackerel scales."

The driver, made uncomfortable by what he must have supposed was the coded conversation of lovers, said, "Certainly, Colonel," as if he were being trusted with an ordinary military secret.

Lloyd swung around impatiently, ordering the obvious and the impossible: "Steer clear of anything that might cause a puncture!"

Two roadblocks and one flat tire later, they arrived in Chaumont, testy with the unconscionable delays. They were eager to know if the bacilli they carried in Jeanne's vials had survived the journey, or died before their motion could be examined under the lens. The return trip, for all its problems, had been made in less than twelve hours.

Prudence Plume, the American nurse least afraid of confronting the French woman with hard news, came down from the ward and around the corner of the barrack; she waved to them in the street, where they were stretching their legs and looking at another tire that had gone flat.

She took Jeanne's hand and pulled her back along the street. "The Germans," she said. "All of them. They all have it. It started with Wolfram. All over his back. I thought at first it was just bedsores because he can't turn over, you know, without rolling himself right onto the floor, but then it spread around over his chest, red marks the size of your hand, and his fever is so high that his mind is gone."

They were in the building by then and moving quickly down the stairs, Jeanne in front, heading for the basement room where Colonel Hanson had ordered that all the German patients be sequestered after Armond made his critical report to the Chief Surgeon. "The food," Prudence went on, "it was running through them like water, and now they're not eating anything at all. I was sure you'd know what to do, but you weren't here. Nobody understands them. And another train came in with fifty more of our own; there weren't beds enough in the ward, so we've got some in the hall, and the doctors were raising all kinds of hell with us for spending any time at all down here, and now look what we have."

Prudence stopped to inhale at last. She had got it all out at once, supposing that she and the other nurses might be accused of negligence or just letting these men die because they were the enemy.

Wolfram's one arm was moving slowly back and forth across his body as if using his last energy to operate a handle that pumped his failing heart. His temperature, Prudence said, had peaked at 105, but since the day before, he'd had no more sweat to give, and now looked gaunt and dessicated, the great red blotches gone purple under his flaking skin.

"Stop moving your arm," Lloyd gently ordered. He pushed the torso into the center of the bed. It gave him no more resistance than a bag of leaves. Wolfram must have understood the command. Only his hand moved now, flopping back and forth over his navel. And Lloyd saw that it was, in fact, keeping time with his heart, whose pulse he took against Wolfram's neck at the carotid.

Lloyd knew he was in a death chamber. He had seen the same symptoms in Ferté, perhaps the same fever in an earlier stage. He was sure there was a contagion here. Miasmatic, the other doctors had presumed. But the Colonel and Jeanne knew more. Before these men acquired their heats and sores, they had frequently gathered on Wolfram's bed, bringing their card game to the amputee, making contact with his bedclothes. But what germs could have been transmitted? The black bands on their arms set them apart as the most sympathetic and cooperative of the German patients. Now all of them wore the face of death, and the secret that ran in their veins was still too small or scarce to be seen.

The letter to Emma said: "It was a good deal more than a premonition."

Lloyd's mail home had never called on intuition, but he could not state scientifically just what it was that informed his dark certainty. It was "eerie," hearing not a peep from any of the once loud and sassy Krauts. As he looked around the room he saw: "every one of them flat on his back, heads to the side on their pillows, staring at me, hollow-cheeked and hollow-eyed, their throats rattling softly with not even a bit of phlegm to moisten their lips. If I offered them water, they tightened their mouths against it. Nor would they eat anything. I thought at first it might be a hunger strike, with all of them acting in unison, but the physical evidence of a common plague was on each of them in the same degree. The dark blotching on the skin, the dehydration, the complete enervation that left them speechless and staring. I knew then that each of them was beyond cure, focusing on nothing. They were staring not in supplication but defeat, and I had no hope to offer them."

He turned to ask Jeanne for her opinion, but she was already gone for her syringes and needles. As in Ferté, she meant to have samples from each of them eventually, fearing that the same invasion force swarmed in the blood of all, but for the time being, Wolfram was the one who mattered. Wolfram, Jeanne's *Stechnadelkissen*. He'd given himself the name. "Ja, I'm going to be your pincushion," he told her, but in German, so the Doctor had sent home for the translation.

Macabre, Helen scolded when the situation was finally explained to her in a note otherwise devoted to the growing popularity of the Lloyd chaise, the hospital bed he'd designed, now in use in all the American base hospitals and several French wards. Not macabre to Jeanne. She spoke the name slowly and softly as a term of endearment. "Mein *Stech-nadelkissen*." Wolfram would have let her do anything. Whatever she wanted, it was all right with him. He was a hero.

As they watched Wolfram fade from this world, Jeanne lifted him several times in her arms, put her cheek against his, and rocked him gently while the others watched without jealousy or any visible emotion. Were there any thoughts in their heads at all? Did Wolfram even know the skin against his gristled chin was not an American nurse or a French nun? Could there be love present in a room where there was nothing sentient to receive it? Not a word passed through his parched lips. His breathing stopped a minute or so before his pulse flickered away. Jeanne fell to her knees at his bedside and wept, her arms draped across him.

Her fists slowly drew together under her chin and she began, *"Gott in Himmel . . ."* Not because German came naturally to her, Lloyd supposed, but out of respect for Wolfram's terrible sacrifices. Lloyd could not be sure whether her call to God was angry and in vain or a thanksgiving for a courage even the French could admire.

She rose from the floor, whispered to Prudence that she should do anything she could to reduce the suffering of the rest of these Germans whom she expected to die within the next few days, and told Dr. Lloyd she was going to work through till the morning on all the samples they'd collected over the past two days, preparing a culture of each. After that, there might be a wait of a week or more. Then they would see what they would see. She hoped it would be the fishhooks or shepherds' crooks she was familiar with.

No car for this errand she seemed to be treating as a private matter. They walked together down through the town over cobbles lit only by the occasional candle in a window. Over the bridge he carried the satchel with the vials of blood, to her side of the river, whose glassy surface under the moon answered the vibrations of cannons far to the north. The sympathetic shimmer stole the perfect reflection of the triple arch and showed the two of them shivering over the water, though they were warm with worry and sorrow.

Jeanne's landlady opened the door for them and hugged them both. "Isn't it so wonderful?" she said. "The man from Reims tells us perhaps one more week, and finished! You are celebrating, yes? All right, *allez!* Don't worry. You deserve. Go on," she said as she pushed them along through the hall toward the stairs. "Everyone asleep," she added, as if to say their secret was safe with her.

In her room, they laid a fire in her little stove with a few small pieces of wood, her ration for the night, and went straight to work, preparing the slides. As she carefully mixed each sample of blood in its own nurturing ox-eye fluid, she was meticulous in her precautions against contamination. She drew from each vial of blood with a clean pipette, and her test tubes had been sterilized in boiling water. When ready, they were hung in a steel rack set in a small container that she could keep at a tropical temperature by lighting a sequence of four-hour candles.

She went about this business with a dexterity and confidence that both impressed and troubled the Colonel. He was not totally reassured by the skill and speed of her work. Rather, it raised questions that he did not ask for fear of insulting her and interrupting or ending the investigation, which, after all, now included Lloyd blood.

As she worked, she began to tell him of a family of lice generated from a small population she had removed from the scalp of a Belgian corporal rescued from a forward position close to the sea, a man transferred temporarily to Base Hospital 15 for guest surgery on a crushed hand by the Colonel's best bone man. There had been hours of repair work on the mangled fingers. But to what useful end if the swimmers in his blood had been introduced by the lice and these microscopic swimmers had released the toxins that killed him?

Emma's hopes of an early return for her Colonel were raised and dashed so many times that by the fall of 1918, each letter from France, before it was opened, filled her with as much dread as cheer, and the latest she carried across the fields toward the bay as if she could produce the desired news by squeezing it for a while in her hand before she read it. Let him be on the ship. Let him leave France to the French and the French nurse.

Her William had told her that the doctors, in such short supply in America, would be coming home first, and she would surely be setting the Christmas table for him this year. Then, in later mail, he began to talk about his obligation to the men in his unit, how it would be faithless to leave them behind after recruiting and shaping them. Nor could he bear the prospect of his base hospital drifting out of service in disorder.

Emma was prepared for another of these tiresome declarations of duty before family convenience, but not for a sketch of the microorganism that the Belgian corporal had carried in his blood to Chaumont, and which had killed him. The Colonel's drawing, finely executed and expertly shaded, seemed to her like a comic illustration in a child's story, placed in the middle of a page. Underneath the drawing: "Excuse a sorry artist's vanity, but some detail is required. We have discovered the shape of a new germ that is passed soldier to soldier by head lice."

What? she thought as she looked at the long, ungainly thing. No eyes in the lopsided beast? How does it see to its mischief? Emma could amuse herself with such a foolish conceit because the Colonel, revealing the bad news only piece by piece in small doses separated by hopeful paragraphs, had saved the very worst for last, an allusion to their own son, which she refused to credit. She had some way to go before the cruel end of this letter. First, he had to tell her that Jeanne Prie had taken liberties in the ward that he could not justify to the Chief Surgeon, General Ireland. These had had remarkable results. Perhaps both lifesaving and fatal. It was too soon to be sure about that.

Jeanne had been feeding her lice under the black armbands of German volunteers. The saddest cases, such as the triple amputee Wolfram, proved to be her most willing subjects. The bands that he thought were tributes to the dead were actually the cover for Jeanne's diagnostic experiments.

The Belgian corporal with the mangled hand and nasty heat had been passed back to his own doctors before he died, but the lice he left behind to Jeanne's research had been fed on Wolfram's arm under the black woolen band. And some of the lice must have been inadvertently passed to the other Germans, and maybe by the most impetuous and avoidable behavior of the Adjutant, to Latoni himself. They would soon know for certain. And from Latoni perhaps to . . . Well, she would understand.

But no, Emma took the omission to mean a possible pandemic, a general contagion. The Colonel was asking her once more to imagine herself present for the terrifying and wonderful sight he had recently shared with Jeanne Prie. He described the several drops they had placed on a slide as a boundless pink lake under the lens, and on this inland sea of shattered corpuscles a vast flotilla of invading canoes ("like the one I've drawn for you"), each with two paddles sticking out on one side, moving left and right, forward and back, incoherently, bumping into one another and bouncing away in new directions.

"These," he wrote, "were not the shepherds' crooks or fishhooks we were hoping to see, the telltale shapes of fevers we have observed many times before and already know how to treat. But something new, sinister in their asymmetry, and overwhelming in their number."

In the end, he told her "Of course I cannot come home before Willie is cured and his own ship sails. If I have my way, I'll be on the same boat, following his case till we're home together. As I told you before, I feel I must be true to the men I recruited, and would hate to hear of a disintegration of order here before the place closes."

Emma finished his report in a helpless rage. It was coming clear to her that the hateful germ had been nurtured in Chaumont at their own hospital, and now her son and her husband were at the mercy of this French angel, as they called her, and her medical cunning. With these details, how could Emma trust any longer in William's good sense and doctoring skills? Though of course he must stay and devise the treatment that would cure their Willie.

Willie's trouble with the French, she thought, could be no more than a misunderstanding, the conflict of a headstrong boy and a humorless intelligence service. Her husband was discounting another outrageous coincidence; she could almost blame him for the unlikely meeting of Willie with the miscreant Latoni as prisoners of the Sûreté. It only made it worse that the Colonel tried to pass off their improbable union on the train as the natural result of their separate scheming against the French effort, as he washed away his own part in the spread of this unnecessary plague. She had been so stupid not to see immediately what his letter had meant.

"Damn you, William!" she screamed into the Great South Bay, and an oysterman turned his small craft toward the shore to see what was wrong this time at the Lloyd place. The Smiths, who were also walking on the beach behind her, came hurrying forward, thinking she must be in distress. When they saw there was nothing apparently wrong, they slowed, and Mr. Smith called, "Have you heard, Emma? Have you heard? It's all over. Signed! Done and done! We're all going into the city, and damn the flu! Will you come?"

"Yes! Wonderful! Yes!" And before she knew it, she'd agreed to ride with the Smiths in to their apartment and watch the celebrations from a balcony over Park Avenue, where some restraint could be counted on by comparison with the raucous behavior expected on upper Broadway. But as soon as the sweat broke on the silver cocktail set in the backseat of the Smiths' limousine, Emma knew what a terrible mistake she'd made. She fell into tears for her son, a prisoner of conscience, wasting in the French jail.

"For God's sake," she said, "they knew what he thought before they sent him over there. And what kind of vicious people are the French anyway? I thought they were fighting the Germans."

Though Mr. Smith was quite put out by the inconvenience, he ordered his chauffeur back to the Lloyd house, where Emma was left again with Nellie, Louis, and her mother-in-law, who had advised against the trip in the first place. Proven right, Helen craftily held her tongue, saving the advantage as a trump to be played in good time.

*T*he day after the armistice was signed, all the Americans held at Ferté-Macé, with the exception of two men charged with sexual assault, were told they would be released into the custody of their own armies. The French were getting rid of the cases that might be embarrassing to them now that the war was over. The son of a doctor with close connections to the Chief Surgeon would be first to go. Any officer could be freed immediately on his own recognizance. Latoni, barely able to walk, stumbled over the straw ticks of the prisoners' common room to the prostrate Willie. "I'm free," he said, "and I'm taking you with me."

The next morning, they were once more fellow travelers, this time on their way to the railway station at Bagnoles de l'Orne. In his weakened and needy condition, it was easy to convince Willie that he should not risk reporting to his former unit, but that he should help Latoni reach his father's hospital, where the needed care would be lavished on both of them. That's where the disease had come from, Latoni said, and that's where they would be working on the bug juice to cure it. If not, he said, he could make big trouble for everyone there.

In the turmoil of victory and the anticlimax following the armistice, no one seemed to care where the prisoners wandered, inside or outside the gates. It was clear to all that the jailers at Ferté had merely been perfunctory caretakers to a population of harmless laggards who were now free to roam the environs of their prison. And those who might make political trouble for them were being transported back to their units. Latoni and Willie were hardly noticed dragging their duffels out to the curb and finding a driver to carry them to the station.

Willie was having one of his better days, his first in several weeks. Latoni was having a bad one. For a while, he would make sense, and then fade off into a bully's threat of trouble for anyone who crossed him.

"You think I can't?" he challenged Willie. "You think I can't?"

He struggled for a moment to pull something from his pocket, a wad of French banknotes as thick as his fist, and riffled them under Willie's nose. The same magic trick he'd once performed for Willie's father, a ransom sum. How could he have made or held on to that much under search and under guard in Ferté?

"Never mind." Latoni put it back, patting the lump it made in his pocket. "Your father and his needle Frog never held that much in their lives."

Then he was all over the map with women, the battles he'd fought in, wonder cures and poisons, with repeated reference to "your daddy and the French shit-finger."

"What are you talking about?"

"Up all night with their noses in blood and shit. And the doors locked."

Madness from the fever, Willie thought, especially the notion of retribution that would follow Latoni's death. Willie forgave the man for the insults to his father. If Latoni didn't have great respect for the Colonel and the French nurse, would he be going back to be cured by them?

Even with his own fever and ravaged bowels, Willie was lifted from his torment by the satisfaction of his private victory in France, maintaining his honor under a cruel imprisonment and examination. Though the questions of the Sûreté had not been questions at all, but accusations. "You are a traitor and a provocateur. Admit it and you may go home." Home? Did they think his home was a tunnel of mud and rats, where fleas and lice stuck like pepper and salt to their human meal? He had confessed to nothing. And didn't this make him some kind of hero, the same distinction his mother had allowed his father?

"Everything's gonna change," Latoni mumbled. "Back to the kind of chicken shit a man can walk through in his sleep. I've got news for your father. He'll be running for a troop ship when he gets through with us.

But you know what, Willie boy? We'll be the first-class passengers. Cured and sent home heroes. Or your old man may never do any doctoring again."

The voices of the two invalids were faint whispers in the Bagnoles de l'Orne station. Then Latoni seemed to be fading away again before Willie's eyes, babbling about the fine quality of a woman he was going to bring to the baths on his next furlough. He was reeling from side to side, trying to balance on his duffel, broiling in the November wind, in a body that could not perspire and was too weak to hold a cup without spilling.

Willie made a funnel of a piece of paper and tried to pour some water into Latoni's mouth, but he coughed it back and the water ran down his shirt. He slapped feebly at the paper and cursed. Willie hoped his new friend would be able to stand and help himself into the coach when the train for the east arrived. The man could not die. Willie had it in mind that his standing with his father depended on his safe delivery of the sick man to Chaumont. If they both got there alive, he would have proven his resourcefulness.

When they rose to board the train, they were too weak to lift the duffels. A shaky old porter threw the bags into a car already overcrowded, and the two invalids stumbled up after them, leaving the porter on the platform with his head cocked to the side like an old dog begging a treat. Willie felt in his pocket for a coin but had no money at all. The man was still reaching out to him as the train lurched forward. With Latoni leaning on him, Willie tried to force his way into a compartment. A Poilu seated inside with several friends held the door shut with his foot and yelled at them to find somewhere else.

Willie, like Latoni, was putting all his hope in medicine and his father and the superior reputation of his father's hospital. But the French were a heartless class of people, weren't they, letting a couple of falsely accused prisoners who should have been in a hospital long ago move off across country on their own febrile powers?

They sat in the car's narrow passageway on their duffels and entrusted themselves to a succession of conductors who would have to direct them from train to train. They arrived in Chaumont two evenings later, half-delirious and requiring assistance out of the car and onto the platform. Only at the hospital, when their identities were finally established, did people begin to scurry and fuss over them. Willie could not understand why his father was allowing the nurses to put him in a basement room with two half-dead Germans.

A few days after their return from Ferté-Macé, with the Colonel in full control of Base Hospital 15, Jeanne had moved all her germ study and serum manufacture out of her apartment and back into the hospital's bacteriological laboratory. The two of them had, in fact, been spending long hours there together after the day shifts had retired. In the privacy of the lab, Lloyd worked calmly and without shame as a subordinate to her gently given orders. He didn't pretend to her knowledge of laboratory protocol.

Colonel and nurse carried on their regular duties by day as if nothing extra were on their minds, but in fact, Lloyd could think of little more than their effort to produce the antidote to what they were calling "Kessel's fever," after the Belgian boy who had been sent home from Chaumont with bones mended and blood poisoned. And Jeanne was patiently explaining as they made their slow way through the half a dozen steps required to reach a serum whose potency they must pray for.

It had occurred to the Colonel that his ignorance in the particulars of the work left them all more than a little vulnerable to her zeal. He was not always sure if she knew something to be true or only wished it so. Her religion might interfere with her science. What if it was really just intuition or the voices of saints that moved her hand?

When he questioned a procedure, she was apt to say, "Aren't you listening?" And then she'd go through it again: "I told you, William. This germ is very resistant to heat. We can boil the solution for several minutes without killing it, and thus be fairly sure we have no other bacteria left alive to spoil our results." He could be chastened into docility, into silence and admiration.

When she shared her knowledge, she did so with the quiet authority of a professor of the institute: this bacterium can only live between these temperatures; this fever takes eight days to develop by injection, but three weeks of incubation after biting by lice; this disease could be transferred by the excreta of lice if the excreta were inoculated in the arm the same way as a vaccine, and this germ can resist a temperature of sixty degrees centigrade. You may be sure a liquid remains sterile, free of animalcules, if you boil it for an hour and then seal its glass container by melting the glass shut. A cork will not do.

His work at Roosevelt Hospital had never been so engrossing or exacting as this. He was eager to learn from Jeanne; his interest in discovering a remedy for Kessel's fever was as passionate as hers. Avid in their secret search, they provoked each other's daring. She grabbed impulsively at his arm after a glimpse of a friendly bacterium splitting in two.

They were sharing more than the phenomena under the lens; there was a mutual humility in their work. The Colonel indulged himself: The bacterium, he said, had been garroted at its midsection by an invisible thread whose ends were pulled by Nature's hands.

Jeanne's eyes lit with pleasure. He was puzzled when she said she envied him this freedom she could never have, this belief that Nature is actually God.

"What do you mean?"

"Yes, many of you Americans have it. You don't really believe your other religion, and this sets you free."

They identified the canoes with two oars in the sample of Latoni's blood brought back from Ferté. First only a few canoes, then teeming with them. "The poor bastard," he said. Thank God, still nothing like this was showing in Willie's sample.

Two of the Germans who had the fever were still alive, but barely. They required constant attention, and this produced grumbling among the American nurses, who said that some of their own boys were made to wait for care while these Germans were pampered. Lloyd was trying to show his staff that this might be a shining achievement of their service, keeping two of the enemy alive against all reasonable hope, that the humanitarian instinct of their medicine was admirably blind, an American example to the Hun, which would set their hospital apart forever.

There wasn't much more they could do for the two Germans. When their temperatures shot up, their wrists were plunged into the coldest water available and cold compresses put on their foreheads. The simplest sort of nursing care was all his hospital could offer them. The nurses were forcing liquids into them, and this was difficult. Water, soup, and mashed food—the only things they were able to swallow. If the cure wasn't found soon, they were going to die.

Jeanne was wild-eyed with fatigue and worry. The butcher of Condes brought her a magnificent large-rumped horse, a bay cob, to use at her pleasure. The men of the motor pool made a stall for it in their garage. Sometimes she rode it bareback out along the river road, but she had another use for it. The Colonel held its head while she injected the animal with a syringe full of the blood of one of the Germans.

One afternoon while Colonel Lloyd stood on the Chaumont Bridge thinking how to explain to Emma new reasons he must stay on for perhaps several months after the peace, even after Willie might be healed and on his way, he heard voices calling down from the upper windows of the village. Women were leaning out, calling to the nurse on horseback as if she were a general in front of a welcome army, as Jeanne rode down over the cobble and onto the bridge. She stopped beside him and said, "It's time. You see the horse goes slowly."

He went beside her, back up toward the hospital, and still the women were calling down from their houses.

"But why do the people cheer? Who are you to them?" he asked her at last.

"Eh bien!" she said. "All these Americans here, a thousand perhaps, and the French think I am in charge. I ride the horse." She waved up to a woman who had thrown down a dried flower.

He thought about what Jeanne had just told him, and the surprising French capacity for self-esteem, until what she'd said began to register as an unnerving truth. He was the CO here, but aside from his orders for sanitation, his steely control, his petty discipline, wasn't he in thrall to her science, her nursing skills, her modestly offered diagnostic talent, her clever interventions? In fact, everything about the way the hospital ran could be seen as much under her influence as his own. When he came to think of it, his orders each day were edited with her approval in mind.

Their work on the antidote to Kessel's fever was a matter between them. It was going forward without the sanction of the Chief Surgeon's Office, as a local response to a local concern, though Lloyd knew full well by then the virulence of the disease and the method of its conveyance from one soldier to the next. And he considered the importance of what they might find to the barracks at Ferté-Macé, unaware that since his visit his son and Latoni and most of the other inmates there had been released.

The Colonel even held the horse while Jeanne drew the blood from its neck. "Keep the glass warm in your hand," she told him. He took the full syringe to the laboratory and discharged it into a half a dozen glass tubes marked by Jeanne in a laboratory code of her own, a jumble of French and German, not all of which he was able to translate. This was the way it had been taught to her, she said, and for some of it there was no translation. For the moment, they were working toward a clear serum of the infected horse's blood. The centrifuge spun, and in time the fluid was ready for the needles.

*O*n November 14, a telegram from Chaumont reached the Moriches farm, addressed to "The Family Lloyd":

> Willie arrived here today. Gravely ill. Have permission to hold him under my care. Letter follows. Pray.
> William

The message sent all members of the household into self-recriminating apologies. Tears falling on every cheek. Even Louis wept and promised to do better by his mother, who spent whole days begging for forgiveness from Helen. And Helen put as much energy into blaming herself for all the bickering that had gone on between them. And they did pray, holding a family service each night in the living room, with Charlotte and Peterson invited to attend.

Charlotte kept a candle of hope burning in the kitchen, even after she'd gone to bed. Peterson wore his change of heart on his sleeve, a little red band sewn by Charlotte, which he swore he would not remove till Willie was home and well. He could be heard in the kitchen speaking of "the terrible price of victory paid with this sacrifice of our own."

And, "When Willie and his Daddy come home, there'll be a bright new day on this farm." Whether he meant it or not, he had said it, and that was enough for Helen and Emma. Peterson had learned a new humility they thought, and this suited him. He was doing extra things, deferential to all, helpful in ways that he initiated himself. Scraping the porch, for example, preparing it for painting the following spring, and straightening up Colonel Lloyd's toolshed. Things that anticipated good news from France and looked toward a happy reunion. All things that might make the family more cheerful.

Actually, they were things the family was too frightened to undertake themselves. For fear of angering Providence, they must not presume on the will of God. They must not anticipate their gain. All of them felt guilty, in some measure responsible for Willie's critical condition. It was as if they were being punished, each for their own slack part in Willie's downfall. Now they were denying themselves the right to celebrate. And in this quiet forbearance, they imagined themselves paying for Willie's recovery. They all felt they should be doing something more, something they could get their heart and muscle into.

Emma had tried to understand what had been wrong on the farm. Not just who was missing, but what the absences meant. The nature of the vacuum, more than two empty beds, two chairs, two places at table. It had occurred to her that the missing men, the senior William and the junior, had been the life and humor, the storm and thunder, the practical joke, the selfish and lovable centers of the family. And their constant battle the boiling pot that satisfied the appetite for hurt and healing. The petty squabbling of the last several months was nothing to the booming arguments of the past, when William and his firstborn went after each other chest to chest with shocking language and ferocity. And the current truce seemed to her a puny and insignificant thing as they waited for the next telegram, which would surly arrive before any letter.

She was wrong about that. A letter dated November 22 arrived on the fifth of December, and it did nothing to allay their fear. The Colonel described the pitiful condition of Willie and Latoni when they arrived, and he told of no improvement since, only the mercurial heats, explosive diarrhea, and consequent dehydration. The Colonel described Latoni's feverish imbecility as not unlike his usual imbecility, though lower in volume: "He cursed me for putting him in the basement with the Germans (the obvious quarantine—Willie is there, too), and said if he dies, there is a letter that will go to the Chief Surgeon that will blame me and explain everything that has been going on here. Raving mad, wouldn't you say? You know how square I am with General Ireland and his staff. I will have nothing to fear from them."

The Colonel's letter went on to say that the two Germans with Kessel's fever had been given a new serum. Latoni had the same germ they did: "We saw it! As for Willie, we don't know yet, but his symptoms are the same. I face the most difficult medical decision of my life."

In Chaumont, all ambulatory patients were being sent on to hospitals farther west. These lucky men were hopscotching their way toward a boat for America, while Base Hospital 15 worked on with a quarter of their full complement of doctors and half their nurses. Most of the American women were already on their way home, and the former bustle of the place was lost. The hallways gave a hollow ring under leather heels, and descending into the basement gave Dr. Lloyd: "the feeling that I used to get at St. Mark's going into the basement of the schoolhouse unprepared for a Greek translation. The echoes were so mournful, the dread of Mr. Crandall's ridicule and grade sheet much heavier than my armful of books."

With Jeanne as his laboratory guide, he took the most aggressive intervention that modern medicine could offer the two German boys—the serum therapy that might have saved their lives. After the inoculations, which were both given on the same evening, they waited in the lab for some sign of improvement in the patients before deciding what to do next.

In an earlier era, it would have been condemned as the most comical quackery. A horse's bloodstream as the factory for an agglutinating potion to be drawn, cleared, and then shot into the arm of a sick man? As extraordinary as the discredited theory of laudable pus, the thick white superation once thought necessary to promote the healing of an open wound.

It was still a novelty for the Colonel to watch Jeanne go about her work. Each new case taught him another caution or caveat in serum

preparation and left him in fresh admiration of her muttering engage-
ment with the microscopic enemies that defied her. The muttering was
a little unnerving. What might she know that she wasn't sharing? Her
independence was a worry. Nothing like his American women. The war
had turned so many of them into alluring and troublesome presences,
but they remained pliant and subordinate when on duty.

Sometimes, Lloyd wondered if Jeanne would end her war in glory,
with a unique medal struck just for her. It was only his fantasy. He
knew Pershing didn't care for medals, didn't believe in them. They be-
littled the valor of those who didn't receive them. And maybe the
French Angel was tempting a different fate. Perhaps she was courting
a final shocking opprobrium. In the end, Lloyd was usually ashamed
of his doubts. But Jeanne was such a contradictory mix of familiarity
and hauteur. Her self-confidence was based on an expert's knowledge;
while her peasant's faith might blind her to the normal rules of medical
practice. He must remember she'd never been trained in medical
ethics, only in the thrill of laboratory discovery. It was his duty to
restrain her.

To the patients, Jeanne was still a figure of mercy, moving so
assuredly through the wards that he was apt to forgive her occasional
concessions to impulse. Her free spirit through all their work and travel
had done nothing to oblige him. He could still hold a gentleman's
reserve with her, even if he could not turn his attention from their work
together.

He, too, had a single purpose in the closing days of November 1918—
to save the two Americans who had stumbled over the threshold of his
hospital a few days after the armistice—Willie and the man he had
dragged along with him. Latoni again. Jeanne Prie was his full partner in
the effort. The notes he kept during this period were scanty, perhaps
because he could not bear to document the wasting sight of his son.

The Provost was called before the men were let through the hospital's
front gate. Like Latoni, the Provost was a career man. They were well
acquainted even before they'd drawn their posting in Chaumont, and
held each other in a mutual, if passive, contempt, as career officers of a

lower rank often do. They both knew they would always step to the order of a higher caste as long as they remained in the army. They might make Captain someday, and that would be it. And as lifers gaining a bar here, losing one there, they recognized and tolerated the compensating dishonesties of their service. They had little enough authority, and this they would not cede.

"You have new orders?" the Provost asked Latoni.

"I've got nothing, you ass. Don't you know the war's over? I'm sick." Leaning into Willie, and barely mumbling, "He's got the same bug. From the needle Frog's pus kit. Any more Krauts here?"

The Provost nodded.

"Shhhhhit! Whose hospital is this?" Latoni coughed weakly and caught his breath. "Don't you recognize his face? Does an American have to lie on a stretcher and bleed to death before you open the gate? It's the Colonel's boy!"

"It wouldn't matter if he was Napoléon's uncle. He can't come in without papers."

Latoni slumped to the ground and Willie propped himself against the wall. "Get my father," he said.

"You don't order me around, soldier." The Provost poked him with his swagger stick. "Don't you salute an officer?"

Willie didn't even try to raise his arm. His back was sliding down the wall, and then he was sitting on the ground beside his friend. A sergeant was summoned, and eventually two majors, both doctors. The sick men were lifted onto stretchers. The Colonel was called. He and Jeanne came from the laboratory, where they had been awake all night staring at German blood under their lens, waiting for the little canoes to be drawn together in a static clump, wondering why the patients were not responding to the serum therapy.

The Colonel, exhausted and afraid, began to ask the wrong questions of his son: "What did they do to you? Why did they let you go? How did you get here?" When they got inside, it was Jeanne who pointed toward the basement, and the quarantine area she knew was appropriate for Latoni, and was all but certain of the same for Willie. Until they were sure of his disease, he could be kept on the far side of the room.

Latoni saw what was happening and began to complain while still on the stretcher. He'd have been yelling if he had the voice, but he could manage little more than a whisper. "You ain't taking me down there. Since when does she decide where I go? If I don't get better"—he was glaring, and warning the Colonel—"you're gonna wish to hell you'd never met me." He was more agitated as he passed the cardboard sign hung on the end of a bunk with GOETZ written in large letters so the staff could not mistake it. And then past the next, which said ZIMMER: "Jeeesus! Goetz and Zimmer."

Latoni repeated the names several times, and then it became Goetzenzimmer, before Katz and Jammer. He liked that. "Hah, Katz and Jammer. Yeh, Katzenjammer, that's good. You ain't putting me next to Katzenjammer."

But they were. All this time, on his own stretcher, Willie was going on in a soft monotone, with his father's head bent over him. Willie was trying to explain how much Latoni had done for him, and how they should give their first attention to the Lieutenant, without whom, he said, he might not have made it out of Ferté-Macé alive. Willie, depleted as he was, had no fear for his own recovery, floating in his fever on the first soft mattress and pillow since home, in the care at last of a doctor and a man he could trust. Pleased to be in a bed in the same room as his outrageous new friend, an officer whom his father must first cure and then come to know better and admire.

The Colonel gave orders for a nurse to be stationed full-time in the basement, and for him to be called immediately should any of the four patients there show a significant change. Jeanne was unusually quiet, not quite pleased with everything that was happening. The Colonel pulled her to the side and explained his thinking; they would withhold the serum from Willie and Latoni for at least a day, hoping by then its salutary effect on Goetz and Zimmer would be evident. In fact, they would not give it to Willie at all until they were certain he had Kessel's fever.

But what harm could the serum do? she wanted to know.

He couldn't tell her for certain, but what if there was more germ than immunity in these shots. Better caution than haste.

"You haven't saved anyone with this disease," she reminded him. "Will you try nothing?"

"What did you decide about me?" Latoni's chin wagged slowly on the sheet.

"Don't worry." Lloyd turned to the miserable man. "You're going to live."

"She doesn't take any blood out of me," Latoni warned. "Do you understand?"

They turned their backs on Latoni and went to Willie's bedside. The Colonel took his son's hand. "This is Jeanne Prie. She's the one we can thank when you're better."

Jeanne tossed her head impatiently. She wanted her new samples. The Colonel lowered his mouth to Willie's ear and told him he was proud to have his son beside him at war. It didn't matter how they'd come to be there.

"Have you forgotten, Father?" Willie smiled up at him. "The war's over."

Neither Willie nor Latoni even winced as Jeanne hit their veins. Afterward, they slept fitfully, but holding on to the idea that their cures were in progress. The Colonel went to his quarters and wrote the letter that followed his telegram. Willie, he reported, was technically absent without leave from his unit. The fact that the war was over and that the French had turned Willie loose would mitigate in his favor. But for the time being, he was under post arrest.

"It is hard to believe that I am both his doctor and his jailor."

On his way to the laboratory to see that more glass was sterilized, it occurred to the Colonel that it was not raining, that it had not been raining for several days, or even a week, and the sky was crystal clear and the air bracing. After Jeanne's encouragement, his words to his wife and mother became more flowery and hopeful, despite Willie's condition: This ancient continent, with the stench of war passing under its bridges, with all its modern misery, is still a reviewing stand for the heavens, and a platform to an ocean that rolls toward America.

He knew that others wrote home of the broken parts of horses and of men floating downriver to the sea. And acres of proud flesh barely healed into the fields' crust, hands rising out of the land like the hands of children in a classroom—Recognize me, headstone here—dead carpenters and poets whose verse, doggerel or sublime, could make them weep. And they put a few grains of the earth as souvenir in the envelopes mailed home, because they were the men who knew, if they got home, they would never be coming back.

Goetz died early the next morning. Willie woke, to see the commotion around the German's bed. Jeanne Prie was leaning over Goetz, closing his eyes. She tried to close his mouth, but no use; it was locked agape at the prospect of the death he'd just achieved. The Colonel arrived and was greeted by Latoni, whose voice was weaker than the night before.

"You missed it. Where were you?"

An arrangement of several pillows held him on his side, facing the dead man.

"I saw it. He didn't say a thing. He just drooled a little. That was it. What does that mean? Does that mean anything?"

The attending nurse, one of the nuns, confirmed Latoni's account.

"I was sitting right there in the chair. There was no sound at all and then this man said, 'The German's dead.' There was a discharge of white mucus from his mouth. No pulse, no breath. I don't know if the breath went first."

"Of course it was the breath first," Jeanne said, comforting the nun. She put her arm around the woman and led her away to find a replacement. The Colonel did the only thing he could think to do—he thumped the backs and chests of the three survivors for the dull echo of congestion and took their temperatures. Zimmer's was 104, Latoni's was 104, and Willie's was . . . He shook the thermometer down again to be sure of what he'd seen, then waited. It was just as he'd read the first time, a little victory, 102.5.

"Superior resistance," he told his son. Or maybe, please God, Willie didn't have Kessel's fever after all.

"Best of the lot," he said.

"What is it?" Willie asked.

"Never mind. You'll be fine. The thing you must do is sleep."

"What will you do?"

"Your best medicine now is faith," the Colonel told him as honestly as he could. "We're not sure what you have."

"The same thing they have," Willie said.

"We don't know that. We don't know that at all."

"But how could you know? You haven't even looked at the phlegm from my throat." He tried to rise on his elbows in protest but hadn't the energy.

Colonel Lloyd did not intend to be questioned this way. Willie was impertinent. The boy would just be frightened if he were told his blood might be full of war canoes, the lethal animalcules that had secreted their toxins in Goetz. Lloyd was less inclined to try the serum therapy again. Perhaps they should wait and see if Zimmer improved.

Latoni tapped on the rail of his bed with the tin cup that hung by his mattress. The nurse for the new shift hurried to his side, but Latoni didn't want a nurse.

"Tell him to come over here."

"Get some sleep, Lieutenant," Lloyd told him on his way out of the room.

"Wait! Aren't you going to cut him up? You're supposed to do an autopsy and see what killed him." Two French mess boys were lifting the corpse onto a gurney, ready to wheel it down to the coal cellar that had been serving as morgue. A coffin would be made, and the body shipped back to Germany. That was the Colonel's order. He'd sent a message to the Chief Surgeon that any German dying in his hospital after the armistice would be sent back over the border. And no one had countermanded this courtesy to the families of the dead.

"We know what killed him, Lieutenant," he told Latoni.

"You knew and you couldn't save him? Then what are you going to do for me?"

The Colonel shook his head slowly, side to side.

"Nothing?"

"You said you would not have an injection."

"I said I wouldn't let her take my blood. Did you give one to the Germans?"

"Yes."

"It didn't do much for them."

"One of them is still alive."

Latoni rolled over slowly and observed the silent and motionless Zimmer.

"Barely," he said.

"I'll tell you what," the Colonel said. "I'll leave it up to you."

"Because you don't know what you're doing, do you?"

The threatened abdication of his responsibility troubled the doctor's conscience. He raised the matter twice in later mail to his family, once to his wife, whom he told: I was ready to leave the decision about the Adjutant's treatment up to him. Maybe because I despised him and did not care to resolve the matter myself. I could as well have let him die at the whim of his own ignorant insolence.

And then to his mother, with whom he was even harder on himself. I am not proud of it. I believe it is the most unethical approach I have ever taken with a patient. Fortunately for the Adjutant, Jeanne Prie's vigorous argument changed my mind. If only . . .

Shown this, Emma was inclined to take her husband's word for it; no longer protesting his incorruptibility, giving way to temptation, taking his first step toward becoming another moral casualty of the general slaughter and pestilence overtaking the world. "He was never like that," she protested to Helen; "he would never let his science or medicine be overtaken by emotion."

"Nonsense," Helen told her.

In early November of 1918, an unusual snow fell on outer Long Island. This followed an extraordinarily wet and temperate fall, which left the soggy land a weakened anchor to the forest. Many of the deciduous trees had hardly turned color when heavy, wet flakes stuck to their leaves and put an insupportable burden on the tallest of them. The tops of the brittle maples snapped off with reports like rifle fire. Whole ash, poplar, and even oak trees toppled in the heavy winds, leaving the woods pocked with craters where their roots had been torn from the ground. Of the shallow-rooted sycamores, there was hardly a large specimen left standing.

Louis, with Peterson as his newly obedient lieutenant, guessed his duty immediately. He went to the two neighboring farms, seeking cooperation in cutting and hauling the thousands of trunks and limbs from the woods to a central site on the plain between the Lloyd house and the bay. Three teams of horses were harnessed and driven into the woods each day for most of the early winter, and the largest piling of timber the Lloyd place had ever seen began to rise. Peterson fancied himself the guiding taskmaster, but Louis was the subtler, engineering brain, the master of chains, ropes and pulleys, fulcrums and leverage.

It was the time of year when farmhands would have been generally idle and otherwise up to drinking and related mischief in the village. The Smith and Crandall farms gave their blessings and the use of their men and teams, because they were just as anxious to have their woods cleared of the mess as the Lloyds.

The way many of the trees had splintered and fallen made lumber companies wary of the remains as marginally profitable. Even if Helen had thought of selling the timber, she had a larger vision in mind. And they needn't concern themselves about wasted cordwood. There'd be twenty winters of firewood just from topping the lesser limbs.

Though the women of the Lloyd house did not actually take part in the raising of this massive pile of wood, they watched its progress with approval. And Helen hinted at the whole family's real intention as she surveyed the work from the camel, watching the horses strain under the load: "Aren't the men going to be proud." By "the men," everyone knew she meant the two Williams who had gone to war. They'd never seen a stack such as this.

Helen believed the absent Williams could be coaxed by telepathic energy to full health and an early return. And the massive woodpile had everything to do with this. Though it was not described exactly this way, because again they did not want to vex Providence with presumption, the magnificent thing growing on the plain was the farm's own war effort, and victory over the most sinister adversity. The harder they worked, the better they felt about their contribution. And when the men came home, Providence would be offered its sacrifice.

After holding up his end of a two-man crosscut all day, Louis liked to observe the new swelling of his shoulder muscles in the bathroom glass, and Nellie teased when she caught him admiring himself. He did seem much larger to her this season; in her loving imagination, he was almost as large as she remembered Willie being.

Louis and Nellie agreed with each other to go easier on their mother, at least until their brother was restored to health and home. In the evenings they took moody walks together through the decimated woods and for miles down the shoreline. Kept home from their schools, sequestered from all contact with possible carriers of the Spanish flu, they had only each other for company, and they made the most of it.

Still young enough to be unafraid of the most fundamental questions, they began to share opinions and beliefs that made them benign conspirators, innocently handling family explosives.

"Do you think Mother and Father have ever been satisfied with each other?"

"Not really," Louis replied, hedging.

"I don't, either."

"She can be such a sappy peacemaker."

"Which only makes him worse."

"Are you very anxious for him to come home? And Willie?"

"Of course," she said, "but I wonder how long we'll have peace when they are home."

"I know what you mean."

"I hate it when Father attacks him."

"I don't think I'll ever marry."

"Oh, Louis, don't be silly."

"Really. Where's the pleasure in it? A book can be far better company than a silent man or an irritable woman. Why not spend your life with books?"

"You silly! Why do you provoke me? A book can't have a child."

"Just so, Nellie."

"But I've seen you staring at yourself in the mirror. Who is that for, that pose of yours? It's not for a book. If I were you, I'd let my hair grow longer in front. Ellie DeVrai thinks it's more becoming that way."

"She's your friend. Why would you mention her? Why would I care what she says about me? No, what about you? Are you ever going to be married?"

She took another dozen steps down the shore before answering rather dreamily, "No. I don't suppose I ever will."

"So what's your reason?"

"I won't find anyone as amiable as you."

Louis pretended he was going to pinch her. She ducked out of reach.

"Nellie, why do you burn the mail you get from Ellie?"

"How did you know that?"

"Everyone knows. Mother knows. And Grandma has watched you from the camel."

"God, Louis! Do I have any privacy at all?"

They went on for a way in silence until she allowed: "Because she tells me things I wouldn't care for mother to see."

"You think Mother would read your mail?"

"We've read Father's, haven't we?"

"What has Ellie told you?"

"Never mind."

But again, she could not carry silence far.

"Louis, do you know what impurity is?"

"Yes."

"So do I. Ellie has explained it to me."

"What is it?"

"It's a boy's habit."

"Yes?"

"And both of Ellie's brothers have it. They're both punished for it. I'm sure she wouldn't say so if it wasn't true. But it can't be such a terrible thing. I mean, they're both quite decent and very handsome. So I don't think we can hold it against Father—for his own trouble with it, I mean."

Now she was waiting for a response from Louis, but he had gone quite silent himself.

"Louis?" she ventured. "Louis, do you . . ."

He stared at her in disbelief.

"Well?"

"What about you?"

"Girls don't."

"Of course they do!"

She was crimson with confusion.

"Never mind, Nellie. No one's going to die of it."

"I'm never going to marry," she said. "Why did you say that?" She was dissolving in tears. "Father thinks Willie may die."

"No," Louis told her, "the prognosis is always worse than the outcome. Doctors always protect themselves that way. Even a father. It's just another habit."

"I think he's too familiar with his nurses."

"That's what Mother thinks. He's far too easy with them."

The Colonel waited a day, though Jeanne had advised the serum for Latoni and Willie on the morning of Goetz's death. Zimmer and Willie showed no change in twenty-four hours, while Latoni's temperature shot to 105.5. He was speaking nonsense again, first begging the Colonel for deliverance, then berating him as useless, and warning him to keep the French vampire away from him.

Jeanne insisted that timely injections could still save two lives, that further delay could be fatal. The Colonel gave way, permitting her to inoculate Latoni while the patient lay cursing their medicine, promising a legal action, but too weak to pull his arm away from the needle. The warm pain of the serum raised the skin at his shoulder into a small red welt. Latoni looked at his arm in terror.

"What did you do? What have you done?"

"Perhaps we have saved your life," Jeanne told him.

Latoni twisted around in his bed to see what was going on with Willie.

"Now him," he said, wanting to make sure they were going to practice a parallel medicine on the Colonel's boy. Something to convince him the game was being played evenly. But Lloyd was leading the French nurse out of the ward.

"No, no, no, no! I want another doctor," Latoni whimpered after them. "The boy gets the bug juice, too, or I want to know why not. You did the German, and now you're doing me."

He whipped his head back again to check the bunk next to him. "Hey, Zimmermann, are you still there? Zimmer? Oh, Jesus! Is he breathing?"

By then, the Colonel and Jeanne were arguing in the hall. Unless she could prove to him that Willie had the same germ, he would not allow this aggressive intervention for his son. And certainly not before they detected some improvement in Zimmer or Latoni.

"The serum did not kill Goetz!" she said. "The delay killed Goetz. He was past helping."

"You don't know that! What right do we have to risk the same result with more men?

"More men? Your own son. You won't give him the same chance as the Adjutant?"

"Keep your voice down!"

Her insubordination could be heard by other doctors and nurses. He was particularly angry that Willie himself might have heard her harmful speculation. He was about to dismiss her from duty for the day and sit her down for a talk. But she was already turning away, still imploring him to think: "Willie has the disease! It does not show in his blood yet! It is in his body, but his blood fights it. When it shows, it will be too late." She was angry. She turned her back on him and would not heed his command to stop. She said she was going to Joinville.

A few minutes later, he saw her riding her cob bareback over the bridge and turning north, as she'd promised. He had no real hold over her unless he wanted to have her arrested by the French police. But what would the charges be? All his American volunteer nurses had signed papers pledging two years of service and obedience to their military doctors. And the nuns from Reims had the hierarchy of their own order for discipline. As he watched Jeanne disappear behind the rise in the road, he was not thinking of military discipline or retribution. It was more like watching the evaporation of a friendship lost to an impetuous dare. He thought it was possible she would never turn her horse around.

He went straightaway to the laboratory, where he might think more clearly surrounded by the antibacillus machinery, the microscopes and the beakers, the slides and pipettes, heat and water, the cob's serum drawn clear, and a dozen distillations and solutions that might nurture a germ or dye it for viewing under the lens.

The lab concentrated his mind. He would not indulge himself in despair. But where was Willie's germ residing? Was it a fiendish troop bivouacked in his liver, in the lymph glands, the spleen? He knew the familiar diseases; was not trained to find the face of new ones. Since the departure of Armond and two ineffectual lab men who followed him, he had no certified bacteriologist. General Ireland would be giving him the credit for the successes that had come from the laboratory here. For the failures, too.

For the rest of the afternoon, the Colonel went back and forth between the laboratory and the basement ward, where Willie slept in a sweaty dream. The boy's heart was pounding along close to 100 beats per minute, while Latoni's pulse raced at 130 in his panic that he was dying, that he was being used in an experiment to benefit the Colonel's boy—such accusation as a threatened doctor was trained to call confusion.

Based on the information he had, Lloyd felt secure that he'd made the right decision for Willie. He was not so sure about Latoni. He chided himself for trusting Jeanne's assumptions. It was not the first time he'd seen her willingness to risk all on the presumption that if she chose one from her store of bacterial attacks, she could add a little intuition to the mix and her saints would guide her in the right direction. This time, he needed her mind, not her faith, and he feared she'd been unable to separate the two.

Now he meant to do the thing himself, without the nurse's aid or interference. He had an urgent, lucky feeling that he would surprise her with a victory of his own. At dusk, he was in the laboratory, focusing his microscope on a newly prepared slide of Willie's blood, almost hoping he would see some new kind of flotilla in formation on the pale lake, in battle ranks. If only there were a signal from the disease itself that it was ready for war. If it would only give him a target, a chance to fight.

With one eye squinting, the other watering painfully, he strained for a clear image. For a brief moment, he thought he could see two ladybug shapes on a collision course, but they disappeared as he tried to improve the focus and would not show themselves again. He slapped at the base of the microscope and his slide went spinning across the room.

It was an awkward moment to have Jeanne return to the laboratory. He turned to her in anger: "What have you got there? Where is it from? What are you doing? Do you think you can come and go as you please?"

She let his short, testy questions hang there unanswered as she went about preparation of another slide. She had a small jar she must have taken from the hospital mess, not even sterilized. It was covered with paper held on by a rubber band. The jar contained a putrefaction that meant nothing to him.

"A stool from Joinville?" he guessed.

"No," she said, looking up with wide-eyed pity. "From Willie."

"But his bowels have not moved for two days."

"No," she agreed, "they haven't moved."

With the split end of a tongue depressor, she transferred a small bit of the feces to the glass plate. She squeezed out some distilled water from an eyedropper, then stirred until the tiny pool of cess was homogenized and thin enough to run across the glass.

"Now we will see," she said.

She inserted the glass in its slot at the base of the microscope and rubbed her eyes for a prayerful moment. He watched her lower the scope slowly and, a moment later, throw her head back in a somber meditation.

"What? What is it?"

She got up from her chair to let him see for himself.

No readjustment was needed. He groaned as he saw the congestion of outrigger canoes covering the smelly little lake. Willie's bowels must have been teeming with them. Perhaps his blood, too, by now.

But why just now? Jeanne could not say. Maybe his blood had been struggling with them all this time, deploying some chemical embargo agent while the tiny craft pumped their toxic bilge into his intestines. Or maybe in preparation of Willie's blood sample, they had applied too much heat and killed the bacilli they had meant to nurture. It was all speculation. Far too much speculation, and still the only message coming from her saints was, "Use the needle."

"I cannot," he said. Though at that moment he was relying more on his own saints or what he might have called "the hint of grace" than on any medical equation. He simply felt safer not doing anything in the way of bacterial interference until they should see what happened to the last two men they had inoculated. After all, weren't Willie's numbers still better than those of Latoni, who'd had the shot?

They were both upset by their earlier argument and were not sure how to retrieve themselves.

He was glad she'd come back, he told her.

"Alone, I am too hasty," she confessed.

Together, they returned to the basement ward. They arrived just in time to see the duty nurse putting a basin under Zimmer's chin.

"He's going!" moaned Latoni. "He's finished. I knew it."

Lloyd noticed how much louder Latoni's voice had become. A further sign of panic? Or could he be rallying?

"I suppose you know what the shit-finger was doing with your boy, Doctor. You should have been here for that show!"

"Be quiet or you'll make yourself sicker," the Colonel warned him again, though his eye was now fixed on Jeanne.

Latoni was right about the German. Zimmer's lungs were full. He was drowning in his own fluid even as he discharged a running measure of it for the last time, a mix of blood and phlegm that almost made the Colonel gag. Lloyd turned away from the continuing flow, and he saw Willie's hand signaling feebly over his head. A few moments later, Zimmer was dead, and Willie, still waving from the wrist, brought Lloyd and Jeanne at last to his bedside. All he wanted was to know that they were doing everything in their power to save Latoni.

"An awfully good man," Willie murmured as his father rapped up and down his back and listened with the stethoscope again for rales.

"The heart of the army, men like him." Willie's eyes watered as he wheezed.

"Son, you've got to try to cough more."

Zimmer, like Goetz before him, was put on the trolley and rolled off to the coal-cellar morgue. Lloyd and Jeanne could not leave the room without passing right next to more of Latoni's nervous insolence.

"The boy gets all the attention and I get none? Just as well. Keep her off my ass."

It was almost as if they'd been holding their breath in the sickroom, avoiding the former Adjutant's spoken filth more than any germ he might pass through the ether. In the fresh air outside the hospital, they breathed deeply again. She reached out and rested her hand on the Colonel's belt at his hip.

"The complaining *merde* is better," she said.

"Yes," he agreed, "but Zimmer is dead."

It wasn't until the following morning that the Colonel decided the serum therapy would be given to Willie. He asked Jeanne to prepare the inoculation, ready to concede she had probably been right all along. By then, Latoni was sitting up, taking nourishment, aware the worst was behind him, sassy as he'd ever been.

"When are you going to do something for that boy?" he asked Jeanne. "It'd be a damn shame if he didn't outlive his father."

Willie lay almost lifeless in a febrile dream of light and shadow whose hero was Latoni. He was not aware of Jeanne's needle penetrating his arm.

In Moriches, the season of goodwill on the farm was near an end. Helen marked the limits of the monument to be built of fallen trees, beyond which she felt its firing could be a menace to the house and the remaining forest. Placing sticks in the sandy loam, she laid out a square of two hundred feet to a side. Within that boundary, Louis and Peterson built a pyramid that eventually rose over thirty-five feet. Louis modestly gave credit to the horses, ropes, and pulleys, but the village marveled that the boy could have accomplished this without heavy construction equipment, and the family was equally amazed at the engineering accomplishment of their house scholar.

Layer by layer, he had built a structure so solid that in spite of its central airway, ignition and consumption were going to be near impossible. The wood was far too green. In this tightly packed configuration, it would hold its moisture and might never season. Louis had left an entryway at the base, through which a small central space could be reached—a tunnel to a little chamber in which there was room to stand and move about. A combustion chamber, he said, in which a smaller fire would one day be built to get the big show going, and Nellie, without thinking, observed that of course the space must be left there, because all pyramids were actually tombs.

There was another telegram, reporting, "Willie no better, no worse." Helen, with her grandson so sick, was far too impatient for the sporadic arrival of letters and telegrams. Once again, she was receiving visions and communications directly from France, a telepathy that Emma believed was honestly felt, however fanciful, because it left the older woman so shaken with fear, and sobbing.

From Willie came the repeated line transferred to her hand as automatic writing: GRANDMA WHY WHY, followed by something crooked like a snake, which she took to be the boy's feverish effort at a question mark. For Helen, the meaning was clear enough. How could she have taken Peterson back into the household after all that had happened? How could she break faith so completely with her grandson?

Within a few days, she called Peterson into her parlor for a difficult discussion of his employment. She said she hoped he had understood that the current arrangement could only be temporary. Once again, the farm simply could not afford the continuing luxury of a driver. He'd done wonderful work with Louis clearing the woods, and for this, the whole family was grateful. She was giving him a bonus for his exertions. But he must understand that with the men coming home soon, it was time for him to push on.

"Push on," Peterson repeated, and it stuck in his craw. He knew what had happened. Helen's recent clairvoyance was much too fascinating for Nellie to keep it a secret from Charlotte, and Charlotte passed it along to Peterson in the kitchen the same day of its transmission from France.

Peterson would not be calmed by the assurance that this time there would be a strong letter of reference to whom it might concern. "Where would I find work with all the soldiers coming home?" His frustration was not so much with the lady and her transparent explanation as with the useless young fool who she supposed had sent her telepathic messages. Only two weeks' notice she gave him. To his credit, the armband he'd worn for Willie did not come off. He would match his honor against theirs. For the remaining days of his service, he responded to Helen's orders with a prim and tight-lipped obedience. And when these chores were done, he continued to look for other ways to be helpful.

He was hardly the study of a martyr working on reprisal. Yet Helen imagined his accommodating behavior must be the cover for a simmering anger. Again, she began to notice things missing from the household. The bed warmer that could normally be found leaning against the Franklin stove in Willie's room. Gone. The new stiff garage broom that

Peterson had recommended and kept on the steps up to his room so that no one else could use it. Gone. Nellie's garnet earrings. Only costume jewelry, but a chauffeur might not know that. Gone.

By the time Charlotte had found these things, all innocently misplaced, several more items had gone missing. Individually insignificant, but cumulatively troubling to Helen, who was still receiving the same message from Willie, now daily. She would never have gone to Peterson with a direct accusation. Her misgivings were passed through poor Charlotte, who had to relay them: "The missus was wondering where . . ." or "The missus was asking, 'Is there a day now you'll be telling us farewell?'"

Peterson made no effort to find other employment. If they eventually put him off the property, they would bear the shame of stranding him at the end of their driveway with his single suitcase in front of their neighbors. Emma suspected he was hoping the family wind blowing against him might shift again. After all, she and the children would not be here forever. If he could outlast them, he might be allowed to stay indefinitely. Though Helen had set a deadline, the day came and went. More of the missing things turned up. She scolded herself for her lack of faith, and let him stay on.

Nellie was the most suspicious of Peterson, and with good reason. One morning as the driver was leaving the house for the morning mail in Moriches, she saw him lingering in the front hallway. From the first landing of the stairway, she watched as he bent over the little gold-framed picture of Willie on the sideboard, the last image of her brother caught before his departure for the city and war. Peterson lifted the frame, put it in his pocket, and looked quickly around him.

Instead of confronting the man, Nellie retreated up the stairs to her grandmother's room, where she told her breathless story, then pulled the skeptical Helen down to the hall to see for herself. "Yes," Nellie insisted, "the picture where we made Willie laugh."

In the hallway, Nellie went slack-jawed. The picture was precisely in its place; Helen presumed by the pattern of dust around it that it hadn't moved at all. They went to the front door. Peterson and the Bouton were gone. Helen was quite gentle in scolding her granddaughter. Such things were understandable with the whole household in emotional turmoil. Nevertheless, she now thought it her duty to break down this family prejudice against the hired man, a prejudice in which she had taken a leading part.

Louis believed his sister's story. Emma was more inclined to think that, led by her unshakable loyalty to Willie, her daughter had got caught in a lie from which she could not escape without unconscionable shame. Nellie might stare at Peterson in knowing contempt, yet he met her gaze and went about his work all innocence. He was in line for damnation, she thought, even more devious than the Smiths' boy on the next farm, who secretly snacked on wafers and wine in the sacristy of the Episcopal church in Moriches and then, in his choirboy's surplice, had the nerve to swallow more of them as the body and blood of Christ.

After his inoculation, Willie slept on, almost comatose in his fever. An unopened letter from Louis sat on his bedside table like an invitation to wake and rejoin the family. Doctor Lloyd had put it there as incentive to recovery. Jeanne was working with another sample of Willie's blood, which had yielded at last to the invasion of the deadly flotilla. Now, close to tears, fearing Jeanne must have been right, that they had waited too long, Lloyd sat beside his son and opened the letter to read it aloud, close by Willie's ear. He thought these might be the boy's last moments, his last chance to receive, however faintly, the news from home.

The letter began as a declaration of love in which Nellie joined with Louis in commanding their brother to fight against the disease that had been visited on him so indiscriminately, so cruelly. Lloyd considered his part in his children's innocence, and he was forced to stop reading for a moment to hide his emotion from the duty nurse standing at the door.

When he began again, he was relating a shocking report from Louis that the hired man, Peterson, had tricked Nellie into telling an unwitting lie about him, and thus could take the part of a faithful and misused employee in pleading for his job. Nellie's word was being doubted in favor of the driver, who had feigned theft of the picture in the golden frame.

"No doubt Father will take Grandma's side in this just as Mother has done. We're depending on you to come home and get rid of the man again. Nellie and I think we must be prisoners of the influenza forever. We can't bear it here much longer. Twice we have snuck into Moriches by way of the beach, but we have to be careful. Mother has her spies. I have built quite a surprise for you. Believe me, it is worth living for. Louis."

There was another message for Willie awaiting his recovery. Colonel Lloyd had read this one, too, orders from the CO of the boy's company for him to be returned to his post at Laon under guard. His unit, still in disgrace, was being used to make regular surveillance sorties north of the former battle lines. This made them targets for a few renegade German snipers who had not accepted the surrender.

Even if Willie recovered, there would be no celebration in shipping home and mustering out. Meanwhile, Latoni was strutting his new health. "I beat your germ." Spreading his venom about Jeanne and the Doctor up and down the line, while Willie, whom he had purposely infected, lay closer to death.

The former Adjutant was already packed for his duty at Commercy, a hospital station manned mostly by career personnel who would be taking over at Chaumont when Lloyd's team from Roosevelt Hospital went home. Latoni was taking his case to the barracks slackers and the latrine lawyers, testing his defense on the slugs of his new post. He was tangling the two stories again, one of graft and one of drug theft, calling them the wild inventions of the Frogs and their shit-fingered nurse, whose poison crabs had been loosed on innocent soldiers. The gossip worked its way back from Commercy to Chaumont through several American nurses who had been sent north on temporary duty.

Lloyd knew the man could eventually talk his way out of all the complaints lodged against him, buttering his way past the company clerks and their paperwork, and the career captains and colonels who would wink at their naughty boy's behavior. Eventually, they'd resettle him in a post in America, someplace entirely new and completely familiar, a little military haven with identical rules and vocabulary, vulnerable to one who knew its weaknesses so well, where he would waste no time establishing another crooked game.

Willie woke for a moment and began to mumble. The Colonel bent close, to hear him say he would not be sailing home on the hospital ship, because he would be traveling with Latoni. Nothing to worry about. The French President had approved the plan. Willie's father had been cleared for the voyage, too. Everything was set for tomorrow. Wouldn't it be grand all playing pinochle together?

Lloyd, afraid that his son's last words might be delusionary nonsense, instead of something honorable and redeeming that could help console his mother, leaned close to his ear.

"Will," he said softly, "do you hear me? Let's think of something fine together. Think. Remember the two rivers? Remember Muskataquit and the river that flows through all of us?"

He was trying to remind him of Emerson's two rivers. His mother's poetry roll in the Moriches living room was always open to the same lines. Willie had been made to memorize them as a young child.

"Say it with me, Will."

> "Thy summer voice, Muskataquit,
> Repeats the music of the rain,"

He imagined his son's lips moving in synchrony. What the boy was saying was, "Yes, they do allow cards on the troop ships. Louis will remove the jokers."

The Colonel was moving ahead:

> "I hear the spending of the stream,
> Through years, through men, through nature fleet,
> Through love, and thought, and power, and dream."

He stopped, realizing that Willie was not with him at all. "Listen to me, Will."

> "So forth and brighter fares my stream,
> Who drinks it shall not thirst again;
> No darkness stains its equal gleam,
> And ages drop in it like rain."

There was nothing coming from the boy's mouth but a thin line of white drool. The Colonel called for the basin, and the duty nurse answered with a sharp cry of alarm. Nothing to do now but wait for the end. He took his son's hand and was pleased by a little pressure in the grip, a small but detectable measure of affection.

His telegram could be a simple statement of fact; a letter would have to follow quickly. With Willie's fingers still pressing his, he began to think: I was holding Willie's hand when he passed away. Together, we had just recited "Two Rivers." Its peaceful lines were still in our ears.

Willie began to murmur again, and the Colonel realized that he was hoping his son would help everyone now by getting it over with. But a quarter of an hour later, he had not given up the ghost, and Lloyd slipped away, hoping for a moment of commiseration with Jeanne in the laboratory. In spite of everything that had happened, he did not intend to make her his scapegoat.

This was how he would explain to her his duty: He would have to write a full report on Kessel's fever to General Ireland. Its transmission by lice, its several known victims and its one survivor. With drawings of the microbes themselves, and a brief on preparation of the therapeutic serum, successful if administered in a timely fashion.

He would tell Jeanne that he could neither blame her for the deaths nor give her credit for the discoveries, because the army did not even recognize her existence here. He must take it all on his own shoulders. He did want her to come and sit with him at Willie's side while they waited for the end, which would not take long. To witness with him at what cost a volunteer may swallow Metchnikoff's bacillus. At least to share in the sorrow and mystery of his loss.

She wasn't in the laboratory. She had left a note stuck to a vial of blood beside the microscope: "*De* Willie Lloyd. *Regarde demain.*"

He supposed she was reluctant now to face what she'd done. He hurried to her rooms. The landlady was not surprised to see him. She pointed up the river, toward Joinville, slapping her thigh with her other hand and rocking back and forth in a comical imitation of riding a horse. The Colonel couldn't be put off so easily. She let him into the house and followed him up to Jeanne's rooms. Nothing there but the bare furniture. The case of lice was gone. No sign of her things. As if she had never existed in Chaumont.

He felt sick at heart and a fool as he walked back to the basement ward to take up the death watch again. The doctors and nurses he passed in the hall nodded or lowered their eyes. He settled into the chair beside Willie, who was still struggling with the same dream: "This is grand . . . all going home together. I've asked the Adjutant to visit us in Moriches." The unconscious struggle for life as life drains away, until there is no unconscious left to carry on the fight. This was the way the Colonel perceived the battle being lost in the bed beside him, beyond the control of medicine, into the realm of spirit.

The next time he looked at his watch, it was well past midnight. He dozed, and woke, pleased to see that, as shallow as Willie's breath came now, there was no sign of discomfort or distress. Whatever thoughts were there were peaceful. The Colonel slept again, and when he roused himself, it was time for breakfast at the officers' tables. His stubborn son hung on. So like Willie to prolong the agony for everyone.

Eggs, toast, butter, bacon! Old delights bestowed again. Satisfying his heavy appetite had its cost in guilt, and he went into the kitchen to have a soft-boiled egg prepared for Willie, thinking if he could get some of it past his boy's parched lips, it might be savored as a last gift. And some of it did go down. The Colonel was sure he had seen the trace of a smile and heard something close to "Thank you." He prayed to be forgiven for wishing his son would get his dying over with.

He could not sit here forever; even in victory, he had a hospital to run. The tedious preparation for turning the command over to the marauding unit coming down from Commercy. He swung by the laboratory for another look at what final bacterial meddling Jeanne might have left behind in her quick escape. Nothing more than he'd noticed before. There was still the vial of Willie's blood marked: *"Regarde demain."*

This was the *demain,* the tomorrow. He might as well indulge her final game. The Doctor was a little careless, splashing the specimen on the glass. Adjusting the scope downward, he was in such an impatient hurry that he cracked the slide; unpardonable mistake of the greenest lab technician. He wiped off the lens, cleaned up his mess, and started over again.

When he had the blood properly under the scope at last, he nearly forgot what he was looking for. The stasis he witnessed beneath him seemed to imitate and confirm the lifeless condition of the body from which it had been drawn. The canoes quiet at last as Willie approached the peace that life had never shown him. The Colonel rubbed his eyes and wondered if sleep deprivation was blurring his vision.

Looking again, he observed three groups of the little craft, three clumps that had been glued together, mired and motionless. He watched a single canoe between them drift slowly across his vision. It struck one of the groups and stopped dead, stuck there like a tar baby. It occurred to him at last that this is what they had been waiting for, the agglutination that, if it was being imitated in Willie's bloodstream, would signal a recovery in progress!

In the basement ward, the Colonel found his son had turned himself onto his stomach. He was complaining of a terrible headache, speaking coherently and pleading to be told that his officer friend had not succumbed. He was not sure he could trust his father's assurances that Latoni had survived and was now in Commercy. Willie turned over and sat up in the bed. He pushed down his covers and looked at his chest and arms in disgust: "My God I'm thin!" Again, Lloyd was forced to turn away from the duty nurse, this time to hide the tears of relief.

By the time Willie was well enough to travel, his unit had finally left their cleanup duty in Laon and departed for the embarkation camps at St. Nazaire. The Colonel was surprised at how easy it was to have his son transferred to his own command. After a special plea of medical necessity and explanation of the logistical realities, the Chief Surgeon's Office had approved the switch and forwarded the required papers. Within a week, the bewildered Willie found himself in a chain of command only three steps removed from the orders of his own father. And as long as he remained a patient, the orders were delivered without intermediary: "Do not get out of bed." "Drink this." "Eat that." "You will not be rude again to the nurses."

The director of the telegraph office himself came out from Moriches to deliver the news from France. He said there was no one else available. Besides, it was a lovely day—cloudy and cold—perfect for a little excursion in his puddle jumper. This, and he knew how anxious they must be for word from over there. Their boy being so sick, he didn't think he should keep them waiting an extra day.

It was addressed to the Lloyd family. He held it out to Emma with a tight smile. The man must have expected her to open it in front of him and share her reaction with the community, since he remained standing there after she had tipped him. It angered her that he would already know the contents while pretending to the usual procedure of innocent transmission. She put the telegram in her pocket, shaming him into his leave.

Emma crossed the threshold, still afraid to tear open the yellow paper. She sat on the horsehair sofa and rubbed the envelope as if this might force the polarity of the news toward positive. By then, the others were sitting beside her or standing over her, taking her light. She handed the telegram to her impatient mother in law. But in Helen's hand, the paper trembled like an aspen leaf. It was Nellie, not Louis, who actually believed in the power of prayer, and she was able to open the news and read it:

WILLIE FRESH AS PAINT
ON ROAD TO RECOVERY

The Colonel's last letter from France was postmarked January 29 in St. Nazaire, at the embarkation camps. It was written in stages as father and son moved south and then west across France to the sea. The pages bore the names of the cities they passed through on their journey.

Chaumont. We departed on Saturday the twenty-fifth at 11:30, one day late, because they sent third-class coaches to take our officers and nurses. These were refused by the troop movement bureau—that is, by me. We make quite a circus now. Three coaches—inadequate but possible—for thirty-four officers and sixty-five nurses. Behind these are five boxcars holding 167 men, then two baggage cars with the bags and rations.

Willie made no fuss when I told him he would ride with the enlisted men. He said he would not allow me to give him preferential treatment. It made me quite proud of him. When we started, none of the cars had any heat because of a single freight car between us and the engine. The weather is cold, flurries of snow and rain. I'm sure the men are suffering in the boxcars behind us. I will check on Willie's condition at Is-sur-Tille.

I don't think I have told you how heavily the disappearance of Jeanne Prie weighs on my mind. I think of her almost as a partner in all that was accomplished in Chaumont. My treatment of her at the end was less than gallant and may have contributed to her flight. I wrote you once that she would either deserve a medal or public disgrace when this was all over. I'm happy to tell you that I have used all my influence with General Ireland to have a special decoration made for her. It is the most beautiful thing, a gold-edged round of silver with the rough symmetry of an ancient Greek coin. In relief on one side is a longhaired, winged lady hovering, and on the other side, a beaten surface that suggests a landscape pocked with craters and the stumps of blasted trees. It hangs from a thin red ribbon. When we locate Jeanne and have a definite address for her, we will arrange for a military presentation. Until then, I keep it with me.

Is-sur-Tille. The journey down the Plateau de Langres was difficult for the nurses and miserable for the men. The poky train took nine hours to reach the place. Here we got rid of the car that had stymied our heat, and they put on two more coaches for us, one a German car with second- and third-class compartments and no heat, the other French, with heat, but filthy.

We had plenty of hot food and coffee served by the Red Cross hut. I walked back to the rear of the train, to find that the men were making fires in the middle of the boxcars. They had improvised heaters with stones gathered along the track. The choice was to suffer in the choking smoke or freeze under their cotton blankets.

I caught sight of Willie shivering in a corner. He was pretending not to see me. He had a dreadful cough, and I was not going to let him catch pneumonia, so I ordered him into one of the forward cars. He was disrespectful, trying to save face in front of his fellow enlisted boys. Of course, the result was that he embarrassed me in front of my command. When I threatened to have him moved by force, he obeyed. You can picture his smirk.

The nurses were still badly crowded, eight in a small compartment in the worst cases. Four of the young administrative officers and I surrendered our accommodations to Miss Galloway, the senior operating nurse, and Miss Plume, common as ever. I asked them to keep a watch on Willie's condition. I think the best thing is for me to avoid contact with him whenever possible until we are home and the old rules will apply.

Dijon. My four young friends and I cleaned house in the French car and I slept for several hours until the train reached Dijon. Here I walked back and found a revel in progress in one of the boxcars. Some Frenchmen at a siding had sold the boys fifty bottles of ordinary wine, and there was already much drunkenness. I felt sorry for their wretched situation and could not blame them much for trying to stay warm, but I was glad I'd moved Willie forward, away from temptation. They had almost burned a hole through the floor of one of the boxcars. I gave fair warning to the NCOs to restore order and actually threatened one of them with the loss of a stripe. I don't think he took me seriously, but I meant every word. The men are too much like horses with the barn in sight. If I let them take the bit in their teeth, I will lose all control.

Bourges. We rolled out of Dijon Sunday morning behind a big Baldwin locomotive with U.S. on the tender and two American boys in charge, with a French engineer as their pilot. I imagined Willie safe and warm in the third coach, next to the nurses' cars. It was a relief to put him and his welfare out of mind and savor some of this last trip across France. At Beaune, we turned to the west for Nevers. As the sky cleared, the morning light on the Montes du Morvan reminded me of your Moran—with a palpable atmosphere that glows. We passed Nevers at midday and pulled into Bourges about dusk.

My troop seemed unusually docile, no one complaining about the cramped quarters, or lack of heat, or hunger. I suddenly felt the hair rise on my neck, and had an intimation of more than mice at play in the woodwork. My curiosity had the best of me. I had to know how our Willie was adjusting to the unaccustomed company of officers. As I passed through the first nurses' coach, the women nodded and called hello from their compartments, but in the next car, they became suddenly furtive when they saw me, whispering and covering their mouths. Miss Plume tried to turn me back to my own car, apologizing for some problem of which I was still unaware.

Entering the next coach, I saw four officers sitting on duffel bags in the passageway outside the second compartment. One of them whistled a warning to the occupants inside, but there wasn't time for them to repair the scene. There was Willie with five of the younger nurses. They had a card table balanced on their laps, strewn with cards and two empty wine bottles. A third, half-full, was being passed around. Drinking directly from the bottle! The bunch of them were too far gone to be startled, and the most brazen of them, a girl I should have sent home months ago, said, "Oh, Colonel Lloyd! Willie is showing us poker!"

I said nothing, and walked back to my coach in shame, supposing that my appearance would have put an end to it. I discovered later that they had gone right on their merry way, opening yet another bottle and continuing the game.

Tours, 9:30 p.m. We changed engines again in Graves, another American monster. The road was blocked repeatedly by slow or broken-down French trains. There were many stops through the early morning, when the officers, nurses, and men gathered around the engine to get a wash in hot water. These toilet parties are a sight I won't forget. Where was Willie when it was time for a bath? Sleeping off his debauch, sprawled on a seat, depriving two officers of their deserved comfort. He doesn't seem to understand that they only humor him out of deference to me. I roused the boy and sent him back to the boxcars where he belongs.

The most awkward thing has just happened. Looking through my compartment window, I was convinced I saw the French nurse stepping down from a train across the platform. I rushed out of the car and chased after her, calling her name, but she would not stop. Catching her up, I grabbed at her shoulder and she turned to me in terror. It was not Jeanne at all, but a woman with a wen on her neck and dreadful teeth. She pulled away before I could explain. So I sit here in the train again, mortified, as several of the nurses were watching through their windows when I accosted the woman. They remain ignorant of my intentions.

St. Nazaire. Here we are down by the sea, waiting for orders to embark. We arrived 5 p.m. day before yesterday. The nurses were sent immediately to the nearby town of La Banc. And none too soon, for on the platform I watched a lewd public good-bye between Willie and the tarty girl who spoke up to me at their poker game.

Yesterday we waited orders, and the officers were looked over for lice. Yes, me, too. We were told the command would be fed and sent to an isolation camp for the night. I kicked like the army mule and we were put to bed right there without further argument. Today we came over to Camp Number 1, and the men were deloused. The mess is better here, and there are showers shared by all.

Tomorrow we will be inspected to see that the men's equipment is in order. As we pass muster, our names go on the list for sailing. But the ships are few and the camp crowded. Some thirteen thousand men ahead of us, and priority is given to the sick and wounded. I shall make sure Willie leaves on an early boat. Not that he is sick enough to deserve it, but because of his continuing determination to debase himself on this continent.

I expect to be here about three weeks and home around the first of March. An officer sailing tomorrow will post this in New York. Use your judgment in sharing it with Louis and Nellie.

Medals

*T*he family had the name of the Colonel's ship several days before he sailed from St. Nazaire—the *John S. M. Booth,* an English merchant ship recently fitted for this service with 2,000 hammocks and 1,500 bunks, a 250-seat mess for officers, and a 700-seat mess for enlisted. Freshwater showers available every other day for officers.

How like an army officer he had become, Emma said, to forward such homely news, to be so preoccupied with the raw logistics of life. Nellie wondered if he meant the ordinary soldiers would be forced to bathe in salt water, or would not wash at all. And Willie, who had been home for almost a week, now a man of the world, said that even salt water would have been a dream on his ship. But that, in fact, men were more like domestic stock, hosed down and disinfected at the beginning and end of any journey they took. Then checked for lice. And were a little proud of the way they smelled in between.

"Shame, Willie!" Actually, his grandmother was laughing openly, and Emma was forced to scold: "Don't encourage him."

In another week, they had the day and approximate time of the arrival in New York—March 17 in the early evening—and Emma was faced with a decision. She could take the family with her to the docks to meet the *John S. M. Booth,* relying on the recent reports that the pandemic was in recession, that the susceptible had already been infected, and the immune could now face the future without fear; or keep them home, continuing to take every precaution against the flu. They could not take the Colonel home with them, in any case; the trip to the city would only be to see him off the boat. After that, he would go to a camp in New Jersey for the final mustering out.

Emma decided they would go. And Helen agreed that the victory and the sacrifices already made demanded a full celebration that should not yield to fear. Even Willie said he would not miss an opportunity to welcome his father home, "where we should all have stayed in the first place."

The women reopened their debate on the usefulness of wet handkerchiefs as masks against traces of the flu germ that might still linger in the commuter trains. Emma took the affirmative; Helen maintained the practice had proven useless. Besides, she said, it was an unattractive display of fear. Their strained politeness drove the children into other rooms or out of the house.

On this occasion, Louis took his brother for a closer look at the pyramid, for which Willie had already offered his highest praise: "You couldn't have made this." This time, Louis showed him the passageway beneath it. They crawled into the little chamber where the tinder would be set and the gasoline poured. "We can tell Mother it's only kerosene." And a string fuse would be laid along the ground and lit at the edge of the pile, where they could scurry away to safety.

At dawn on March 17, Willie took his shotgun, walked to the bay, and left in the family's rowboat, heading for the marshes to the east for a morning's duck hunting. He was to be home by quarter after ten so that they could all leave together on the morning train for the city. At 10:30, Emma, Nell, and Louis were forced to leave without him. And Helen insisted on staying behind in case Willie was in some kind of trouble.

Emma suspected correctly that the boy had never intended to meet his father at the dock, and that he would plead he'd lost track of the time. She was actually relieved that he would not be there to spark trouble with the Colonel at a time of joy. But she hadn't foreseen that Nellie would refuse to be driven to the station by Peterson.

Helen ordered her granddaughter to get into the Bouton. Nellie would not. Louis demanded to be allowed to drive. Helen said no. She relented just fifteen minutes before the train's departure. Peterson climbed out of the driver's seat and was sent to the kitchen to have his feathers smoothed by Charlotte. All parts of the household were either in irritable discord or full mutiny as the reunion day got under way. They made an explosive mixture that might be set off by any flinty soul, and from the kitchen to the backseats of the Bouton, all understood that soul was almost on the American shore.

They walked all afternoon in the streets behind the docks where the troop ships were unloading, pleased to observe and brush elbows with the disembarking soldiery of the nation. The *John S. M. Booth* entered the harbor at four. The pier was opened to the public at berthing. They watched the massive hawsers thrown down and made fast to mooring posts. The whole dock shivered and groaned as the ship heaved against it.

Willie had explained to Louis how it would work. The ratlines first. Then the gangplank for the men, who would be pushed down four abreast, then the officers ambling off as the time of day suited them. And now Louis was explaining the same to his mother and sister.

"Rubbish," Emma said. "The sick will be taken off first. Then the officers will come down with the men to keep them in order."

Neither was correct. The gangplank was not put down, and no one could tell them why. Soldiers were jammed along the rail, waving to the crowd below, but their service hats made them all appear to have the same hairline and their faces at that distance were indistinguishable.

Nellie claimed to see her father waving to them. As it turned out, this could not have been so. Colonel Lloyd, the highest-ranking medical officer on board, was then in hot debate with the general in charge, who was ordering the ship's English captain to put down the ramp and let his men disembark. A city health officer had been lifted onto the ship in a pilot's chair, and after debriefing Lloyd, he told the captain that the whole ship's company was quarantined. The captain looking out for the commercial interests of his line would not disobey the civilian's orders.

The Colonel explained that five men in ship's hospital had developed lesions on their upper bodies, sores that he could not identify, and that one of these men had died during the crossing. He could not say if they were witnessing a miasmatic contagion, infection by contact, or a non-contagious disease that would warrant release of the men to shore. Until more was known, he could not recommend dropping the gangplank.

The general, infuriated with this stubborn ignorance, shouted at him, "Would you have every man on board infected?"

"No, sir," Lloyd said calmly, "nor would I wish every man, woman, and child in New York City put at risk by our negligence."

The General said the Colonel would come to his senses or risk losing his commission. And Lloyd assured him, "If that's all it's worth, I wouldn't give a penny for it." A final war story for the hearth, one his women could scold at while they swelled with pride, one even his children could admire.

The family waited until dark, then went to their apartment on Twenty-third Street and spent an impatient night. The next morning, they were back at the pier, and, informed of the quarantine, were disgusted. They waited around till noon, then left for the station to catch the afternoon train for the country.

When the Colonel reached New Jersey, he assumed command of his family again. He ordered them to stay out of the city, to come to meet him in the family car at the Moriches station. And Emma obeyed as best she could. She and Helen were waiting on the platform a half hour early.

"Not there," Helen said, "here. He'll be at the back door of the first car. Just here. Where he's always gotten off."

She planted her feet firmly where she was sure she would be the first one to touch him, and then made another prediction. "The first thing he'll say is 'Where are the children?'"

Yet another reproach to Emma, but what could she do? She couldn't make them get in the car with Peterson, who should have been gone from the farm long before this. The train was visible half a mile distant, where the track seemed to come to a point. As the engine approached, Emma saw her man spreading the rails apart, into a **V**, forcing his way home. The flat face of the train came gliding toward them, pushing its light, swaying slightly side to side, and she thought of the Doctor shifting his weight from foot to foot, impatiently. His headlamp on in the middle of the afternoon, scrutinizing a new case. She was as anxious to see him as she was fearful of his arrival. The engine's bell came clanging past, knocking aside a new silence between the two women. Helen had positioned herself perfectly.

As the train came to a stop, the Colonel, with all brass polished, was looking directly down on them with a grand smile. His mother would not be budged from her spot, and it was difficult not to bump her as he lifted his baggage down. He clapped his hands and kissed her warmly on both cheeks, then took Emma into his arms, and she wept happily for a moment nestled against his neck.

He pushed her back, holding her by the shoulders to examine her more closely, as if the reunion they'd awaited for so many months might escape without being properly felt or reciprocated. They looked into each other's eyes a little bit like strangers. A new heaviness at her jowls, maybe too soon like her mother's face. A stiffness to his jaw that she took to be a part of his officer's disciplinary kit. Was there a squint to her left eye that he did not remember? Maybe a nervous thing that could be easily patched up with a little belladonna. She she noticed new weight at his girth, surely added since the armistice, the indulgence of the last several months.

"Nellie and the boys?" He turned his question to his mother to keep the reunion in balance.

But Emma answered for her: "They're getting things ready for you at the house," she said.

He rode to the farm next to Peterson in the front seat, complimenting him on the fine appearance of the car while imagining a banner of sheets hung across the front porch—WELCOME HOME COLONEL LLOYD—and a party of several dozen friends gathered around a punch bowl, bursting into "He's a jolly good fellow" as he crossed the threshold.

Going up the drive, he said the woods looked far better than he'd expected. "Someone's done a remarkable job."

"Thank you, sir." The driver took credit, though not loudly enough for the ladies in back to hear.

"My God! What's that?" Lloyd was amazed at the size of it.

"That's Louis's project. He's so proud of it. It's for you, William. To celebrate your return."

"Peterson helped a great deal," Helen put it. "Indispensable, really."

"Thank you, ma'am."

No banner. Nellie stood in the driveway, hands raised in delight. Louis was on the porch steps behind her, expectant but restrained, as if waiting in a reception line for a handshake. Willie was nowhere in sight. A few minutes later, they were gathering in the living room. No company. Charlotte was there, and she was fussed over by the Colonel as she beamed at the walking display of leather and medals. She was promising two duck for dinner, brought in from the bay by Willie. And Mr. Lloyd's favorite custard with caramel at the bottom.

A few minutes later, Willie came down the stairs and made his entrance. "Father! You must have taken the packet boat! But you're home at last. Welcome!"

It was not condescension, but equality the Colonel heard from William. He'd anticipated some distance from the boys, but not to this degree. He took a glass of sherry and suggested all the others have one, too, including Charlotte and Peterson.

"You, too, Nellie."

"William!" Emma and Helen protested in unison.

"She's old enough. This is a special day." He poured her glass himself. She was the brightest thing in the room. When the others were finished with him—especially his wife and mother—he wanted to go for a walk with Nellie, to let her keep asking her generous questions about the people who had made such an impression in his letters, about all the months of his life they had missed, new secrets of medicine laid bare to the world. They couldn't begin to know his exhilaration.

"To the victorious end of the Great War," he said. "To the beginning of . . ."

"The next one?" Louis asked softly.

Lloyd would not be provoked. "Well, Louis, let's have a look at what you've done." They all marched out across the front meadow. As they approached the pyramid, the Colonel stopped to marvel again.

"That's wonderful! Two thousand dollars' worth of logs there if there's a toothpick. But why did you stack them the way a pharaoh would? It will only be harder to get them on the trucks."

"They're not for lumber, Father. They're for you. For tonight."

"Nonsense! You must be mad!"

"Grandma says it's quite all right. She says it's Moriches's sacrifice to you. For all you've done."

"We'll see about that."

Before they had heard the rest of his adventures with the general on the ship, voices were being raised, and by the time they reentered the house, they were all yelling at one another, with Emma pleading for peace. Charlotte and Peterson came out of the kitchen as the Colonel's argument rose above the others.

"By God, no one's going to torch that wood while I'm in charge here! Do you hear me? That's a small fortune you've gathered there. It's not for burning!"

Helen climbed to the first landing and looked down on them. "Children!" And by this, she meant everyone but herself. "Children, the logs are mine and I will decide what happens to them. Stop this quarreling. There is too much to be grateful for. Get yourselves ready for dinner."

There would be no fire that night, and Louis supposed that in calling the wood "logs," her thinking had now changed in favor of a sale. Shamed as a wastrel, he walked away to the beach and made plans to leave. He must convince his mother that it was necessary for him to be in Cambridge for the spring and summer to prepare himself for his last college year. To make up for the time he had lost as hostage to the flu. And let her put it over to his father.

Willie heard something different in his grandmother's brief remarks —that she was not ceding control of the place to anyone. She had once told him that he must go into the world to make himself before settling here at the farm in his turn. Now he suspected that had changed. His brief and dangerous time in the service gave him sway with her, a new power in the coming struggle he expected with his father. The Doctor would return to his hospital and his practice in the city. Willie had no intention of returning to New Hampshire, to the campus his father so despised. If it came to an argument, it was right there in one of the old letters. No, the field was open here for work and play. He must show them all a little work and make his intentions clear.

Nellie was the one who best understood her mother's fear, and something perverse in her made her steer to the heart of it.

"Father," she said, "I want to see the medal. The one that was made for the French woman. The nurse with the odd name."

"The woman didn't have a real name," Helen remarked. "She kept changing it. So what could anyone believe?"

"Oh, yes," Emma said, "the one who was so ambitious. And careless in the laboratory."

Dr. Lloyd listened in wonder that his censored army mail could have taken them so close to the center of his recent life, and so far from a fair appraisal. It was amazing to see how much had been added to, how much interpolated from, the simple news he had written.

"After supper," he said. He would look for the medal after supper.

"Now!" Nellie insisted.

"Nellie." Helen grabbed her granddaughter's hand and led her into the parlor. There was no privacy there and Helen didn't seem to care; she was making it clear she wanted the subject changed.

"Nellie," she said, "I know what you've been up to."

"What, Grandma?" Why shouldn't they all see the medal?

"Never mind that. What did you tell Willie to say to me?"

"Nothing." Nellie was a useless hand at lying; she was almost trembling with shame.

"Yes, you told him to tell me that in his fever he kept thinking, How could I have disappointed him? How could I have taken Peterson back into service? Nellie, look at me. Look me in the eye. What do you take me for? That was very naughty. Did you think I wouldn't see through that?"

Doctor Lloyd felt the lecture in the next room was being delivered as much for himself and the rest of the family as for Nellie, and he was uncomfortable with it. Millions of men had died, but his family struggled over the employment of their pathetic driver, and the tedious business was continuing into peacetime.

Lloyd took his wife up to their room to give her the several presents he had gathered for her in St. Nazaire. It was not lost on Emma that her gifts, two maudlin prints of children at play with hoops, and a plaster reproduction of a child ballet dancer, had been plucked from street stalls at the last moment in his last French city. She said they were lovely.

The Colonel took her hand because the moment obliged it. She drew shyly away and went to the window. Not to pull the shade, as he'd expected, but just to stare for a moment at the silence of the world. He was pleased that he was not expected to perform his passionate gallantries just yet. In fact, it was a relief to see how grateful she was that he was not pressing a sexual advantage at reunion. She was so obviously confused by all the contradictory stimuli of his homecoming.

After the plentiful dinner and the first round of stories from France, with French officers taking the parts of amiable buffoons and Lloyd as the modest agent of reason, anticlimax fell on the table as a palpable depression: no bonfire, the children's stubborn reticence as they were each called to account for their last eighteen months, and, when they were not forthcoming, the officious announcement that it was time for young people to be off to bed.

The children recognized a stuffy military hegemony that must be put to rout at once, before it became habit. Nellie struck again at the vulnerable place: "You promised, Father. You said after supper you'd show it to us."

"Your father is tired."

"No, it's all right, Emma. I did promise."

Emma began to clear dishes, as if this had been her regular wartime chore, and when her husband returned with the medal and laid it on the polished oak table, there was a collective holding of breath.

The thing was truly beautiful, stunning in its miniature perfection. It reminded them of a Saint-Gaudens figure. A portrait in low relief of classical elegance and beauty, like the lady on the dime, radiant, lit, and draped like a saint.

"It's gorgeous," Nellie said. "It *is* a Saint-Gaudens, the figure."

It was no coincidence that none of the men and all of the women in the family knew what Nellie meant. The women were the ones who had gone to an exhibition of the sculptor's work and had swallowed hard at the news that his favorite model was also his mistress. The rare beauty had shared his summer life in New Hampshire and had even entered the home when his wife was in residence.

"I want one!" Nellie said. She lifted and turned it to look at the desolate landscape on the obverse. The golden edge, rounded and thin, around the silver field gave it the rich framing of a craftsman's masterpiece, and she was reluctant to put it back on the table. As Louis tried to take it from her, her lips swelled in a pout and she pulled it back to her breast.

"The only way to earn one of those . . ." the Doctor began. He seemed unsure how to go on. "The only way," he said again, "is with a life of service." But how was he going to keep order here if a tear came so easily? There was a pretense of blowing his nose, which fooled no one. Nellie, surprised by her father's sentimentality, called their attention to the medal again.

"What's this? What does it say?"

"Nothing," the Doctor assured them.

"Yes, feel. It must be her name."

She was rubbing her finger over a tiny semicircle just above the golden rim.

Just a decorative line, Lloyd supposed. He hadn't even noticed it before.

Nellie went after the big magnifying glass in her father's secretary, and was soon back and thrilled with her discovery of a hidden message, reading under the lens: "Combris Fils et Cie., Chaumont."

"Father, this was made in Chaumont! Where you were!"

He said he supposed it must have been, that it didn't surprise him at all. Some of the finest handwork in France could be found right there. But how was the thing going to find its way to the saintly woman who had earned it, since she had disappeared and left no forwarding information? Nellie would not relax her covetous hold on the medal. If Jeanne Prie was not found, she could imagine this becoming her own. Emma and Helen admired the piece more than they dared say. They made no further comment.

In the days that followed, Emma found ways to discourage the Doctor's occasional bedroom ardor without denying him altogether. If his mind was in France, she could wait for its reunion with his body here in America. Until then, his touch would seem only lustful and vexing. But his reaction as she turned to the wall for sleep was more like indifference than frustration. She knew he had other problems in mind.

Their plan had been to stay in Moriches for the first week, then move back to the city so that he could rearrange his working life. They would let the children come and go as they pleased until their schools began again in the fall. That way, Helen would not feel so suddenly deserted, and the Doctor and his wife might have some time alone to mend the injustice of their long separation.

Lloyd came home from his first trips to Manhattan with glum reports. Roosevelt Hospital did not renege on its agreement to take him back as attending physician, but it must be on new terms. He would have to share the old position with three other doctors, and his duty must include night work. He was not to take this as a demotion or an insult, but in good grace, recognizing the new realities at the hospital since he took leave.

Leave? Hadn't they asked him to go? To do his patriotic duty? No, he was told, they had given him the opportunity. And they were proud of him for having taken it. And now they were making room for him in a crowded table of organization.

Lloyd made an appointment for the next day with the man to whom he'd left his practice and office on East Sixty-first Street. Not sold it, simply left it in his care. And here he found the situation more honorable but equally troubling. He liked this young doctor whom he'd chosen from the interns at Roosevelt. The style of the office had changed, though—less time for the long consultation so important to older patients, and many of them had left in Lloyd's absence.

Meanwhile, the efficient doctor had acquired a good list of new, younger clients, and these would not want to be switched off to the returning army man. The Colonel must depend now on calling back his old people and finding new ones in midcareer. All this he told his wife, and she did not quite trust it. It sounded more like a premature excuse for failure than a commitment to succeed. "There's plenty of time," she told him. "Why are you in such a hurry?" She had been hurt by the little slights of his wandering attention. And she probed nervously for the more specific causes of his distraction.

"Do you blame me for the change in the children?"

He didn't exactly deny it, though he said they had free wills and whatever they would make of their lives was now up to them. He had come home thinking he had so much to tell, so much to explain, and each time he began, Emma looked to him like a deer sniffing danger. Her fear annoyed him. And in truth, there was nowhere to go with the excitement he held inside him, because it was, in its fullness, a secret. And it was not so much about the past as about possibility.

What could he tell her? Emma didn't want to hear more about the collaboration in the laboratory. When he spoke of the woman who traveled with lice, of his high regard for her, he might as well have been telling Emma it was fascinating to ride on a sewage wagon. But she was not so naïve as to think the war had destroyed his powers of discrimination. If she were a more confident woman, she might have ignored her own suspicion. Instead, it came straight to the fore.

"It was humiliating," she told him.

"What, dear? What was humiliating?"

"Showing it to your mother and the children! As if they couldn't see through to what it really is."

"What the devil are you saying?"

He saw no need of unnecessary explanations and confessions. "The thing is not a medal," she said firmly.

"But of course it is."

"It's not a medal, and you know it! It's a piece of jewelry!"

"Your mother can hear you. And the children."

"So much the better." And she raised her voice to a higher pitch. "It's jewelry. And the army didn't order it made for her. You did! It's so obvious, William."

"How can you talk this way with no knowledge of the facts?"

"I have eyes to see, don't I?. And your mother and the children— they're all talking about it."

"What are they saying?"

"Made in Chaumont, William. And ordered by you."

"Let them talk."

"Then you don't deny it?"

"Why should I deny it? I thought she deserved a medal, and I had one made for her."

"You lied to us, William. Your letter said—"

"But I didn't want you to have the wrong idea."

"And what would the wrong idea be?"

"The devil take it! If you must go on with this attitude about it, I won't discuss it with you."

He turned to leave, but she wouldn't give it up.

"William! How could she deserve a medal in any case?"

"You haven't a notion what you're saying. I won't discuss it."

"From what you've told us, she was a deserter."

"The war was over."

"Willie could have died."

"Emma, it was I who almost let him die. She saved his life."

Emma calmed and took his hand.

"No, no, no, dear," she said. "She made our boy sick. It was her doing."

"Emma, slow down, and think what's happening here. Everything you're saying is based on what I wrote to you. Why would you have more faith in my letters than what I'm telling you now?"

"You have just confessed to misleading us in your letter."

"And from the way you're behaving, I see how right I was."

The argument had become a circular sophistry that had nothing to do with real life, and Emma found a tangent that could open it to more useful debate.

"Well," she said. "I suppose you'll eventually do the right thing."

"What would that be?"

"I mean after a few months. When you recover from all the excitement of your service. William, it's not so surprising that you're still distracted."

"Oh yes?"

"No. And everyone understands your discouragement. When you've settled in again, it will be more clear to you. After all, there can't be a ceremony now. She's disappeared. As time goes on, you will recognize who deserves your medal."

If she was thinking of herself, she never said so. He assumed she meant Nellie, who had begged shamelessly for it. Still, he thought the insinuations were the most unpleasant presumption he'd ever heard from his wife.

/ /

The Peterson situation, so long in question, was solved in a week. The Smiths down the shore had just lost their handyman-driver to his sick mother in Chicago, who moved him in with her after finding him a job as a dairy deliveryman in her city. Mr. Smith came to the Colonel with a delicate deference, as if he might be asking for a family heirloom, and to his surprise, he was encouraged to make his deal with Peterson, and sooner rather than later would be more convenient. The only tears at his departure were shed in the kitchen.

The great pyramid sat sodden and permanent in the front meadow, and Helen was sorry now that she had ever allowed it to be built. From the camel, it spoiled the field of vision that had always been wide open to the bay. She made it known to them all that she wished it were gone, though she would allow neither side the victory that would remove it and make her a partisan. Neither fire nor sale. The Doctor said she enjoyed some dotty notion of herself blindfolded and holding up the family scales of justice.

Louis was no longer interested in the argument, supposing it was settled. It took only a little persuasion by Emma to convince the Doctor that his second son could use his time that spring and summer to better advantage in Cambridge, reading in preparation for the following semester. Louis was gone by April, and this left only Willie and Nellie with their grandmother Mondays to Fridays. The Doctor and Emma joined them on the farm at weekends.

Emma supposed the Great War and her man's part in it were no longer the powerful fixations they had been. She was making it clear enough that a reestablishment of intimacies would be acceptable. He suggested with his own mute signals that he preferred weekends in the country for such activity, when the week's enervating tedium came to an end. No, she signified in return, her face to the wall again in Moriches, she could not bear it in the same house where her mother-in-law slept only a door away. An abstinence continued that actually suited them both. They were each pretending to a resentment that neither of them really felt.

Nellie, beside herself with boredom that summer, had to make do with Willie for conversation. His tales from France, usually stretched beyond credibility, were no longer amusing to her. She did not believe that he would have written anything crude and insulting on the wall of his cell at Noyen, and his claim to a friendship with the Adjutant, Latoni, she assumed, was just to antagonize their father. In that respect, it succeeded marvelously, and now she wished her brother would stop.

Before a Saturday dinner at the farm, Nellie pestered her mother for something special to put on for the evening. Emma had nothing to give her that would fit. She didn't understand what her daughter was driving at, and Nellie wouldn't say. She waited till Emma had gone down to table, then went to her parents' bedroom. She knew her father kept the medal in the top drawer of his bureau. More than a dozen times, she'd been there to look at it, to take it up in her hands and stare at it, to put it around her neck and then examine it in the mirror, to imagine herself in front of a division of soldiers, all standing at attention as it was hung from her neck. She put it on and went down to dinner.

The Doctor was looking down at the plates he was serving and his mother was offering unwanted advice about the appropriate size of everyone's portions. Willie saw it first; he winked and ran a forefinger across his throat. Emma, who thought she must be missing something, looked across the table at Nellie, first in astonishment, then approval.

"Why Nellie, look at you! That's quite lovely on you."

Nellie turned her head away in mock insouciance as her father took notice at last. He put down his serving utensils and stared in disbelief. Without a word, he stood, went to the back of his daughter's chair, and lifted the medal from her neck. He carried it back upstairs and replaced it in the drawer.

The Doctor came back to the dining room as if nothing had happened. He sat down and introduced the price of flax as a topic of conversation. He put it to Willie: "You're interested in working here. Is it possible the farm could ever sustain itself again with flax as staple crop?"

Willie wouldn't have the foggiest idea. It was a mean question on that account, and the Doctor knew it. Seeing all the eyes on him and accusing, he withdrew it.

"Never mind."

He was silent through the first course, brooding on the injustice being done here, the disrespect for something decent beyond their understanding, or their desire to understand. Emma could tell he was seething, though she had no idea the family was in real danger of disintegration.

"Mother," he said as Charlotte brought in a lemon pudding. "Mother, let me ask you. If you were visiting the Smithsonian Institution, say, and you were standing in front of an open case that contained the clothing that President Lincoln wore on the last night of his life . . ."

"Yes?" Nellie said.

"I'm asking your grandmother."

He turned back to Helen.

"Would you have the temerity to take up his top hat and place it on your own head?"

"I doubt very much the case would be open," Helen said.

"The answer is no, of course you wouldn't. There would be some sense of reverence."

Nellie was looking shamefaced into her napkin.

But the others were staring at the Doctor again in unanimous disapproval.

"For heaven's sake, William," Emma said. "What does that have to do with anything?"

He slammed his fist into the table. "Everything!" he shouted. "Why would you toy with the woman's medal? She was a saint! She did miraculous things! Pure in every passion!"

He could not abide these indulged and frightened people who could not credit what he was saying. He believed his wife to be the least tractable of all. She was so certain that ox eyeballs and lice could only be the working tools of a witch. But it was Willie, man of the world after his heroic survival in the French military's penal yards, who dared cross him now.

"Father, are you being a little melodramatic? Wasn't she quite filthy in her work habits?"

A few weeks later, Dr. Lloyd began to receive the most flattering reports on his military service from the Office of the Chief Surgeon, General Ireland. The General had always been quick to compliment Lloyd. Now he was told that his hospital unit had been the only one authorized to wear the commendation patch designed by Pershing's staff for exceptional volunteers. And Ireland said he felt Lloyd deserved something more, to recognize his personal contribution.

After that, there was a note on Ireland's personal stationery. The General said he'd had no idea of the last discoveries Lloyd had made in his laboratory. "Your report on Kessel's fever has been read with much admiration and wonder. My people have never seen this bacterium before. We had some difficulty translating the German sections that were mingled with your French. You never mentioned you spoke Hun. I can't blame you for keeping that quiet. Once we got hold of your meaning, it all made sense. I hope you won't mind that I've given your name to some textbook people, and to the historian on our staff. Will soon get to the rest of the Base 15 laboratory reports. I am much intrigued by all of it. You are quite famous in this office, and I hope to see that fame spread to a wider audience."

Emma told her husband he must take these compliments and use them to advance his career. Why not show them to his hospital colleagues? It might give them a second thought about the shabby way they were treating him. Yes, and an article ought to be written about her husband. The light reflected off him might penetrate, she said, into the dim halls and minds of Roosevelt. It would be something he could frame under glass and hang on the wall of his own office.

What was she thinking? No doctor could do that. It would flout the profession's canons. Besides, such conceit was totally inappropriate. Yes, she admitted, it was a silly idea. But her dismissal of his colleagues as dim only showed how far she was from understanding his situation. In her criticism of them, she was belittling him, as well.

As the Fourth of July approached, word spread across the island from the Moriches post office and drugstore that the Lloyd bonfire would resemble nothing the South Shore had ever seen before. It was a rumor, and Helen's denial only served to spread the false word faster. Willie did nothing to discourage the expectation, and it was assumed again that the family's reticence was a ploy to keep the crowds away. No locals believed such a restriction could apply to them. All the parts were in place for a reprise of the grand celebration.

At dusk on the Fourth, the uninvited began to gather again at the tree line beyond the front meadow. Doctor Lloyd went out to inform them that there would be no fire. As he approached the woods, most of them turned away and disappeared behind trees, ashamed of their curiosity and trespass. A few of the more brazen stood their ground to hear his denial. They could believe the word of Dr. Lloyd. But who, hiding in the woods behind, would believe them? Word and counterword spread through the underbrush as total darkness fell, and the forest was still full of men, their shy wives, and their children, all eager for high flame.

It was a night of low atmospheric pressure, clouds, and sheets of lightning that went dancing across the horizon over Fire Island. The electric storm kept Helen awake and going back and forth from bed to the camel's screen, alert for the work of any arsonist. She was teased over and over again into premature accusation by the heat lightning's repeated flicker.

When a fire-starter finally did appear, she was not aware of his work. He had crawled through Louis's tunnel and poured perhaps several gallons of gas at the center. An explosion was heard, which Helen thought might have been thunder. Light flew around the pile and into the sky, but she never saw it. The fire was out before Helen was at her screen. She said she had seen two men supporting a third, his arms over their shoulders as they helped him away and into the woods.

The pile was far too wet to burn. It was never going to burn. Packed together the way it was, unable to dry, it would sit in place for years if not dismantled. The next day, Louis found some charred bark at the center, clear evidence of the attempt. The whole town knew who had done it. The young man had permanently disfigured himself.

Under the low atmospheric pressure, the fumes of the gas he'd poured had crept along the ground with him, and when he set his spark, he was kneeling right in the edge of his explosion. His face and hands were horribly burned. The sight of him from that time forward, cleaning the waiting room of the Moriches station or sweeping the station platform, was a reminder to all of his mischief. Later, as sympathy shifted, the face of the unmarried man, all brittle and shiny planes drawn tight over the diminished flesh, was more a reminder of the place of the

Lloyds in the community, and the great nuisance that still sat in their meadow, growing punkier as the years passed.

At the end of July, the Doctor heard from General Ireland again. The Chief Surgeon was more effusive than ever, astounded by what he called "the majestic simplicity of your work in the laboratory at Chaumont. The making-do with materials that had to be scavenged in the neighborhood. The inventions and resourcefulness of a man raised in the country as you apparently were." The letter continued:

I don't think it's right for the English and Belgians to be taking all the credit for field development of vaccines that originated with you in that poorly equipped laboratory. There was no one there trained for that exacting work. With all your administrative duties, how did you manage? My daughter is fascinated by the riding horse you used as factory for your serum, the preparation of the ox-eye fluids; it is nothing short of miraculous, and you did it not once but five times! Five previously unknown strains of fever. Five bacteria identified, drawn, and beaten with sera you manufactured on site. This is news we are going to be spreading through the medical corps and among the public.

You are a civilian now, but I trust you will obey one last military order. You will appear on August 7 at noon in front of the New York City Hall to receive a decoration from the Chief Surgeon of the U.S. Army. Your former CO, Colonel Hanson, will be there, and his adjutant, Gerald Latoni, conveniently stationed in New Jersey, will have orders to attend. Please send the names of others it would please you to have on hand.

Yours with greatest admiration,

General Ireland added a postscript:

We are not forgetting your invention of the Lloyd chaise, or your introduction of asepsis into our field manuals as the prescribed treatment against gas gangrene. Congratulations, William. One more thing. I was aware that a three-way vaccine had been prepared for paratyphoid A and B and B typhosis, but how, with your meager materials, did you concoct the four-way serum against the new fevers you identified? Marvelous. One day soon, I want you to come down to Washington to give a lecture on all this at a symposium of our bacteriologists.

Emma, in looking back for cause, gave far too much credit to that evening of the Doctor's furious assault on the family's irreverence. Deeper, she feared the intention to ask her for divorce must have been born months earlier in France. Other irritations merely served as convenient excuses for this pitiless and devastating action he was taking against her and the children. To destroy everything. To have their names removed from the Register. To shock and infuriate his mother, for whom he had spent his life proving his worth. To humiliate his wife in drawing rooms from Washington Square to the end of Long Island. For all this, Emma was inclined to look for fault in herself, and in the end, to compare herself unfavorably with a gypsy medicine woman.

She discovered he had been making plans to leave long before he mentioned divorce to her. In papers she found after he was gone, she learned that as early as May he had asked the hospital to allow him another extended leave. This time, they gave him no guarantee of a position on his return. Early in June, he had booked passage on a Cunard ship that would sail from New York in late August.

Emma remembered very clearly the day she found his ticket, June 17, 1919. And there was no return accommodation. Emma could not understand why he would leave this where she would see it, right next to the medal in his drawer. Of course she would have to ask what was going on. She was furious.

"In Mother's house, Charlotte puts my socks away. I didn't mean for you to find it," he told her. "It didn't occur to me that you would go rummaging through my bureau."

"And when was I going to find out, William? On the day you sailed?"

"Emma, sit down. We'll talk about it now. It's no good. You're not happy. I'm not happy. I'm going to ask you for a divorce."

Happy? She was stunned. Did he think one had to be happy in a marriage? A marriage was forever, happy or unhappy. All the people they moved with, city and country, knew this much. Of course they were happy. Or happy enough. And "going to ask"? Did that mean sometime in the future? Or was he asking now? She hid her face behind her hands, too frightened to weep yet. His hand on her back, consoling her, was only a hateful thing.

He spoke of the wood again, more wistful than angry, as if her lack of support for his position had helped turn the whole family against his will. She didn't care a whit what happened to the wood. Well, she should care, he told her. There was just no unity of purpose in the family anymore, and if she could not be loyal to her husband's position of clear common sense, what was the use of this life they shared?

She fought back. "Listen to your*self.* Is this the flimsy stuff that our marriage hangs on? An argument over a woodpile? No, I won't listen to this. Have you told your mother about it?"

"I think she already knows."

This threw Emma into a passionate fury. "Think she already knows"? He had told his mother before he told her? Outrageous!

She told him to get out. The way he had gone about this—the ticket already bought and set in front of her—she doubted his mind could ever be changed. In fact, it was only a few minutes later that her thoughts raced to the indignities ahead, to self-protection and the children's welfare.

"Of course you will have the best lawyer," he said. "I'll call Delafield tomorrow. You can't go wrong there. I don't want anything, Emma. You must have it all. You, and eventually the children."

Emma looked at him as if he'd lost his mind. She considered the heartlessness of such a generosity. It was a martyr's nonsense that he should have nothing. His mother would never allow it. Nor would Emma. Let her children's father go begging? It was disingenuous of him to suggest it. She suspected he had gone senseless with his wartime infatuation. It was an insane and selfish romanticism, of which she had not thought him capable.

/ /

The Doctor was unable to keep the news of his honor from his family. Willie brought the letter home from the post office, and before it was opened, Emma had guessed the contents. The prospect of his celebrity left a spark of hope. She thought it might give a new push to his stalled medical career, and provide the confidence he needed to come back with chastened heart, and apology, to her care and love.

Instead, the whole thing only made him more morose and testy, even mean-spirited with her, a quality she'd never seen in him before. His brooding that day led him to a solitary walk—he would not even let Nellie go with him. He kicked at the sand on his way down the beach, struck viciously at the sand flies, and came home with his forehead slapped red. For the rest of the weekend, he lounged on his bed and would not let Emma into the room until it was time for her to retire, when he took himself downstairs to sleep on a sofa.

At the Sunday meal, before his trip back to the city, Willie suggested that if he did not want the medal, he should say so, he should renounce it, and he would only be the more admirable in his family's eyes. Emma and Helen would have none of that. Of course he must accept his medal; why wouldn't he? In spite of the Doctor's intention to leave her, Emma had secret hopes for a family celebration in the city; indeed, she clung to the private thought that this could change everything.

On the seventh, the family took the early train from Moriches, all of them uncomfortable in the muggy morning, heading for worse city heat. Colonel Lloyd, in uniform again, appeared to be suffering even more than his mother. She was formal, head to toe, and said she felt like melted sugar being forced through the nozzle—the boned guimpe at her neck—of a confectioner's bag. Louis, in the city since the night before, met them at the station and they set off together in a taxi for lower Manhattan.

The Doctor's first intention on receiving notice of his award had been to refuse it, to explain to the General where the credit belonged. He put that plan aside when he thought of all the explanations that would be required of him, and the investigation that might follow if Latoni was provoked again by recalling the French woman. It only piqued him further that Emma had so little trouble in reading his thoughts.

"You deserve the credit, William, not her. She was reckless; she might have destroyed your hospital." The Doctor's dark brow sent his mother from the living room before his anger could spill over to her. Emma, left alone to be attacked, did not withdraw. She believed she was maneuvering bravely against the grand mistake of his life.

"Listen, William. That miserable little man cannot hurt you. He's lucky he's not in the stockade somewhere. He'll have to stand there at attention while you receive the honors you deserve. And that's an end of it. Your victory in front of him."

Again, he realized that her partial analyses were based on the very information he'd provided her over the months of his service. He oughtn't to blame her for a shallow understanding. But he had brushed aside her arguments and went off across the fields again on his own. Now in the taxi, his shame grew as the minutes before the ceremony dwindled away. If he could get through this day, past the reviewing stand where Latoni already waited with a false salute, or perhaps a disrupting accusation, he believed there might be an honorable way out.

Presently, the pomp of a trumpet and the presentation of the colors raised the hot hair on his neck, and pride took over in that moment he had planned to save for demur. Hanson introduced Ireland. Ireland made the effusive speech. The medal was pinned to his chest. He was not asked to speak. In the face of superiors, one was allowed only a silent, dignified humility. Puffs of smoke rose over the black camera curtains, and a reporter called rudely, "Lloyd? How do you spell that?"

Afterward, Latoni looked past Lloyd's face as he shook his hand with a force meant to crush the fingers. The Doctor was ready for it and gave as good as he got as the man whispered in his ear, "How many have you lost, quacker?" It took the Doctor a moment to understand that Latoni had not been referring to his shrunken practice, but was asking how many civilians his recent medicine had killed.

Emma thought General Ireland's remarks had been disappointingly unpoetic and that the medal itself lacked elegance. It was a small pewter triangle impressed with the obvious caduceus and hanging under a tricolored bar of red, white, and black. Never mind; they were all puffed proud when it was pinned to his chest.

Their little disappointments were saved for the train ride home, when they supposed his closed eyes and deep breathing meant he was fully asleep and could not hear any carping that would diminish his day. He did hear them. He heard Nellie observing that a triangle contained only 180 degrees, the little circle the French nurse would receive contained 360. He was reminded that he must send along a check to her school's capital campaign.

The Doctor gave up his small practice to his associate again, with little hope of ever recovering the loyalty of patients twice deserted. He packed minimal luggage, which his sickened wife complained was more like the duffel of a tradesman than the suitcases of a professional man. That's the way he preferred to travel, he said. In steerage, and once in Le Havre, it would be second- or third-class coaches or no class at all. All this to make clear that it was not a grand tour he had in mind, but a hair-shirted homage.

Emma spoke to a doctor at Roosevelt who specialized in nervous disorders and was told that her husband's behavior—withdrawal from family, from society, from his ordinary standing in the world, and questing after a grail in the clothes of an outsider, a stranger, could be symptoms of a melancholia whose clinical evidence would be sleeplessness, loss of appetite, and, if it continued, the gradual appearance of a palsy in the head and hands. More agitated than ever, she denied that any of these symptoms applied. She did not speak to the specialist again.

Lloyd left her in their city apartment on the morning of August 23 and boarded the Cunard liner that afternoon. Papers for the divorce were being drawn up by her family lawyers, as he'd proposed. Whatever they wrote, he signed. This begged the much larger question of the codicils that might follow his mother's will as a result of William's outrageous and selfish mistake. In the meantime, his cash position was adequate and money beyond his need for this journey had been transferred to a bank in Paris.

The weather was fine, a high-pressure system followed his ship over the Atlantic, and they moved through a sunny haze over a glassy surface for much of the trip. For the first time in his life, Lloyd felt the scorn of stewards. They did not do favors for steerage passengers. To speak with grammatical precision or self-importance in the bows on a lower deck only invited their ridicule, and along with the ship's insolence, Lloyd accepted vomit in the sinks and filth in the toilet bowls as the just deserts not of poverty but of a passenger in penance.

He supposed Emma would go back immediately to Moriches, suffering his mother's company during this humiliating time. To be with her children Nellie and Willie, she would say. But that would be short of the full truth. She would go back to make sure of what she suspected. She would go straight to his bureau to confirm that the medal was missing. At that very moment, it was in the warm palm of his hand, on its way to France. So Emma would beg the children to return with her to the city. Nellie would go with her. Willie would not.

The Doctor's remote diagnosis of the family dynamic was accurate in every particular. The smooth passage was giving him no opportunity to show off his fine sea legs and iron stomach. He shared his small cabin with a smirking college boy who asked for stories of the war and then interrupted them with architectural interpretations of Chartres Cathedral—which the young man had never seen. The Doctor's fresh air was limited to the narrow outside passageway on the same level as his cabin, and covered by the cantilevered deck above. Here he placed the only seat available to him, the folding chair he carried from his cabin each morning. And there he sat to study his Baedeker and his maps of France.

His finger starts at Chaumont. He puts himself in the mind of Jeanne astride the cob, riding north toward home. Does she stop overnight in Joinville? Tell someone she is on her way next to St. Dizier or Houdelaincourt? About Crouen, the home she claimed, he has asked anyone who might know, looked in gazetteers, atlases, tourist maps. No one has heard of the place, nowhere is it written. How can he guess her route if it has no known destination? Crouen? Is he misspelling it?

"You're forty-six, William!" That's what Emma had said. His mother, too, in her own way: "How old are you, William?" Both trying to shame him out of this mad journey. "Where are you going?" He wouldn't tell them. Or couldn't because he didn't really know. "Will you *stay* there?" He had no answer. They were incredulous.

His ship made Le Havre on the evening of September 5. He spent the night there and set out for Chaumont via Paris, just as he'd promised himself, on the hard seats of second-class rail coaches. He was dressed in well-worn gabardine pants and a blue work shirt. His boots were a friendly old pair from numerous hunting seasons on Moriches Bay. Repeated saltwater soaking and drying had left them almost white and well molded to his feet.

The accommodations and the clothes were an invitation to treat him as a common Frenchman. He was disappointed to find that his disguise did not work. He was given away in half a dozen details of hygiene, personal effect, and habit. His mouthful of perfect teeth in a world where the normal tooth was snaggled or missing or eaten with dark rot. The golden rims of his glasses. The clean-shaven face. The gold pocket watch, whose wondrously narrow profile declared itself Swiss. And the fact that he read its hands so furtively and frequently, betraying himself as a man who measured his day in small blocks of time, each of which would have a cash equivalence.

The Doctor's hope had been to shed his officer's pride, to practice a rapport with the common people that would serve him well when he reached Chaumont. Melt suspicions. Make him a friend in the taverns. Get a conversation started over an ale. Was anyone familiar with the name Crouen? A town maybe? A place too small to be on the maps? He supposed his so-so French might be admired at least for its effort, as it had been among the French officer class. Here he was mistaken again; the common Frenchman was even less tolerant of an assault on his language than the ordinary American.

They took him for an eccentric Yankee who dressed poorly and was badly in need of a guide. Their reaction was far more a threat to his purpose than a shock to his self-esteem. There was one man who asked him where his farm was. Lloyd was quite pleased until the fellow made it clear he supposed Lloyd owned the farm and was only out from Paris for a day to see that his tenants were obliging his trust in them with an honest husbandry.

Poor connections and the ordinary confusion of the French railroad cost him three days to Chaumont. He was able to sleep twice, once while propped upright between two missionaries of a Protestant sect from America whose charge was a season on the French rails. They were not familiar with his Mr. Emerson, but they seemed grateful for a respite from the intransigence and scorn of their usual Catholic audience. In exchange for his polite sufferance of their credo, they watched his luggage while he slept. His only other slumber of more than an hour was in the crowded waiting room in Bourges, where he woke with a small boy's hand reaching into his pocket.

In Chaumont, he passed by his hospital, raised his eyes to its whole facade, as if the building would remember him. The only sign it gave back was the lettering raised over the door again, L'HÔTEL RIVE HAUTE. There was no indication of occupancy. Only a concierge in a greasy brown jacket standing in front to announce the dismal obvious—there were vacancies. The man had been trained to say, "Here, here is the place you want," but the Doctor had no intention of staying there. He was soon over the bridge with his two small suitcases and standing at the door of Jeanne Prie's former landlady.

She was amazed. *Dieu! Vous encore!* And then she seemed to be saying, Have you come down so far in the world? The chief of the hospital, like this? No car? No driver? Your people are gone long ago. You are hungry. Come in. Hurry up! What do you want here? *Qu'avez-vous?* He was overwhelmed as she rattled on in her greeting of contradictions—impetuous, scolding, solicitous, impatient. It was more difficult making himself understood.

He wanted a room for the night. He wanted the room that the nurse had stayed in. No, it did not matter that it had not been cleaned. She said she had not even gone back into the room since then. Not even to change the sheets. Fine. Just as it was when the nurse left it? This was more than he could have hoped for. No, no, no. She mustn't change a thing.

The woman's face lit with a sudden recognition. "You want to see the nurse," she said with a sly grin and an accusing finger raised against his chest. "*Trop tard.* You cannot. You are too late. Do you remember?" Once more, she mimed Jeanne's departure on horseback. She made him sit at her kitchen table, served him a vegetable broth and a crust of bread, then poured him a tumbler of wine as freely as water.

After fussing over his food, she began to speak rapidly again, so quickly and with abbreviated slang, only a native could have followed her. It was clear enough she was scolding him. Attacking with her finger in his face, raising her voice in a whipping staccato of criticism. He thought she was saying that he should be ashamed of himself, coming back here. After mistreating the woman. Not a cheap lady to be trifled with. What did he expect? That he would use this house for his pleasure again? No, she would not allow it. He could stay the night and then he must go. Out! Out!

When she slowed, he was more certain of her meaning, though his translation lacked idiomatic ease. He wanted to pay her something. "Yes," she said, "how much do you pay at the hotel?" She thought better of her question. "Never mind; you will pay what I tell you. Out tomorrow! Coming and going! Here and there! Shame! The nurse left for away. That's always!" The finger waving in his face like a speedy metronome slowed to an obbligato of sorrow for their mutual loss. "You will not find her. She doesn't want it. That's always!"

Could he make the old woman understand: "Do you know where she is? Do you know where she went?"

This only set her off again into a stinging list of bad names for him. If she despised him so thoroughly, why had she fed him, and why would she allow him a room for the night? Perhaps it was only for the opportunity to observe and rebuke him. What could the old lady know? He'd be off the next day, following Jeanne's trail all the way to Crouen, perhaps close to Germany, maybe farther north to the Belgian border, wherever the mystery village might be, the place too small to be noticed by the state's geographers. If justice were blind, she'd put Crouen on their maps one day. After the medals, one day a clarifying beatification and a shrine where they least suspected it. He caught himself gathering wool again. The woman waved a hand in front of his face.

"Crouen?" he asked her.

"*Oui!*" she answered.

She's heard of it!

"*Crouen? Oui!*"

"Where? Where is it?"

Now she was confused, waving her hand against his nonsense. He took the maps from his luggage and spread one on the kitchen table. He pointed to Chaumont. She nodded. Then he tried "Crouen?" again. He spelled it for her. She looked up at him with a vacant grin.

He was pleading with his whole face, hands raised.

She became angry once more, and was off on another tirade. She told him about her daughter in Contrexéville, who expected to go to America. *Très jolie!* Instead, the American soldier gets her with child and goes himself to America. She said he must go to Contrexéville and see her for himself, then decide.

Decide what? If he would have the girl himself? Even a country missing so many of its men could not be so pathetic.

She said, "No more is always." Or something like it. He was ready to go up to his room, Jeanne's room, to look for anything she might have left behind. To sleep in her bed. As if he might pick up the trail's scent in her soiled sheets.

The old lady came up the stairs behind him and tried to follow him into the room, but he stood in her path, then sent her away muttering. She had not lied. Not a chair had been moved. There was dust on everything. When he turned back the bed's counterpane, he could feel the dampness, even see a little speckling of mildew. He sniffed at the pillow. It made him sneeze. He pulled the sheets down and noticed stains at the center. He stripped to his shorts and climbed in.

He was rolling over and back, gradually turning the dank bedclothes warm in the restlessness of his fantasy. He doubted Crouen would be his final destination, only the place where they were sure to know Jeanne's whereabouts. She would have gone to some university town large enough to nourish her curiosity and contain her energies. That might just as easily be in Belgium or Germany as in France.

How was he going to travel? If he knew how to ride, he would hire just a horse and go farmer-style, as Jeanne had done. A car would only spoil his chances, speeding past hundreds of people who might have aided her journey or noticed her direction, people who could help him. He would miss the signposts that she would have studied and been led by.

Trains would be hopelessly bound to their tracks. He had it in mind that he must learn by going where he had to go. That her journey, if he followed it slowly enough, would make itself clear to him. Though he would never admit it, the whole affair hung by this slender thread of his intuition, and the occasional advice of a stranger.

What he had in mind was a horse and simple carriage, light and well sprung with single traces, its seat closed under a small cab against foul weather. He had a clear picture in mind of just such a gig. He used to see it displayed for hire in front of the hostelry across the river. He didn't care what it cost, even if they made an American buy it before they let him drive it out of town. The horse, too, whatever it would be. Anything that wasn't lame. First thing in the morning.

He must have been rolling around in the bed in a distracting way, because the woman below began to knock on her ceiling, and he was shamed as he recognized his stubborn state of arousal in the musky sheets. What would the woman downstairs think now?

His dreams that followed were of easy and rewarding travel, no turnstiles, no tollgates, only the godspeed of friendly publicans and righteous farmers. Unthreatened, euphoric, he sensed he was being honored by those he passed in the road for his ennobling mission. On waking next morning, he was reminded of Mr. Peck's frequently repeated adage to his St. Mark's boys: "If your dream is light, the day before has passed in purity." As an adult, he found it not fatuous, but consoling.

It took two days to hire the single sulky and find a driving horse. He spent the equivalent of a hundred dollars, knew he had been soaked, but considered the money well spent. After an argument and another outrageous settlement, he was allowed to stay a second night in his room. Though not before he had promised to include Contrexéville in his itinerary. He set off for Joinville in the afternoon.

The horse walked out on the lazy side of brisk but moved with good form, and could be coaxed into a trot with a slap of the rein on his backside. The Doctor made a feint once toward the carriage whip. The horse sprang to the side and ran into the ditch, and Lloyd never reached for the whip again.

The road ran due north, following the west bank of the river. In an hour and a half, he'd passed Bologne and was in Vignory. He stopped in the town center, tethered his horse, and sat on a bench, waiting for someone to approach and ask his business. Strollers on the common gave him a wide berth. He called to one of them, who stopped reluctantly to answer his questions, but first he would have to answer himself.

"Who are you?"

"I am a doctor."

"Where are you going?"

"I don't know."

"You wait here," he was told.

The man was gone, over the green and down the street on the other side. Ten minutes later, he was back, two others with him. "This is our mayor," he said. "He will speak to you."

The mayor introduced himself, then presented the other two as the town clerk and a councilman. "I will show you your office," he said, motioning for Lloyd to follow along with them. "It will be no problem for you. The people pay what they can—eggs, cheese, vegetables, bread . . ."

"Meat!" the councilman interrupted.

The mayor looked alarmed. "And the town pays the rest," he went on. They were taking him up the steps beside a poultry shop and into an office with a tiny waiting room.

"We had two doctors here when we needed only one, and now we have none. This will be your office. You can start tomorrow if you like."

"I think Madame Genseille has cancer," the clerk said.

"Shut up," the mayor told him. "What about your own wife?"

The man threatened to run against the mayor in the next elections, and the councilman promised to back him.

"Taisez!" The mayor hushed both of them. "What will the doctor think of Vignory?" He turned to Lloyd. "You must buy a house, but this is no problem. You will bring your wife; you need an assistant."

"The town will give her milk," the clerk added. "Just as we do for the water engineer and the sweeper."

The mayor told Lloyd to ignore the man, and he began to extol Vignory's bracing and health-giving climate. The Doctor discovered later that they knew who he was, knew that he'd been boss of the military hospital in Chaumont, and were allowing him the anonymity of his transparent disguise to humor him, to keep him at whatever cost in Vignory.

Had they heard of Crouen? Could they show him on a map?

The city fathers looked at one another as if they doubted anyplace could have such a name. They advised him to stay in their Hôtel de la

Gare that night. They would introduce him to his patients in the morning. When they saw that he had no intention of accepting their offer, or even staying with them for another hour, the mayor pointed him across the river to Vouecourt and Roches, and the other two suggested he keep straight north beside the river all the way to Joinville and beyond.

On separate postcards to his mother and estranged wife, he described his new French hosts as curiously deceitful. "They deny the existence of a place, then send me in two directions to find it. *Incroyable!* Several months ago, this was a nation of patriots. Now they are all at one another's throats again. *C'est la vie française.*"

The Doctor continued due north for no other reason than consistency and a suspicion that a straight line of travel would have appealed to Jeanne, as well. He passed Gudmoi, where a tinker told him he must surely run into Crouen if he kept to the same road. Five miles beyond, close to Fronville, a woman in black, who was walking south, waved him down. She seemed surprised that she had got him to stop, but asked if he could please carry her across the river to St. Urbain. She said if he was looking for Crouen, he must pass through Joinville. He must listen to all she could tell him about Joinville, because the place could make much trouble for a foreigner if he did not know whom to talk to— Monsieur Goncourt at the Goncourt Café-Tabac and any Lanvelle, her family name. He must avoid les Tamierres, les Mormonds, les Nogents, and les Fronds. The surnames were offered with scorn. These people might lie, steal, and cheat him if he gave them the opportunity.

Madame Lanvelle was a small woman, and Lloyd let her squeeze next to him on the driving seat, where it was easy for her to point the way. She had lied, too. St. Urbain was not her destination. Just a little farther, she told him, but soon they had gone several miles east to Poissons, where she showed him a few small coins and said these should be enough to take her on to Germay, seven miles distant.

Was she going to Germay?

Yes.

Yes, it turned out, and still farther.

The compounded dishonesty only amused him. This was just the sort of detour he'd anticipated. Byways and gossip enough to redirect him. Did the name Jeanne Prie mean anything to her? How about Lucienne de Crouen?

She said the names sounded familiar. She thought perhaps the two of them could be found in Lezéville. And at last it was clear that Madame Lanvelle's real destination, her home, was Lezéville. It was after dark when they arrived at her cottage. Her daughter, her only family surviving the war, was waiting for her in the open doorway, large-eyed and hollow-cheeked. Thin, like a tight-wound spring when she saw what her mother had caught and brought home.

They made a bed for him in their attic room, where a squirrel had to be chased out to create a credible vacancy. For supper, they killed their rabbit and picked a squash, the only September yield of their garden. While they prepared a meal for him, they tried to convince him that Joinville was altogether a place to avoid. If he stayed here, they could give him work and a home.

Not in the attic, the daughter promised. It was no use wandering about France with no destination, she said.

He asked again about Jeanne Prie and Lucienne de Crouen. Without coaching, the daughter covered her mother's story with another layer of invention. She believed they had lived here once but had moved away because of their *brouille*, their dispute, with Riesere at the café.

"Jeanne and Lucienne are the same person," he told them.

"You would know better than we about that." The older woman shrugged.

They were showing him how easy it would be to step into another man's family. Always the same. So many men missing. He saw with some shame he was even to be given a choice which generation he might choose for his bed. Anything to keep him here making the hay, milking the cow, making the garden produce its quota. At breakfast, Madame Lanvelle suggested that two meals and a night's lodging must surely be worth his morning's help patching their roof. He obliged them, climbing up with a broom and a pail of tar, and they shouted instructions at him from below with petulance, as if he were theirs for good.

"Look, you silly cabbage, where you have missed!"

"Tomorrow, he will do around the chimney," said the daughter, as he came down the ladder.

But he was leaving them. Their voices grew louder with complaint and censure as he readied his rig, and when he trotted his horse out of their yard, they called on several saints to plague his journey for his ingratitude. He assumed the woman's information about Joinville was equally prejudiced, and probably useless. His maps showed him there was no shortcut; he must retrace his journey of the day before.

The following evening, he sat in Goncourt's Café in Joinville, well fed, and studying the clientele for a likely informant. He'd had a double dinner at the small hotel across the street where he'd taken lodging for the night. Now he relaxed with a Pernod and water, sipping like a regular with elbows on the bar.

"Doctor Lloyd," Goncourt greeted him.

He had hoped to reveal his identity and mission slowly, perhaps after buying a drink for the man who sat next to him. A fellow on his other side took his cap off to speak: "The road to Lezéville can be dangerous this time of year, eh?"

Lloyd, surprised again, asked why.

Down the bar, another said, "You never know what you'll find asking for a ride that way."

The others joined in laughter, and Goncourt, probably afraid the Doctor would leave and spoil the evening's business that could be attracted by his presence, poured him a complimentary drink and wished him health.

"Animals in the attic over that way?" someone asked.

More laughter.

"No! The squirrels get put in the soup."

"The squirrels prefer that to her bed."

Across the café, a man who had been keeping to himself rose and brought his empty beer mug to the bar. The others turned, their eyes fixed on him as he came. He was curly-haired, stocky, and proud, striding across the floor, surely a hero of the eastern front. His lips were swollen and a scar ran from his cheekbone to his chin. He carried himself as if he'd won a war single-handed, and the others in the room paid him the honor of a sudden silence. He wore a frayed shirt of faded purple, sleeves rolled, and his sunburned face and arms shone like polished stone in the dark room. He was coming straight for Lloyd. At the last moment, he reached around him to set his glass on the bar and spoke into his ear.

"You people came too late, and now you come too early."

With that, he left the café, and the others began to speak again, softly at first, and then in normal voice, as if their conversation was safer as the man receded from them. Goncourt told Lloyd he should not concern himself with the departed Monsieur Thivet. "Justin Thivet has no café. I don't know why he comes here."

For a while, the Doctor sipped in silence. He supposed Goncourt had given his patrons a signal to leave the American alone. But when Lloyd asked the fellow next to him for directions to Crouen, the rest took it as a cue for group participation. They'd been waiting for their chance, and all began to speak at once. They were interrupting and contradicting one another, and Goncourt banged his fist on the bar, calling for quiet.

"These fools don't know anything about it," he said. "They will lead you in circles." But they knew something, and Goncourt obviously preferred that they keep it to themselves.

Lloyd left the café, supposing his goal must lie farther to the north. He believed his method of search had proved itself useful, if demeaning. In bed, he gave thanks for his faithful gray horse, which had not gone lame, and which might have to pull him all the way to Belgium.

There is no rationale for his turn to the east from Joinville. He only knows he is not welcome where he is and the farther he gets from the hospital where he was chief, the more likely the people will be to allow him to blend with them. And the more apt they are to listen to his story, to his description of the woman he seeks. He could go north to St. Dizier, but on his map, that town is peppered with a dozen churches and crosshatched with streets, all indicating a place of such size and sophistication that formal introductions might be required.

He was halfway to Houdelaincourt, in the village of Saudron, when he sensed he was way off course. He couldn't say why, but he knew something was wrong, and that he was going to turn back. He found a house that would give him bed and a breakfast, and he took an early-evening supper in the village's only café. By now, his effect on the people was almost humorous in its predictability.

Once more, their initial reserve was close to rudeness. But when they had established his education and his rootlessness, when he told them he was not sure where he was going, he became their prey. Here two old fellows plied him with generosity at the bar and then declared the availability of the schoolmaster's position in the village.

In France, he was a wanted man everywhere. Everywhere except Joinville, where they had almost pushed him out of town. The only place where he'd been made to feel he'd be one man too many. That's what was wrong. That's why he was going back. The two old salesmen for the Saudron school job did not give up easily. They made him promise to visit the schoolhouse in the morning, and said he wouldn't be disappointed in the quality of his dozen students; the granddaughter of one of these men was a state-recognized scholar of botany.

Next morning, Lloyd was rolling west again, behind the steady trot of the gray, and thinking this time he would ignore Madame Lanvelle's advice completely. He would make Tamierre's Bar-Tabac in Joinville his center of operation. This time, he meant to stay in the town until they became used to him, until he became more than a curious embarrassment, until they gave in to his persistence and began to answer his questions with candor. It might take several weeks. Though with that much time, they were likely to satisfy his curiosity on their own, without his being intrusive.

At the hotel, they gave him the same room as before, on the second floor, front and center. Its small balcony over the street made a useful observation post, where he could stand behind the curtains and follow pedestrian and street traffic. His first evening back in Joinville, Monsieur Tamierre welcomed him as if the town had been expecting his return. He called Monsieur Mormond from the back of the room to join them in a beer and a salute to the Doctor's war duty in Chaumont. Lloyd recalled Mormond as another name Madame Lanvelle had warned him against.

This man was a bit of a peacock, especially proud of his memory for the several hundred local families and their intertwining histories, their *brouilles,* their feuds going back generations, and the blood connections and intermarriage that confused the *brouilles* and fortunately made the social fabric a piece of knitting rather than a quilt. *Comprenez?*

Yes, Lloyd understood, but what could Mormond tell him about a place called Crouen?

"Not a place. Can't you understand? It's a family."

"Do you know this family?"

"Certainly. Everyone knows them. The daughter brought them a certain fame. He was the undertaker. He's dead, of course. The mother still does laundry."

"But where can I find the daughter?"

"Doctor Lloyd, why do you play this game with us? She is no stranger to you. She worked with you at the hospital in Chaumont."

"You mean she lives here in Joinville?"

"But she is not alone, monsieur."

"Where is she?"

"The house is over the canal. The little farm is beyond that. They are happy enough."

"Her laboratory is here in the town? Her colleagues?"

"What are you talking about? She has no laboratory. She has no colleagues. The Sûreté sent a man here to look for her. Now they are looking for him. Do you understand?"

Even as Mormond gave Lloyd specific directions to the house, he was warning the doctor to stay away. The man, he said, had been with the Special Attack—no helmets, just knives, bare knuckles, and the occasional grenade—and was still fighting the war. "You should stay away from him. I told you, they are happy enough."

Lloyd's sudden depression was visible in every corner of his face, which had lost all animation. It gave the lie to the selfless purpose of his travels.

"*Un peu fatigué, monsieur?*"

Mormond tried to pour him a pastis, but he covered his glass. He walked to his hotel a little wiser about his nurse. It made sense to him now that she would have set off so often from the hospital for Joinville; it was her home, after all. That she would have known the people so well. That the national celebrity he'd imagined for her was simply an obvious familiarity in her local countryside and villages.

The next day, he went on foot rather than show off his horse and surrey. It was a walk of several miles, but it was nothing to find them. There was a Jersey cow grazing untethered in the yard, two goats, and a few chickens. A kitchen garden with several rows of greens still producing, and some tomato plants with the fruit more green than red in September, unlikely, he thought, to ripen before a frost.

The cottage was enviably peaceful, a square pile of ancient whitewashed stone, thatched, its casement windows shuttered against the midmorning sun. Dead nasturtiums hung from front window boxes, and the shoots of a wild rosebush by the door were flowerless, brown, and sere. A man and woman were watching him from the field beyond, leaning on pitchforks beside the haystack they'd been building.

As he came closer, he could see their clothes were dark with sweat. He recognized Jeanne first, short and robust, her face sunburned, her bare red arms well toned from her country labor. He could tell she was still cutting her own hair, which was chopped into another careless thatch. And something else was the same, the brown army pants. Her wet blouse was hanging out of them and unbuttoned at the top. A shameless airing against the heat of the work, and she made no effort to cover herself on his account. Perfectly at ease in the hay field, she stared back as if to ask, What do you want? Why are you looking at me?

By then, he had recognized the man as Thivet from his night in Goncourt's café. Justin Thivet. Her husband? No one had said so. Thivet spoke first, with an open contempt.

"There is no one sick here. We have no need of a doctor. Why don't you check the tongues chez Lanvelle?"

The man stuck his own tongue way out and said, "Ahhhh," right in Lloyd's face. Jeanne grabbed Thivet's arm and shook her head. "Not this," she told him, "not this again."

Lloyd said he would like to talk to her, that he had something to show her, something to present to her.

"Where do you keep your experiments? Who do you work with now?"

Thivet stepped between them.

"She doesn't have to speak to you. She did nothing wrong. They send people to ask her questions. Some of them never go home, eh?"

"Could we talk at the house?" Lloyd asked her.

"As you like."

"*Non!*" Thivet said.

But she pushed past her man and led Lloyd back to the cottage. Inside, there was even less than he'd expected—furniture minimal and rough-hewn, a plaster crucifix over the door, and a faded print of Virgin and child over the mantel. The downstairs was a single room with two chairs, and two storage boxes against the walls served as guest seating. She told him to sit and then brought him a glass of milk.

Should I drink it? he wondered. Are the cow's teats clean?

Jeanne sat facing him in one of the chairs and told him to get on with it. Directly behind her, Thivet's face appeared in the window, his gaze set on Lloyd, and he remained there the whole time they were speaking. Jeanne must have known the man was watching everything, but she never turned her head. Her blouse was still loose and revealing in a way that would have shocked his family.

He had a hard time beginning, and she helped him.

"Don't worry. This is my house. But what do you want, William? Why do you come here now?"

He couldn't bring himself to state the selfish truth—that he was eaten with envy and mad to commune with the woman who hid behind this bucolic mask. Sitting on the chest, he supposed that a thousand lice, labeled with the diseases they carried, must be compartmented within a smaller case beneath him, along with her microscope and the glass paraphernalia of her craft.

"Look at you, William. Still afraid. Even afraid of the milk. You don't believe I keep the cow clean?"

That she could still see through him so easily was only a further incitement, another challenge to shed his reserve and get to the business of the moment, which was no business at all. He pulled the gold medal from his pocket, carried it across the room to her—Thivet watching every step—and hung it around her neck.

"For what you did," he said. There was hardly time to whisper a prepared line of praise in her ear.

He knew it would be red flag to Thivet's bull. She removed the ribbon immediately, and right away the man was standing in the doorway. There was no chance to explain the medal's full meaning to her. Thivet was blocking his exit with a leer that invited Lloyd to move in any direction he dared.

"*Non!*" Jeanne told her wild soldier again. "The Doctor is leaving."

Thivet stepped aside and the three of them went outside together, Lloyd watching his back as Jeanne led them across the yard to the grazing cow.

"*Regardez, Suzanne,*" she said. "See what the Doctor has brought you." Jeanne hung the medal from the cow's neck and admired it there for a moment, then turned and went back into the house without another word for him. Lloyd turned down the path to the canal. Thivet chuckled and stood watching the Doctor's retreat until he was out of sight.

In Manhattan, the news of a divorce within the lists of the social directory had a crushing effect on the families involved. It was as damaging to the rogue husband's mother and her family as to Emma and the Delafields. It was a kind of death without funeral, and it produced its full share of censure and pity.

For Helen, it was as if a daughter had died. That would be Emma, whom Helen's close friends would not dare mention in Helen's presence. And for Emma herself, it meant that the world she knew in the city had ceased to exist. People would not embarrass her with invitations to any of their gatherings, and if they did, she would not have embarrassed herself by accepting.

Emma never had been one for parties, but through fall and winter seasons, the opportunities had been plentiful, for bridge, for teas, for dinners, and the chance to refuse was the expected privilege of a woman of her place. She could be expected year after year at the Christmas Assembly. She kept the Assembly invitations as souvenirs, and her dance lists from those occasions. As a child, Nellie had liked to rub her fingers over the embossed lettering and read the names of all the men who had honored her mother, sailing her over a grand ballroom in their fast waltzes. A researcher in the family archive could see that even the Christmas Assembly invitations ceased after 1918.

Nellie was several months late starting back to Chapin in 1919. It was not the school's fault, but her own fear of going back to face the teachers, who would fuss over her grand misfortune. Worse were her friends, who had the story of her father's second expedition to France from their parents. Whether cold to her or overfriendly, Nellie couldn't abide them either way, and for much of that season she stayed home and cried with her mother. She was missing her second consecutive year of school.

Emma thought it would be cruel to force her to go back right away, and the chance to commiserate appealed to her. When other ladies walked out of their apartments and took the air up Park Avenue, Emma, with Nellie in hand, ducked over as far as Lexington before she felt free to venture uptown in the protecting bustle of commerce that spilled from the markets onto the sidewalks. When they weren't weeping together in the apartment, they read to each other from a long and uplifting novel of a crusading woman who was breaking through the teary adversities of an undeserved singularity to a final honor.

Helen was taking Emma's side in every issue raised on the way to the pending divorce, and Emma wrote to her at Moriches, blaming Nellie's depression and school problems squarely on the Doctor. She told Helen she'd had nothing but the one postcard from William, and so she had nothing to pass on to her, or to either of her sons. Helen advised her to be a realist, to find a cause, a passionate avocation, and involve herself in it for life. It was her information, she said, that some abandoned women tortured themselves with the notion there was a second chance to launch themselves in society. It could only frustrate them and make them bitter forever.

Helen did not tell Emma that she was receiving more mail from the Doctor, ever dutiful to his mother, even in his shameful wandering, mail that would only have been gall in the draft that Emma was being forced to swallow. William wrote that with some difficulty he had found the French woman, Lucienne de Crouen, and presented her with the medal in a small ceremony at her country home. Lucienne, he said, had received the honor with all the modesty he'd expected of her. "It must have touched her deeply, and in ways she could not express."

And yet, he said, he was concerned about Lucienne's welfare. All celebrities have their detractors. And if prophets are seldom recognized in their own countries, imagine the skepticism in their own villages. "Lucienne has a man who works for her in the fields and around the house. A grizzled veteran whom I think she keeps there to protect her, nothing more. After all, there must be residual resentments from the war, whose fickle winds blew her across conventional boundaries. When I presented the medal, my encomium was brief but, I think, to the point: 'Your enemy was the microbe; your flag was science.'

"I won't leave Joinville till I'm satisfied that neither state nor army, nor some false friend, can bring her harm or disgrace. I remain here in her town, though out of her sight, as a potential witness to her honorable service. It seems beyond reason, but I believe she actually thinks there are people close by who would like to see her prosecuted and her reputation destroyed."

One morning, Emma looked in her glass and said to herself, I'm glad he's gone. He doesn't deserve me and I don't deserve him. The family was amazed at the swift change in her outlook. The arbitrariness of the turnaround filled her with a new pride of self-control; she was pleased to think herself contented. She showed a nerve they hadn't seen before, volunteering at Roosevelt Hospital, taking chances in rooms where she was forbidden, bringing conversation to men and women with uncertain complaints. Purposely risking her health, and without fear. Hadn't William done the same?

When Nellie called her transformation "a gallant generosity," Emma reminded her that she neither wanted nor deserved pity. It would only deny her own responsibility in the divorce, which she was ready to declare. She told the children they should feel free to communicate with their father their full affection, that some passions went beyond selfishness and could be admired for their honesty; they should look at his life that way. If this was a pathetic sophistry, it was completely ingenuous and had the marvelous effect of making them all spring to her side of the family equation, drawn to her selfless courage.

She simply decided one day that she would no longer burden the children with a choice of right or wrong in their father's disappearance. It was neither right nor wrong. It simply was, she told each one of them in separate sessions without tears, in a cold appraisal of reality. Without respect for their father, they only diminished themselves, she said.

"Nellie," she told her daughter, "I was wrong. We cannot go on forever blaming your melancholy on him. It will take you nowhere. And believe me, you are going places, all over the world."

For Louis, she forecast a life of intellectual achievement, but first he must give up his resentments. A great weight of anger, she predicted with acumen, would prevent him from being the editor or writer he was capable of becoming. She knew him perfectly and understood why he would never confess to such an ambition. Far too great a chance of failure. His pages were still secrets locked in a desk.

In the case of Willie, he came to her. He told Emma before anyone else that his forced conscription and time in France had not been the disaster the family supposed it to be. He was glad for the experience. He knew now that a near-fatal disease was a chance to be reborn in the world. This was as near to transcending his complacence as her son ever got, and she took the opportunity to tell him that while talents came in many wrappers, his father had been trained to recognize but few of them. "You were made for the fresh air, Willie, not for an office. Forget your quarrels with him. That's the way to begin. You have nothing to fear from your father."

She'd never been such a Pangloss. By setting the whole family free to their desires this way, she had unwittingly focused their loving attention on herself. They worried so much about her loneliness, fussed and visited so often, that she had to scold them into staying away. She was going into the hospital every day, making her mercy visits, breaking rules right and left, sliding past the nurses' stations, immortal as any microbe hunter.

Lloyd settled into Joinville in the same room in the small hotel across the street from Goncourt's Café. He engaged the room for three months, and this planned tenancy was immediately a subject of discussion in Goncourt's, Tamierre's, and the hotel's small restaurant, where the Doctor took most of his meals. For the time being, his gray and surrey were a nuisance. He wanted to walk the streets and country roads, not to make a showy display when he went about the town.

He reached an agreement with the hostelry two blocks from his lodging, whereby they would maintain the horse and carriage. In return for this upkeep, they had the right to offer the gig in rent until such time as the Doctor should ask for its return. A very favorable deal for the hostelry, which was owned by Tamierre's cousin. The arrangement did immediate service to Lloyd's reputation as a fair businessman and gave him new standing in the town as a man they'd be pleased to trade with.

But Lloyd was not there for business, and his daily routine left everything about him open to speculation. A tourist? They couldn't be deluded into thinking a tourist would settle in Joinville. An American doctor in love with France, waiting for a license to practice among them? Only a fool would believe that. He took breakfast and the morning paper at the hotel before walking out into the country. Was he just rusticating? Using them to ease his new life as a widower? It was Emile Nogent in Goncourt's who speculated that the Doctor's wife had died, and in transmission of this report across town to Tamierre's, it became a matter of fact.

Often missing lunch on his walks through the country, Lloyd was in the habit of double supper portions at the hotel restaurant. Then it was off to Tamierre's, where they were becoming so used to him that the regular customers left a stool in the middle of the bar for his use, the better to seek his advice, and comfort from their incurable complaints—rheumatism, headache, dyspepsia, or urination reduced to a painful trickle.

Tamierre saw the Doctor's uneasiness when cast as the café's medical adviser, and sometimes he arranged his escape, taking him by the arm to a table at the side of the room and offering his own conversation, or the company of someone else he assumed would suit a man of Lloyd's education. It was not long before the Doctor was introduced to Masirot, the retired teacher and principal of Les Petits Oiseaux de Joinville, the primary school. He was the man, Lloyd discovered, that he should have gone to in the first place.

Masirot was in his seventies, lively and talkative and a fitting conversational companion, ready to explain his admiration for the most remarkable student he'd ever taught, Lucienne de Crouen, or Jeanne Prie, as he preferred to call her. She had chosen that name for herself, he said, with some help from him. But that, he said, was something else altogether.

Masirot had retired from the school ten years earlier, though he'd been there and in his prime as a teacher when Lucienne entered the little academy in its first grade. He remained her teacher until she left after her third year. "Much too quick for the other children," he said. She had returned to him for encouragement and advice long after she escaped Joinville to live in Belgium with her aunt. His was her safe house when she returned for visits with her brother, Roger. Until Roger had his accident and was found floating in the canal.

"You must understand," Masirot said, "the parents were soft in the head, and not gentle on that account, but morbid and dangerous. The father was the poor man's undertaker. He rubbed his children's faces in death. Shut them into parlors and bedrooms with his corpses." After each embalming, Masirot said, their mother went into their rooms at night, wrapped in a sheet and wailing as a ghost on its way to hell for a sinful life.

"Jeanne told me something like that," Lloyd said.

"You didn't believe her?" *Eh bien.* The boy came to my school, as well. He didn't have her spirit. He couldn't defy them. There was nothing to be done for him."

He spoke as if he had been Jeanne's surrogate father, a relationship that had never been hidden from the Crouen parents, who were not pleased with it. Masirot might still be the one Jeanne would go to in distress. Or with one of life's troubling mysteries.

The Doctor was onto something now. He understood how fortunate he was in this new friendship. If he could just bide his time here, if he could just wait patiently for the details, the old schoolmaster would reconstruct the life of his nurse in all its unlikely turns, right up to the moment. It didn't matter how long it would take. Lloyd had all the time in the world.

Justin Thivet came into the tavern, and conversation stopped along the bar. He looked across the room at Lloyd, called to Tamierre to draw him a dark beer, and sat alone at a far table. No one joined him and he spoke to no one else, only stared from time to time at Masirot and the Doctor.

"This isn't his bar," Masirot said. "Someone told him you were here, and he has come to see for himself."

"Should I be worried?"

"The Germans were."

"He had a fame of his own? The Germans knew him?"

"It was different in Bulgaria, you understand. Hills, cover, raiding sorties. Trenches, but not like ours. They knew his face well."

In the several weeks that followed, Lloyd made a closer friend of Masirot. Just as he'd hoped, the old man made an open companion, offering his opinions and his knowledge like a cautious historian, always distinguishing between the two. His information made a credible fit with what Lloyd had learned from Jeanne herself. Though he knew she had lied to him when she said she was from Crouen. From Crouen the father, yes, and out of Madame Crouen. But there was no such town.

Masirot acknowledged there were parts of Jeanne's life that one would never be certain about. She had left Joinville so young and in such nervous distress that even she was not completely clear about her childhood. The parents had angrily removed her from his school over a matter of historical fact. They insisted the Children's Crusade had been ordered by the voice of God heard in a church in Contrexéville, the father's birthplace.

"And the more recent time in Belgium?" the Doctor asked on another occasion. "After the Germans had stormed in?"

"I think she would like us to believe there is a patriotism that is ignorant of uniforms and boundaries. If we can't accept that, the rest is none of our business."

"Yes, but do you accept that?" Lloyd asked him.

"Of course the Sûreté cannot accept it. They are still investigating so long afterward. It can be dangerous work for them, with Thivet so adept at hiding his indiscretions."

"But you—do you accept?"

"Monsieur Lloyd, it is a matter of trust. You've seen enough to decide for yourself. If you don't trust, why are you here? She is not an exact copy of Joan of Arc, you know. She is of her own time."

Why would he say that?

"Because, for Jeanne d'Arc, religion and France were cloth of the same thread. For Lucienne, nothing was so simple."

"But why must you compare them?"

"You know very well she compares herself. Her name, her saints, her voices, her mission above all, her father's distrust, the martyrdom of her body to her cause."

"Her body?"

"To heat, but not to flame, monsieur. She is no Jeanne d'Arc."

Masirot's presumption did not sting the Doctor, but woke him to the exciting truth of her nature. Others knew, as well.

"What of her name?" he asked, to slow the man down.

"I told you," he said, "she changed it herself." He explained that her aunt, visiting from Belgium, had seen the damage being done to the children. She took Lucienne to Domrémy that she might be inspired in her adversity with the example of Jeanne d'Arc. Lucienne was eight years old at the time.

"She came into school the next week quite full of her trip, and so excited. But disturbed by the statue of Jeanne she had seen at the pre-served home of La Pucelle. The sculpture was short and full and plain of face, kneeling in cumbersome armor. What was the matter with the statue? I asked her. It had hair that flowed like a swollen river down to the buttocks, she said, while everyone knew that Jeanne d'Arc's hair had been short and black like her own. Otherwise, the statue was a replica of herself, she said, in every detail. Even her aunt had said so.

"It overwhelmed her. Even as a small child, she felt chosen. It made the other children resentful. I thought I could take the pride out of her with a switch. I was wrong. I apologized. She said she understood why I had done it and would try to hold her tongue and not condescend to her mates. We were fine after that, until her father heard I had doubted the word of God in Contrexéville."

Lloyd felt his eyes filling in appreciation of the man's humility and the wonder of the child; his satisfaction in finding another who had deferred to her, and so early in her life. "Remember," Masirot said, "she was only eight. After Domrémy, she was much harder on herself. Her sums had to be perfect, and everything just so in her copybook. The exercises I gave her were just busywork compared to the ideas that were already turning in her head. One day, she asked me if I knew that tiny animals lived in the water and that some of them could make us sick. And they could only be seen through a curved piece of glass. I was able to answer yes honestly, but little more. I found her a book about Leeuwenhoek and his microscopes, and his animalcules. When she learned that he had only been a janitor from Delft who had taught himself, what could stop her?

"Her myopic parents could not tolerate any of this. As her knowledge passed theirs, they only beat her more. She and her brother had to cringe in a corner and wait for a revenge that never came. Lucienne had returned from Domrémy calling herself Jeanne. If anyone in the school forgot, she would say, *'Je vous en prie! Je m'appelle Jeanne!'* It began more like the contraction 'J'en prie,' and that's what the teachers called her; to humor her and ourselves. To her, it was Jeanne Prie."

She liked that, Masirot said. She didn't want to be a Crouen any longer. And the next year, she had enlisted his help in running off to live with her aunt. The parents were pleased to be rid of her. After that, the name had changed back and forth with the necessity of the moment. At the hospital where she started work as a child maid, she had been Jeanne Prie. When she was older and went to the laboratory in Brussels, she changed back to Lucienne de Crouen in case they should check on her birth records. Besides, de Crouen sounded more credible. When she left the Germans, she feared that name would be inconvenient as she took up residence in Chaumont. She became Jeanne Prie again.

His nights at Tamierre's continued through the middle of October. Several times a week, Masirot showed up in the bar. The Doctor stopped in every evening after his supper at the hotel. If the schoolmaster was there, Lloyd settled in for an evening, plying the old man with beer and steering the conversation around to his school and favorite pupil as child and woman. If Masirot was not there, Lloyd had a hurried pastis and took his leave. Thivet came only once a week, on Friday nights, sat there long enough to cause a self-conscious silence in the bar, had his beer, glanced at Lloyd a few times, and walked out.

Masirot explained that the regulars in Tamierre's were the older ones, who had not been in the fighting, and some of a certain age who might have volunteered but did not. These men could be made to feel guilty by Thivet, who made no secret of his contempt for them. They had cursed the Germans from the safety of their bar stools while salving their consciences with Tamierre's ale. Little wonder there was no one for the veteran to talk with here.

When Thivet was well out of hearing, they made themselves feel better by speculating on the allegiance and the purity of his woman, Masirot explained. They took advantage of all the years she was gone from Joinville to let their imaginations play with her reputation. They knew she was celebrated somewhere else, but the Sûreté had asked many of them questions about her, and these questions linked other names with hers, some of them German names. Plenty of room for speculative invention.

"Why do you tolerate them?" Lloyd asked him. "Why do you come here?"

"Where else would I go? To Goncourt's, where they are all heroes? No," he said, "I come here to know what the old men are saying, to follow the scandal. To see who starts the next lie, and who has the nerve to repeat it. You notice they say nothing when Thivet is here."

"If you are such a friend to her, why doesn't he sit with you? Why doesn't he speak with you?" The Doctor had not meant to be rude, and the questions did not throw Masirot off stride.

"William," he said, "is naïveté an American trait, or just your own affliction? I knew about her from the beginning. Sometimes she still listens to my advice. Of course he mistrusts me. Furthermore, I sit with you!"

The Doctor sensed something to be gained here, and he overreached again: "How in the world could she settle for him?" Not just that, but for him in a barnyard. A woman of her mind, with a belligerent like Thivet?

A pathetic question. He could have been back at St. Mark's, asking a classmate what Edith Sands could find to admire in a dandy such as Huideckope, looking for an answer that favored his own prospects.

"He trusts her," Masirot said leaning across the table to see that his point was taken. "He believes her." As if that were a distinguishing attribute and sufficient reason. Something that separated the soldier from the Doctor.

Two weeks passed without Thivet making his Friday appearance in the bar. Lloyd assumed that the veteran had decided he could not scare him away from Joinville merely with the menacing stare, and why should he come anymore to a place where the mutual dislike was so palpable? Thivet would probably be quenching his thirst at Goncourt's. The Doctor thought it would be time soon to make a second sortie to the cottage across the canal. First, he must see the old schoolmaster again. He was counting on his friend's good offices for a second and more dignified approach to Jeanne.

But Lloyd had been far too facile in his judgment of Masirot. He had taken him for a fellow easily plied with a beer, a bit free with opinion, a man who escaped a more rigorous scholarship by giving his life to children. Further, the Doctor was presuming on a friendship that existed only in his own mind. No less than the old man had wished him to believe. When Masirot showed up in Tamierre's again, he made no more than a grunt in Lloyd's direction, took his beer to his own table, and sat with his back to the room.

Lloyd had to force his company. Could he join monsieur? "Si vous voulez."

Had something happened?

"Rien de tout." Nothing at all.

Justin Thivet had not been around for some time, Lloyd said. It was this easy to turn the conversation innocently in Jeanne's direction. Again, Masirot was indifferent. He drank in silence till his mug was empty.

"Monsieur Lloyd," he said finally, "why should I talk with you anymore? I gave you every chance to be honest with me. And how did you respond? With deceit. I was forthcoming. You withheld. You showed yourself ignorant, as well. What can I learn from you? Nothing of value. You want to use me. Do you think I would betray her for your sake? She is going to have statues."

Lloyd sucked the air too quickly and beer followed into his windpipe. He coughed for several minutes before he could speak again. There was time to consider Masirot's attack. Even so, his only response was a stammering dismay. Couldn't the man see that he held Jeanne in the same reverential esteem?

"Monsieur Lloyd," he began again. "Did you think it was a secret from us? You take honors and a medal for the work she did? And you come here with a trinket for her? Don't you know this is the same she has faced all her life? That one day she will overcome the Sûreté and the likes of you? Perhaps in St. Peter's. Several hundred years from now, when we are all dust."

For Masirot, she was Jeanne after all, and on her way to sainthood. A grandiosity that would be held up to mockery either here or among the young veterans at Goncourt's. Lloyd wanted to say that he had suggested as much to his own family of skeptics in America. But in the schoolmaster's mind, the Doctor would still have been a lewd interloper tampering with the making of grand French history.

How did this square with what Masirot had claimed with such assurance only two weeks earlier—that she was no Jeanne d'Arc. "I thought it might provoke you to argument, monsieur. Your silence only showed your disrespect for her and your ignorance of our history."

Lloyd was shocked by the hostility more than the insult itself, and unwisely he said, "What would a teacher of children possess of a real historian's knowledge?" The answer came in a surprising flood.

"Monsieur, I thought you would have known that Jeanne d'Arc's reputation has swung this way and that with the politics of passing centuries. The view of her depends on which text you start with, the Armagnac chronicles and the record of the rehabilitation or the record of her original trial and the Anglo-Burgundian histories."

Tamierre's other customers turned to listen as the rebuke in kind rang across the room. A few of them came and stood around the table, ready to cheer on the debate.

"To the Anglo-Burgundian alliance, she was strumpet and heretic, virago and witch. And so she remained through the Renaissance. Among the English, too. The False Maid. Do you know why?"

The people looked at the Doctor in dismay. If they had come across the room to see a cockfight, one bird already lay wounded, refusing to fight, or unable. They watched as Masirot raised a spur and struck again: "Because, monsieur, she was too low in origin for those aristocrats. *Bien sur,* a face and figure were woven into tapestries, but there were no grand monuments to the Maid in that time, no drama to celebrate her."

Lloyd sat dumb, waiting for him to finish.

"Perhaps you have read *La Pucelle d'Orléans, Ou La France Deliverée*. No? You surprise me, Doctor. A silly epic that made her a laughingstock for most of another century."

Lloyd tried to leave. As he stood, someone behind him put a hand on his shoulder and pushed him back into his chair.

"You are bored with this, Doctor? Even *mes petits oiseaux* learned this much without squirming in their seats. Won't you wait for the bell?"

"So. What happens next?" Masirot went on, close-up in Lloyd's face. "For the Philosophes of the Enlightenment, Jeanne was a charlatan who dropped herself into French history like a battle machine from the clouds. Too self-righteous for them. Then the Revolution, and it only got worse for her. The best they could do was name a cannon for her in Orléans . . . a cannon that had been cast from her destroyed bronze monument.

"All of this, Doctor Lloyd, and still she couldn't be kept down. Napoléon needed her. He brought her back as the central figure of French nationalism. And in the next hundred years, she rose to her full glory. And with the restored monarchy, she became useful again. And so she was to Foch in your war. To soldiers and kings. What sniveling mutineer would dare raise his head in the land of the conquering Maid?"

Willie? Could this man know something about Lloyd's family? The others looked to the Doctor again. He had no answer for them.

"That's it?" he said at last. "I thought we were discussing Lucienne."

"We are!" the old teacher said, hitting again, harder.

"They are!" a man piped up in support, sharing some kind of victory.

"Shut up!" Tamierre told him.

Masirot ignored them, never blinking, staring into the Doctor's confusion. "It took them five hundred years to make Jeanne d'Arc a saint," he said. "Should we worry about Lucienne's reputation today?"

"Still," Lloyd recovered, "we have to put the record straight. Set it down honestly in the first place. So those who follow might make a valid judgment."

It was a homely truth, but enough, he hoped, to salvage a bit of honor.

"Honestly? Honestly?" Masirot was indignant. "Were you listening? There were two records I told you. Which one was honest? Do you suppose someone said to himself, Now I am going to write a dishonest account of the Maid? No, the only question for you is this: Do you leave it to the judgment of other courts, other centuries, or do you make an honest woman of her for yourself, from your own information?"

Lloyd wondered for some time afterward just what he was meant to take from that. Probably not what an ordinary American might suppose "make an honest woman of her for yourself" to mean. He knew the French turned their verb *faire*, "to make," to a thousand uses. But which of them had Masirot intended?

In Moriches, Helen was delighted to have Willie staying on at the farm. He was talking more and more like its manager, even suggesting the reintroduction of flax as its staple crop. Something to amaze his critical father on the old man's return, a return that the whole family considered inevitable. Helen knew how to treat such uninformed enthusiasm with a care for the boy's self-esteem. She welcomed his ideas and then let them die of their own impractical weight as Willie acquainted himself with the realities of farming in the modern age. In the meantime, he was happy with his sweat pouring into the ground he turned with the other farmhands, harvesting the sugar beets and mangel-wurzels.

It was a pleasure for Helen to see her big grandson at peace with himself at last, exhausted and happy at the end of a day, with Charlotte serving supper, pouring him an ale as if he were the first William Lloyd himself. He sat at the head of the table, proud as his father and grandfather had been that their land lay under the flyway of the Canada geese, promising his grandmother that Charlotte's fingers would be sore with plucking feathers in the coming season. This was as sure to bring a wail of martyrdom from the kitchen, a tradition worth preserving.

What a bountiful land, Helen thought, what a lucky boy! If he would just forget completely about his troubled army service and let go of his contact with the man at the New Jersey depot, Latoni, who had been such a nuisance to William. Willie, she supposed, was trying to prove to all of them there was another side to war, where regulation gives way to common sense and private duty. The situations that men like Latoni and himself had to deal with through no fault of their own. That's why he had invited Latoni to the farm, to prove to his grandmother how wrong his father had been about the man.

Helen had another mailing address for her son, this time in Joinville. He had written of his intention to stay there indefinitely. She sent an immediate reply. "Write to your wife, you selfish boy." She was intrigued by his description of the "testy little grammar school master," who had been so amusing and informative about Joan of Arc.

It gave her the chance to respond with the Spiritualist's view of the Maid of Orléans, not quite claiming it as her own opinion since the Spiritualists were presumed to be allied with that old wizard, the Devil. It also gave her the opportunity to quote from her recent reading: "'A constant stream of inspiration flows down from the invisible world upon mankind. There are intimate ties between the living and the dead. All souls are united by invisible threads, and the rhythm of universal life. So it was with our heroine, Joan of Arc.'"

Helen noted the synchrony of their mutual concern with the same mysterious woman and, anticipating his too-rational response, warned him that only a man bound by the limits of scientific arrogance would call this mere coincidence. Nor was it just coincidence, she explained, that Latoni had walked back into his life again so long after the man's disgraceful dismissal from St. Mark's.

"Willie is showing so much initiative. You'd be proud. I hope it won't worry you that he has signed for a loan to plant seventy acres of soybeans next spring. I know we've never done soybeans. Nor has anyone in the region, for that matter. He says they will one day be the main source of vegetable protein in the world, and the old Lloyd place can be a leader in this revolution. However quixotic, this time I'm giving him his head. It's so thrilling to see him taking hold, and taking charge.

"One other thing. He only told me after the arrangements were completed that his note would be cosigned by Latoni. I see no great harm here, because Willie has promised me that neither the farm nor any of its equipment could ever be claimed by the man as collateral. You see Willie has some common sense."

/ /

Doctor Lloyd supposed his mother must be feigning indifference to this piece of filthy news, that the whole thing might be a ruse to bring him back across the sea. His resolve could not be shaken so easily. He was furious, though he wrote only that she must deal herself with the boy's foolish arrangement and Latoni's crafty insinuation of himself into the family business. Obviously, his motive would be profit at Willie's expense, or worse.

There were more important things happening in the world just then. He said he did not wish to frighten her, but that afternoon would come the turning point for him. And perhaps the most dangerous venture of his life. A man stood in his way, a man not worthy of the woman he held hostage under the guise of protecting her from governmental inquisition and community lie. The man must be confronted in his own house. If no news followed in the coming month, she should accept her son's silence into eternity without unnecessary mourning. "Turn that balance of affection you hold for a wayward son to the benefit of his former wife and his children."

Everything was in order in the Doctor's mind as he crossed the bridge and walked around the long horseshoe curve of the canal, toward the rowboat mooring. Unarmed and alert, going bravely, supposing that a rifle would soon be trained on him. The letter he'd just posted to his mother was not melodramatic, but as honest as a schoolboy's full confession. He was anticipating his own death. It was a suicidal mission. And he was as proud of all this as he was scared.

Masirot's lecture on Joan, which had made him a fool in the bar, now gave his legs purpose and his mind the peace of a decision long delayed and now irrevocable. A decision reaffirmed by voices of his own. At long last, he would present to Jeanne what not even a war could bring out of him, an unconditional faith rising out of all the contradictory evidence. He must or there could be no faith at all. No, not in religion, or your silly superstitions, he imagined himself yelling at his mother, faith in the nurse!

Of course, he had accepted he was no match for the knives and knuckles of a man as practiced in killing as Thivet. So much the better. If he were not the weakling in the match, what could be gained here but a bully's empty victory? Ahead of him, behind a church, he saw a garden of gray stones—rectangles, some with circular tops and squared shoulders, obelisks, with letters carved and numbers. A whole row in the rear, next to a fence, had been recently planted and were sparkling white.

A moment later, he was, in fact, whistling past a graveyard, "K K K Katy," though through his dry lips, the sound was hardly sibilant. Ashamed, he blew harder and produced a champion's noise, but so far off-key that he abandoned the effort altogether. And the reality of the afternoon came into focus, the cottage visible in the distance across the canal.

He could see no one in the fields. Thivet, he supposed, would be sitting at a window, calm and confident while Jeanne went about the distaff by default and without complaint, waiting for the day her trials, real or imagined, would be over. And she could flee her confinement and jailor, be off to the city where she belonged, whichever city it might be.

The scene took a sudden and alarming turn, as if out of a dream and into the trap of the waking world. It was the sight of the rowboat's oars angled up in the oarlocks, their paddle ends pointing toward the cottage. These frightened him and redirected his mind. He was ashamed of himself for having told his mother so much. His lifelong habit of total honesty with her, in conversation and on the page, now seemed like a childish addiction. There came a time when fealty was outweighed by an adult duty of silence in distress. What right had he to predict his own death and throw it in her face as if it were ordinary news of the season? The weight of deserting his family grew heavier with each of his silent denials of responsibility.

These thoughts gave gravity to each step along the canal path, and held him to his course. Wasn't it appropriate that a selfish man go forward into the shadow of death? Implicit in this was the long chance of a purification through valor and survival. Once in the boat, the oars felt strangely light in his hands, and the water gave no resistance to his stroke. He was across in a single pull, and climbing up the bank on the other side.

He stood for a moment behind a tree, regathering composure against the rapid and palpable pumping of his heart. Though he would already be in the man's sights, he would not go on his belly or crawl. There was no cover between him and the house. He tried to think of the rest of his approach as a measured wedding march, his own, with the bespoke bride already at the altar—well, the honeymoon cottage, never mind a church. Unconditional, or interest evaporated again, and for good.

All very well to whistle shame into courage, but the violent side of the day turned in another lobe. Thivet looking down his barrel through the window, or, just as likely, he'd be waiting behind the front door for the first footfall over the threshold. Then a flashing palm. Knocking Lloyd's nose bone up toward his brain, one of those tricks a killer is only waiting to pull out of his training kit.

The Doctor tumbled backward as Jeanne screamed at the maniac to stop. But Thivet was not like a dog that could be leashed by voice. He followed Lloyd down with a flying knee to the groin, hands at the ready to grab the skull and beat it over and over again into the floor, multiple concussive forces that left him senseless, or dead, or wishing he were. Please, not the trickling of blood, letting the life out of him slowly. But even this better than a vegetable life, and the humiliating pity of the nurse.

The cow was bellowing in the front yard, the ribbon and medal gone from her neck. Lloyd knocked at the front door. There was no answer. He waited, then knocked again, louder. He walked to the side of the house, the cow following him, still bellowing, nudging her nose into his back. He gazed over the fields; perhaps they were kneeling at harvest, or below the hilltop in the distance. No movement, no sound. He went to the door again and pounded harder, cursing the anticlimax. Had they fled? No death match. No bride at his wedding.

He pushed open the door and it slammed into the wall.

"*Doucement*, monsieur."

It was a plea from a man near death, small and plaintive, not a plea for life, but for a peaceful passing already in progress. Though a peaceful passing was going to be impossible. Thivet lay alone on his cot at the back of the room, curled into a sweat-drenched fetal ball. He said he had a headache and that he could not eat or drink.

In only a few weeks' time, his rugged face had hollowed to a skeletal outline, and the flesh of his arms rested flaccid and harmless on the sharp edge of the cot. His head was crawling with lice, though he was too far gone to notice, or care. Lloyd, who had witnessed the symptoms so many times, had no hope for the man. The stench was awful. He must have been lying for several days in his fouled sheets, with no one to help. The little wood case was on the table, all its drawers open and empty, the tiny glass containers scattered about. A few clothes were strewn on the floor, and some scraps of food. "What happened to you?"

He couldn't expect honest answers from Thivet, but the exhausted wretch was curiously willing to speak, however softly. "Monsieur, the cow is in pain. She must be milked."

Lloyd rolled the man over gently and pulled the filthy sheets from the cot, though very carefully, because he knew the tiny shape and purpose of the life that swarmed in his intestines and in his blood. He set a fire in the stove, which was cold, and carried water in from the well. After washing Thivet, he boiled the sheets and hung them to dry outside. When the bed was made again, and after he tried to force a boiled egg into his patient's mouth, and some water, he sat down beside the man.

"Where is she?"

"I can't tell you much," Thivet said. "First you take care of Suzanne!"

The cow's bag was swollen and she bellowed in pain. Lloyd managed the chore, though he hadn't milked since a boyhood summer in Moriches. It was remarkable how the sound of the milk ringing against the steel pail soothed the animal. The Doctor was more astonished by his misjudgment of the man inside, who had shown more concern for the animal's misery than for his own life, which was almost over. He wondered if Thivet had taken the medal from the cow's neck and disposed of it.

When he reentered the cottage, Thivet had fallen asleep again, and the Doctor had some trouble waking him.

"Where did she go?" he began again. "How long has she been gone?"

Thivet could not say with any assurance.

"I know she would not desert you in this condition."

"Monsieur, she left me," he said sadly.

"Do you know how you became sick?"

He must have considered this a more dangerous question. Even in his rheumy eyes one could read his still-skeptical appraisal of the Doctor. Perhaps he was deciding that even a fool, if he would milk a suffering cow, must have a bit of heart in him.

"She told me to use only the chest under the window, never to go in the other one. There was sickness inside it."

"And you opened it anyway."

"Monsieur, I assure you that is not how I became sick."

"How do you know?"

He smiled weakly at the Doctor's ignorance.

"I know her secret," Thivet said.

"And what was that?"

He had to stop for a moment to gather his strength again. Lloyd gave him another sip of water.

"Nothing," Thivet said finally. "Her secret was nothing. There were hundreds of little glass boxes. I opened every one."

"Yes?"

"Nothing."

"What do you mean?"

"Her secret was she had no secret. Every one of them empty. There was nothing there, monsieur," he confided. "Her experiments were a hoax. Of course she didn't want me to go into the chest. She was a fraud."

"But how did you get sick?"

"That *is* her secret," Thivet said. He raised his hands in front of his face in the failing light and manipulated one with the other until he had made an X of two fingers and spread the rest wide. He raised the sign a few inches above the sheet.

"What is that?"

"The witch," he said.

Thivet went much quicker than Lloyd had expected. His breathing became shallower, until it could hardly be felt. The Doctor kept a candle burning through his deathwatch, more as a votive than an aid to futile treatment. Without the vaccine, there was no treatment. Jeanne would have done her best, but without adequate facilities, it would have been hopeless. If she had stayed to the end, she might have been accused in the death of another soldier, and this one of some celebrity.

In the middle of the night, there was the characteristic white fluid from his mouth, a gasp, and the heart beating for a minute or two after the last breath. Thivet must have been waiting to make his witness against the nurse before giving up the ghost. In vain, because his testimony was never relayed beyond his tainted jury of one.

Lloyd did not hesitate. With a fire poker, he pried a loose board from the floor and set a pile of twigs directly under a joist. He placed the burning candle beneath this. With the first crackle of the dry wood, he opened the shutters and door for draft. Then he was on his way swiftly across the canal. By the time the fire was in full light, he was in his bed in the hotel, and ready to feign surprise at the town's alarms.

The reports the next day were of the hero burned to death, probably smoking in his bedclothes, and tight on the wine from the cracked and blackened gallon jug found in the ashes. The Joinville fire force hauled water from the well, and when that proved too slow, they tried a bucket brigade from the canal. All too late. No one thought of blaming Jeanne. Masirot told the police she'd left Joinville several days before, on her way to Nancy, where she expected to find work in a hospital.

Lloyd believed Nancy was the last place she would go, simply because Masirot's purpose was to mislead anyone trying to follow her, probably to send them in the opposite direction. The Doctor had a new intuition about Jeanne. He supposed she must have had her fill of country life as she'd waited for the bitter and superstitious charges against her to shrivel and disappear. She would be ready for a city again after all the provincial gossip.

A few days later, Lloyd had his rig back and was on the scent again, actually following his own nose more than any trail that Jeanne might have left. Passing the stone walls of the burned-out cottage on the far side of the canal, he cringed at what he'd done, though it was no more than any public health official would have recommended.

There was no way he could have explained, or made people believe that he could be saving Joinville or the whole of Lorraine from a scourge. Anyone handling Thivet's corpse might have spread Kessel's fever across the countryside, breeding new generations of the disease-carrying lice as it went. They would have called him mad, and Masirot would have turned them against him long before the pandemic was under way.

Far better this way, he thought, as the gray pulled him toward St. Dizier on the long journey westward to Reims. It might take him two weeks, time enough to rededicate himself to his own Saint Joan. Masirot had been right, but only to a point. One needn't weigh state's evidence in a case where the relevance of sovereignty was denied; one only had to cast out doubt and remember the woman's passion for truth.

Jeanne would have had mixed feelings for Thivet's rabid patriotism, which could never have tolerated a science without national boundary. Especially in wartime. Who *could* tolerate it in wartime? Was there anything to match the bullying brutality of the Huns? Though they might have pointed at Justin Thivet and said, Yes, there's your man. But Jeanne would never have used him in one of her experiments without a vaccine on hand. And not unless he had volunteered. Obviously, he hadn't. He had broken into the little boxes against her wishes. He would never even have seen the lice, hard enough to detect if he'd known what he was looking for. No telling how many fevers had been competing to take his life before Kessel's took charge. Once he had disobeyed her and become sick, there was no point in telling him what had happened. He would only have been more of a liability, his imminent death certain to bring new suspicions and attacks on her.

In Moriches, Helen was sharing all of her news with Emma. Nellie had been sent back to Chapin for the winter term, having decided she preferred the sympathy of her classmates to the silence of an apartment, which by then was frequently broken by her mother's complaints of her laziness. She was a good student and had begun to write heartfelt English themes on the behavior and mistakes of nurses in wartime. These were passed in the faculty sitting room among her appalled teachers, who called for a conference with her mother. Emma considered this a voyeuristic concern and none of their business. Instead of showing a tear after that, they began to tsht-tsht. Which Nellie actually liked better than the intrusive sympathy of their sidelong glances.

For Helen to share all the news with Emma meant the most painful along with the merely distressing. And this included the Doctor's report that after some months of aimless wandering, unable to find himself, he had gathered useful information in Reims. He'd discovered that some of the most advanced work in European medical science was under way again in the defeated country. In Koblenz. The next week, he would be going to Paris to get his papers in order.

Impatient, he was selling his horse and surrey and trusting himself to the trains again. "It's not too late to thank you, Mother, for the few words of German you forced down my unwilling throat in childhood. I almost believe you knew you were preparing me for the war and its aftermath, though I wouldn't have you take this as a concession to your spiritualistic claims."

The Doctor's long correspondence to his mother on the journey that followed seemed almost too humanitarian, too much like an excuse for Germany's behavior and for his own. Surely, to his former French colleagues, it would be a premature conversion. Though he made no such apology for the woman Helen knew he was chasing across the border.

"I have not seen one well-nourished child here, though the German cities are clean as wax. The people, dazed by their defeat, wear the faces of prolonged suffering. In Zell, I was welcomed into the house of an older officer who had been in the war of 1870. He lives with his wife and fine servant and a dachshund. They took me in to warm myself by their dining room fireplace. They had survived the struggle on war bread, potatoes, and occasional bits of meat. For all the deprivation, their home was neat as a pin.

"The old officer assured me the Germans were not *böse Leute,* not bad people. He couldn't understand why the world hated them so, and quietly I told him just why. They had been the first to use poison gas and the first to bomb open cities. This shocked him. He believed the French were about to enter Belgium, so the German army had to do the same. The French, he said, had treated the German prisoners far worse than the French had been treated in Germany. And believe me, I have seen convincing evidence this was quite true."

For Helen, these were brand-new ideas and not quite trustworthy. She read on: "My host thought the U-boat campaign had been justified when England put foodstuffs on the contraband list. When you look at the starving children here, you wonder yourself. The man couldn't believe the number of merchant seamen his navy had murdered or left to die in the water. He did say he had always suspected the Kaiser of personal ambition. His wife had disagreed with him until the Kaiser's desertion in defeat assured her, too, that he was a traitor.

"Before I left, he held out his hand to me across his table, saying, *Dann aber wir sind nicht Feinde*'—'but we are not enemies.' The wife sat next to him, rigidly erect, the fear of a rebuff clear in her face as her husband asked me for this crumb of sympathetic comprehension. I'd rather have lost my right hand than not offered it in return."

Emma, shown this evidence of her husband's misplaced graciousness, was disgusted but would not criticize. Would he write next an apologia for the wholesale German slaughter of the world's next generation? It seemed to justify her children's past sniping at the vanity of the war, and it made her long effort to uphold the Doctor's service a thankless mistake.

Before they had fully digested the meaning of that news, he was writing from Koblenz, giving a post office box as his address, another sympathy note for the vanquished: These people will not crumble in defeat. Order reigns everywhere, and cleanliness. The river shipping is neat, large in volume, and altogether impressive. You might as well try to dam the Rhine as prevent this country rising from its ashes.

Until Germany sees the light, world peace is insecure. It's up to Americans to wipe the scales from the German eyes. The French and English hatred is too deep, in proportion to their suffering at German hands. But every injustice done to the defeated now will only delay civilization's advance.

Lloyd meant all of it. Helen saw how nicely it fit with his own plans and she resented the bald selfishness of it. He didn't have to tell them; they knew the woman was there. If Koblenz was his new home, why couldn't he give them a home address? Because he was with the woman, and using a post office box to avoid embarrassment for all. Helen and Emma were both quite sure of it. From then forward, they might refer to the Doctor as "they." And several weeks later, their suspicion was justified by a letter from him that began "We . . ."

In Reims, it had taken no more than a tour of two hospitals for Lloyd to find a bacteriologist who had been acquainted with the work of Lucienne de Crouen in Brussels and Paris. The man's employment had overlapped with Lucienne's service in both cities. A smile played across the fellow's face as he tried to describe the experience of working with *"the chasseuse des microbes."* The woman whom Pasteur had called "the doctor without degree." The smile meant something disapproving, but what?

In order to survive in that world of proud scientists, he said, she had been wise enough not to argue with her mouth, only with her slides and her results. She was always working at the edge of some great man's experiment, on some problem that would help to confirm a larger finding. She was not given these assignments, but was ingenious at inventing them for herself, and found time for them in the course of the other work she was required to do. And she never claimed a victory in her own name. Her reports, written with precision in any of three languages, were always turned over to the *directeur* for his own signature. Given to the larger glory of the laboratory.

"And the problem?" Lloyd asked.

"It is difficult to explain," the man said. "There is a point at which a series of small martyrdoms gather a name, and this becomes a liability to those in charge. When an assistant's quiet advance begins to be a nuisance."

"Yes?"

"Well," the man said, "I suppose one can't tolerate such an unchecked ambition, no matter what disguise it wears. There must be limits. She did very little to stop the rumors of her own importance. One couldn't have her stealing a corner of this room and that for projects that had never been authorized in the first place."

"I'm sorry, sir," Lloyd said, "but I'll have to carry the Devil's brief here. This would all seem quite impossible unless she had some support. But if true, quite admirable."

"Oh, she had support!" The man winked. "You wouldn't believe the number of friends she made . . . or the things that were said. Wherever she went! Of course, the same thing was bound to happen to her when she moved to the institute in Paris."

The French were such masters of slanderous innuendo. Lloyd would not let himself be tainted by the man's sly eye or his oral exclamation points. "But what happened to her?" he asked.

"She made great contributions at one of the American hospitals. In Chaumont. There was some trouble, which has not been resolved. The American doctors there were quite charmed by her, and perhaps a little gullible. I think she's hors de combat just now. You're not the first to come looking for her, monsieur."

"Anything else?"

"Sometimes Lucienne heard voices." He shook his head. "Which made it quite easy to discredit her when she became difficult."

"She *could* be quite emotional."

"You knew her, too?"

The Doctor didn't try to deny it. "I think you know where she is," he said.

The man became suspicious. "You stay here," he told Lloyd. He disappeared for a moment and came back with his superior, who took charge of the interview. They asked to see Lloyd's credentials. When they had examined his passport and established with a third party that he'd been the Doctor in charge at Chaumont, the first man was red with shame, or anger, and would not speak.

His superior talked freely, with little regard for Lucienne's privacy, or her reputation. He was told that she had most likely taken herself into exile in Germany. Perhaps in Koblenz, where a study of a new combination vaccine for childhood diseases was under way. Koblenz, headquarters of the Allied occupation, where she might feel safer under the wing of some Yankee protector. He winked at his colleague.

They were dismissive of whatever work she could be doing, saying the Germans had always got their blood theory wrong, and the war had done nothing to deflate the arrogance of their science. Lucienne would probably be quite at home there, the superior said disconsolately. Yes, the other affirmed, she would know how to use the carelessness of their methods to her advantage, to shine forth from the shadows of their mistakes. The results were apt to be altogether undependable.

Lloyd, wondering how far they would go with this, knew how to put an end to it: "They make fine microscopes. Isn't this a Zeiss?"

"No one denies they're good glass grinders! But my God! When it comes to analytical observation, theorizing, rigorous proof, who touches the French? Pasteur! Roux! Bordet!"

His partner whispered to him that Bordet was Belgian.

"Yes," the superior replied, snapping at his own mistake, "and not quite reliable at that!"

That was it, all Lloyd was going to get from these people, though more than enough to turn him around to the east and across the German border. He was certain they knew she was there. Their hesitation in declaring it without doubt was only out of fear that she might fly back into their lives with work that would discredit their own. It astonished him that they could be so aware of her talent and ignorant of her generosity. Their work, he supposed, driven by competitive spite, would never serve the world. It was destined to failure.

Before Germany, as he had written to his estranged women, he had gone back to Paris to have his passport fixed. He'd had enough of his useless disguise. A haberdashery clerk tried to put him in plus fours, but he bought creased corduroy pants and a jacket cut with a pinched waist, as well as a pair of informal brogans, all of which still left him more cousin to a tradesman than a professional, but sporty to his taste and anything but impoverished.

The trip to Paris was unnecessary, as it turned out. Crossing into Germany on the train was a snap; he saluted a Frenchman, with a German trainman looking on in humiliation at their disrespect for his border. In Lloyd's hurry, all modesty of approach was forgotten. He hired a car and driver in Trier and drove up the valley of the Mosel in a single afternoon, stopping only in Zell, where the old German officer had invited him into his home.

The last miles before Koblenz were a blur of contradictions, a neat countryside of farms and tidy villages, and country folk walking slowly all along the road, their heads hung in shame, as his cocky driver sped past with only a horn for the inconvenience of their thousand miseries. Lloyd could rebuke himself only gently for his lighthearted journey through their disgrace, a journey whose grail was nothing he would find there, but something he was bringing, a simple act of his own volition that would heal the past and justify his flight from home, a declaration of his own.

On arriving in the city, he dismissed his driver and took a room in a respectable hotel on Vasserstrasse. The following day, he was able with little effort to locate the Koblenz Institute for the Study of Infectious Bacteria. He did not wish to surprise Jeanne in her professional surroundings, so he waited outside for the closing hour. The workers did not come in a rush, but wandered out one by one. They walked stiffly and solemnly, and Jeanne was not among them.

The Institute's rooms were beautifully situated over the banks where the Mosel met the Rhine, and by noon the next day, Lloyd was walking back and forth at river's edge along the promenade's elegant iron railing, keeping a watch on the office building's door at lunchtime and again that evening. Once more, he was disappointed. The harebrained childishness of all his plans and travels jarred with each clap of his hard leather heel on the unforgiving pavement. The black Rhine ran away beneath him, as fickle as family blood turned to water. His undeclared devotion to Jeanne was mocked again by the falling German night.

On the third evening, she emerged from the building. His hand jumped with a palsy of love, impulses that defied neurological decorum; he thrust the hand into his pocket, jammed it against the lining until it was still. She looked beautiful at this distance, more lovely in her straight-backed pride than he had pictured her, erect and animated in a city of dejected men.

Still, she gave no quarter to fashion. Her black hair looked chopped again, shorter than ever. In this morbidly conservative town, the dark trousers and jacket she wore, which might have blended nicely with the clothes of her male colleagues, were, on her full, short figure, provocative, positively bohemian. To the Doctor, they said she owed this world nothing more than she had already given it. To all men, they announced her independence; to women, the right to walk in whatever company she pleased and to take according to her desire. In the flush of his excitement, Lloyd forgot for the moment that this was also the costume of sexlessness—the clothes of her sanctified sister from Domrémy?

He was elated, though someone had followed Jeanne out the door and kissed her warmly on both cheeks. It was nothing to her. She threw the end of her scarf over her shoulder with a gesture so unconcerned that Lloyd was stuck in place for a moment, stunned by the indifference of it. She was halfway down the block before it occurred to him that he was meant to follow.

Jeanne was walking away from the river. She made a left at the first corner, a right at the next, then went straight for three blocks and left for two more. If the city's grid was a chessboard, she moved across it with the queen's whim and freedom, a celebrity denying a destination, as if bound to keep moving for her own security. If she knew she was being followed, she would probably enter a restaurant or public place.

Instead, she stopped for a moment in front of a small stone building with an elegant door of dark wood and hand-wrought strap hinges that ran across its full width. Along with the metalwork over its windows, it gave the house the forbidding look of a medieval stronghold in the midst of the more ornate and less defensive architecture of the quiet residential street. She looked over her shoulder once, then entered the building quickly.

Lloyd came up to the same door, surprised that she had walked in without even turning a key. He waited for a while outside, taking courage by comparing the death of a million soldiers to the puny consequences of the next hour. It helped only for a moment. There could be no false step this time, no room for misunderstanding. The last day he had confronted her, he'd lacked heart and face. Today, that's all he came with. That day, she had thrown his gold-rimmed piece around a cow's neck. Today, he was giving her no chance to throw his pearls before swine. He carried no flower or trinket for a bribe.

Her door knocker he recognized as Portuguese, the brass casting of a hand holding a ball, which, when he swung it against the metal plate behind, sounded more like an attempted break-in than the arrival of polite company. He looked up and down the sidewalk, thinking he must have disturbed the peace of several households. There was no answer. He knocked again, softly this time with his knuckles. He thought he heard the sash being closed behind the iron bars overhead. Nothing more.

Standing alone in the street, he wondered if she had seen him following her. He thought of Justin Thivet left to die in the cottage in Joinville, of the young Kessel smiling after his surgeries, thinking his body mended while the war canoes swarmed in his blood. Wolfram and the two Germans in the basement ward, Latoni and Willie, all carriers of the same brand of canoes with outriggers, the ones that had escaped from Chaumont. In portage across France on the backs of the tiny-legged carriers, which had traveled in the luggage of the lady upstairs. Could there be more of them with her in Germany? She had just shut her window and pulled her shades.

Why, in that fortress of a house, did the door push open so easily? Once inside, he realized that only the facade of the building was solid. The broken plaster walls showed large patches of lath. The rubble of demolition was scattered through the abandoned rooms of the ground floor. A stairway, torn partially away from the wall, hung at a slight angle over the hallway. He grasped the railing and started up.

There was another door at the top of the steps, suggesting the old residence had been divided into separate living quarters. He rapped solidly. There was the sound of another door opening inside and a toilet flushing, then her voice speaking French.

"Go away! I don't want to talk to you. I told you I don't know who started the fire. You have no right to come in this house." She shifted into German: "This is not France; this is Germany!" The guttural diction was a rasp on his conscience. Could there be any true color to a chameleon? Pressing him from behind, ordering him to knock again, were the lectures of Masirot on the fickleness of truth, and his own philosophers of Massachusetts, who had warned rational men against foolish consistencies.

He had made his choice, and he called through the door, "I know who started the fire."

The door opened quickly, and Jeanne pulled him into the room.

The questions came tumbling, serious and trivial.

"What are you doing here? What are you wearing?"

"Did Justin suffer? Dead before the cottage burned?"

"What is that on your cheek?" Just a smudge; she wiped it away.

Who else was she hiding from, besides the Sûreté?

Had the fever taken his son?

If she was hiding, how could she live in a house with no lock on the front door? What kind of house was this? She could break her neck on those stairs.

Who told him she was here? Not those saps in Reims?

They calmed and looked at each other more closely.

"Who dressed you in these clothes? she said. "They're French, aren't they?"

He told her he was sorry for barging in without warning.

"You're not sorry," she contradicted softly. "No more than you were in Joinville."

"I haven't given you a chance to dress," he said.

She looked down at the sash of her bathrobe and waved an impatient hand at the inconvenience of her clothes, which were lying across a chair at the side of the room.

"Dress for what?" Once she got home from the institute, she didn't go anywhere.

"Dinner. You tell me where."

"I don't want to go to dinner. I don't want to go anywhere in Koblenz. Neither do you."

She was in tears when Lloyd described Thivet's last hours.

To explain herself, she began with the house. It had been built by a landlocked sea captain, a widower who sailed out of Bremerhaven and was gone eight months of the year. With his neighborhood fully aware of his long absences, he had needed a well-armored place to secure the kroner and chattel of his voyaging. After his death, the building was split into two apartments. And during the war, the downstairs had been occupied by squatters, who made a wreck of it. The owner was allowing Jeanne to use the upstairs rent-free until he might choose to rebuild the quarters below.

"You're not paying attention," she said.

He was asking irrelevant questions and not waiting for their unimportant answers, interrupting before she was finished with the last.

She brought him up short, asking what his wife was thinking, with him off traipsing Europe like a gypsy. He explained the divorce as best he could, not trying to deny the cold-hearted half of his flight from New York, or to place any blame on Emma. The solemn thrust of her lower lip suggested she was filing away each apology for further deliberation.

"*Eh bien.*" She jumped forward into another gear and put a kettle on the enameled stove that heated the room. She sat him down at her table, gave him a piece of dried fruit, and took the chair across from him, watching him chew and savor. Was she admiring the way he relaxed into what might be his new home?

He thought her smile more beatific than affectionate when she raised her eyes to his and said gently, "Again, you want to make acquaintance with my lice?" And again, the resonance of this confounded his reason as it stirred his groin, doubling back between lewd and vulgar and the respectable excitement of scientific inquiry.

He was out of his chair, coming around the table, lifting her by the hand until she stood facing him. He reached for her robe's sash, began to tug at its simple knot, but she pushed his hand away and held it at bay. Then she led him out of the living room and down the hall, showing him the other rooms.

"There is this," she said, opening the door to a small chamber with a twin bed and a bare, lumpy mattress. "I could make it more comfortable."

Jeanne continued down the hall to the end.

"This is where I stay," she said.

It was a generous space with two large windows at the back that gave over a fire escape onto a courtyard garden of untended flower beds and overgrown with shrubbery turned brown. There was a four-poster bed centered against one wall. It carried a faded blue canopy printed with the Chinese willow pattern. The bed must have been the old captain's gift to himself from his part in the Asia trade. On a small finial at the top of the headboard hung the gold-rimmed medal.

Lloyd leaned over to remove and examine it again.

His family was right: It was small enough, elegant enough, to be jewelry. Not really a medal at all, but a lovely trinket. Emma was right, too, that the pretty thing would never excite a discussion of war bravery or honor, only compliments on its cunning and unique design.

He held it out to her and asked, "Why don't you wear it?"

"You said it was a medal. Do soldiers wear their medals?" She was annoyed.

"I had it made for you," he confessed. "In Chaumont. There is no other like it."

"Really? Why didn't you say? I almost left it on the cow."

She took it from him, put it around her neck, and admired it for a moment.

"It's quite nice," she said. "Are you expecting to stay here?"

He took her hand, felt how calm and cool it was in his nervous fingers.

"No," she said. "Words, say something. It's no good just to slide onto the bed. Who will you be here? Are you a doctor? Will you do research? What will you expect of me?"

"Can I presume? These are all things that might depend on you."

She went to a cabinet over the sink and brought out a ripe blue cheese and stale crackers, then poured a tall glass of wine they would share from a bottle that had soured. It tasted fine to him.

"Take your shoes off, William. Sit up here."

Again, he was determined to lead, not to follow. But for the moment, he did what he was told. They sat on the bed. Where to begin? He was at great pains to be open, not to be caught again in hesitation and doubt. He started with the day early in her service when he had followed her into the fever ward and watched her bend to whisper and make her sign on the brows of three men who were about to die. She was reluctant to talk about it, leading him back to the question of faith.

"Your religion floats in the air, William. It leaves you free to censure as you will. It makes you a forgiving judge. That is your problem. My religion has a body, face and hands, and words for me to follow. That is my problem."

"But that wasn't faith, what you did. That was an accurate prophesy of death. You knew something. What was I to think?"

"You thought I might have let them die? To prove my wisdom to you?"

"No," he said. "Would I have kept you if I thought that?"

"I don't know," she said. "You were confused."

They talked late into the night by the light of a single candle. She spoke of the sorrows she had for her time in Chaumont, the shame for her failures and mistakes, the escape of Kessel's fever from her control.

"But you made us quite famous," he argued. "You never misused any of your patients."

"You still find it necessary to tell me that? I never broke my word to you. The Germans volunteered for me?"

"I never doubted you," he lied.

"Yes, you had doubts. About my science, and about my loyalty."

"At times," he admitted. "But I made you this." He reached out again to the gold-edged piece. Shouldn't this prove his final faith in her?

"And what about Thivet? Do you believe what I told you?"

"Yes," he said.

"But why? Thivet didn't. Others don't. Don't you agree that the circumstances are against me?"

Masirot had taught him. "I don't have to have a reason that can be verified by you or any other."

She put her hand on his face, let her fingers slide down over his mouth. "That's enough words," she said.

She took him by the hand and led him down the dark hall to his room.

"Tonight," she told him, "this is where you stay."

"Thank you," he said, pressing his lips to her forehead, letting her go.

"We'll know soon enough," she said, "if our Gods will tolerate each other. One usually knows at the breakfast table." And she went silently back to her room.

Before he fell asleep that night, he called down the hall from his bed through her open door: "Will you stay here . . . I mean for good?"

"Of course not," she called back. "I hate these people. We will go back to France. When she allows us."

He was buoyed by her generous inclusion of him in the long-range plan. There were no diseased lice here. They had been destroyed in Joinville. She had been testing his nerve again. He was only a little surprised to notice that after making the bed he had desired, with a lifelong finality, there was no one in it but himself. At peace with their continence and the pleasure of anticipation it assured, he fell away into the sleep of the just.

He had no idea what time it was when the three French officers broke down the door. He was in the hallway, standing in their way, their flashlights blinding him.

"Where is she?" they demanded, pushing past him into her room.

The window was open and so was the garden gate. Jeanne was gone.

They threatened Lloyd with a lot of foolishness. He could be arrested himself, they said. He called them worse than Germans with all their bullying nonsense, and after he showed them his credentials, they holstered the serious threats and took cover in their bureaucratic mandarin. But if they wanted to speak to her, why didn't they go to her office at any lunchtime?

They had no answer for him except to say, "There is new information." They could have been a bunch of commandos left over from the war, used to attacking at night. If they hadn't had pistols on their hips, he would have thought them no more than buffoons.

But behind the faces of moralizing clowns, there could be malignant deeds. Jeanne knew that. She was gone. Lloyd saw his duty now to stay in Koblenz and protect the temporary home. He wouldn't be bored here. There was work to do, starting with the garden, where he thought rows of small boxwood could replace the dead shrubbery.

That afternoon, he worked in the cold, stripping the flower beds of their dead vines, preparing them for the next spring's planting of bulbs and other perennials. He'd have some things already flowering to brighten her return. She might be gone for quite awhile, but she'd be back. His Joan had yet to escape the stake and pyre that modern France had planned for her.

Dr. Lloyd began writing to all his family again, to the boys, to Nellie and Emma. They were less anxious to respond than he was to reach out to them. Without rubbing their noses in his contentment, he was eager to share experience. From 1926 to 1930, his wife and children understood that he had returned to Joinville with Jeanne and settled there for the duration. The French had given him a license to practice medicine, and charges against the woman were not pursued. Jeanne was happy with a little laboratory of her own devising, in another cottage by the canal. She was corresponding with a researcher in immunology at a hospital in Marseille. Lloyd kept a small office in the town and eventually found humor, satisfaction, and humanity in the trade of a diagnosis and prescription for a dressed hare or two dozen eggs, or an ancient walking stick, from those who had no francs.

From time to time, through the years, Lucienne and her doctor friend were seen wearing black armbands. It was presumed these were in observance of the anniversaries of comrades lost during the late war. Though sometimes the two of them strolled along the canal, hand in hand, with the black stripes of their mourning on display for no one but themselves. She had given him two names for her, and he used them both: Jeanne, when he was feeling affectionate and loved in return; Lucienne, when he was annoyed with her. When all went smoothly, which was most of the time, he was William; when he overstepped his claim on her, he was Dr. Lloyd.

Nellie and Louis made plans to visit their father and his nurse in the summer of 1931, but Louis got pneumonia and the trip was postponed. A year later, mail from the Doctor stopped abruptly. Nothing sent to him was answered. Eventually, one of Nellie's letters was returned, marked "Address unknown." The nurse, too, had disappeared. Inquiries to the American embassies in France and Germany were answered with a polite but vain concern. As time went on, Emma and the children could only presume the Doctor dead.

Dr. Lloyd had drifted away on a fever whose culprit was not visible under the lens of any microscope of that era—a too-willing volunteer to Jeanne's science. Against her advice, he had scratched his arm with a serum prepared from the blood of one of his own patients. She had intended it for use only if one of that man's family had followed the fever toward the death that had taken him. Lloyd supposed he might prove it safe for prevention in a healthy man. In her anguish, she screamed at his foolhardy heroics before taking him in her arms, rocking him gently in his last hour, forswearing in his name her experiments and the work of her life.

Jeanne left almost everything behind in the cottage on the canal, her papers, all the records. The Doctor had supported her; now she would have to sustain herself. She sold the cottage and wandered back to Chaumont, where she took her old room in the boardinghouse with a single payment that allowed her there for life. She cleaned rooms in the Hôtel Rive Haute, work that found her sometimes on her hands and knees.

Jeanne had taken her microscope with her. It sat on the table in her boardinghouse room. She did not consider this a betrayal of her promise to the Doctor. For the time being, she didn't have to look at things that moved, or swam in serum, or teemed with an evil threat, or hung together in dead clumps. One could marvel at the same ambiguity of the quick and the dead in a single human hair, a translucent duct of mysteries, or in the magnification of a grasshopper's wing, cells in a weave of infinite patience and care, beyond understanding.

*T*he people of Moriches waited impatiently for the Great Fire that was meant to follow the Great War. They could as well have been waiting for the Second Coming; the event was that stubborn. Their faith said it must happen; physics said it could not. Louis's fine engineering had left no breathing room between the logs. As seasons passed, the pyramid grew more pulpy and sodden, until Helen no longer needed to pass her annual warning against trespassers on Independence Day. While it spoiled her old view of the bay, the pile of rotting wood was comforting to her sense of control.

Every year, she sent a pair of Christmas geese and a small gift of cash to the station attendant who had burned himself defying her. Before Helen died in her sleep on the camel in June of 1928, she was reassured by a bay fisherman that she needn't worry any longer. The pile, he told her, was "ripe as a pier."

Emma understood what had mattered most to Helen was a concentration of will and wealth that would maintain the Lloyd longevity on the Moriches plantation. Relying, against common sense, on William's return, she never altered the will that left her estate to him. There was much legal fuss before the court accepted the Doctor's death and passed the property to Emma and her children. Emma, fearing her own death, which came only several years later, wasted no time ceding her interest in the place.

Willie was no farmer; his efforts at Moriches had more to do with an awkward thrust, this way and that, for self-respect and honor than with any understanding of vegetable husbandry. Without the moderating influence of his grandmother, he floundered, and turned to whiskey and excuses. In his defense, all the farms in that region were soon to be called "real estate."

Nor did Louis have any desire to struggle with a farm, not even in Moriches. Louis was a bookman, familiar with classics and amused by recent novels. He met the small crowd from Harvard who came to New York with their short-lived quarterly, *Hound and Horn*. He made himself useful in their editorial offices, and he was once asked to dinner at the home of Lincoln Kirstein, a party to which the poet Edward Estlin Cummings had been invited.

That evening went badly for him. He was overfull in praise of his host's thesis that American painters of that generation had only replaced an Academy of the Right with an Academy of the Left, trading abbey knights for Frigidaires and photographs. His emotional seconding of what had already been said, too much like an echo, produced a cold silence at the table.

Far worse than that, on self-aggrandizing impulse, he told an epic lie. Knowing that Cummings had been early to France as an ambulance driver, he quoted for him a poem that he claimed his brother had written on the walls of a *camp de triage* at Noyen. It was the blank verse that ended with three initials, which he changed for the occasion to w.r.l. for Willie Rolfe Lloyd. Across the table, Cummings said nothing. Louis, who was never a plagiarist before or afterward, was not asked to return. He was told only later that he had stolen the lines from the man for whom he recited them.

Louis's salad days arrived in 1934 when *Hound and Horn* accepted his provocative essay called "The Limitations of Marxism." Though that proved to be the last issue of the quarterly, the piece made a gratifying buzz through the brownstones of East Sixty-first Street. Louis gave up a long bout of morbid rustication in Moriches and opened a bookstore on Lenox Hill in Manhattan. He took to the particulars of shop keeping as if they followed seamlessly from his youth and breeding.

Nellie came down to Manhattan from a Poughkeepsie education in high spirits and with a new group of women friends for life. With Louis, she conspired to save their older brother from his involvement with Latoni. But the Latoni problem solved itself. His affairs branched beyond military graft into the streets of Little Italy, where a civilian bullet finished him. Still in uniform, he was given a soldier's burial, a late hero of the Great War.

Nellie and Louis worried for their brother. They consulted doctors about his self-destructiveness and nervous depressions. Willie drank; Willie spent. His warm nature and enthusiasm brought him a pretty, sweet-tempered wife, who followed him to the end, investing her life as faithfully and imprudently as he spent his money.

The weight of taxes, the prospect of cash for the estate, and the separate interests of the three siblings almost guaranteed that this generation would sell out the tradition begun by their distant forebear Richard Lloyd in 1678. Willie wanted the cash to go cattle ranching in Nebraska—his investment was lost in a blizzard, with Willie almost freezing to death in a generous and foolhardy effort to save one of his herd. And Louis had no intention of holding on, at the expense of his own interests, which by 1935 included a difficult wife who did not get along with any other Lloyds. And eventually, not even with Louis.

Nellie argued in the name of her ancestors against the sale of the old plantation. By then, she had married, too, happily and for life, as it turned out, to a man who did well as the American president of an English shipping company, and who would have supported her share of the Moriches home as a family retreat. She cried when outvoted, though she could hold no grudge against her brothers for the neediness of their less favored lives.

Nature and vandals had their own way with the place before the sale was completed. Thieves and ordinary trespassers entered the house at will, rummaged in the attic, and stole papers before Nellie had a chance to remove all of them. In the hurricane of 1938, water rose over the meadow, lifting the pyramid of rotten wood from its twenty-year squat, dumping the logs into the violent wash. As the wind and water rose, the massive trunks of wood came tumbling into the house with a new cast of uprooted trees, knocking the camel's stone legs from beneath it, smashing over the cage, splitting through walls and studs, and leaving the whole place at a sorry tilt as the tide receded.

When the land dried, the dilapidated house sat as an obvious invitation to flame, and some ordinary son of Moriches—one could hardly call him an arsonist—put the torch to the place. The village had the kind of spectacular fire it had known before Doctor Lloyd went to war, while his remains lay somewhere in France, as blind to the harmless desecration as to the shifting reputation of his nurse.

It was a reputation glimmering in the ashes of an old war. And on the lips of a professor in Brussels, making peace with his God before death, regretting his dishonest use of the Maid from Joinville in the publications that had made his name known across the world. A mouth agape in Neuilly in memory of a child under Jeanne's care who rose from a coma to speak again, a raised hand trembling before the Virgin in Reims while heart went out to Jeanne Prie, somewhere awaiting final judgment.

If anyone cared to look, the record of her achievement could still be found in two military archives, German and American, disguised under the titles of the officers she had served in the course of the same war. Waiting for the attention of a scholar before dry rot or the scythe man of old files took her deeds and her two names into oblivion. In Joinville, she had already been raised to "the Second Saint of Lorraine," and a marble carver from the Vaucluse was hired to sculpt her in full height for the town square. Which led to an argument as to whether she had ever worn pants. There were many who swore she had not.

In the restricted halls of French Security, where her file was inactive but not actually closed, word of Lucienne de Crouen's late martyrdom was an affront to the state. From Paris, word of hidden source was spread again through Lorraine, reminding the people of the death by fire of their hero Justin Thivet. In Paris, Jeanne Prie was still the Colonel's whore.

Author's Note

Among the papers left by my mother at her death were two caches of letters from her father. I'd been told that his life was split in two by the Great War—his first forty-four years, exemplary and obedient; and the last fifteen when he divorced and disappeared into the mist of family secrecy and shame.

After the war he had taken up with a nurse from abroad, unnamed and consigned to contempt. She was never introduced to my mother or her two brothers. What I was supposed to think of this lady who, it was said, had worn men's pants, was given me by innuendo—that she was coarse and not worthy of my questions about her origin or end. This hard line against the nurse was relaxed as my mother reached her final years, and she began to picture her father's foreign lady in a more flattering frame as a woman of parts, of languages and science.

Later, with discovery of the letters, my grandfather's case could be reopened. In a shoebox was all the mail he'd written home from the St. Mark's School in Southborough, Massachusetts, dating from his twelfth year, 1885. Behind the box was a folder holding typescripts of correspondence to his wife and his mother from "somewhere in France," some 150 pages describing his World War I service as a doctor.

Though parts of this correspondence appear here, this story is not biography but fiction. My grandfather's name has been changed as well as the names of his family. Nor is the story an accurate account of his children's lives.

I am indebted to Paul de Kruif's *Microbe Hunters* for portraits of the earliest explorers of microscopic life and disease; to Herringham's *Physician in France* for accounts of field bacteriology labs; to Charles Lightbody's *The Judgments of Joan,* a study of the shifting reputations of Joan of Arc; and to e. e. cummings's *The Enormous Room,* the serio-comic account of his World War I incarceration by the French for suspected mutiny.

Special thanks to Dr. Salvatore Amari, Dr. John Koh, and Phil Ehrenkranz.

A Note About the Author

JOHN ROLFE GARDINER is the author of three previous novels—
Great Dream from Heaven, *Unknown Soldiers*, and *In the Heart of the
Whole World*—and two collections of stories, *Going On Like This* and
The Incubator Ballroom. He is the winner of a Lila Wallace–Reader's
Digest Writer's Award. His stories frequently appear in *The New Yorker*.
He lives in Unison, Virginia (near Washington, D.C.), with his wife, Joan,
and his daughter, Nicola.

A Note on the Type

This book was set in Fairfield, the first typeface from the hand of the American artist and engraver Rudolph Ruzicka (1883–1978). In its structure Fairfield displays the sober and sane qualities of the master craftsman whose talent has long been dedicated to clarity. It is this trait that accounts for the trim grace and vigor, the spirited design and sensitive balance, of this original typeface. Rudolph Ruzicka was born in Bohemia and came to America in 1894. He set up his own shop, devoted to wood engraving and printing, in New York in 1913 after a varied career working as a wood engraver, in photoengraving and banknote printing plants, and as an art director and freelance artist. He designed and illustrated many books, and was the creator of a considerable list of individual prints—wood engravings, line engravings on copper, and aquatints.

Composed by Stratford Publishing Services, Brattleboro, Vermont
Printed and bound by R. R. Donnelley & Sons, Harrisonburg, Virginia
Designed by Margaret M. Wagner